Praise for Aidan Higgins

"His characters, eccentric, tattered, inconsequent, slowly and powerfully burning up their lives, are unwieldy and magnificent. . . . Aidan Higgins is a writer of great originality and strength."—*Sunday Times* (London)

"*Langrishe, Go Down* is clearly the best novel by an Irish writer since *At Swim-Two-Birds* and the novels of Beckett."—Bernard Share, *Irish Times*

"Aidan Higgins is a born writer, in love with language and what language can do."—Frank O'Connor, *Sunday Independent* (Dublin)

"Higgins writes with genuine Irish bitter poetic intensity. . . . He reminds me of novelists who used to write for the sake of writing, to achieve what Nabokov called 'aesthetic bliss.' Higgins helps to revive language."—*Spectator*

Books by Aidan Higgins:

Flotsam & Jetsam

Aidan Higgins

Dalkey Archive Press

First published in Great Britain by Minerva, 1996
Copyright © 1996 by Aidan Higgins

First Dalkey Archive edition, 2002

Vanessa Vanhomrigh's letters in "*Rückblick,*" are reprinted from *The Works of Jonathan Swift,* v. 19; ed. Sir Walter Scott (Bickers & Sons, London, 1984).

Library of Congress Cataloging-in-Publication Data

Higgins, Aidan, 1927-
    Flotsam and jetsam / Aidan Higgins.— 1st U.S. ed.
      p. cm.
    ISBN 1-56478-316-2 (acid-free paper)
     1. Ireland—Social life and customs—Fiction. I. Title.

PR6058.I34 F57 2002
823'.914—dc21

2001058131

Partially funded by grants from the Lannan Foundation and the Illinois Arts Council, a state agency.

Dalkey Archive Press books are published by the Center for Book Culture, a nonprofit organization with offices in Chicago and Normal, Illinois.

www.centerforbookculture.org

Printed on permanent/durable acid-free paper and bound in the United States of America.

For Zin again

Contents

I

Flotsam and Jetsam

As Largs in Scotland is to Glasgow so is Kidd's Beach to Kingwilliamstown in the Eastern Province of South Africa – a quiet seaside resort.

The grunting of baboons hidden in thick woodland that reaches down to the lagoon sounds a warning note of rampant wilderness; as does the four-foot shark decomposing on the hot sand; as do the putty-coloured 'Non-White' youths displaying swaying stallion's erections on the dunes. Now they are scrummaging with two free and easy African girls; the girls screeching in a stupendous surf that bursts over them, their excitement barely contained in the briefest of bikinis.

An incoming rip tide smashes on the reeling shore with the force of toppling masonry. Kidd's Beach is not safe.

We walk there at sundown, looking for driftwood, buy a bottle of Oude Meester brandy from the hotel off-licence, use Coca-Cola as a mixer. Cattle breathe close to us at night, scratching themselves against the clapboard walls, and every sunup gives us more of Bruckner's 'thunder dawns'. Rise up! Rise up! The skin tingles.

One day in a clearing away from all human habitation we came upon a group of African men breaking in a horse, a coal-black stallion whose twitching pelt glistened

3

with the sweat of fright as a little brown manikin with his shirt off struck and struck again at the stallion's head with a tarred, knotty rope-end. Emitting gusty whistling through the wide wings of its nostrils, the stallion reared up to expose its thundering great progenitive parts. Rolling a bloodshot eye it backed, kicking up dust, straining on a lunge rein held by another African.

We strangers from overseas salute them civilly, but they do not respond nor seem to see us, a white man and his woman walking at dusk. It was the time of Apartheid when 'Non-Blankes' were invisible to 'Blankes', and were forbidden to swim on their beaches or sit on their public benches.

Mr Vaschel had sleepless nights. He lay on his back in bed listening to the gale blowing itself in over the Sound, the scratching made by the privet against the small window set high in the wall, the breathing of his fat wife Kate, and could not sleep. Motoring down on the previous day he had witnessed two disturbing incidents. First he saw two cars run off the road pointing in opposite directions into wild country. A scattering of people, white and coloured alike, stood about with indeterminate expressions and restless as though waiting for an ambulance to arrive and the accident to be completed. Then the crowd parted for an instant and he caught sight of the victim. It was a coloured man, an elderly person: someone had thrown a coat over him covering the injury. He lay there, as still as death where it had found him, his face pressed to the asphalt, his limbs quite naturally disposed though not yet at peace. The ghouls hovered over him, their shadows mingling, the thin summer clothes stretching forth in the wind. Sand also was being blown over him so that he could have no peace; death and burial were arriving at the same time. Mr Vaschel let in the clutch and drove slowly through, trying not to see, swallowing his spittle. But before he had time to compose himself the second incident was upon him. He saw, between parted trees, two donkeys struggling. The field, as it flew by, seemed to carry them forward and upwards as if onto a platform, there to display to advantage the incredible erection of the male gruesomely mounting and the female submissive and with downcast eyes. And then nothing but scenery again, the bridge and the flooded river. But this was not the cause of his sleeplessness. Not this, nor the sea, nor the air always disturbed, nor the annual holiday again. It was some distress, other than these, which would not let him sleep.

By day he ranged far and wide, passing through the various deserted beaches and across the high dunes overgrown with scrub. In the rocks he came upon a young shark decomposing, a wound twelve inches long in its side, its obstinate mouth closed for ever. He walked as far as the wreck, the thousand-ton coaster *Frontier* which had gone aground on the rocks one clear night, for no good reason, with a cargo of sugar and tyres, all hands saved. And on the public beach in view of all (though it was deserted but for the three of them, himself unseen) he saw a coloured girl in a red costume provoking a coloured man with her straps undone and her breasts bare, prone in the surf, allowing the waves to wash her against him, the saucy piece, but he was apparently having none of it. And Mr Vaschel, high and dry on a sand dune, felt an erotic twinge such as had not visited him for many a long year.

He saw the second river dried up short of its mouth, and over the estuary the ibis birds flying, dark and awkward, with beaks curved like scimitars and their wings thrashing the air. Out of more than curiosity he returned to where the young shark lay, already opening, prodding it with a stick so that its gases escaped with a sigh and out came its intestines, oozing back into the water. For his was the 'angelic' nature of the pampered boy who must seek consolation in wounds: an inclination which had bequeathed to the grown man a positive love of disfigurement. He welcomed the stye in the eye, the swollen members, the bandaged face and arms as actors welcome masks. Similarly the timid, should they care to search, can discover for themselves in the bodies of whores irregular traces of human aspiration on its off-days: a wild and brutal chaos undreamed-of in their more cautious politic. For respectable women could be found – various enough to suit nearly all tastes – who would be prepared to negotiate, to trade (even in marriage) a present for a past, or at least to make that past 'safe' for interlopers. But here, with his stick feeling in the dead fish and his eyes wide open to it, was an archaeologist breaking the seals of neglected and forgotten tombs, to read in the rigid bodies and perished features the impossible extent of his own decay. Here was one of those who, turning away from what is considered normal and permissible but which has refused them, finds in perversion themselves, even as archaeology finds a living past buried in the unconscious body of the present (which is Time on its way somewhere).

Years before, after his long bachelor existence had at last come to an end, he had found reason to say:

'For the first time in my life I seem capable of pure sensation, and you ask me to forget it!' And she, Kate, the infected charmer, had lain there in the ruins of the marriage bed, rolling her eyes at him in disapproval if not actual disgust, whispering:

'You are cruel ... you certainly are cruel. I wasn't expecting that ... I wasn't prepared!'

A toast to her 'beauty' tossed off recklessly in the long

days of courtship, 'I cannot hollow out a space big enough for you to occupy' (presumably in the heart) had rebounded on him with a vengeance in her early middle age, when she had begun to put on flesh like a schooner clapping on full sail. She lay in bed upstairs as a rule, issuing orders from that sanctuary, dropping her 'darlings' on all and sundry, heavy as stone, himself included, producing her coffins of polite alternatives, bidding the children to come to her bed, giving the day's orders to Amalinda, counter-ordering and shouting downstairs, her voice raised high as though haranguing invisible curs. She drank a glass of milk regularly before dropping off to sleep and enjoyed a hearty breakfast shortly after waking. Holding a slice of cake in one fat hand, she looked up at him, Innocence-surprised-in-a-deed-of-cupidity, a hand cupped to her ear, saying in mockery:

'Hark, do you hear the sea?' But he looked down at her, unsmiling, his life's partner, smelling misfortune escaping like a gas leak. Gone was the period when he could say, *Last time it was no good; I wanted to struggle with you, not to argue. You would not let me.* Gone was the woman he wanted to struggle with; and in her place this veritable mountain of flesh, which had the additional grossness of being a generally accepted fact. He went down, to sit in a catatonic trance in his study, unable to work. To be able to rise at last and go to bed, and be unable to sleep.

Kate Vaschel was the only daughter of Carl Theodor Richter, lawyer, and Hilda Berenice (née Bone) Richter. The father, aged seventy-five, had long retired from his profession, while the mother, aged sixty-five, was bedridden.

Kate was at pains to represent their son-in-law to the Richters as a bona fide character, gruff and downright. Whereas, as far as they were concerned, he was inaudible and underhand: his remarks at table being generally of a cynical or deprecating character, delivered as 'asides' which they only half caught, and between husband and wife the fiery glances flew. She told animated stories – entirely fictitious as far as they were concerned – delivered *sotto voce* and as though mimicking his honest-to-goodness inflexions, where he 'came across' in a manner which they might be expected to consider reassuring; Vaschel the bluff squire in riding-breeches. And with this farce she persisted.

In accordance with a long-standing arrangement which none had the heart to disrupt, the whole party, Vaschels and Richters alike, spent three weeks at the sea each year, drinking coffee and brandy and praising the view. Add to this the coloured girl Amalinda, maid of all work and namesake of the murderess who had done away with her own child.

Old Mrs Richter sat at table, her face troubled with some hidden and enduring grief. Some dislocation of the spirit, added to the ruins of a distinguished carriage, gave her the semblance of a dilapidated monarch: a Mary Tudor, as it were, wasted away under life-sentence in the Tower. Some such unheard-of dislocation of history or nature seemed to pervade and undermine her spirit. Shaking before the absolute and inevitable, too long covered, too carefully hidden, she looked slyly out at the hurly-burly before flinching away, the worms that had eaten her nerves and her fortitude down to the bone still breeding in her face. No sooner had she finished picking at her slops than she was pushed from the table by 'the devoted Amalinda', eyes upturned in stark amazement as though she (Mrs Richter) had just begun to grasp one of her son-in-law's insinuations – the rest of the expression, dawning certainty, being lost as she was propelled violently through the doorway: Amalinda's spine dead straight and her buttocks grinding fiercely together.

Mrs Richter's bedroom was downstairs and sparsely furnished. A wardrobe rested there on the bare boards with
a chest of drawers and the bed itself on a rectangle of
faded blue carpet. A commodious chamber-pot was generally apparent under the sadly drooping edges of the bed
coverings, almost magnetic in its importance to the
general picture of Mother Richter abed, as though the
parts of the iron bedstead and herself, covered in glad
rags and a nightgown with a ruff, constituted the filings
– the mesmeric field – which 'made' the whole happy
unit. She seldom offered to quit her bed, being content
to sit or lie there like a hen in a dust-bath, hale and
hearty enough at sixty-six, though decked already in the
habiliments of a slovenly old age, plucking at her beads,
engrossed in the women's magazines, a set of false teeth
in a glass by her head. For her, the 'beautiful thoughts'
of the world were confused hopelessly with the framed
sentiments found embroidered on cloth at seaside cottages – grisly mottoes which ran to predictable jingles
very much in character with the damp air outside and
the stained ceilings within: a boredom caged within four
walls, as within a tormented soul, raging to be allowed
out.

She preferred to lie before the open window and listen
to the sea, trying not to hear the dreadful outcry coming
from her daughter above. Sometimes Simon would come
and sit on her bed 'to keep her company'; but these
were visitations she did not greatly relish, well-intentioned
though they might have been. She complained to her
husband:

'I do wish he wouldn't sit there . . . he tightens it down.'
And sometimes, made frantic by his calm and patience,
by the uselessness of the gesture – for it aggravated her
until she seemed on the point of suffocating – she wanted
to scream at him:

'Go away! Go away; I want no patched-up horrors in my room. Go and look for Nelly Deane ... Maybe she'll give you a touch of her seaweed!'

But in the meantime he visited her and she tolerated it. She was a little wizened-up creature in a cloth cap out of which wisps of hair stuck at all angles, for all the world like the wizard of Ferney in his last decay. Blinking and screwing up her crow's-feet the better to propose her momentous questions, she shifted in bed: her veined and parchment-like hands, wherein a sluggish lymph moved, hesitant and old, fidgeted on the covers. Her jaw sagged a little as she prepared to break silence. And then the 's' sounds came whistling forth as from the nozzle of a badly trained hose. Would the bread suffice until tomorrow? ... Was the wind ever going to drop? ... Could he say the time? ... Had the clothes dried yet? ... Had the boys come home? ... Until at last, weary of this little game, she relented and let him go, sinking from sight beneath the coverings and leaving only the grey mound of her wig visible, her old breathing filling the room. She knew Simon Vaschel had been a casual child: his birth an accident – neither of his parents (since deceased) had wanted him. From the beginning, therefore, already a casualty he was to search all his life for a consideration withheld from him from the start – rummaging in locked drawers, white in the face, breathing fast. She alone knew this: she, Hilda Bone, by all despised. Recapitulative suffering was her particular middenheap. Occasionally she wept, her face to the wall and the coverings in upheaval.

Then, like sorrowful music interrupted and again resumed, the sea commenced hammering again on its one persistent chord, washing in over the yells of the players, pounding even rocks down to powder.

By the sea Mr Vaschel walked alone with his troubles, though what these troubles were he could not say. To his right hand the sea was burning; from the horizon heat vapours arose; and every night sleep refused herself to him until four or five next morning. About the house the donkeys and their young were straying, cropping the grass, eyeing the visitors, all gutta-percha prick and lantern jaw. Their moist long-suffering eyes sought him out until they bored into his own. Carl Theodor Richter continued to discuss world finance in his slurred old man's voice, as though his mouth were crammed with fudge. Signor Coreggiato sat opposite, nodding his head every so often, a glass of brandy balanced on his bulging thigh. Signor Coreggiato, the pineapple king, seemed to lack a neck, for his inflamed face was screwed down flush into the great barrel of his chest without noticeable interference. He had straw-coloured hair as coarse as grass which stood on end so that he resembled a caricature of one of his own pineapples. Simon Vaschel excused himself after a while and left. He walked among the rocks which thereabouts had always reminded him of Aran and wildest Mayo, where as a young fellow he had spent many pleasant holidays. The track burned under his rope-soled feet, wet grains of sand blown in by the sea adhered to the uppers. Forlorn shapes of nature surrounded him only, like the landscape of Rousseau's *La Charmeuse de Serpents*. Littoral and hills were giving up the ghost before the onslaught of implacable heat: all the harsh or accommodating shapes of land and home erased. But darkness would fall, none the less, obliterating all, and the consistency of day go down before the vast inconsistency of night, in which no man slept. But into which he crept. Damned for daring to have children (for he had children, two males, at first all gut and squall and ignored by him; more recently turned baboon, spending all their free time in trees, still ignored by him), damned for his activities in the antique trade – into which he was securely rammed, like a cement block into a cement wall and indeed unthinkable otherwise; double damned for courting the bewitching Katherine Richter, who had lured him to his destruction and then changed herself into another person; so that early Kate remained innocent and could wash her hands of the whole affair. So that late Kate could say to her cronies:

'He doesn't fit in, it's a speciality with him that he doesn't fit in.'

But, alone on the rocks, his thoughts were beautiful – terrible too – burning holes in the sky. Looking across the plain which contained donkeys, themselves turned towards the dunes and sub-tropical hills dissolving under the heated breath of the sky, he thought: Is there any darkness where she lives for me to perish and rise up again? Or do all those who go down with a tradition imagine their life to be a hearsay? As though enacting a scene from Grand Guignol, he saw a wan and ghastly figure exposed in braces, timid as a sessions clerk, and there his lion-taming lady letting herself out of an outsize girdle – exposing a backside which seemed to be stricken with elephantiasis, stating in a warm voice her fondness for whisky and hot milk. Oh Vaschel! – Here at last, embodied in this pale creature, was one of nature's cuckolds, created specially for that office. Perhaps he thought, felt, this: I am going through a period when I may touch nothing. Then I can say nothing either, seeing I have lost faith. Lost passion.

After such walks he returned more depressed than before. Arriving out of a declining sun, the rapid twilight over, darkness had begun to fall. Heavy night birds were flying in from the sea playing their nocturnal rattles; or perhaps the noise came from bullfrogs in the pools. Above his head a cloud in the shape of a man floating, spreadeagled and ominous, face down. Mr Vaschel stood below in the light of the open door, his shadow enormous behind him. Arrived! That hungered figure! That minister of God's retribution.

He had been engaged in the antique trade for a greater part of his life than he cared to remember. Running a small not remunerative business hard by the hospital in a fashion that carried vagueness to the point of amnesia. During his working day he sat in a room at the back, divided from his shop by a curtain round the edge of which he observed the customers' reflections in a mirror before him. Potential clients strolled in and out, confused by the lack of service, for he would not rise for everyone. It was worse still when he did and appeared in person to engage a customer in one of his marathon discussions, leaning over the trays with a black wideawake set on the back of his head and as though dressed for the street: so that they felt doubly awkward, awkward because they were detaining him, awkward because of the trend of the discussion, which touched on every conceivable subject except the one they wished to consult him about. ('Pistols,' he would say, brushing them aside, 'are not my line,' and begin to talk of Benjamin Constant.)

The Georgian façade of the hospital loomed over his premises at the junction of Lower Stephen Street and Johnson's Place. A small lettered sign announced ANTIQUES in faded paint. A chiming bell guarded the door, which for that reason was always left open ('Charon,' said Mr Vaschel, 'with a defective larynx'). In the convex display windows stood some of the collection of Simon Vaschel, Esq., lithographer and gent. The coins of Greece and Rome, designs by Pistrucci and Briot, the suspected Rembrandt and the genuine Modigliani, red coral crucifixes the size of a little finger (French, XIV century), the Crab and the Scorpion, the Balance and the Waterpot.

'All the counters,' he said, quoting some authority, 'of passion and rejection.' Inside, Mr Vaschel droned on about Daudet, who lived in a windmill. Baudelaire and his ilk were, with him, in high disfavour, for he believed in the classics and the Great Tradition, Homer, Dante (he read neither), Balzac, free trade and the might of England.

'How can one determine to be wicked?' he would say, as though proposing an unanswerable question. How can one?

If he was not actively engaged with a customer he put up the shutters for the day at five o'clock or earlier, locking the shop and dropping the key inside the letterbox on its long string, walking to the number 2 bus stop down William Street. By those walls, those seas, those thoroughfares, those public conveyances, went Simon Vaschel, a competent keyless citizen, innocent and alone.

Looking into his own past as down the barrel of a gun, he sought for a man (himself) who, opposed and outnumbered, would receive the blows of an aggressor as though beating his own chest. He had not found him. His heart, fattened on some unconventional pasture, had left him out of things, like Nietzsche in the bitter Alps. Not that he would have approved of the comparison, not that he resembled Nietzsche in the least. Kate might well taunt him with:

'The exceptional person does not lurk in a glory-hole' – a glory-hole here being synonymous with a child's 'secret place' – for Berbers and fierce Kabyles, hidden in the mountains of Algeria and owning allegiance to no man, could not have been less accommodating than this lone citizen, lowering under the mountain of his choice.

It was about this time that he began to have distressing dreams. Fed on insomnia, they came in the early hours of the morning where sleep had at last overtaken him, to reveal a side of his nature foreign to his family and associates. He who had not craved erotic pleasure for so long – for his bachelor existence had been a marvel of prudence and restraint, and his marriage much the same – witnessed in dreams, and then participated in, orgies and bestialities the likes of which, for sheer variety, this world has rarely seen. Coloured girls were involved with donkeys, with jackasses, the wretches got up in outsize cravats like Dr Unrat in *Der blaue Engel.*

From these exercises, Mr Vaschel awoke stricken with remorse and drenched to the skin – to find in the pale window the privet already creeping and day well on the way, so that he could sleep again. Passive at first he was witness to these noctural rites, terror-stricken and yet tempted. Until at last, no longer passive, he launched himself in. Immediately a half-familiar figure began to emerge – a coloured girl like the rest – inadequately clothed, her breasts coloured white and her lips parted: the destructive image of Amalinda, his wife's mother's servant and his own. To the strains of wailing and percussive instruments she was swept past and the dream ending. Time and again he was to lose her among hair and thighs, at first carried towards her and then away. In the morning the privet shook above his head as though nothing had changed and he felt the sour taste of frustration in his mouth. Time and again he forced himself back into sleep in pursuit of her; until at last the longing proper to his dream was answered by the longing proper to his conscious self, and seemed indistinguishable. He began to notice her then: for dreaming or waking she had roused him up.

Amalinda Pandova walked this earth as though her clothes were a positive burden to her: a burden, moreover, from which she might any day burst. Her head was rounded and purposeful like a statue's, outlined with its fuzz of hair through which the shape of the skull showed, her ears were pierced for small brass earrings. She had a small discoloration under her right eye the size of a florin. It was not known whether she had any male admirers, but she went on odd Sundays in the company of one of Signor Coreggiato's girls to the missionary church Star of the Sea, near the refuse dump – a rectangular building of wood without ornament or bell. In a word, she seemed a thoroughly respectable girl. Only in dreams had she thrust that disguise aside for him, with her clothes and her status as a coloured servant, lowest of the low, and gone towards him, mad as himself, for she had discovered at the same time a particular style, most refined without a doubt, in the accomplishment of the coarsest transgressions. Sometimes, confronted in the dream, her hands were about him and her skirts about her neck, staring him out. He drove in then as though berserk, his mouth open, his arms outstretched as if to receive a beating.

One night without dreams all sound stopped. He knew then that the hour for whatever had to happen between them had already struck. In the silence he heard a tap running. Something within him was injured – unnatural blood dripping into him. He rose up at once and went straight out; his bare feet carried him unerringly towards the tree. Hardly stopping he came out of his pyjamas. Beyond the branches he saw the roof of her hut shining against the galactic spawn. As he stood at the door he noticed the shapes of the donkeys all around in the building sites. The tree, extending its arms on either side in an unbroken series to the ground, outlined itself against the plain, across which a white mist was slowly moving, like the brackets in church into whose sockets the faithful screw their candles. Bowing his head he

pressed the latch down and entered, a white Hermes soon
to be transformed into a ruthless Centaur. All his life he
had been a careful man and no one could take that from
him: first a careful child, then a careful son, then a careful
father; and the claiming that is done with a heavy hand
was truly unknown to him.

A shaft of light from the open doorway bisected the
bed, over which her uniform hung on a peg. The heavy
odour of a coloured person rose to meet him, more
persistent than carbolic or Lifebuoy. This dim abode of
condemned spirits was her lair. And in its darkest corner,
under the rafters, he sensed his dog rose sensing him. To
reach her he would have to penetrate forests and mangrove swamps; no matter, no matter.

Amalinda lay on her stomach on muddy-coloured
blankets with her eyes open watching him. Her dark skin
radiated light as from a pool; she was naked as the Tahi-
tian girl in the painting. He left the door and went in.

Time withdrew itself from under him as he took her
ankles and pulled her weight towards him until her toes
almost touched the ground. He leant down, trembling,
his heart pounding, putting his hands on both sides of
her neck. As he laid his hand on her he saw below her
woman's dark and anonymous flesh – a brown bay into
which he was about to cast himself and be drowned for
ever. In the end it was to be easy; only thinking about it
had made it impossible.

Into her ear he whispered something. She replied into
the pillow and appeared to be smiling. They lay side by
side covered in sweat, light draining from the corners of
the window and the south-wester blowing again.

He awoke in complete darkness and found himself
alone. The door was closed and above his head the clothes
peg swung empty. She was in the kitchen then, although

day had scarcely begun, in her green uniform and white headband as innocent as pie, kneeling before the stove and feeding it sticks. He watched the sunlight breaking through the keyhole and under the door. His pyjamas, retrieved from wherever he had thrown them, lay folded over a chair. Looking for wild oats then, had he found garbage? He felt nothing. The south-wester continued to blow hard in over the Sound. It would be a wild day. He rose and dressed himself in his pyjamas.

As he came through the door the jackasses let loose their atrocious bray, derisive and as though pre-arranged. The sea was pounding on the rocks. The sun was up.

In Old Heidelberg

In the Café Wagner an angelic choir composed of ex-Luftwaffe officers stood by the counter in the soft and shining leather of their airmen's boots, tweed jackets completing a dress which included the remnants of a uniform without wing or star; arms linked and their countenances full of an emotion not unlike horror, they sang 'Denn wir fahren gegen Engeland'.

Perspiring freely, the proprietor went about among the tables serving his American custom Münchner beer. Across the way the Gasthaus Roter Ochse shook to the strains of 'Gaudeamus Igitur', accompanied by the free thumping of beer mugs. In the lobby more American tourists gaped at the folio guest-books black with signatures of famous men, including their own Mark Twain. The high wail of 'Stille Nacht' came from a back room, played apparently on bagpipes. Kliger and Gluck were bawling for their *Wiener Wochenausgabe*.

In the corbels and drains of Heilige Geist Kirche pigeons huddled in freezing proximity to stone quarried before Lipperchey had invented the telescope and exposed to the elements ever since, the lime of their droppings now invisible beneath them in thin snow. Snow had fallen all over Heidelberg on this, the twentieth day preceding Christmas on the Christian calendar, 1949.

She made her way along the Neckar embankment, keeping to the inside of the kerb, dressed in a heavy duffle coat, snowboots and a scarlet stole. The river charged past below her left hand at nightmare speed, west-bound, black and swollen already with Swabian snows. High into the sky on her right loomed the damp façade of civic buildings, from the cornices of which melting snow had begun to drop into the street.

At length she saw the spires of the Church of the Holy Ghost meandering towards her and beyond that the twin onion-shaped domes of the bridge towers, Moorish and out of place against a turgid northern sky full of snow. She crossed the chill bridge entrance below the portcullis and stopped before a small door set into the wall. She touched the bell, heard nothing at first, then it began to ring high up in the building.

An insistent wind fought against the vacuum created between the tower suspensions. One wing was inhabited, the wing below which she stood, its fellow served the purpose of municipal lumber rooms, in former times perhaps *garde-robes*. Loose snow blew up from the gutters below the teeth of the portcullis. A car passed on the opposite bank, going fast towards Neuenheimer-Strasse. As she put her finger to the bell again a door opened upstairs. She withdrew her finger and waited. After a pause footsteps began to descend within the tower. She walked to the centre of Neckar-Strasse and looked up and down. A headless Heidelberg already ankle deep in snow. Remote sounds of festivity came from the Roter Ochse below the lock. She walked to the door again and struck it with the flat of her hand. It gave inwards. She was confronted with a Franciscan figure dressed in a heavy brown overcoat and brown muffler, holding a candlestick. A figure of doom.

The weak light left much of the face in shadow. A stiff crown of hair stood on end as though meditations of an intense and pious nature had been rudely interrupted. The face below showed neither surprise nor pleasure. It might have belonged to a disobliging churchman of a bygone time. A person, moreover, whose chief character-istic seems to be one of waiting and who, whether priest or defunct, is obliged to regard the living with a certain amount of apprehension, and almost resentment, as if by living they delayed the Judgement Day – as in a sense indeed they did. The gaunt features resembled to a striking degree those of the poet and priest *manqué*, Antonin Artaud, who had lost his reason in Dublin Bay. They stared at each other without speaking.

'Now,' she said at last, 'do we come in?'

The hallway smelt as usual, sawdust and ash wood, which in the fire would give off an aroma of English gin.

'Is that you, Ellen?' he said, holding the candle aloft.

'No,' Ellen said, 'not at all. It's Julie Récamier. Do I perish here or do I come in?'

The narrow hallway was blocked by up-ended branches of generous girth, into one of which a small axe was sunk. They began to ascend the spiral stairs, the young woman called Ellen leading.

'When did you arrive back?' he said into the dark.

'This afternoon,' Ellen's voice said. 'We got the connec-tion at Mannheim. It's snowing much harder up there. They were saying the Fulda is frozen in parts.'

'You must keep climbing,' he said. 'I'm living in the bedroom now. I have a fire.'

He heard her panting up ahead.

'Father, needless to say, detested Berlin,' her voice called back. 'All the tarts of Charlottenburg accosted him

every time he stepped outside the hotel. I saw some
theatre. Berlin is not so awful under snow, but miserably
cold.'

Crossing the dark landing they went up a step and
entered the bedroom. It was a room lit in the daytime by
a single window and largely destitute of even the most
necessary furniture. One picture hung on the wall, not
his but a copy of Carpaccio's *St Ursula's Dream*, which
seemed itself to reflect on a diminished scale the contents
of the room. It had the same elevated bleakness of setting
as the painting, the same ferns on the windowsill, the
walls high as a barracks. Fairly in the centre stood a
Renaissance double bed with a high flying canopy. In the
painting the martyr was alone in it, one ear cocked; a
little to one side the angel was quietly entering. Both
seemed bedchambers tottering on the edge of catastrophe, as if all their adhesive properties had been
pulverised out of them. In one respect the room differed
from the painting. Four carriage lamps hung from
brackets about the four walls, throwing repeated circles
of light. An immense wood fire burned in the grate,
around which plates were arranged warming, *Leberkäse*
and a litre of red wine.

'Can I offer you something?' he said.

'Certainly you can,' she said. 'You may embrace me.'

'But do you trust me?'

This was by way of being an old chestnut. When she
had first come to the bedroom he had asked that. She
had answered then:

'Of course I trust you,' and looked demure. Almost
unasked she had come to his bed, stepping without com-
punction out of her clothes. Her skin, prickled and damp
as if awaiting abuse, suggested not a woman's unbeholden
charms but rather the bleak skin discovered in fowl
beneath their feathers, all tendon and loss. Meat too

roughly exposed bracing itself for the hatchet. Ellen's flesh had an almost mineral sameness about it. She kissed as though determined to be lost: a touch bitter as quassia.

Towards the end of the previous summer he had become involved with this sullen young woman, who was some years his junior. Of Irish extraction, but licentious, she had narrow hips and the projecting knees of a boy. She preferred tweed suits to the usual feminine frocks and frills. Undressed she resembled a Graeco-Roman athlete, chill and somewhat masculine in spareness of line, a lay figure to which pubic hairs had been incautiously added. He was in a fair position to say, for had she not undressed before him almost at once, needing no encouragement? She had come across the bridge on that first warm day with a red rose in her buttonhole and a scowl on her face, asking permission to sunbathe on the roof. Her full name was Ellen Rossa-Stowe.

He had seen her first at the Kunstverein in the University, standing chewing her lip in the midst of the Braque collection. He had taken notice of her then because she was dressed completely in tweed and even carried a tweed handbag, and looked as though she were covered in feathers. Later he saw her again in the Moufang Gallery in Rohrbacher-Strasse peering myopically at Munch's *Self-Portrait*. And there and then, not being able to contain his curiosity any longer, formally accosted her. She was excessively near-sighted, but houses of assignation were nothing new to her, and into his thinly baited trap she trod lightly.

At an age when other little girls had scarcely discarded their dolls she had already discarded more than she could well recover. Germany suited her down to the ground. Unknown to her prudent parents she had the run of a bachelor's tower. She liked to trail around the three tower rooms dressed only in a pelisse, through which parts of her person could easily be detected, tiered at bust and hip. When aggravated or deprived of what she wanted, a perpendicular furrow came between her eyes; pinching in her lips then she contrived to look displeased. As she stood erect in the bath the same distracted furrow reappeared, projected lower and behind, in the cleft of her tight crestfallen buttocks: here again the same grim cast of countenance, peevish and deprived. It seemed altogether dubious whether the hidden parts of her nature included anything as commodious as a womb. Or if it did, that chamber would of necessity be cramped as a mouse's ear, a bypath of herself, disused and to all appearances forgotten.

Not for Ellen Rossa-Stowe the amorphous breeding of issue; matching her bitter kiss was an embrace which had a wild recoiling quality of the bolting horse biting on its snaffle. In her the convention of woman's boundless attractiveness had experienced a radical upheaval. She applied face make-up with determination and rapidly, employing a blunt object that resembled a shaving stick, as if she would have done with it for good and all. Sometimes she appeared on the streets wearing make-up several shades removed from what was becoming to her, alarming the public with the livid complexion of one stricken with jaundice.

On her flat thighs an object as intrinsically feminine as a suspender belt became asexual as a holster. And yet, and yet, through all this masculine armour, the female in her could not but betray itself.

She spoke of Dublin's flea market and autumn in Herbert Place, the red traffic eye suspended across an avenue of leaves and the drunks accosting her in Ballsbridge. She mentioned two painters she had known. Her flat in Mespil Road overlooked the Grand Canal and a hospital out of which coffins were carried at a judicious trot by orderlies in white.

'What a place!' she said with affection. The view from the front was all *Passage Cottin* by Utrillo, the view from the rear was like a circus moving in.

He took Ellen for long excursions out into the municipal wilderness – on one occasion walking her clean over into Fischbach. Somewhere outside the village they had to cross an enclosure which contained the elements of both scrap-heap and knacker's yard. An odd assortment of abandoned agricultural machinery had fallen among the wreckage of trucks and cars. Rusted chassis struggled with the grass which fought its way tenaciously through axles and dismantled doors. A barn or disused factory of mean proportions stood some way back among trees. Sliding doors, long fallen from the rollers, had in the course of time virtually disappeared into the ground. In the gloom of the interior skeletons of animals lay among harness parts. Bones of a sepia colour rested on twists of horsehair padding which had spilled out in profuse disorder. A bonfire of rags and dried dung stank and smouldered against one wall, as though ignited days or even weeks before and then forgotten. Locked in the tangles of grass, deprived of bonnets and wheels, two or three Ford Edsels had begun to disintegrate.

They crossed over into a meadow waist high in summer grass. Halfway around it they came upon the lake. The ground sloped away suddenly and there was the water, hidden by the high ground and a brake of trees. It was the afternoon they saw a lammergeier.

It was also the afternoon that Ellen, who up till then had been sunbathing sedately in her briefs, stung by a fit of harvest lust or perhaps driven wild by whatever uncontrollable spores she had in lieu of more placid genes, rolled back, arched her spine like a salmon, unpeeled herself in one continuous movement, rolling back into a sitting position and then forward onto her knees. Tossing aside her briefs she said, low and unbridled:

'Come on. Corrupt me now, damn you! *Verführe mich!'*

Irwin Pastern was a painter who had exhibited in Berlin and London. He had his first one-man show when he was forty-two. For a living he worked in a cramped office overlooking a small railed park, longing for his brushes, his fifteen-inch diameter frying pan, his peace and his tower. In the premises of Spüllicht and Ausgus, Quantity Surveyors, he had tried, with his head buried in his hands, to recover from innumerable hangovers.

He was forty-four years old and a bachelor. When in motion his long legs seemed to precede his trunk, tentative and stealthy, after the manner of wading birds. The palms of his hands were of a higher colour than the backs, raw in appearance they spoke of a sluggish circulation – the fault of a too sedentary existence and long hours at the drawing board. He had stiff black hair which stood on end, disdaining a hat. He went in for out-of-door herringbones, loose-cut tweeds which hung in a depressed fashion from his emaciated buttocks. His nose was long and beaked, discoloured winter and summer, for he enjoyed but moderate health.

When the urge came upon him he locked himself up in his tower and worked without ceasing. Delicate colours emerged as though wrung out from their darker background and the spectator was lured into a drenched metropolis or into a rain-sodden countryside, over which presided the half-materialised demons of retribution, their faces uncertain and their hands empty, the guardians of a land in an uneasy stance, out of which floated children and apple-women and the poor of Mannheim dockland – half familiar and half forgotten, holding onto the Bar of Justice with their thin hands, looking back to a land (where they were certainly lost) or facing out of the picture – bemused little faces picked out of the surrounding dark by his brush and patience, fainter and more hopeless than the prisoners wilting under endless litigation in a canvas by Forain.

He first laid down a foundation of black and out of this primeval bog, in a month or two of excavating, a misted scene at last emerged – grey, bled-off, revolving slowly within the frame, colourless as a dream, an image of the caul itself, a thin piping out of utmost darkness. And it was on these Zöllner's Patterns of paint and canvas that he hung, when his strength was up to it, his better fancies.

Sometimes his figure was seen skirting the grass and disappearing through the doors of the Graphisches Kabinett on Karl-Ludwig-Strasse. He took his lunch in restaurants chosen at random about the Green, occasionally taking a paper bag with him into Dr Moufang's Collection, dropping his crumbs before Marc and Klee.

In the Café Wagner he seated himself as far as possible from the counter. Lowering his head as though mortally ashamed to be caught eating, he bit into a sandwich smothered in mustard – his free hand reaching out for the glass of wine, feeling along the wood while his eyes were averted. He studied the *Rhein-Neckar Zeitung*, a cigarette lit before he had finished swallowing the last morsel. His movements were leisurely, abstracted, the motions of a man who had ample time to spend.

It was his custom in summer to walk to work. Skirting the Odenwald and entering the park by the gate furthest from the zoo, he timed himself to reach the centre by five past eight at the latest.

Beds of flowers abounded in the park and a couple

of low-lipped fountains with ornamental lead bulrushes. From the centre a series of lanes radiated out in six or seven different directions around the perimeter, and from these lanes, invisible to each other until almost converging, came the pedestrians. They had to cross a humpbacked bridge and pass along a short avenue overhung by trees to re-enter the town by the main gate under the motto, *Impavidum ferient ruinae* . . .

At any time between 8.03 and 8.30 the unknown young woman might arrive from the Mönchhof-Strasse lane and pass ahead of him over the bridge. Sometimes he sat on the cement edge of the fountain and waited for her. When the fountain was working he was obliged to remove himself a little to the rear, where he took up a position against a clinker-built ramshackle pavilion and from there watched her come, preoccupied but stepping with some deliberation, veiled in spray.

On rare days it happened by chance that their steps converged and he walked behind the free unit formed by her shoulders and moving hips. He saw a line of faint hairs on the calves of her legs. It seemed to him that she was a woman as outside his time and experience as, say, Catherine de Medici. Unlike those who, under the guise of an unappeasable sexuality, offered or seemed to offer the 'consumer goods' of their person as if it were a commercial product and he its unchanging customer. She, on the other hand, seemed to him infinitely touching, a creature removed from woman's narrow style and from temptation. She rarely looked at him (and perhaps even then she was merely looking in his direction), whereas he found himself bound and compelled to her by an affinity as tenacious as that of copper for oxygen. Her presence – leaden, serene and descending – had a quality impervious to change (although it was already doing so, even as molten lead will alter shape ten or more times in its passage down through water, before it comes to rest, but still remains lead). Her body was made up of chemicals and iron as well as flesh and bone; something in the movement of her hips, in her advancing, suggested a displacement that was also marine in character. A like paradox of movement and displacement was implicit in her walk: a denial that the body could ever be impoverished, and with it a refusal to ever care. The motion which she offered to his eye, but more precisely to his heart, was no longer physical motion; it had about it the appeasement of that which is not only still; of that which is inorganic. Her clothes did not seem to conceal her, but to this too she seemed indifferent. He quaked at the subdued eroticism of her gait.

The fountains played; the sun shone. Classical statues stood neglected in groves, a stately thigh here and there overgrown with moss and roses. All the birds sang together in Schloss Park Schwetzingen.

At night of all the other Opels crossing from Ufer-Strasse, he recognised hers, braking hard on the far side and then slamming into gear on the bridge. As she drove under the portcullis she gave a single blare on the horn and went on through, parking some way from the tower further along the embankment.

After a while he heard her slow step crossing below and the sounds of the front door opening. He went out then and stood waiting at the head of the stairs. Shielding the candle with one hand and peering down he said: 'Yes, who are you?'

He heard someone stumble in the dark below and her voice complaining. The door banged shut and against his hand he felt the banister shudder as she began climbing.

Her head appeared at last. At first there was nothing but a spiderweb trembling where the light fell, then, after an interval her face appeared in the dark recess, upturned, unsmiling, without coquetry.

'These impossible stairs again,' she said, out of breath. 'Is there never light for me?'

Besides the exceptional whites of her eyes something shone and jangled against the banisters: the dark glitter of her spoils.

'No, Anna,' he said, raising the candle. 'The bulbs are all blown.'

She came in then and he helped her out of her coat and lit more candles. She sat on the worn sofa and began drawing off her gloves. Then he set out two whiskies and sat down beside her. Alter or begin again.

She, Annelise von Fromar, was the naturalist who swam alone in Lake Garda and climbed alone in the Dolomites. Cremona, Mantua, Milano, Bergamo, each of these towns in turn had seen her, consulting a timetable under the arcade of the Palazzo del Capitano – the foreign lady with a halt in her stride and the long imponderable nose of Leonardo's Beatrice d'Est. Tall and composed, she wore a loose-fitted travelling coat, her hair was pitch black and combed low down over her forehead in a fringe. She had prominent dark eyes in a pale face and went in for fawns and wood colours, muted tones. In her hands the common accessories which women carry in the way of handbag or umbrella became the Crook and the Flail: forbidding emblems of sovereignty and dominion. Hers was a sad elongated face; its curious texture recalled Canopic jars – the pureness and semi-transparency of faience.

A cold wind from the river drove against the walls, agitating the window in its frame and the four candles dripped grease. The large fireplace held too much wood. After, Annelise would cook *Leberkäse* on the long toasting fork while he cranked the gramophone and a harsh rasping voice would fill the room, singing against a night-club orchestra.

The Dukes Elect of Pfalz crouched in their niches on the bridge and mooring lights shone here and there on the river as Piaf began again, '*Histoires du Coeur*'.

One day Annelise happened to pick out a book from his shelves and a photograph detached itself from the leaves and fell at her feet. She picked it up. After a pause she asked:

'Who is it? . . . Your father?'

'Yes,' Irwin Pastern said, glancing at it.

'He looks very purposeful.'

He took the snapshot from her. Father's hands were clasped before him on his stomach, one grasping the other's wrist so that the veins stood out. He was in uniform. His head was thrown back, eye-sockets, nostrils and upper lip alike were deeply shadowed; perhaps the total effect was one of purpose. Irwin remembered him as quite an old man, dozing in a deckchair under the walnut tree, his speckled old man's hands fidgeting on the covers of a book. Sunken into the chair with his head resting on his chest he seemed to have pre-deceased himself; a general by defeat made memorable, as it were, but still out of place (as silicified wood ceases to be part of a forest in order to become the property of a museum).

'Purposeful,' Irwin repeated, 'No, I wouldn't say that. Mother insisted that he was a fool. She said he would drive her into the grave. For her he was "the unfortunate", as if God's finger were on him. Perhaps it was. He was certainly contrary. I remember when I was a child he once promised to take us to a local gymkhana. But promises meant nothing to him. At the last moment he said no, it would only be a disappointment for "the lad" (that was me). He knew gymkhanas and furthermore he knew

Baron Rohe-Macht, and this particular gymkhana would be worthless. My mother said, "But what does it matter? Irwin has *never* been to a gymkhana." But he shook his head and repeated that it would only be a disappointment. Mother said, "Let him cool down. Leave him to me." And shortly after that he came back and announced that we were going after all. He would arrive at the interval when the prizes were being presented in the marquee, that was the best time. There would be no one there and we would "have the place to ourselves". Do you understand that? We were being offered the best of something that did not exist, that had been refused existence. A gymkhana in its purest form. The field cut up by non-existent hooves, the jumps still left lying where they were knocked by non-existent riders, flags and tents everywhere, papers blowing about the field – every evidence of a crowd. But no crowd. No crowd, no riders, no horses. Can you feel that? I believe that was his general notion of Paradise. Circumstances did not come together in the proper way to allow it to happen.'

'Is he still alive?' Annelise asked.

'Not at all, he died when I turned twenty-seven. Father was never really healthy. He joined the Belgian Army in the Great War, as it was called, and fought for "Brave Little Belgium". The result was, he got a lungful of chlorine for his pains. Afterwards he had to be very ingenious to survive at all, contrary or not. Did you know he introduced neon lighting into Ireland? At one time he even sold fishing flies of his own manufacture in a basement store. He did everything in his time, except succeed. I don't think success interested him much. He was a great reader, mainly history. He adored Marcus Aurelius. He had talent of a sort. He could draw like Doré ... well, better than Spitzweg. Painstaking draughtsmanship was his forte, with Victorian gravure effects. He did a pencil sketch of a dead soldier at the front that was unnerving, being offered the bays or a palm by some supernatural party, I think an angel. Anyway, he called it *Der Engel von Mons*. Without the angel it would have been effective. How all Victoriana quaked before that Blessed One on the battlefield – ages before the really terrible wars broke over us. Poor Father!'

One grey day he had done away with himself, took his own life. It was Michaelmas time. The weather had begun to turn raw and wet. He was then in the building trade. Up to the end he was engaged in throwing up a line of identical labourers' cottages in the pursuit of some municipal dream. Into the first installed gas oven he had put his head, turned on the juice, covered himself with his coat and took his last whiff of gas. So they found him, spilling from the oven, survived by wife and son. As it happens in the marches of history that a people, lacking a voice, lose themselves and are forgotten, so he had been forgotten.

'Poor Father,' Irwin Pastern said again. 'Is it much of an epitaph? But who, for that matter, can expect any better?'

'What about your Ellen?' Annelise said.

'That walking marvel!' he said. 'Let me tell you. She had long nicotine-stained fingers and the nail-biting habit – a type of latter-day Dagney Juell and *most* promiscuous; at all events a most consummate dissembling whore. We looked for order, not hers and certainly not mine, but between "arrangements" that never quite came off we hoped to achieve a balance. We never achieved it. All that remained after the first flush was a communion of irritations. Trying to be in two places at the same time exhausted me. The effort of communication became itself an act of love, or Love's poor relation. She was greatly attracted to men, but what she hoped to find there I could not say . . .'

He showed Annelise the view from the turret roof. Fetching out chairs he began to talk, as the tower shadows lengthened across the river, twilight already upon them, and from Neckar-Strasse other voices came, upraised in anger.

She sat opposite him, her chair tilted against the parapet. He told of his mother who had had a horror of obesity and had tried to live on a diet of stewed apples and bran. He told her of the street musicians he had seen in London, into whose bald heads pennies were sunk as though with a hammer, playing their accordions to the queue for *Modern Times*. He spoke of the young girls he had seen on a flat roof at Untertürkheim from a passing electric train, how they lay out in the sun, the pair of them on the threshold of puberty, dressed only in knickers, pressing each other's still non-existent breasts and laughing at the train. He told of the Hauptbahnhof at Munich; how it appeared at four in the morning with the down-and-outs stretched on newspapers like the dead laid out in the morgue. He spoke of the psychic artist Sylviana Bertrand who had work accepted by the French Salon for no better reason than she had claimed to produce paintings under the 'psychic guidance' of a Tibetan monk. He spoke too of Paul Klee at Kairouan and what he had seen there, the red-brick wall thirty feet high and the hundred mosques and the 420 columns and the Arabs distilling oil of roses, and how he – Klee – had begun to use colour.

She sat quiet opposite him, outlined against a moving sky, while he informed her that Charcot had been the first neurologist to take women's hysteria seriously, and that in etymology 'hysteria' means 'womb'. He told a story from Montaigne; how Persian mothers uncovered themselves to the chin when they saw their sons fleeing from battle, shouting: 'Where are you running to? Don't you know you cannot hide in our wombs again?'

He spoke of the poor of Mannheim, suggesting that pain was a fact beyond justice, not to be calculated, for in the rags and distress of grinding poverty he had seen hints of that desperation and encroachment which proclaims the breakdown of appearances, and in that square was cast back into the jungle where superstition – and religion – was born.

'Perhaps nothing ends,' he suggested – 'only changes. At least this much is certain: for every human being on earth life ends in themselves.'

He made a grimace into the dark. He had spoken at random, fabricating, contradicting, embellishing, extolling, deriding, rapid and slow, about every subject that entered his head, as though he were constructing something elaborate for her, while she sat there like inert matter – a sailor's grave of stones (his recollections), a cairn which he, a passer-by, kept adding to.

Three gulls were performing aeronautics fiercely overhead, squalling in the freemasonry of the air. On the river an insistent voice was mangling Schubert; it was a song from *The Winter Journey*, a female voice, feeble, not young;

> *Ach, und fällt Blatt zu Bo-den,*
> *Fällt mit ihm die Hoffnung ab,*
> *Fall' ich sel—ber mit zu Bo—den . . .*

At last her voice spoke across the gap between them. He heard the rustle of her skirt as she moved and then a strange voice saying out of the dark:

'Nothing can be much worse than poverty. It's just ugly and frightening, and from it one can learn nothing. A year after Willie left me I hadn't a thing. I don't mean I lacked comforts. I was reduced to actual want. Bread and cheese kept me alive and I drank nothing but water. I found a hide-out in Bellevue Park which seemed safe and slept there under my coat in the leaves. It was just off the footpath and in the mornings I would wake and see the feet of all the people of Berlin going to Mass – because there was a Catholic church down near the railway line. I went there one morning to get out of the cold. It was warm inside and candles were lit everywhere and up on the altar a priest was moving about as in a dream, and I sat at the back propped up between the pews – a true "fallen" woman. Someone was limping around doing the Stations, an old woman with a pot-shaped raffia hat with artificial berries in it. I was against the wall and Christ's feet were protruding a little from the Crucifixion and the old one was genuflecting and then standing, the beads flying in her hands, then genuflecting again, her lips moving fast as if Lucifer had his prongs into her. Then all at once she leant across me without even an "*Entschuldige!*", as if I wasn't there, breathing turnip jam all over me, and kissed Christ's plaster feet. The berries nodding away like mad Yes-yes-yes-that's-the-style. Holy Mother of God, and her hair all anyway; and I thought, *God, the faith of the poor and the lowly – it's not very fattening* . . .

'I used to go to the Spree to wash and also to try to keep warm. The street spraying machines were out at that hour, the drivers jumping off to struggle with the hydrants. Then, when the winter began, I had to move into a hostel. I ate even less after that and my health began to go. Shortly afterwards the nuns took me in. Two of the sisters had a pious practice of coming to my cell at midday to pray before the window, looking at me from the corner of their eyes. They were simple and kind, but the only way I changed was to get one ear bigger than the other, I mean the one I slept on. I have never slept so much in my life. When I left, I felt strong enough to come on here on foot – '

Annelise stopped.

The leaves of the beech trees on wide Anlage strained backwards as he walked to the station. The hands of the clock stood at 4.25 as his ticket was punched at the barrier. Some office girls went before him dressed in their finery, drawn tight across buttocks and bust. At the end of the platform he saw Annelise waiting, standing by an open carriage door.

The 4.30 slow for Mosbach drew out of Heidelberg for the millionth time, bearing Herr Irwin Pastern and Frau von Fromar to a house of assignation some way down the river.

As the carriage windows slid across the viaduct he saw an expiring sun low in the sky over the sheet-metal factory and the lying-in hospital and thought, *I am too old for this any more.*

Annelise sat opposite him and then alongside him, looking out of the window and saying nothing, her fingers locked in his. The secret fragrance of her flesh came to him, suggestive of both nettles and mignonette.

The non-denominational boys' school flew past, flying the German colours. He began to study the framed panels of advertisements in the carriage. Facing him below a crude illustration of a gentleman looking anguished was printed the legend:

KAUFT BASTEN SCHUHE
DER SCHUH FÜR FUSSLEIDENDE . . .

The next panel, black on green, with a symbolic female, announced:

KRÄUTERSAFT

(the woman was stark naked, arms upflung in triumph)

FÜR MAGENLEIDEN!

The panel next to this was blank except for a scrawl in indelible pencil:

TO HELL WITH THE JEWS!

He looked away. Near the lock between Ziegelhausen and Neckar Gemund a long-legged brown girl in scarlet shorts was tending an upturned rowing boat. The image crawled past. The whistle screamed as the train began to climb through a pine forest. At each of the short halts on the line an inspector appeared, to protect the alighting passengers lest in their eagerness to be away they should do themselves a mischief. Between the peak and brim of his cap on a dog-collar brass was inscribed his office: SCHAFFNER.

As the train began moving again the Schaffner swung himself aboard through the open door of the guard's van with consummate agility.

At last he was crying,

'Hirschhorn! . . . Hirschhorn!' Herr Pastern and his paramour alighted and went slowly towards the barrier. In the street outside a barrow man with a tableful of shrimps and crabs was shouting in a raucous voice and making wild signals:

'Eat! . . . Eat! Stop starving yourselves!'

Hirschhorn smelt pleasantly of pine and eucalyptus, mixed with the stronger odours of a river port. Below, between a medley of shirts blowing on a clothes line and a darkening balustrade, they saw a smooth stretch of the river flowing slowly west. The sky had grown darker and the streets were still steaming after rain.

Through the open door of a pork butcher's shop, Herr Pastern saw a stout little butcher with his back to them raising a cleaver. Folds of skin stretched over his stiff collar. As they passed he brought it down and the folds of skin subsided. They began to descend steps going towards the river. Moss and iris grew in profusion along the walls.

The cottage was situated on an eminence above the men's bathing place. The garden was overgrown with grass and the centre slats had fallen from a reclining seat. Out towards the centre of the stream a tar barrel had been moored in the channel. The sky was overreaching the land and cries from the late bathers carried up from below. Above his head, pressed to the darkening window pane, he saw the pale shape of a fish. He thought to himself: *I'll probably run away when she gets out of her clothes.*

As though struggling in the depths of the sea towards a surface ever withdrawing from him, receding because of the very insistence of his longing, his chest rose and sank, rose and sank, rising ever higher to sink ever lower; his lungs contracted, his eyes dilated, fingers shook at his nostrils – his mouth a dark cavern deprived of air; then the dreadful wheeze was expelled. He whispered to himself: *I am too old for this any more.*

Then he saw something white moving in the glass of the door and heard the sound of bare feet approaching; she came on towards him. As though set on some irrevocable course, and already falling, he kissed her mouth.

'I love you, Strephon,' she said. '*Ich liebe Dich.*'

She received him as a Roman suicide might take his sword; in the language of military strategy, he had achieved a 'peaceful penetration' at last.

He lay on his day-bed with eyes half closed; somewhere in the tower voices were chanting in what sounded like

Latin; light was ebbing from the high room, but he was uncertain whether it heralded night or the beginning of a darker day.

Lifting his head he saw a shape crouching inside the threshold of the open door. As his eyes grew more accustomed to the gloom he identified this as a pair of riding-breeches thrown down in disarray with stained linings exposed. He was conscious of his property about him, mute companions scattered throughout the three rooms leading from the turret stairs. Wood was piled banister-high in the hall waiting for the winter to come round again. His apparatus, with blank rolls of canvas, stood neglected in a corner of the Round Room. The dark-breathing tower was all about him and he was entombed in it as within a generous vault; immured within its walls which were older than the bridge pillars themselves, erected by one Carl Theodor in 1756; abandoned now by all its former tenants it seemed restless under this last occupation. Somewhere a board creaked or a door stirred. He distinguished the remote sounds of elm boughs scraping on the outer wall, fingers arranging something on his grave.

The turret door moved again on its rusted hinges and sand and dust scuffled in the drains. Silence persisted then until he moved in bed, sighing and restless.

At last he rose, covered himself in a blanket and climbed painfully upstairs, passing out onto the roof where cool air engulfed him. He leant over the parapet on the river side.

The old bridge lay deserted. Beyond it a plume of smoke ascended slowly from the Odenwald. The river went out sluggishly under the piers. In the distance across flat lands sown with asparagus, beyond the yellow stretches of the Pfalz vineyards, over the horizon, misted and winding among trees, was a shaft of light that marked the Rhine.

The nearer bulk of the tower seemed lost in innumerable river reflections. Over its placid surface a multitude of gnats, perceptive of the soft hour, performed haphazard patterns. A pasty whey-coloured river drifted reluctantly by, matched by a low ceiling of discoloured reluctantly moving cloud, which as it passed seemed to remove from river and town all the dejected masses collected there, rather as a 'transfer' will withdraw from the master stamp (once subjected to water) and leave a pale and sundered imitation, between which, for the brief space of the impress, an unresponsive reality has coldly intervened.

He stood looking vacantly about him, feeling the air of a bland summer day rest on his face, while his bare feet sank into the leads, as into tar. He thought of Hoppner and the exhaustion of perpetual day, the Arctic sun moving in a never-to-be-completed circle overhead. He felt too as though the hour were being perpetuated in order to torment him, adding to itself endlessly while his feet sank further into the soft lead; so that he stood in a place made derelict, watching formations of cloud deploying over Heidelberg spires. While he himself, at a geographical remoteness equivalent to death, witnessed processional day unrolling itself effortlessly, coming on from the horizon without interruption, formal and performed, but as though in mockery.

He felt space shift under his feet and had a vision of himself gripping the stone parapet above the drop as he might have held the ornate balustrade of a galleon plunging into the head of a storm; a ludicrous figure staring wild-eyed out over the void, hair on end, capillaries erupting on his florid cheeks; a scared face outlined for an instant against rolling cloud, then whipped back and gone.

Bowing his head as if under sentence he drew away from the stone, pulled the blanket about him and went down. Among the bedclothes he found a pair of trousers and a pullover. He dressed himself in these and pulled on a pair of brogues with burst-open heels. In the low-ceilinged kitchen he began to prepare a meal.

Twenty minutes later he was on the platform again. Evening had sunk a little, but not much. The temperature had dropped. The gnats had gone.

He recalled a freezing night soon after his tenancy had begun. He had stood then, key in hand, before the outer door, his head thrown back and his jaw at an acute angle to the ground, staring up in consternation at the tower he had foolishly rented, which had just moved in front of his eyes. He stood before the door into which all manner of hasps and bolts were embedded, dwarfed but insubordinate before the mass of swaying verticals, ready to plunge his small key (a Yale) into the only refuge he knew in an indifferent if not hostile world. High above his head, projected against the night sky, he saw the walls almost gaily in motion – as though the dense shadows thrown down to earth by the tower walls were not sufficient to moor it, but merely served the purpose of hawsers. Parted already by the prodigious strain exerted against them they had begun to fall away in terrific slow motion. Soundlessly, occurring coldly against a real sky full of October's sharp stars, they had begun collapsing, like something witnessed in the extremity of fear, watched by a person who had become paralysed, incapable of lifting a hand.

Berlin After Dark

He wore a widebrim fedora and carried a cane, suggestive of wealth – a stout man in a hurry along a grey tranquil street. Clenching his free fist, bulky and determined, he favoured the centre of the pavement following a course west along Kissinger Platz. Opposite the Delphi Cinema he altered course and bore briskly down Auguste-Viktoria-Strasse.

He examined himself with solicitude in a shop window. Hot disgruntled eyes stared back at him, a heavy moustache trimmed above a bitter mouth. Herr Bausch's deportment was admired by a variety of women. He walked in a surly loose-kneed fashion as though adjusting his stride to the inconveniences of a cavalry sabre. In point of fact he was uneasy on foot and alone, without his chauffeur Ned, and seemed himself to walk in chains.

Satisfied at length he advanced towards a tobacconist's sign. As the door clanged shut behind him a bilious winter sun broke free of cloud. Aloft on a hoarding the haggard features of the actress Lotte Lenya, four times larger than life, stared with depersonalised venom over all and sundry.

All the ladies of Berlin might fall for Herr Bausch but he could not repay the compliment. Girls in general, troubled by the scarce music of their years, bored him outright. Wedded women of a certain character were his allotted prey. As nothing less than a dashing kepi or a General Lee slouch hat could do justice to that sepia-coloured visage and hunter's lope, so nothing less than a double blooding could satisfy his keen sense of the kill; the weak shriek of the outraged wife echoed, so to speak, in the dismayed husband's *basso profondo*.

Herr Bausch had a coarse weatherbeaten face and small almost lobeless ears which were laid back along his skull like a boar's. The pale stubble of a military haircut stood up, once free of fedora and feather, like aftergrass on his bullet head. Below it his features squeezed themselves together in a veritable snout, on each side of which were arranged little bloodshot eyes. It was a face that might have revealed nothing, given away nothing, had not the over-impressionable human physiognomy betrayed him. As certain burrowing creatures, in order to gain their ends or to exist at all, are resolved down to one anxious or bitter form of themselves (the burrowing snout and its fellow darkness), so his features seemed to narrow down to one place and one gesture: his was a face falling back to a function. As winds in their persistence stretch and sharpen boulders, and as these in turn indicate free access to territory beyond, so the features of Herr Bausch spoke of only one preoccupation, and that preoccupation, venery. Venery not so pure, not so simple. His nostrils could still expand under temptation although he would not see forty again.

He was driven about by his chauffeur, Ned, in a highly polished Hispano Suiza, fitted out with every conceivable comfort, including a pile carpet into which the legs of delighted lady passengers sank to the hocks. This dread-nought was but one of the indulgences he permitted himself once he had amassed his fortune.

He had begun his career inauspiciously as a junior cement worker in a small factory in Breslau, Silesia, some time before 1930. The lowest ebb in his fortunes came early in the 1930s, for with the Depression he lost his job and the factory had to close down. In 1934 he had no option but to join the Party and was to be seen soon after strutting around in the brown uniform and peaked cap of the National-Sozialistische Reichsarbeitsdienst – his one cue for salvation.

Within a year he was offered a rank on a reserve basis and became, with Herr Speer's blessings, more or less free to continue with his own projects. Together with a comrade named Herisson he bought up requisitioned lorries for haulage contracts between Breslau and Stettin. These machines were to become a familiar sight on the Breslau–Stettin road, overladen and underpowered, the doors and tippers inscribed with the legend:

BAUSCH UND HERISSON

Fuhrunternehmer und
Zementhändler

BRESLAU–GLOGAU–KÜSTRIN–EBERSWALDE–STETTIN

By 1936 he had his own cement factory. As one of the pioneers of the Reichsarbeitsdienst he was in a position to perform favours for the Party, in return for which he was declared *unabkömmlich* and spared the doubtful honour of carrying arms or the ignominy of digging irrigation ditches. In addition, thanks to his own exertions, he was able to secure Reichsarbeitsdienst haulage contracts in eastern Prussia.

Contracted to Todt, of the Reich Roads, he could begin to consider buying property in Berlin. Soon afterwards he did so, acquiring a fine house on Königs-Allee in

Grunewald, with a view of the wood. The war was approaching, but Herr Bausch found himself for the first time in life comfortably off, and chose to ignore it.

The island of Sylt, and Bavaria, were the regions where he took his summer pleasures.

Stimulated after immersion in the harsh waters of the North Sea, Herr Bausch lay prone in the shelter on a cement block the size of a gymnast's 'horse', reading from a paperback novel of erotic content.

Every ten seconds the flat report of the surf striking the beach and exploding forward came to him. That morning, under eyebrows stiff with salt from his diving, he had watched a dark fellow of uncompromising mien splashing a concupiscent Swedish girl, both in hilarious undress, some way down the beach. Almost dissolving in such effervescent whiteness, she had exposed all the drenched and tantalising fissures and ramps of her female person.

Removed from the polyglot uproar of Westerland Casino, Kampen lay quiet. Every conceivable amenity of undressed nature abounded there, including the nudist colony. In his mind's eye, Herr Bausch saw kilometre upon kilometre of deserted sand dunes open to such sport, overhung by cliffs and backed by meadows and stray Friesian cottages upon which storks roosted.

His own gross bulk and the purposeful arrangements of spine and buttock (free of bathing drawers) created in conjunction with the block a truncated and obscene effect. Fixed and stern, it seemed as though his member was embedded in the cement, which took on the property of a prodigious root or membrane doubled under him and upon which he lay passive – something by which he could immediately be recognised, as the monsters of antiquity are recognised by a particular vice or the unicorn by its extravagant horn.

The type of women that Willie Bausch was attracted to belonged to the wealthy and idle cast who had grown familiar with sumptuous surroundings but had not yet lost prosaic appetites. He was addicted to these as poultrymen are addicted to Perigord geese. One of the temptations he could under no circumstances resist was the lustrous flesh of a lady with an imposing carriage and, say, an income exceeding 15,000 marks to set it off.

Hot in the pursuit of this daemon, he had obliged some such ladies to connive at their downfall. His generosity was at the best of times as lame as that of the poultrymen, they who must subject their charges to the indignity of *gavage*, stuffing them with more corn than they can well manage, if necessary thrice a day, with the aid of a funnel or stick. So that more than one of his ravishing dupes had made a début in high German society in a condition almost as wretched as the geese, who are in any case obliged to enter a dining room backwards, skewered and despoiled, exposing a monstrous great liver now dilated to half the size of a football. Prior to this, Herr Bausch's ladies, reduced now almost to *foie gras* themselves, were laid down and submitted to a conditioning as brutal.

By turns prodigal and mean, now withholding tips, now dispensing them with grandiose impartiality, he was both welcomed and feared by the staffs of half a dozen night clubs in Hamburg and Berlin. In the St Pauli district of Hamburg, in Greifi, in Zur Wilden Sau, he was known but not respected. In Berlin he favoured Resi and the Krehan Bar, near the Bahnhof-Zoo.

Coming in from Helmstedt he passed fields sown with winter crop; mangolds and swedes fidgeting in their long chill trenches, and on all sides upturned clay and sodden fields bare of cattle; a pastoral scene that always left him at a loss and unhappy.

Leaves were scattering over the Autobahn. As he reached the entrances to Berlin the lights came on. He could not keep his feet warm, but was almost home.

Berlin had always been faithful to him, and it was there he had enjoyed his first great success. He was to leave behind a memory – a fading wake – of coups accomplished, gargantuan dinners, ten-mark notes floating down the Spree; an almost carnival prodigality to which all the favoured ladies would be obliged to submit in time.

He might well feel pleased with himself and with Berlin, for there he had graduated from the old hand-to-mouth existence to the grandeur, presumption anyway, of an almost patrician order. Berlin bars and Berlin women were to protect him as if he were their talisman. The hotels and cabarets he patronised had imparted to him a hue, an effulgence, analogous with their own plenty. It was an aura difficult to place, redolent of Opal cigar smoke, the dulled odour suggestive of repletion that over-polished mahogany and intractable brocade exudes, and something else besides – a pressure as positive (though itself intangible) as the suspiration of the hotel heating system. It had about it the guarded and sunken quality, somehow associated in the mind both with relief and with untimely death, of a game-lick come upon in thick bush. A wild animal resort bereft of animals must seem to the curious human eye as tenanted, as charged with their outraged absence, as the very track itself must seem loud with their presence. And Willie Bausch's own presence was not without that hint of menace. Formidable and heavy in his lion-tamer coat, he drove a small herd of servants down the steps of the Adlon, tripping over baggage, out into the street. Dispatched on its way with their curses, his cab went bowling down the Budapester-Strasse bound for the Krehan Bar.

The women who accompanied him on these excursions were no lightweights; pallid brunettes as a rule sat in the cab with him, with hair falling over the collars of their fur coats, narrow featured, prim of mouth, lethargic, with standard tempting legs ending in pointed shoes, their hands lost in a muff, about them hung an air of faded elegance. To oblige him sometimes they would consent to open their coats, only to discover his hot hand under their armpits drawing them down. In simulated recoil then, exposing their gums in wild protestations, they panted in a ferocious whisper:

'*Nicht jetzt, nicht hier . . . nein, nein, Willie, bitte nicht!*' Until with an instinct as hot and avaricious as his own, they consented.

Later at night, muscles bulging and cigar in hand, he would visit the wilder houses and permit himself indiscretions. Solid and barrel shaped he sat among the whores, thumping his thigh and bellowing in a fashion difficult to sympathise with. Presently they too, despite their bored manner, became infected and began to roll their eyes, with their backsides and mouths never still, as if they were targets being continually readjusted to a nicer range.

'See my all-togethers, Willie!'

Willie glared and brought down his fist on the table so that all the little fingers of *Mampe halb und halb* shook together. As he began to lead them pell-mell into the lewd territory he dreamed of, the atmosphere so forthrightly induced – redolent as it was of excreta and iron – became as insuppressible as the brawl of the gorilla house.

At some hour, on some bed chosen by him, he had injected a full head of lust into a more or less willing victim. One of the pale suspicious temptresses had permitted the snout and the bristles to intervene between her and the light and suffered embraces as muscular in character as therapeutic massage. And who can say, perhaps under such sub-feral conditions his rufous virility seemed an inestimable consolation. Not for him the *Verba dat omnis amans* common to the world's keen lovers. Rolling on his femur as if adjusting his aim, he bore down, heavy and inflexible, until safely embedded in still-living subject female flesh.

An amiable divorcee who had lived for many years in Buenos Aires, and was connected in some way with Ufa Studios in Berlin, had on one memorable occasion accompanied him to Bavaria. Built like a puma and with eyes which seemed all pupil, she had a way of staring him out as though estimating the bore of a gun trained upon her. She proved to be one of his better stud selections.

'Oh indeed,' she said, crossing her legs. 'Bavaria?'

'Lower Bavaria,' Willie said.

'How low?'

'Yes,' Willie said, 'the savages. It will amuse you. They eat out of a hole in the table, drink and play Tarock all night. The air! (spreading out thick fingers). The *Knödel!* (raising his eyes heavenwards). Yes, you will enjoy it immensely. We need not trouble Ned. Leave it all to me. We can take our time.'

'But, dearest *Schmutzig*,' she said, 'I have no time.'

'Nonsense!' Willie declared roundly. 'Stay a few days and see. Dingolfing will be a real cure. You can bathe in the Isar. I'll telegraph Herr Wirt today.'

'You are so persuasive,' she said, looking at him with her puma's eyes. 'I suppose I need a rest after Berlin. Tell me, must I leave my maidenly qualms behind?'

'Rich!' Willie roared. 'Rich!' and guffawed violently.

They drove out of Berlin's thin sun over cobblestones,

Willie impassive and very upright at the wheel, wearing motoring gloves rolled back from the wrist. The puma was dressed in a severe grey-and-white costume with a leopardskin toque.

He drove at a moderate speed all the way, changing gear when required with the solemnity of a bishop adjusting his gaiters. Towns came and went. Willie offered few comments, being content to puff at his cigar; his passenger offered even less, staring out of the window and missing nothing.

In the valley of the Isar a stream of warm air surprised them and Willie let down the hood. Rushes waved along the river with white butterflies in attendance. In the garden of Gasthaus Zum Koglerwirt a small brown-faced wrinkled man with a shock of blond hair hurried to and fro dispensing beer.

'Herr Wirt,' Willie said, nodding sagaciously as though he had created not only the Zum Kogler but Herr Wirt as well. He looked at his watch and then at his passenger.

'We have made good time,' he said with evident satisfaction. He unrolled one glove to shake Herr Wirt's hand. Indicating her with an inclination of the head he said: 'Herr Wirt, allow me to introduce my ward. Countess Gerta Kroll!'

Dressed only in a towel the puma advanced recklessly across sand and into the river until it reached to her knees.

'Look!' she called, and whirling, flung away the towel.

'Very nice,' Willie said, pulling at his tie.

When it grew dark they sat in the tap room like true lovers and were served beer by Herr Wirt. Willie ordered Moselle for dinner. It appeared in due course through the hatch to be followed shortly by Frau Wirt in person, all smiles, who made a bow and said:

'*Guten Appetit!*'

Before they had quite finished an encouraging Szege-
diner Gulasch, a trapdoor opened a few feet from where
they were seated and a blast of damp hot air, compounded
of rotten beams, horse and *Pschorrbräu*, almost overbal-
anced the 'Countess', who happened to be sitting with
her back to it.

Willie half rose in his seat and saw over her shoulder a
brawny arm, evidently female, supporting the trapdoor,
out of which a frass of strong light gushed in all directions.
Glaring across the table at him, a glass suspended midway
to her mouth, the 'Countess' whispered:

'*Mein Gott, was ist es nun schon wieder, Willie?* . . .'

'Wait,' Willie said without taking his eyes off the arm.

A wildly excited male voice of deep and resounding
register could be heard hallooing below. Above this came
a succession of ringing blows falling heavily on some
metallic surface, followed by more cries and then a ponderous fall.

'Can they be dismantling a train in the cellar?' said the
'Countess' under her breath.

In the widening aperture Willie saw a fuzz of yellow
hair which seemed to be standing on end. As he watched
it began to ascend until a face duly appeared below it.
He found himself staring into a pair of innocent blue
eyes. The head sank again until he saw nothing but hair
and he heard her voice say in coaxing tone:

'Helmut, please go easy on the cylinders.'

This time (for she had risen a step as she called) Willie
saw a dirndl cut low enough to be considered frontless,
and a bosom upon the peaceful slopes of which beads of
honest sweat rose and fell, rose and fell.

'Well?' said the 'Countess'. 'What is it?'

'They are adjusting the carbon oxide.'

'Carbon oxide,' repeated the 'Countess'. 'Why in God's name carbon oxide?'

Willie reseated himself and began to attend to his cigar. 'I believe to elevate the beer,' he said.

The vision had by this time completely emerged and, bending in a dangerous manner, was closing the trapdoor. Through clouds of cigar smoke Willie saw a model worthy of the brush of Rubens approaching. Midway between the table and counter she made the sketch of a curtsy, exposing if possible even more bust, and went tripping behind the beer pulls.

'Halcyon days,' said the 'Countess'.

After an interval some locals filed in. Seating themselves along the wall they began ordering rounds of beer. Sucking long clay pipes and looking blank, they were served decorously by the young woman from the cellar.

Shortly after ten o'clock Willie and the puma began to retire. Three-quarter way up the stairs he heard the voice of Herr Wirt bidding him goodnight. Turning he saw both of them side by side below, one plump and one wrinkled, their hands upraised as though surprised in the act of taking leave of air passengers – raised not only above their own 'station' by embarking in an airliner, but above their thinking for ever.

'*Gute Nacht, Herr Bausch!*' they cried. '*Gute Nacht, Gräfin Kroll!*'

Willie, taken by surprise, raised his hand also.

'*Gute Nacht,*' he said civilly.

The following afternoon a telegram addressed to the Countess Kroll arrived from Berlin. She read it quickly once and said:

'Well, friend, that's that ... I must leave tomorrow morning.'

Willie objected in a 'thunderstruck' voice.

'Yes, yes, it's quite impossible,' she said.

'If you must go,' Willie said, 'of course I'll drive.'

'No,' she said, 'that won't be necessary. Ufa have started casting in Munich. There must be a train. It is a pity. I have enjoyed it here. *Komm, lass uns zum letzten Mal schwimmen gehen . . .*'

Next morning they drove in bright sun to the station. She promised *von sich hören zu lassen,* once back in Berlin again; but instead of that was to spend the best part of a year making a film in Salonika. Willie mentioned that he would probably stay on another day or two.

'Then you behave yourself,' she said, striking him lightly with her glove. (He had in fact scented game again.)

'*Eine Ehre für unser Haus, Herr Bausch!*' said Herr Wirt.

The puma leant out of the carriage window and raised her hand as the train drew her away.

While searching for his collar stud in the bedroom on the previous day, Willie had unearthed a curious document from behind the cabinet. It was written in pencil on the lined pages torn from a school exercise book and was signed, 'Ida'. Now Ida, as he had been inquisitive enough to find out, was the name of the girl with the Susanne Fourment bust. Ida Schindler. Moreover, she was thirty-six, married but no longer living with her husband, a good-for-nothing named Joseph Schindler who was reputed to be dissipating his energies at a great rate about the neighbourhood, had as a consequence lost most of his trade (he was a master carpenter) and was in the process of losing Ida by divorce. Willie read the letter through once more in the privacy of his room, his flesh creeping. It bore neither address nor date and ran without paragraph indentation throughout:

Oh you happily married husband!

    I wish you lots of luck with your young wife. Are you not ashamed to sleep next to the woman? It must please you to see again a naked undressed beautiful body which excites you so that you can boast about it in the Inns. You old potbellied man you are probably on top of her as with Josepha the half-dead one. Even from the altar you were looking about for another one. You were on top of every dungheap in Vilsbiburg that was the 'thing' whatever it may have been so long as it was female. You cannot blame me for the consequences of our marriage. The fault is with your tramping about and with the innkeepers. And that she is so much more capable than me you will have to forgive. She will have to be more capable still to pay your 300 marks drinking and whoring debts like I did. She will probably have to carry your collars to the Isar perhaps she also has the honour to wash your shat-into trousers which you have shat into and vomited upon when you were drunk it is no wonder that it stank so in that little room. If they pulled you down from a whore you would certainly still deny it well that denying was invented by a fool so it won't help you. I should have thrown you out at Josepha's place I should have known you sooner. You shall not have a happy hour of death, on your last deathbed you will have to ask me to forgive you for what you have done to me made unhappy for all my life. The sun does not shine on any more evil man than you. You will also have to come to Vilsbiburg to show off your woman but the people are not interested in you, they are too accustomed to your tramping about, you do not show anything new. How glad the company down there are that they are rid of a burden but how long. Have your things fetched otherwise I will throw them out but you will not enter my hut any more. I must ask you what has happened to my snuff money will I not get it. I will probably have to bring this to the police. You will probably have none you will probably still be celebrating your honeymoon Ich hätt' dich früher kennen gekönnt die Leut' haben mir's wohl *erzählt*...

(Here, in mid-stride, the first page ended as though the writer had broken off in speechless rage).

The second page began:

In all the years that you were married you were on top of every beggar woman in the place ah I was horrified by you. You will probably have the same inclination as with Josepha Olsacher. At least you have got one again to sit before you where you are working she has got the time she has nothing to do but serve you. Do not try to blind the people they know you are black enough already but she will never pay your debts like I did for being good you have pushed me out naked into the world my own people vouched for me so that I did not perish, not my own husband. If love falls on a dungheap, as it can well be said to in this case, there it lies. She will be only too glad that she has got a man and the children a father rejoice that you got one woman at least who is your equal birds of a feather flock together. You would probably have kept that Josepha whore if the devil had not fetched her. The money she gave you for her tombstone you spent on drink and she is still without one it is very embarrassing if the people can hold something like that against you. Perhaps that fate will also befall you one day. Your half of the hut was not worth 500 marks every penny that I had to pay for you you shall atone for I have done more towards the hut than you. The people said that you only married so that you could get along easier but it isn't true for you would still manage with all of Vilsbiburg on your hands but not with that woman who you have made unhappy for all her life. Probably you will go with this one also into all the Inns as you did with the Olsacher the people are horrified by you. Bugger! Schweinkerl! Ausg'schamter, Gleichgültiger! Eh'brecher! *I wish you lots of luck.*

Ida.

Willie longed to know her; within that useful volume of flesh what a heart was beating – a compliant furnace! Vulgar, if you will, Willie admitted, stroking his nose; but he and she were alike, of the same abject and bellicose blood. He decided there and then to order coffee in his room that night. It could be tactfully arranged. With what a roguish look he would say:

'*Dein Dirndl ist so anziehend, Ida* . . .'

Perhaps drawing it down a fraction, perhaps pinching her bottom. And Ida, who was in any case all dirndl and bottom, would succumb. When a woman of passion finds herself loose in a man's bedroom, Willie assured himself, nature is bound to take over. *Ja, Enthaltsamkeit macht das Gemüt zärtlicher!* He took a bath towel from the bed-rail and set out for the Isar in high good spirits. Dingolfing had surpassed itself.

Prompt at 10.30 that night he heard a discreet rap on the door and a voice saying:

'*Der Kaffee, mein Herr!*'

He threw open the door and was confronted under the low lintel by the same periwinkle eyes and generous front, which seemed to be tilted at him. She carried a steaming object before her on a tray.

'*Der Kaffee, mein Herr,*' she repeated, staring submissively at him.

Willie dragged his eyes away and noticed coffee and biscuits arranged on perforated paper.

'Bring it in, Ida,' he said backing smartly away. '*Bring es herein!*'

Ida carried in the tray and Willie closed the door behind her with his foot. The fruit hung, still unplucked, from the bough. Then begin!

They performed a ponderous gavotte by the window: it ended in the usual fashion under the heavy quilt. In the asylum of the bed and of her arms his nostrils knew again the once-familiar odour of a feminine labouring body, pungent and soothing as the tang of split Baltic pine (even though she stank of *Kaiser-Schmarrn*, sweat and unliberated tap-room smoke). Moved more than he would have liked to admit by the ardour of her moist honest-to-goodness embraces, he had the uncomfortable sensation of being at once whole and dismembered, and all in one operation; as a shoal of fish (his nerves and evasions) caught in the haul, believing themselves free but no longer so, become more and more distressed as they come together and are dragged frantic at last out of the *Gegenströmung*.

No longer the great god Pan or even the sham-squire Bausch, Willie renounced for the time being all his presumptions and in a fever embraced all his past – the thick cotton stockings, the nailed boots, the terrible bloomers, all flung aside and disregarded – and sank without trace into Ida Schindler's prepared white featherbed as into an ancestral sea.

Next morning he began the return journey to his mansion in the Königs-Allee.

Into an international set of loose or fallen women he once more led his preoccupation, as a skipping Croat gypsy might lead, with ball and chain, his unreliable performing bear. Meekly the women submitted, as though no other course were open to them. Signorina Bikken-Mikkelson of Genoa fell, Egberdine Broeze of Halsingborg, Conny Mol of gay Vienna, Jantze Nieuwenhuis of the Hague, Maria Augusta Siebrito of Wesermünde, Smartrizk Herbst of Bucharest, four dashing American ladies – Maura Veening of Altona, Jeanne Pronk of Butte, Montana, Mrs and Miss Stan Crooker of Toledo – these were numbered among the fallen. Add to this, Antonia Maria Burger of München, Grietze Voms of Köln, Corn

Schillersort of Olomouc, Gerta Kroll of Berlin, Sietske
Schouwstra of Rügen, Schwester Waltraud Ebenda of
Oberammergau, and on the same day, Helen Stöhnen
of Graz, Mrs Tom Forrest of Swiss Cottage, and in the
end, Frau Baronin Mathilda Schaffrath-Wilge of the
Power-House had resoundingly fallen.

Risen apparition-like from these splendid beds, and
from others too numerous to mention, Swedish beds,
generous Austrian and over-generous Lithuanian beds,
Romanian beds and deep White Russian beds, from these
lairs had Sextus Tarquinius Bausch of Silesia risen, to
claim in the end Annelise von Fromar as his Lucrece.

They were married in a Protestant church in Berlin.
But hardly was the ink of their signatures dry, hardly had
he left the Registrar's office with Annelise on his arm,
when the guns began to go off and the Panzer divisions
went careering into Poland. Königs-Allee shook to the
sound of marching feet and swastikas and brass bands
broke out like a plague all over the city. The phrase
'Hitler's Germany' had had as little meaning for Herr
Brausch as the phrase 'God's good earth', or even 'Satan's
Hell'; he would still survive, despite unspeakable odds.
But now he found that this unspoken truism was no
longer true and the whole structure of his pre-war *Besitz-
giere* had begun to collapse in front of his eyes.

A considerable business which he had coaxed out of
virtually nothing was about to be swept from his grasp. As
a 'purely temporary measure' his lorries were confiscated,
camouflaged and refitted with canvas roofs; after which
they disappeared from the face of the earth. As compen-
sation he was given a staff car and was obliged to drive it
himself in the capacity of a reserve quartermaster, following with very ill grace in the wake of the victorious
German Army through Belgium and Holland.

The niceties of Mine and Thine had never troubled

him overmuch, but with the departure of his lorries he lost even that fundamental sense of self-preservation which should have warned him to tread carefully. And once again the gamble paid off, for a while at least. He who had been no true National Socialist at heart – as the Party was well aware – began now a form of single-handed espionage, a movement which, and this made it awkward, did not bother to distinguish ally from enemy. The loss of his business, his profitable connections, his bank account all taken from him by a gang of goose-stepping blackguards, this was more than he could endure. He began to speculate on the black market.

At first he smuggled silk stockings from France into Germany. Then knitting machines from Saxony went back into France, with sunflower oil from the Ukraine. Growing bolder, he bartered sewing-machine needles in exchange for American cigarettes and saccharine, and then bartered the good will of Sweden against all the loot he could lay his hands on in the Low Countries in the semi-illegal, semi-immoral, highly profitable 'gift parcel' trade. At one time he would be a receiver for a 'Pan-German Dye Trust' and at another a manufacturer of synthetic petrol. Later, as an old friend of the production foreman (who supplied him with a wagonload of candles), he appointed himself trustee and chairman of a curious combine: the 'Staatliche Kerzenmanufaktur, Werra.'

All this came to an end in 1943 when his connection with the haulage trade landed him in Russia. There to his discomfort he found himself in the midst of the German retreat. Intoxication with property had led him to a high peak that had been quite invisible to his eye in Breslau – his cement worker's eye; but now the same intoxication was to force him down the other side, into a valley without sun.

His presumptuous marriage, as if it too constituted part

of his 'property gains' and could be lost or liquidated, ended. He was obliged to get rid of the house on Königs-Allee. Then he could no longer visit Berlin. Losing heart he did not bother to trace Annelise. She in turn refused to get in touch with him. Then Berlin and Annelise sank on the horizon, under brimstone and fire.

After that Willie Bausch went wherever his cupidity led him. In 1944 he was discovered by an old comrade from Silesia standing outside the Reserve Bank in Paris scrutinising the face of the building, and boasted at once of two lines he had running simultaneously in Venezuela: flints for cigarette lighters and razors that could cut both ways.

Lebensraum

I

Fräulein Sevi Klein left Germany in the spring of her thirty-ninth year; travelling alone from Cologne to Ostend, she crossed the Channel, and from Folkestone to London found herself in the company of sober British citizens. She took a reserved seat facing the engine on the London train, her feet on the carriage floor as settled as ball-and-claw furniture, both fierce-looking and 'arranged' after the manner of such extremities, curving downwards towards a relentless grip. Her hips and spine conveyed the same impression, but reinforced, becoming the downturned head of a dumb creature with muzzle lowered as though drinking; her eyelids seemed an intolerable weight. Her knees were pressed modestly together, she had hands of remarkable beauty and dressed in a manner suitable for someone possibly ten years younger. At Victoria Station she hired a cab, read out the name of a Kensington hotel from her pocket-book and was driven there with a moderate amount of luggage strapped into the boot. This was in the summer of 1947.

Sevi Klein walked the streets with the rolling gait of a sailor. In the National Gallery she stood minute below the paintings of Veronese, marvelling at his immense hot-faced women. Here she had met her match, for she was a lady herself down to the cockpit, but below that a snake chitterling or a chitterling snake.

Inevitably she walked into trouble at night on the Bayswater Road. The whores told her exactly what she could do with herself in cockney and French, a dark one pouring baleful abuse into one ear, brandishing a copy of the Sierra Leone *Observer.* She said:

'*Vergess es,*' thinking she preferred the Brinkgasse. Several times she was accosted by late gentlemen passing in Palace Avenue, until she took to scaling the fence into Kensington Gardens. She sat on the cement edge of the Round Pond with both feet submerged, the red glow of her cigarette reflected in the water between her legs; leaning forward until the monotonous passage of ingoing and outgoing traffic on Bayswater Road became dulled and remote. After a while she heard only the wind in the trees and the stirrings of the geese across from her. At last she threw away her cigarette and sat with the edge of her skirt trailing in the water, hearing nothing.

Her flat was a dark place into which an uncertain sun never entered, but in summer loitered for a couple of hours on the balcony before creeping away. She opened the full-length windows to sit drinking coffee in the sun, dropping her ash through the iron grid, staring into the chestnut tree opposite. On odd Sundays the terrace resounded to the deafening strains of an itinerant drum-and-accordion band.

The whores continued to be suspicious of her. A free-lance who lived in the basement next door had noticed her nocturnal habits and irregular hours of business and passed on the information. She roamed the streets with an air free yet constrained, like a castaway. Growing attached to Kensington Gardens she liked to spend whole days there in summer dressed as briefly as decency would permit, sitting on a deckchair under the hawthorns. She read constantly and brought out a covered basket of sandwiches and cold beer. She enjoyed drinking but missed the bitter Kölsch beer of *Vater Rhein.*

In dull weather the gardens were deserted at evening save for old women exercising dogs. Then she went sauntering down the avenues of trees beyond the equestrian statue, heading for the Serpentine, a small figure silhouetted for an instant where the lanes ran together, dwindling, shapeless, then blotted out. Her favourite pub was by the Queensway Underground. An already strong thirst was improved every time she passed the entrance and caught the dead air carried up by the lift. Then the gates crashed to on another lift full of pale commuters – the light vanishing as the contraption sank from sight.

One evening in June of that year she had drunk a little too much again and was flushed and talkative; meeting her reflection in one of the mirrors behind the bar, she knew it. The mirrors created an hexagonal smoke-filled confusion, and in these the patrons would sometimes encounter unexpectedly their own befuddled stares directed back at them from unlikely angles between shining tunnels of bottles. There upon the reflection of her own features another's strange features sank. A question was directed at her. Looking up she came face to face with a Mr Michael Alpin, late of Dublin, the doubtful product of Jesuit casuistry and the Law School. As far as the eye could see the patrons, with downcast eyes, were drinking their anxious beer. On one side a drunk repeated:

'Fizzillogical . . . (inaudible) Swizzer-land . . . Yesh, shir,' and a sober one said over and over again: 'Really I don't know whether to buy that house or not . . . now really I don't.' An elderly gentleman who had blown his nose too hard had to leave his drink and retire bleeding to the toilets. But Michael Alpin looked down into the small crucified face under the love-locks with the accumulated arrogance of a man who had made cuckolds (this was far from being the case, for he had emerged out of a past barren as Crusoe's as far as passionate attachments went). Would she care to join him in a drink? Would she? Nothing daunted, she gave him one quick look and said:

'Very well, thank you. I think I could.'

With some such preliminaries their life together had begun: in smoke, uproar and the sight of blood as if in the midst of a bombardment – to the skirl of a barrel-organ in the street outside and the look of incomprehension on his face (for he knew not a word of the language), while she chattered away in German.

They left arm in arm at closing time. He informed her that he had thrown up his profession and gone to seek his fortune on the continent of Europe. Morose and unsettled, he wore the air of a conspirator passing through enemy territory at night (although everything about him suggested furtive though arrested flight – a figure of doom superimposed on the landscape in dramatic photogravure). Plunged in a gloom out of which no succour could hope to lift him, Alpin the versatile Bachelor of Arts was twelve years her junior.

They set up house together in Newton Road, Paddington. Her forthright manner both perturbed and enchanted him. He himself had attempted to expand his hopes by the guarded necessity of having innumerable alternatives and had almost succeeded in abolishing them altogether. In the following summer they crossed to Dublin. They were seen at the Horse Show where Sevi's curious manner of dressing was noticed by the press, her photograph appearing in the next morning's newspaper over the caption: 'MISS S. KLEIN, A VISITOR FROM COLOGNE,

PHOTOGRAPHED IN THE JUMPING ENCLOSURE YESTERDAY.'
After that they moved to a hotel twenty miles down the
coast, driving through the pass one evening in a hired
car, hoisting their baggage onto the Grand Hotel counter
and signing their false names with a flourish: 'Mr and Mrs
Abraham Siebrito, Cascia House, Swiss Cottage, London,
NW3'. There they came together at last steadfast as man
and wife, though he was almost young enough to be her
own long-lost son, and no marriage lines had ever been
cried over them.

They lay together at night listening to the freight trains
pulling through the tunnels, exchanging confidences.
She spoke of a wet night at Enschede on the German—
Dutch border. Woken in the early hours of the morning
by bicycle bells and noises from the drunks in the lane
behind the hotel, she had heard a monstrous voice roar
with a blare almost of ordnance, and in English:

'Run! Run! Run from me!. . . But do not run in a circle!'
He mentioned a Negro whom he had observed buying a
newspaper outside the S-Bahn in Berlin, and how the
action of selecting money from a reefer jacket, dropping
it into the vendor's box, taking a newspaper, thrusting it
under his arm and entering the station, was performed
to a rhythm almost ballad-like – a flowing series of poetic
actions, he said, as appropriate as the equivalent in an
uncorrupted community, performed with the 'rightness'
of hundreds of years of repetition behind it; the same
economical gestures he had seen put to another use on
Inishere when the islandmen were launching the cur-
rachs. Into a mechanical and self-conscious milieu the
Negro had introduced something as natural and unex-
pected as the village pumps encountered among the
chromium and neon signs on the Kurfürstendamm.

'But why not?' she said. 'After all, the Negro has been
a city man since the invention of printing.'

'But not as a free man, Sevi,' he said. 'Not free.'

'Free?' said Sevi faintly, '*Herr Gott!* Who's free?'

Then she slept with her knees drawn up, drawing on oxygen as the dying draw on air. From such deep sleeps, recurring over and over again, light as sediment, heavy as evidence, she was not so much woken up as retrieved. He did not attempt to touch her, for there were depths into which he did not care to penetrate. Apprehensive of a bitterness and venom half perceived or guessed at beyond her habitual kindness, beyond her ability to be hurt, while he himself was attempting the impossible – to hold such contradictory elements together in his love. Every day he feared he would lose her, and every night he feared he was going to bed alone, seeing her bound so: the distress of a frontier people obliged to present their backs to grievance and opposition. About her hung an air of demolition; taking herself so much for granted she seemed immune to her own destruction. Her presence admitted no other alternative; she could only be relieved when she was let go. Since he held the scales in his hand, perhaps he felt also that she was disappointed in him. Looking for an arena where she could be put away, she had not found it in his cold bed. Even though his love was offered *in extremis*. Even though he was himself invaded and all his neutrality violated.

She went for long walks alone; returning late at night, re-entering the sleeping village, coming to the hotel where her lover lay sleeping. As she ascended the stairs the building seemed to shake, so that he awoke to become the unborn child in her womb, and the whole resounding house her stomach. She stood outside the door listening before taking the handle in her hands and tearing it open. He started up in bed. Standing with the light behind her she hissed into the dark bedroom:

'*Michael, bist Du aufgewacht?*'

Sevi chain-smoked everywhere, taking volumes of Proust
into dinner, dining on prawns. Rain kept them indoors
for days on end, arguing on the stairs; she went out only
to exercise her dachshund, Rosa Flugel, or to attend Mass.
She came down to dinner in a housecoat of faded blue
denim such as greengrocers favour, ate rapidly, reading
from a book propped up before her, arranging prune-
stones in an absent manner on the cloth. He loved and
desired her, incapable of the most rudimentary caution.
He felt a tension in her which would not permit her to
age – holding her years like a pendant about a no-longer-
young neck. Thus she came to invoke for him the
incautious women of the eighteenth century, talented yet
promiscuous, half whore, half wife. Thinking of Sevi he
remembered Madame de Warens, and made himself par-
ticipator in what he had lost. When he touched her flesh
it seemed infested with another life. Sevi too was a woman
never at rest, so that intimacy with her seemed hardly
possible; she had travelled all her life and would probably
continue to do so until the day of her death – his own
intervention swept aside; so that she would always be out
of reach. If sleep and death, as we are told, bestow on us
a 'guilty immunity', then travel does too, for the traveller
is perpetually in the wrong context; and she was such a
traveller. Sevi Klein belonged by right to that unfortunate
line of women found in history (and almost extinct in
their own time) which its progress, in an unreasonable
search for attitudes, abuses; at least there was a certain
melancholy in her eye which suggested she was part of
such an abuse. 'Unrelated' in the way that the sentiment
'Pray for the Donor' in churches is unrelated to the disorder of death itself and to the imminent horrors of the
Ewigkeit, or to any condition such sentiments affected to
cover, one waited in vain for the 'real' Sevi to appear. She
smiled no reassuring modern smile but now and then

produced a rare and archaic one of her own, a smirk that unpeopled the world. Sometimes the expressions so calmly uttered by her in the English tongue contained inaccuracies open to the widest interpretation; and towards these breaches in the walls of common usage his fears were constantly running, without, however, ever being able to close the gap. An act of revenge for her threatened to be a clumsy and unusually indelicate operation. Sooner or later in all her own undertakings wild flaws appeared, disorderly and complete. Gored by the Bull of Roman Catholicism she had once made a pilgrimage to the Holy City, where an ardent male citizen had attempted to assault her indecently in a prominent position on Sancta Scala, in the course of Passion Week ceremonies.

She had only to think, 'Now I have something extraordinary in my hands', for the object, no matter what it was, to collapse on her. She said:

'In Paris it was like this, I thought that I was going to faint outside the Musée Grevin. The brightness of the streets had made me dizzy. I tried to ask for a glass of water in a shop there, but I couldn't make myself understood; they gave me a box of matches instead. Every day I passed that place they came out to laugh at me.'

No, she knew nothing of the larger resources and confounding quality of female tears, and thus could sneer in character:

'*Verliebte lieben es, in Gewahrsam genommen zu werden.*' Of her no timid lover need ask, beg:

'Am I debauching you, or are you debauching me?' because as a young girl she had already spared him that embarrassment. '*Wir glauben nicht an die Legende von uns selbst weil sie im Entstehen ist . . .*'

Justice hardly seemed to apply to her, her own nature

not being porous enough, or lacking the space, the safe margin, for a change of heart, or for forgiveness.

From the beginning their relationship had proceeded erratically in a series of uncalculated rejections. She could be relied upon to say:

'Look, I haven't changed'; as if this justified her as a 'woman in love' instead of condemning her as an out-and-out impostor. It was as though she must live a little ahead of herself, in the condition of having to be continually roused out of her absence. It was true also that Sevi still escaped him. Another damp morning would begin, day breaking wretchedly, and without many preliminaries she would stand before the window, looking out on the sodden and discoloured earth, thinking her own thoughts. Both beaches lay deserted; gulls were collected over them, veering about, crying. The scavengers were collecting muck on the foreshore where Sevi had bathed naked. Her impatient form, damp hair and piteous skin! That part of me that is not me, in the person of another. There in a dream he had embraced her.

She crept back into bed beside him without a word and soon was asleep again. As he too began to sleep he was advancing into her, and advancing was troubled by a dream.

In the dream – in the dream! Hastening along the road among a crowd of pilgrims – never fast enough! Dreaming, he heard real cries coming from the rear, and blows. The pilgrims were taking to the ditches. He flung himself in among them and found his hands fastened on a woman's skirts. He was a child. Someone was passing, but it was forbidden to look. The pilgrimage to the queen was interrupted because she was coming in person on the road, hell for leather among her entourage. Power was passing, shaking the air. From the ditches on either side the bolder spirits were peering, whispering. He uncovered his head and looked.

At the level of his eyes and striding away from him down the crown of the road he saw a heavily built woman dressed in a transparent raincoat worn open like a cloak, above it a bald pate. In the ditches they were whispering in astonishment among themselves. Then the dream carried him abruptly forward into the town.

In the last part of the dream all were dispersing from the town rapidly, as though threatened. He found himself, adult now, hurrying out hand in hand with a girl who was unknown to him. The town was under shell-fire but the queen and her court had to remain behind. In great fear for himself, he felt the ground shift under his feet and his heart race as though to outstrip the danger. But the first shell was already airborne. He sensed it coming through the clouds of dust raised ahead of him by the feet of the pilgrims. It exploded up ahead in the crowd. He plunged on – almost racing now – hoping that the next would pass over his head. The smoke of the first explosion came drifting back, and as he went forward into it he sensed, low and directed, the dropping trajectory of the second. Then he saw it. Silently, almost casually, a white object was lobbing towards him, gathering speed as it turned down. Too late already he flung up his arms. The shell crashed through the walls of his chest, firing itself point-blank into his soft unmilitant heart. Localised and unhinged his last soundless yell went up. A blinding detonation followed, casting him out of sleep.

He awoke trembling in the grey light. Beside him Sevi huddled lifeless. He touched her; she groaned once and turned over. Incurable, incurable! So it would continue until all the charts of the body were stowed away, the record of its blood and its thinking completed, and the light of the eyes extinguished. He felt then as he or another might feel at the hour of death when the loathing borne by the suffering flesh goes out like a sigh to the objects the dying person stares at, and all the refuse collected together by that person in a lifetime brought up to date, stamped with a formal seal (corruption itself) and made part of the universal collection; so that the disgust with the Self, total and languishing no more, is transmitted to inanimate objects – sinless as well as free in space and time – and the dead person freed at last from the responsibility of feeling.

II

The coast road entered the hills beyond Shanganagh, climbing in the half-dark between cedar and eucalyptus. In the light again, houses appeared, designed like citadels and displaying Italian names. Built into the granite above the beach, they gazed without expression over the bay. The beach resembled a sand quarry converging on a sea. Semi-naked bathers descended wooden steps on its blind side, going down and shutting from sight the mock-Italian frontage, balconies and awnings, the chorus of eucalyptus trees.

They came on the coast train in the season, appearing first on the horizon in the most purposeful and heroic shapes, the women numerous and always protesting. Crowds of them lay on the shore all day in extraordinary attitudes of repose, while from above more and more were descending with the measured tramp of the damned. No wind disturbed the incoming sea or the prostrate people, and in the glare all that could be delineated was destroyed. Shore and sea merged, dog and clown were swallowed up in inextinguishable fire. On the high stan-

chions of the tea-rooms the bearded John Player sailor
was burning, remote and lugubrious in hammered tin.

So the days drew out, tides entering and leaving, the
heat continuing, the floating bodies aimless and inert on
the water. Time appeared as a heavy hand giving or taking
their life away, falling anyway, impartially on sand, on
feeble walls, on tired summer trappings. And the smoke
going straight up from the stands; and the children crying
(a sound blood-dimmed and heavy to the ear, as though
conducted there not by the air itself but by brass or
copper); and the damp elders prone everywhere. For
Saturday had come again and Saturday's tired population
was at the sea.

All who arrived at the beach from sloblands and city
came shaken with a suspended summer lust, to hold a
commemorative service on the summer passing and the
free days. Submitting to chance freedom but performing
the act diffidently and as though enacting a scene obviously 'beyond' them. A company coming down resigned,
without too much enthusiasm and without too much style,
into the Promised Land. The bulk, unconcerned with fair
play, knowing in its bones the awfulness of any dealing,
lay claim to their territory as graveyards lay claim to the
dead. So these citizens were to claim this beach, lying
there like an army fallen amidst its baggage; ground molli-
fying them, taking them into its secret at last, completing
them. Admitting at the same time that under the name of
'Hospitality' is concealed various disorders; heavy bodies
saying in effect, *This is our ground; let us exploit it* (the
resources of a spirit seldom fired conceiving only this
drear Heaven of abject claims). So they descended in an
uneven line all through summer, no individual shape
an heroic shape any longer, but all the shape of the
common plural.

One evening a member of the *lazzaroni* appeared on the beach. Destitute and unwhole, escaped from the tenements, he had made his way out of the station, dressed in an ancient overcoat which reached below the knees, found the steps, and arrived. The bay water was dead calm; an odour of eucalyptus hung in the air. The young ladies who had come from the hill convent were just collecting themselves together, preparing to leave. He had watched them from his perch, unseen and pawing himself doubtfully, without ever taking his eyes away. Spread below him he saw an intoxication of green uniforms and then a flurry of undressing, and then bare flesh, then girls shouting and swimming, and now dressed again and going. While the face hung above them, chalk-white where paralysis had killed it, the bleak jawline and the bared teeth presented as component sections of the human skull, the profound bone base of all emotion glaring back its final indifference. The freak face stared down, motionless and cold, negligent as features gouged in putty, with a stare which took in the area and then destroyed it – the observer himself lost somewhere between unrelated head and unrelated body. Confronted with this all would be left in doubt, waiting for the final kindness to put it right or the final unkindness to annihilate it. The bay water remained calm; smoke rose blue into the air from the cooking stands; the nuns, careening themselves at a decent remove, were showing an emancipated leg on the Feast-day of St James the Greater.

Nuns apart, the people were to become aware of him as they might have become aware of the stench, the effluvium, which surrounds and yet contains discarded and putrefying matter. Not deformed in any striking manner, there remained something foul about his person, an uncertain wavering line drawing him down and compelling him to be recognised. They were looking at an imbecile, one of themselves, a person loose and lost, a young fellow in his mid-twenties – a 'fact' in the way a multiple exposure in photography is a fact, something irregular yet perfect, perfect yet a mechanical abuse of itself. Beyond that he was nothing, could be nothing, for there was nothing left over, no place where they, weeping with solicitude, could put their hands and say, 'This at least is ours.' He was like something they could not recollect. He was a disturbance in their minds. The normally healthy, when their health breaks down, speak of being 'in poor shape'; but he, who had seldom been healthy and never been normal, was poor shape incarnate. He was the Single One, a neuter.

A tenement child had lured him to ground level with her sly eyes, with a movement of her head which was partly a deliberate soliciting and partly that dumb invitation we tender a beast. He crept out after her, the child turning and grinning, spilling water from her shining can. So he found himself among the people at last.

He began wandering about, head shaking and feet uncertain – a nameless fear. A tall and disjointed figure fashioned by all manner of winds, whose every movement was apprehensive, trailing his wake of misery behind. His stare lacked momentum, falling short of the object before he could 'take it in', painfully slow hands closing on the dog's head after the animal had moved, closing on air. His touch was more an experiment than an act of possession. The eyes he turned on them were dark and liquid, barbicans in his shattered face, guarded and half closed like the identical crenels of a tower: that old and wary perspective of eyes behind which the senses stood armed and uneasy – a minute suspicious stir in the wall's face. None could pity, or deplore or 'place' him because he could not be found, could not find himself, lost and swallowed up by a continual and forbidding silence. No way remained open to remind him of a former disturbance which he could have gone back to and reclaimed – as a dog draws back its fangs from the security of the kennel, so this creature was drawing back from the appropriating touch on the arm which would identify him as a poor blind man. His feet were the first to despair, dragging the shadow, shadow in its turn flinching from the outstretched 'charitable' hand. He was struck at such a pitch of intensity that he had to be heard to the end.

Those who were leaving made to pass him, but in their embarrassment wheeled round to face him, at a loss and unhappy, clutching at their possessions and saying to their children:

'Come along now . . . oh now come along!' not even knowing where to look any more. Then he covered his face, churning in the sand, cancelling himself with his own hand. The shadows on the cabins were locked together for an instant and then wrenched apart. They did not wish to see him or be witness to this distress, for among them he was an effigy and a blasphemy, something beyond the charity of God or man. Perishing so in his own presence, he seemed to be devouring himself. Existing outside perspective, he could not be considered as an equivalent to themselves.

Thrown out of order and at a loss the herd was in full retreat, their dreadful faces turned about, their mouths wailing soundlessly. And then nothing. Silence fell. He went alone through it, ignored. Their silence, no longer a retreat, became an intermission – a trying situation out of which all hoped presently to advance, voluble and unrepentant, back into the good life out of which all had been cast. Presented with this figure of doom their Christian feelings had fled. Here was no blind man, only

one who did not care to remember; this patient brought
no dreams to the session.

And so, little by little, life returned and darkness fell.
All the living were out and about as though nothing had
happened, blown hither and thither by the high winds of
commiseration, holding aloft their stupendous banners,
being obliging, running messages (their obligations
running before, to rob them), being spiteful. Spiteful!

Save the patronage of their kind names. They went
down blind into the dark pool, the shadows falling everywhere and the ending never likely. They went down. Dark
clouds were forming overhead. Look here! Look there!
Unkind life is roaring by in its topmost branches.

III

The late summer when he had watched that had gone
for good. Now it was winter: late evening-time in an Irish
October. The short winter day was drawing to an end. He
sat on the sea wall and watched her tramping along the
bluff, heralded by piteous cries from some climbing goats.
She came trailing into sight after a while, crossing below,
barefooted, trailed by her low German hound; she
resembled a person who never intended to come back.
He watched her, a dark blur by the water's edge, her
shoulders were moving. He leant forward (could she be
crying?) and saw she was writing with a stick on the sand,
the palimpsest. *Das ist des Pudels*, she wrote, and below
that one word, *Kern*, in a crabbed backhand. That was
that. The tired eye had begun to close; soon they could
go their various ways. It was not as if light had been
drained from the sand but as if darkness had been poured
into it. Now almost invisible he sat aloft so that Sevi came

for the last time, walking slowly against the sea and against the last light, penetrating him as an oar breaks water. But not stopping, retreating, descending stairs of sand, going out slowly followed by the dog. He watched her evaporating, crawling into her background, not declining it, deliberately seeking it, lurching away from him to stumble into a new medium (a way she had), beating down the foreshore like a lighter going aground. Her hair undone went streaming back from her head; for an instant longer she remained in sight, contracting and expanding in the gloom, and then was gone.

The tide rose now until it covered the entire shore. Shallow yet purposeful water embraced the extremity of the sea wall. Invisible gulls were complaining, worrying, somewhere over its dark unpeaceful depths. Anxiously the pier lights waved a mile to the south – a remote outfall of light more dingy than the sky, now dropping, now drowned in intervening wave. Michael Alpin walked out of the dark construction of the wall, broken here and there by heavy seas. He stood over her scrawlings, her last abuse. Unbuttoning himself he took his stance staring out to sea, his lust or love in the end reduced to this. Retreating to the wall he laid his face against its intolerable surface of freezing stone. As he began to go down the false surf light and the remote light along the pier, diminishing, swung away.

There is no commencement or halfway to that fall: only its continuing.

North Salt Holdings

The remains of Miss Emily Norton Kervick were committed to the grave one cold day in March of 1927. On that morning – the third – a Mass for the Dead had been offered for the repose of her soul, and she was buried without delay in Griffenwrath cemetery.

The day previously the body had been laid out on its high bed in a room too full of the stupefying odour of arum lilies. It had been her bedroom. The furnishings were not remarkable. A fierce wallpaper design of bamboo and prodigal shoots appeared to contract the walls on two sides. Within that area and resting on the bare boards, white and sedate, decked with flowers, stood the deathbed. This bed, notwithstanding its panoply, notwithstanding its character of unmistakable intent, or its occupant, seemed to move on its castors at a slow, almost imperceptible rate of its own – as small craft in a difficult roadstead will creep from their moorings.

Then the room shook under the tread of mourners. They came unsolicited on the first day, a mixed bag of male and female gentry come to pay what they described as 'their last respects'. Wearing the appropriate expression they took up a position by the bed-head. They were not relatives but locals. And every so often they so far forgot themselves as to make that hurried, somewhat cupidinous gesture of piety – blessed themselves. Emily-May's forbidding manner had repulsed them in life and now, destitute of sense, it finally routed them.

This corpse, so exact and still, was impervious to all human compassion; their presence seemed superfluous or worse – as though uninvited they had arrived at the wrong funeral. In the hotpress her linen lay stored and ready; her cases stood packed in the next room. It did not seem that she had died and escaped them; on the contrary, dead, she had come to stay.

She offered no help herself, being content to lie there, grey and heavy, dressed in a monk's dark habit which even covered her upturned toes, clutching rosary beads cumbersome as manacles. The head was thrust back into the folds of the cowl, out of which an arrogant warrior's nose and pronounced cheekbones appeared in a scarred and discoloured face. On her chest, in addition, was balanced a phenomenally heavy crucifix. In posture she resembled a Crusader in a tomb, seemingly just on the point of rising up violently and dashing the Cross to the ground: the general effect being more military than strictly religious.

Warily the survivors circled this ambiguous deathbed, half conscious of the permutations it had already undergone, hoping it had gone through them all. Now boat-like on no high seas; now solid and as though cast in rock like a tomb; now shrunken to the dimensions of a litter. So they could make nothing of it and had to retire baffled. A day later the bed itself lay stripped and empty. Death had borne the last disquieting image of Emily Norton Kervick down with it into the grave.

I

Forty-five years before, in the hopeful 1880s, a couple by the name of Kervick bought Springfield House outright from the Land Commission for the purpose of farming and raising a family. Springfield House was a freehold premises in the barony of old Killachter, situated one mile from Celbridge village and the ramparts of Marley Abbey, whilom home of Hester Vanhomrigh.

Two decades later this couple had passed away, unmourned and almost forgotten in their own time, leaving behind as a legacy for four unprepossessing and unmarriageable daughters, a seventy-two-acre estate so fallen into neglect that it had to be parcelled out as grazing land. Over the years the rockery and vegetable gardens had merged to become a common wilderness. In the orchard the untrimmed branches sank until lost in the dense uprising of grass. Four spinsters grew up there. They were christened, in order of appearance: Emily Norton (known as Emily-May), Tess, Helen, Imogen.

Imogen Kervick had the nondescript face of a plaster Madonna, pallor and all. Her small opportunist mouth daubed with dark lipstick recalled the 1920s, and she favoured also the trenchcoats and the hats of that period. Her movements were at once prosaic and portentous; she conjured up lascivious dreamy knees for herself, and a heart full of vicissitudes, the morals of a rhesus monkey. From her a declaration of love would have to be as detailed as a death sentence; fortunately the occasion never arose. Imprisoned in her own particular folly, she refused to behave as if there were any such condition as *âge dangereuse* or any such policy as relenting. She preferred to represent herself as if lodged within a ring of persecution – making considered motions with the hand, waiting only for the faggots to be lit under her. Sometimes, laying down her knife and fork, she wept at table, her eyes wide open and no tears falling.

It was into this unlikely subject that Cupid had discharged his bolts. Some years previously she had created a modest stir by indulging her fancy with a pallid youth named Klaefisch. No one had ever looked at him before, least of all a woman, least of all with favour. He came from Bavaria. He had one good lung, and resembled a gawky version of Constantine Guys. It was she who persuaded him to live with them, but outside, like a dog, in a clapboard and tar edifice that stood on raised ground. Here Otto Klaefisch came for peace and quiet, for free board or a little love – if that was to be part of the price; but mainly in order to complete his three-year-old thesis, *Das Soziale Schicksal in den Novellen Theodor Storms.*

Throughout that summer the swallows went shrieking overhead, and Imogen came and went from the house with tray after tray of food. She walked boldly into the pavilion and came out later carrying pages for typing scored with a bold Gothic script. Did he make attempts on her virtue in there? Nobody knew. From the frameless window the face of the nine days' wonder peered, the sun glinting on bifocals and the corners of his mouth drawn down.

Gliding past of an evening they heard his nasal drone punctuating the dark. It was Otto reciting Schiller to himself. (*'Der Mensch muss hinaus in's feindliche Leben,'* muttered Otto darkly, *'muss wirken und streben!'*) Indifferent to them, he was travelled, well read, uncommunicative, loose-living, free. But this idyll of late-flowering love was of short duration.

For one short summer only Otto tolerated her ardours. For one season only were they treated to the unedifying spectacle of a spinster-virgin in rut, their shameless sister. Then one day she found herself alone again with the three resident she-devils. Otto had departed with his thesis, finished and bound in dark blue leather.

The weeks and the years passed almost unnoticed. The weeds grew upwards, rotted, passed away. The wheel of the seasons spun round; quite soon she had forgotten him. Like her sisters she was lost in a career of unblemished idleness. She had some sort of an understanding with Helen. Sometimes they talked to each other for hours at a stretch. When she and Helen came to speak together, each had to rise to the surface in order to say what they had to say, after which they sank again to their respective depths.

Tess was the eldest but one. Of her let it be said, she played Demon Patience for her nerves, liked to work in the garden for her health, drank gin for preference, enjoyed outside contacts, was Joseph's employer. She had red hair, buck teeth and a child's high voice. Tess was a Patroness of Adversity, and a pawn to the others' kings and queens. She is not in this story.

The third daughter was Helen.

Helen Kervick was a collector of dead things, right from the start. She discarded dolls (capable of modestly lowering their eyes) in favour of rabbits strangled in the snares and overrun with lice and fleas, and these she disentangled and buried with her own hands. It was they, dumb disfigured creatures, who got all her compassion, as she grew up. She went her own way, inventing games for herself alone that required no partners. All her life that tendency would continue – the game that required neither the presence nor the assistance of a second party.

'I just live for the day,' she said, 'and I try not to think of anything much . . .'

She sat often in the windowseat in the sun, sometimes

manufacturing dark rings under her eyes with a typewriter brush.

II

Emily-May was the fourth, the first-born, the heaviest by far. In her distant youth she had been a holy terror on the tennis court, performing in a headband and one of Papa's discarded cricket shirts, worn moody and loose, panting about the court, perspiring under her armpits. Languidly she moved to serve. Heavily she served, elaborate and inaccurate, recalling to mind the high action of obsolete field-pieces. She toed the baseline, measured Tess's ground with a merciless eye, served. Into the net went the ball. Again. She threw the service ball high into the air, squared at it, refused the strike, re-caught it! At a third or even fourth attempt she might be induced, with much caracoling, to make a stroke – the sun flashing on the racquet and the ball once again crashing into the net.

All through summer endless games of singles were contested with the patient Tess. Rallies were infrequent. Some of the high returns had to be retrieved from the beech hedge with a long stepladder. Tess kept the score.

'Thirty-fiff!' she cried in her intolerable tennis voice. '*Thirty-fiff!*'

Missel-thrushes came floating down from the great trees into the evergreens. Dusk crept around Springfield. The sun descended into the wood. Tess served again. Emily-May, model of rectitude, crouched in the Helen Wills Moody position. Dim figures stirred again. It had all happened in the long ago.

Otherwise Emily-May's gestures betrayed few emotions. Her gestures and progress, reduced to a minimum, were as uniformly dull as her clothes. Her face, a full pod of flesh, was bulky and uneasy; her manner was so abashed that it could only be seen or thought of by degrees. For there are such faces. Her entire corporeal presence had the unknown quality of things stared at so often that they are no longer seen. Her condition was one of constant and virtually unrelieved embarrassment. Here was a person who had run out of enthusiasms early on in life, and in the halls of her spirit, so to speak, toadstools grew. Imogen, who detested her, had appointed herself Emily-May's biographer and amanuensis. But all the thin slanders assembled by her bounced harmlessly off the sebaceous elder, whom few cared to address directly. Emily-May took ridiculously small steps for a person of her bulk and moved rapidly, pigeon-toed, from thickset hips with a repressed fury that was painful to see. Physically she belonged to what Kretschmer called the pyknic type (all arse and occiput). Add to this a disagreeable set of countenance and an uncommon air, for a lady, of suffering from hypertrophy of the prostate. The creature had commenced to put on flesh at an early age, and as well as that found herself prematurely bald before the age of thirty. Those unhappy people who speak of being 'thrown back' upon themselves, in the sense of being confounded, would perhaps have understood her best. For she was a throwback, stem and corolla risen to new heights, bound to please no one; one single forbidding link, alive and growing into itself, casting a brave shadow in a world loathsome beyond words, from root to flower.

Poultry abounded in the back yard, a hundred yards away from the house. Everything from fidgety bantams to turkeys, spurred and fierce, savagely disposed towards all, were allowed their freedom there.

Helen was greatly attached to the hens and their little

ways and liked nothing better than to spend hours
observing them. This she did with the aid of a collapsible
camp-stool, moving about from point to point in their
wake, and then sitting stock still in her battered old hat,
not knowing her mind between one beat of her heart
and the next. Endlessly patient she sat there, Crusoe with
his beginnings. The hens themselves seemed to live in a
lifelong coma, disturbed only by the rats who sought to
catch them on the ground at night; or by Joseph, ready
to lay violent hands on them by day – for though Helen
herself was a vegetarian both Tess and Emily-May were
gluttons for spring chicken served with new potatoes.

While they lived the hens collected grubs, flies, took
dust-baths, waited for the cock to rush upon them and
have his way; sometimes they ventured far afield into
the meadows. The evening was their time. They seemed
happier then, a little surer of themselves. They sang in a
cracked unhinged key that rose, more lament than song,
hesitated (they were sure of nothing), broke off before
the phrase ended. Up the ramp at dusk they stumbled
after the white cock, and one by one they dropped inside.

They were early astir in the morning in the dock-and-
pollen-infested yard, scratching and rooting about, emitting sad droning cries, *Key-key-kee-kee-keeeeee*, that then
trickled off into silence. One of their number would
sometimes take fright, call out three or four times, then
stand petrified as all the other red hens froze about the
yard. A dog was moving behind the wall; a hawk was
hovering above, preparing to fall out of the sky and rend
one of them. Then that danger too seemed to pass. The
first one would move again, dipping its head and
clucking. Then one by one all would resume their activities as before. They seemed pleased with the filthiest
surroundings – the lime-fouled henhouse or the pig

troughs. Imogen it was who fed them. They got into the mush the better to enjoy it.

Helen spent whole days among them, listening to their talk; in it there was neither statement, question nor reply; and this characteristic greatly pleased her.

Helen sat indoors, uncomfortably on her raised seat in the upper cabin, lost in *The Anatomy of Melancholy*. The last daylight swam in the clouded pockets of the little window, as from a bathysphere, before her eyes. Evening clouds were moving across that portion of the sky visible to her. She was thinking of Emily-May, about whom she was attempting to write something (closing her Burton and shutting her eyes). Her eldest sister, who from the tenderest age onwards could be seen lurking in the background in a succession of family snapshots, invariably surprised in a slovenly pose, off guard, her weight resting on one hip – effacing herself, so that she became more distant than a distant relative. But she did this so well it had become almost indelicate to notice it. Well, she had been foundering in some such confusion all her life – a life lonely and shy, subjected to a process of erosion that had reduced her in some irreparable way. Until at last she came to resemble that other person trapped in the snapshot, a version of herself perpetuated in some anxious pose and unable to walk forward out of that paralysis.

The cabin was flooded with a white afterlight, an emulsion reflected from a non-existent sea. The sun was setting. Evening benediction had begun. Helen stared through the glass and never saw the dogs moving cautiously about the yard, for her mind's eye was fixed on other things.

In the hot summers and sometimes even in winter, Emily-

May went bathing more or less every day, naked into the river. Grotesque in modesty as in everything else, she crept down to the water, both chubby hands shielding her various allurements, overpowering as the Goddess Frigga at the bath. Avoiding the main current (for she could not swim) she floated awkwardly downriver in the shallows, using one fat leg as a keel, touching bottom, floating on. At such times she was happy, no longer caring that she might be seen and find herself in the Court of Assizes on a charge of indecent exposure, and she no longer feared that she might drown. The noises of the river delighted her, the sensation of floating also, the nakedness too. Her nerves relented, she let go, she was calm, she felt free.

Thus did Emily-May indulge herself all day long in the summer. After these excursions she had the whetted appetite of a female Cyclops. Shoulders of beef, haunches of lamb, fish and poultry and game, washed down with soup and beer, all these and many more condiments disappeared into that voracious crop. She lived in indescribable squalor among the scattered remains of Scotch shortbread, preserves, chewed ends of anchovy toast, boxes of *glacé* fruit, rounds of digestive biscuits lurid with greengage jam. Indoors and out she ate, day and night, winter and summer, odds and ends in the pantry, lettuce and bananas with cold rabbit by the river. But little of what her mouth contained was by her ferocious stomach received, no, but from rapidly champing jaws did fall and by the passing current was carried away, *secundum carnem.*

In her lair, safe from intrusion, Helen wrote into her daybook:

As a person may mime from a distance 'I-have-been-unavoidably-delayed', by a subtle displacement of dignity, such as the wry face, the hapless gesture of the hand etc., etc., so Emily-May's manner of walking has become the equivalent of the shrug of the shoulders. The fear of becoming the extreme sort of person she might, in other circumstances, have become has thrown her far back. The pattern of a final retreat runs through her like a grain in rough delf.

None of this high-flown Della-Cruscan pleasing her, Helen broke off, closing her book and putting aside her pencil. She looked out. The yard gates stood wide apart. Great dogs were lifting their hind legs and wetting the doors of outhouses – acts mannered and ceremonial as in a votive Mass. Peace reigned in Griffenwrath. Then far away in the fields someone called. Helen threw open the window. Amazed, the dogs took to their heels. Helen drew in her head and went quietly downstairs.

III

Joseph the gardener sat drinking stout under a prunus tree out of the heat of day. The shambles of his awkward feet lay before him, side by side and abject in their thick woollen socks. He had removed his boots and laid them aside. A smell of captive sweat pervaded his person and something else too, the stench of something in an advanced state of decay.

Joseph killed silently and with the minimum of effort. His victims the hens had scarcely time to cry out, before they were disembowelled. Fowl and vermin were dispatched with equal impartiality, for he was their slaughterman. He was a great punter too. His speculating on the turf met with an almost unqualified lack of success, but this did not deter him in the least. His drab waistcoat blazed with insignia – half were seed catalogues and half rejected betting slips.

A passive and indolent man by nature, he spent his working day among the moss-roses and privets, or kneeling among the azaleas – weeding, praying, farting, no one knew. He spent much time in such poses, and it required quite a feat of imagination to see him upright and on the move. Yet move he did – a crab but recently trodden on who must struggle back to find first its legs, torn off by an aggressor, and then its element. His balance was only restored to him when in position, in servitude, behind a wheelbarrow, say, or a rake. He knew his place, and kept himself to himself.

Labouring in the garden, on which his labours made so little impression, he kept his Wild Woodbines out of harm's way under his hat, with the lunch. He was their gardener, he was indispensable, he knew it. Joseph the mock-father lay sleeping under the prunus tree, pandering to a chronic ataraxy.

He was the person who saw most of Helen, all that there was to be seen of Helen. She spent most of her time indoors, drawn up like a bat in daylight behind the window curtains on the first floor. Groping in the earth sometimes he felt her eyes fixed upon him. Turning to see, framed in the darkness of the window where the progress of the creeper was broken, the white face of the recluse staring at him. Half-risen he then attempted a salute (as if taking aim with a gun) from which she turned away. The gesture could not be repeated. She was reading.

The other three women seldom saw her, lacking either the energy or the interest to raise their tired eyes. They passed to and fro below, plucking at themselves and mumbling, exercising soberly about the various levels of the garden, fond of the tangled grottoes, trailing through shade like insane persons or nuns of a silent order.

A great impressive hedge, a beech, eighteen feet high, ran the length of the garden; beyond it lay the orchard. Alongside this hedge Emily-May had worn a path hard and smooth in her regular patrols, tramping down the pretty things, a veritable Juggernaut, the coltsfoot, the valerian, the dock. It bore her onward, at night shining under her like a stream. Her shadow moved below like a ship's hull.

At long intervals Helen too appeared in the garden. After winter rain she liked to walk in the orchard. Joseph spied on her, marvelling as the grey engaged figure urged itself on among the stunted trees, appearing and disappearing again, like something recorded.

At other times she left the window open and gramophone music started above his head. She sang foreign songs in a melancholy drawn-out fashion, more chant than song, and not pleasant either way. She sang:

> *Es brennt mir unter beiden Sohlen,*
> *Tret' ich auch schon auf Eis und SCHNEEEE!*

Joseph covered his ears; this was too much. Night once more was falling on this graceless Mary, on her fondest aspirations as on her darkest fears – the confusion of one day terminating in the confusion of the next. Joseph, in his simplicity, believed that she had been something in vaudeville, in another country.

Urge, urge, urge; dogs gnawing.

IV

The apartment was cluttered with an assortment of casual tables on which stood divers bottles and jars. A submarine light filtered through the angled slots of the Venetian blinds, dust swirling upwards in its wake, passing slowly through sunlight and on up out of sight. A frieze could be distinguished, depicting a seaside scene, presented as a flat statement in colour as though for children (the room had formerly been a nursery), beneath which at calculated intervals hung a line of heavily built ancestors in gilt frames, forbidding in aspect as a rogues' gallery, leaning into the room as from the boxes of a theatre.

Out of the depths of a tattered armchair Helen's pale features began to emerge, as Imogen went towards her, to the sound of defunct springs. A miscellaneous collection of fur and feathered life moved as she moved, flitting into obscure hiding-places. High above their strong but unnameable smell rose the fetid reek of old newspapers. In one corner a great pile had mounted until jammed between floor and ceiling, like clenched teeth. An unknown number of chiming clocks kept up a morose-sounding chorus, announcing the hours with subdued imprecision. Even in high summer the place gave off a succession of offensive cold-surface smells: an unforgettable blend of rotting newspaper, iodine, mackintosh, cat.

Here on this day and at this hour was Helen Jeanne Kervick, spinster and potential authoress, at home and receiving. In the gloom her voice came faint as from another person in a distant room – a weak and obstinate old voice:

'And our dead ones' (she was saying), 'our parents, do you think of them? When we were young they were old already. And when we in turn were no longer young, why they seemed hardly to have changed. They went past us in the end, crackling like parchment.'

She stirred in her antique chair. After a while she went on:

'Do you suppose they intercede for us now, in Heaven, before the throne of Almighty God? Now that they have become what they themselves always spoke so feelingly of – "The Dear Departed" – when they were alive? Oh my God,' she said with feeling, 'what will become of us all, and how will it end?'

Imogen said nothing, watching Helen's long unringed fingers stroking the upholstery of her chair. The friction produced a fine dust that rose like smoke. Beyond it, in it, Helen's voice continued:

'Ah, how can we be expected to behave in a manner that befits a lady? How can we? Everything is moving' (a motion of the hand) 'and I don't move quickly enough. Yes, yes, we envy the thing we cannot be. So, we're alive, yes, that's certain. It's certain that we're old women. At least we stink as old women should.'

It was the beginning of a long rambling tirade.

Like all Helen's tirades, it had the inconclusive character of a preamble. As she spoke, pausing for a word here, losing track of the argument there, the captive wild life began to grow increasingly restive.

'We take everything into account, everything except the baseness of God's little images. What a monster he must be! We've set ourselves up here like scarecrows and only frighten the life out of one another when we come up against ourselves in the wrong light. And in winter the damned sky comes down until it's hanging over our ears, and all we can think about are the mundane things of the world and its rottenness. And then there's that bald glutton Emily-May having seizures in her bottomless pit, and we can't even distinguish her screams from the noises in our heads.'

She stopped, and sat silent for a long time. Then she said:

'When one lives in the country long enough, one begins to see the cities as old and queer. It's like looking back centuries.'

She went on:

'Listen, have you ever considered this: that Crusoe's life could only cease to be intolerable when he stopped looking for a sail and resigned himself to living with his dependants under a mountain – have you ever thought of that? No. Trust in Providence, my dear, and remember, no roc is going to sit on its eggs until they are hatched out of all proportions; or if there ever was such a bird, I haven't heard of her.'

From by the door Imogen's voice called something. Drawing closer then and pointing a finger, she said in a child's high voice:

'Dust hath closed Helen's eyes.'

Something hard struck Helen's forehead and she allowed herself to fall back without another word. She heard feet lagging on the stairs and after that silence again. Pressing fingers to her brow like electrodes she bent forward until she was almost stifling. A heady smell of dust, undisturbed by time, and the parochial odour of her own person entered her throat and filled her eyes with unshed tears. Something began to ring, blow upon blow, in her head. She straightened up again with a hand to her heart and listened.

A distant sound of wild ringing in the air.

It was the workmen's bell in Killadoon that was tolling. Faint and drifting, carried hither, finally ceasing. Almost, for there was the aftertone. There it was again, the last of it. She felt relieved. The men had finished another day of labour and were departing on their bicycles. From the shelter of the trees she had watched them go. That heavy and toilsome lift of the leg, and then away, slowly home under the walnut trees, past the lodge gate, down the long back drive of Colonel Clements' estate, home to their sausages and tea.

Blood was groping and fumbling in her, pounding through her, greedy lungs and mean heart. 'Bleed no more, Helen Kervick, bleed no more!' the blood said. No more the thin girl-child, become the anaemic spinster; no more of it. She rose and dusted her person. Where now?

She crossed to the window and peered through the blinds at what remained of the day. High-scudding cloud, the wood, sky on the move, feeling of desolation. Already she regretted everything she had said to Imogen. Yes, every word. It was all vanity and foolishness. And herself just a bit of time pushed to the side. That was all. She heaved a sigh, allowed the slat to fall back into place and stepped back.

The door stood open. Dusk was everywhere in the room. The landing lay below her, bathed in a spectral light. She stepped down onto its faded surface. Her mind was still disturbed; she was thinking of the departing men. They dug in the earth; they knew it, through and through; it was their element; things grew for them. One day they too would be put down into it themselves, parting the sods and clay easily, going down like expert divers.

'The faith,' they said, 'have you not the faith?' She had not. It was something they carried about with them, not to be balked, heavy and reliable, like themselves. She felt at peace in their company. They were solid men; but their faith was repugnant to her. Their stiff genuflecting, as if on sufferance, and their labourers' hands locked in prayer (for she had gone to Mass to be among them) – their contrite hearts. Out of all this, which in her heart she detested, she was locked. And yet they offered her peace. How did that come about?

Here Tess, tired of waiting for the evening cock-pheasant to put in an appearance, strolled out from behind a tree in the field below and began to move along the plantation edge, as though she had intended something else.

V

Members of the Kervick family, too old now to have any sense, strolled vaguely about the house and along the landings, appearing suddenly in rooms sealed off since the death of their parents. Sometimes their heads showed in the currant bushes; at other periods they stood under the plum tree with their mouths half open. They began to collect loganberries industriously in a bowl by the loganberry wall. They cut wasps out of the last apples and worms out of the last pears in the Fall. There was a time when Helen could scarcely walk into the garden without flushing out one of them – such was their patience – collapsed onto a rustic seat and lost in some wretched reverie or dolour. For the combined misery of the Kervick *Lebensgefühl* was oppressive enough to turn the Garden of Eden into another Gethsemane overnight.

Plucking up courage, they would set off for unknown destinations on high antiquated bicycles, pedalling solemnly down the wrong drives and out of sight for the day. Dressed in her Louis XV green, Tess was bound for the back road and Lady Ismay's gin. Emily-May herself was off again to paint in Castletown demesne. In the course of a long career over 400 versions of the house and reaches of the river, drawn from the life, had been accumulated, most of them duplicates.

At a bend in the front drive, where the paling interfered with Helen's line of sight, watching from the window, the cyclist (it was Emily-May, gross and splendid with a hamper strapped onto the rear carrier) jerked forward out of perspective as if sliced in two – the upper section travelling on, astonished and alone, with augmented rapidity. It was not unknown for one or both of the cyclists to return in a suspicious condition; but unsober or not they never returned together.

Alone and safe from intrusion now, Helen crouched in her sky cabin. Alternating between it and the windowseat, she relied on her mood and on the waning light to inform her where to go. Indeed at any time of the day or night the curtains might part and Helen Kervick palely emerge, clad from head to toe in *bouclé* tweed, clutching her Burton or translations from the Latin masters, making her way to the bright convenience on the upper landing. Her head was sometimes seen suspended from that window with hair swinging in her eyes. After dark she closed the curtains carefully behind her, extinguished the oil lamp, passed down the main stairs to the hall, ignoring the dim print of Lady Elizabeth Butler's *Scotland for Ever!*, arriving on the gravel dressed for walking. In the windowseat in winter she bore patiently the cold and the affront of continuous rain, sighing down her life for the last time again – on the garden, on labouring Joseph, on the parallels, on the flying rain. Stay Time a while thy flying. *Air!*

VI

Towards midday, the weather being fine and bright, early March weather, Joseph appeared with a tremendous rake and began to scuffle the gravel before the house, but without much heart and not for long. Somewhere a window went up and a sharp voice called his name.

He did not appear to hear: an image dark and labouring in the weak sun with a halo of light above his head, outside the world of tears and recrimination, his gloom cast for all time. But there was no escaping.

'TEA!' the voice screamed.

Joseph came to a halt and removed his hat.

'Oh come along now, Joseph!' the high bright voice invited mellifluously.

Emily-May freewheeled by Paisley's corner for the last time and soon had passed Marley Abbey on her right hand. Vanessa's old home. Swift had gone there on horseback, jig, jig, long ago. Emily-May went coasting on into the village. She ordered half a dozen Guinness from Dan Breen and began, on account of the gradient, to walk her bicycle uphill towards the great demesne gates. She passed the convent where with the other little girls of First Infants she had studied her Catechism. Later, in First Communion veils, models of rectitude, they sang in childish trebles, *O Salutaris Hostia* and *Tantum Ergo*. Bowing her head she passed in silence through Castletown gates – the skeleton branches rigid above her, Emily-May descended into her nether world.

Core, Hart, Hole, Keegan, Kervick, Coyle. Damp forgotten life; passing, passing. Some had lived at Temple Mill, some at Great Tarpots, and some at Shatover. Molly North lived at St Helen's Court: she had long black hair and was beautiful, unlike Emily-May who had tow hair and was considered hideous.

She passed through. Beyond March's bare trees she saw the sun hammering on the river: the water flowed by like a muscle, the summer returned, something turned over in Emily-May and she became young and voluptuous once more (she had never been either). A few minutes later she had reached her secret place behind a clump of pampas grass. She spared herself nothing. Trembling she began to undo her buttons and release her powerful elastic girdle. She, a stout Christian who could not swim a stroke to save her life, pulled off her remaining drawers, charged into the piercing water and struck out at a dog-crawl. The damp morning was like so much sugar in her blood. The bitterly cold water ate into her spine as the main current began to draw her downstream. Under wet hanging branches she was carried, dropping her keel, touching nothing but water. By fields, by grazing cattle, by calm estate walls, Emily Odysseus Kervick drifted, the last of her line, without issue, distinction or hope. She could not cry out; frozen to the bone now, steered by no passing bell, she floated weirwards towards extinction and forgetting. The river carried her on, the clay banks rearing up on either side, and there she seemed to see her little sisters, grown minute as dolls, playing their old games. She saw Tess clearly and behind, holding her hand, the infant Imogen. She screamed once, but they neither heard nor answered and after a while they ran away. Suddenly, directly overhead, Helen's crafty face appeared. She looked straight down, holding in her hands the fishing lines. As a child Emily-May had a passion for writing her name and address on sheets of paper, plugging them into bottles and dropping them in the river below the mill. She imagined now that Helen had remembered this too, and that Helen alone could retrieve

or save her. But when she looked again Helen had
become a child. Innocence had bestowed on her sister
another nature, an ideal nature outside corruption and
change, watched over by herself – drowned, grown more
ugly and more remote – so that the decades and decades
of her own life, past now, seemed a series of mechanical
devices arranged at intervals like the joints of a telescope
held inverted to the eye – to distort everything she
inspected and to separate her from life and from whatever
happiness life had to offer. Brought sharply into focus,
it became clear that Helen had not escaped to a later
innocence, not at all, but in growing up had merely
adopted a series of disguises, each one more elaborate
and more perfect, leaving her essential nature
unchanged. As they stared hopelessly into each other's
faces something altered in Helen's. For an instant the
child's face was overlaid by the adult face known to Emily-
May – this one a mask, long and perverted. It stared down
unmoved on her wretchedness – naked, 'presumed lost'
– itself empty of expression, disfigured now, as though
beyond participation. (Here Helen herself closed her
Burton and rose up sighing. As her foot touched the
floor she drew down the chain with a nervous disengaged
hand.)

But the dark gulf was already opening for her sister.
Swept towards it by an unbearable wind, courage and
endurance (she never had either) ceased to matter. Emily-
May saw that and closed her eyes on the roaring, the
ROARING. The rockery and roaring gardens were
together under the weeds, the untrimmed branches in
the orchard were lost; lost until all, prostrate and rank,
sank from human sight.

Asylum

The Flowery Land

All the leaded windows of the house had blind views, with the exception of a front dormer which rose above the wall. To the rear the view was blocked by profoundly dense undergrowth and a melancholy fowl-run. The house was surrounded on three sides by Killadoon Wood, its timber radiating out until it had covered as many baronies. The eastern boundary of the wood was the river, the western the estate wall under which the Brazill family lived rent free. Tall elms converged on the house, their leaves scattering on the pitched roof of faded slate, clogging the eaves' gutters. The house was the front gatelodge, a narrow two-storey edifice built slap against the boundary wall of Colonel Clements' estate.

Into this house were born six children, four boys and two girls, of whom five survived – one of the boys dying in infancy. The eldest child was christened Edward Pearse. The father was the lodge-keeper and chief steward on the estate, a corpulent man with a walrus moustache of a pepper-and-salt colour, grave and insufferably cautious by nature, who always wore leggings. His wife, tall, red-headed, of erratic temper and devout, had a stiff straight back and a passionate eye. Her husband was called Ned and she was Clare. She wore men's boots and tattered cardigans, with her hair screwed into a tight bun at the nape of her neck. All week she laboured without ceasing. Lit by the fire, beads of sweat stood out on her forehead which she disdained to wipe. Doubled up and panting she struggled with the awkward churn, milk slopping here and there on the tiles. On Sunday she rested – Got her wind back, as she said; on that day she darned the socks and patched and mended the clothes.

The figure of his mother, angular and undemonstrative, standing at the clothes line with pegs in her mouth, seemed to Eddy Brazill the embodiment of security and plenty. She had only to put a hand out of sight for a moment to take out oatmeal cakes and ginger biscuits. So it was while he grew up; labouring year followed labouring year and from the ten tall chimneys of the Brazill home smoke ascended clear of the trees, fading into a wash sky.

From his bed, Eddy could hear of a morning, far off in the wet woods, the clap and echo of a shotgun – then his mother's:

'There's your father' – so restrained and proud. Ned Brazill was allocated a regular supply of cartridges, in return for which he donated a brace or two of grouse, pigeon or pheasant in season to her Ladyship's larder. As a consequence the Brazills ate very well, and Eddy's young palate became early accustomed to delicacies such as roasted game-birds or river trout served with butter and parsley.

His earliest memories were associated with a shadowy kitchen into which no sun could ever enter, his mother cooking soda bread on the range, the sight of his father's stout gaitered legs. A dead rabbit hung upside down from a hook on the ceiling in the company of onions. An assemblage of black frying pans of all shapes and sizes clung to one wall. From his chair, in bib and tucker, he commanded a lateral view into the blue haze of the wood.

Even before daylight he had lain awake listening to the noises stirring in Killadoon as the wood began to wake, followed by the erratic sounds of his mother moving in the bowels of the house, preparing breakfast. The lids of the kitchen range were removed one by one with the disturbance of iron manholes rolled aside. Then it was the primus's turn to begin its roaring and the clothes line came squeaking down. Da went padding past then in his stockinged feet.

At the end of the stone-flagged corridor beyond the dusty bells, a meal of porridge, scones, marmalade, eggs-and-bacon, with a pot of tea, was being set out for his da. A door opened and closed. The shaving mirror was drawn out to its full extent from the wall and a kettle of boiling water poured into the basin.

Then in the darkness feet were pounding again on the landing: Father's boots heavy on the grave, stamping the earth down – sullen, importunate; and darling Mother far below.

At a tender age Eddy was dispatched with a satchel and a younger brother to the convent, where the nuns were to take over his education.

'*Who is God?* . . . *Who made the world?*' These and other even more confusing questions flustered him greatly and he was considered backward; a spindle-shanked fellow with a clown's face and his mother's outrageous hair.

'You are a dunderhead, Eddy Brazill,' said Sister Rumold with finality.

But it was his father, more than the nuns, who taught him finally to read and write: the father bequeathing to the son a fair round hand together with his own homespun wisdom, for what it was worth, together with his prejudices: all of which were innocent enough. Thus Eddy came to know of the Land Act of 1870 and of the infamous and unprincipled William Sydney Clements, third Earl of Leitrim – murdered, in retribution, by some of his own tenantry. Ned Brazill followed de Valera's politics and would proudly admit:

'Yes, I'm a Dev man.'

He spoke against Mussolini, whose army at the time was engaged in the wholesale slaughter of Abyssinians, saying:

'They're only poor bloody savages.'

He was a devout Catholic, a member of the Men's Sodality, and cycled to evening devotions twice a week. The people, according to him, had turned away from God, and Almighty God would not tolerate it much longer. In the meantime he taught his son how to cast for trout and to shoot:

'Fire agin the grain of the feathers,' Ned said.

The slow river with its whirlpools and shallows taught the son to be quiet, to wait. The wood gave him a predilection for cover. With the nuns he had the reputation of being an 'underhand' boy, and he was constantly beaten by Sister Rumold.

In his ears echoed always the mournful marching songs of a defunct Ireland. The pipe-and-drum band played 'O'Donnell Abu', a music frantic and scornful, lost in the wind buffeting the cyprus trees about Griffenwrath. The legendary Fenians, the villains of the Cosgrave administration, the heroes of the Tailthean Games, Tommy Coniff and the Wild West, Tombstone and Cody, buffalo-hunter for the gandy-dancers, Charley Reynolds, and Wild Bill Hickok himself, with his buckskins and his saffron hair, all these met together miraculously in the main street of

Celbridge. Over the bridge strode a cowboy dressed in buckskin, followed by a Red Indian girl with a red feather stuck in her hair. Up and down the main street he went, cracking his bullwhip and not saying a word. The girl, fringed buckskin to her knees and high-heeled boots with fancy tops, a brown face and blue-black hair, stood opposite Deas's Harness Parts holding at arm's length an egg up-ended on a spoon. Down the main street swaggered the cowboy cracking his bullwhip and not saying a word. All Celbridge were out in amazement. He smashed six eggs in succession out of her hand, standing on the opposite pavement by Breen's Hotel.

Nor was that all. The dead of the Rebellion were buried all over again one bitter Sunday in Griffenwrath, and volleys and orations fired over their graves.

The Brazill family drove to Mass in a pony and trap every Sunday and Holy Day of the year. The yellow shafts of the trap tilted up, the little pony could hardly sustain them, high-stepping it down to Celbridge. The two gawky sisters sat in front, pious Misses in sunbonnets and organdie. The three brothers sat to the rear, hair sleeked back, their raw hands on their knees, furtive and uncomfortable in reach-me-downs. Ned Brazill drove, holding a long whip in one hand and sporting a bowler, staring peacefully ahead. After Mass he liked to retire to the toss bank above Coyle's Cross and mix with the men, uniform in the sobriety of their Sunday blue, for the purpose of gambling.

Between them the Brazills consumed a roast of prime beef to celebrate the Sabbath, garnished with homegrown vegetables, cress or leeks. Ned drank a bottle of stout with this meal, into which one of the daughters was sometimes bidden to put a heated poker, 'to bring up a head'. The gravy boat passed sedately from hand to hand. Evelyn tittered over some joke with the imbecile Essy. A froth of stout moved on Father's moustaches as he ate. The red hen hesitated on one leg in the doorway.

Then Father pushed his chair back a little from the table and crossed his legs, looking down the table at his ravenous family almost in bewilderment. How could any man ever have whelped such a litter? Afterwards Eddy retired into the wood to read the Sunday supplements in peace.

At the age of nine, choking in an Eton collar, he was confirmed by the Bishop. His infancy lay behind him after that and he had to move with his class to the National School across the river. It was a stone structure over-hanging the water presided over by two notorious whippers, one called Mr Sands and the other called Mr O'Mahon. Eddy Brazill resolved at once to make himself unobtrusive. He kept his mouth shut and was beaten by Mr O'Mahon for insolence, opening it to say the wrong thing, whereupon he was flogged by Mr Sands for stupidity.

Chastisement, chastisement, he never seemed to get enough of it; how long ago had he grown immune to it? He sat at the back of the Religious Knowledge class with his head down listening to the sound of the river flowing out under the dirt and knots of the floorboards, and was told to stand in the corner for dreaming. In all he spent two years under the iron rule of Sands and O'Mahon. It was not a happy time. During that period his mother died.

Dragged across the threshold by his father, he saw his mother's head propped up among the pillows; her eyes were shining and her long hair unbound like a bride's. He went to the foot of the bed and stood there, holding onto the brass bed-rail, not knowing what to do or say. Indeed, he had never seen his mother in bed before, for she rose long before he was awake and retired after he was asleep. She, who had never suffered a day's illness in her life, or at least never taken to her bed on that account, seemed now strange and remote, with the quilt drawn up about her shoulders and her hair loose. She had never ceased working all her life and began her death as though it too were merely a continuation of labour; she had become smaller but still seemed to be engaged on some difficult but not uncongenial task. He heard her loud breathing and saw how flushed she was; he watched, his hands gripping the brass rail as though he could hold her back from dying, although he knew it was useless. Between his hands he saw his mother's face, worn out, timorous and grave; and then he could bear it no longer and began to cry. She reached her hand out slowly and said:

'Cum 'e here then.'

He crouched by her side, taking her hand, and she went on:

'Nay matter, my love, God's been very good to me, and I'm reconciled . . .'

And Eddy wept on her hand and was afraid to look at her. She was dying of diphtheria and nothing in the world could save her. Two days later she was dead. She lay there stiff and cold on the Tuesday. It was early summer, a numb day of silence and diluted sun. Sounds seemed to carry a long way, and the priest prayed *Requiem aeternam.*

The turf carts which had passed the house at night, toiling from the Bog of Allen in all weathers down the rocky road to Dublin and back again, were drawn in a slovenly manner by little white-bellied donkeys with big heads. The load was much higher than the shallow sides of the cart and covered in tarpaulin. Two weary carriage lamps lit the shafts and tail boards, their candles fitful behind blurred glass. The drivers walked by the donkey's head on the journey out, with the traces trailing and, drunk at times, dozed on their sides on the floor of the empty cart under sacks on the journey home. All his life long they had been rumbling past, causing the same commotion, the axles ungreased and the wheels loose, man and beast alike sunk in a half-sleep out of which there seemed no waking.

After his mother's funeral the old lullaby changed to a dirge, ground out to the same painful motion of the wheels. *Your-mother-is-dead, yourmotherisdead, your-mother-is-dead, yourmotherisdead* . . . He lay on his back in bed listening to it, the blood and the life draining from his heart; until it seemed that in his misery he had gone underground with her – down with her headlong into the grave.

A year later he left his schooldays behind him for ever, and was apprenticed to Mr Flynn in the forge. He was then fourteen years old. In the forge his face became as habitually black as a sweep's. He wore a leather apron and was never without a cigarette butt between ear and cap. He lifted the hind leg of a massive dray horse and drove nails rapidly into its hooves, gripping the spare nails between his teeth like a true blacksmith. The horse stood patiently on three legs, breathing down his neck, aquiver as flies crawled over it, no gelding either, lethargic mounter of mares. Eddy finished the job with the rasp.

'Gran' die, thanksa be-ta God,' he said to Boland's vanman.

'Ay,' Boland's vanman said, spitting, 'Gran' die for a big blonde.'

For five years Eddy Brazill laboured in Flynn's forge. Black in the face, beating showers of sparks from the anvil, peevish, he cursed his past and his future. Five years during which his father, grown feeble, was pensioned off, dogs died, Mr de Valera went out of office, his brothers left home for England, and Evelyn went into domestic service. One bright day in the spring of the last year he took the bus to Aston Quay, walked round the corner into the B. & I. shipping office and bought a single ticket for Holyhead and London. Four days later he stood in the kitchen, cap in hand, a cheap suitcase by his feet, attempting a sang-froid which he did not feel. A ready-made suiting of indigo serge, double breasted with a vent behind, hung from his shoulders stiff and unaccommodating as sandwich-boards. A puce tie and green knitted cardigan filled in the gaps of the blue. A poor-quality white shirt, pinched in by a Woolworth's tiepin, gave an odd flounced effect. The tie was worn outside the cardigan and extended to the navel. The shoes were a wild ox-blood hue, with pointed toes and perforated uppers. The mop of hair, clipped into ridges and cones, vanished over the crown of the head in damp undulating waves. Brylcreem shone on his ear tips. The total effect was stunning. All – all – from the Brylcreem wavy hair to the sharp affronted shoes, proclaimed in no uncertain terms the migrant Irish day labourer surprised on the day of his setting forth. He stood on familiar stone; clearing his throat, he spoke in a hollow voice into the gloom:

'I'm off now, Da.'

The father came forward from the depths of the kitchen. Essy appeared, hanging halfway down the stairs. Son and sire met in the centre of the kitchen. The old man's head was lower than his own; ancient Atlas world remover with the globe shaken from his shoulders. Old Brazill, a decayed ill-favoured rheumatic man, partially blind, almost wholly deaf, bent double with lumbago and the years, contrived still to move about with the aid of a staff the size of a crozier, which he grasped at a point above his head and propelled himself forward as though punting. The waxen flesh of his face was stretched tight across jawbone and temple. His face was a network of discoloured veins, jumping with every laboured breath as though his life were being read off on a graph. When he spoke the scrawny neck shuddered and the jaw sockets were agitated. Tufts of hair sprouted from his flared ears and from his nostrils. His eyes were rheumy and uncertain, focusing doubtfully, straying. The lids were scaled and heavy. Effort and fatigue had rotted him away. He made to release the staff, as if to embrace his son, but thought better of it. He leant on it, opening and closing his mouth, the sour breath of a seventy-seven-year-old issuing from his lungs, baleful as the fumes from a jakes. Out of this ruin a lifetime ago, hope and sperm had gushed. With failing senses he had watched his wife and children go, one by one, into the world and into the grave; obstinate to the last he still hung on – a stagnant pool about to be stirred for the last time.

'You take care Eddy,' the voice said. 'You take good care.'

Eddy saw a spark appear far down in his father's eyes, down in the Sargasso Sea; it came whirling up towards the alarmed pupil. Some convulsion of the spirit was taking place, forcing the eyes out of their sockets, full of some nameless apprehension, a dread of unknown, foreign places, of uprooting. Horror-stricken it fled past, leaving his features more awry than ever. Old Brazill swallowed and tried to speak. Eddy grasped the staff below his father's hands, glaring speechless at him. Transfixed they stood eye to eye. From a great distance Eddy heard the tale being recited, over and over again. *Fine times we had together . . . fine times . . . don't let them get the better of you . . . I'll pray for you . . . I'll be thinking of you . . . and write to us some time*, the hopeless eyes beseeched him.

Then Eddy Brazill went out of the kitchen for the last time.

Perivale Prospect

The London Labour Exchange officials began by asking would he work on the railways. Years later the same question would come up, an irresistible association in the mind. Was it because he looked undernourished, had flaming hair and was Irish? Was there an unwritten law that Irish labourers are attracted to railways, as the ailing to lung charts, or gadflies to dung?

No, Eddy Brazill said; with the best will in the world he would not work on the railways; could they perhaps offer something a little better? The man looked down among his papers, moving them here and there, sceptical of opportunity for the semi-skilled. Would he work in a factory? He would. Very well, the man said, making a note. A vacancy existed for a promising aspirant of slightly above average intelligence in a cosmetic factory in north-west London: how would that suit him? Behind his own head Eddy Brazill saw in his mind's eye the elevated blackboard with VACANCIES printed over it. Scrawled upon this in chalk and in haste, as if executed while the very men he was advertising for were already advancing upon the writer, appeared the legend:

TURRET-CLOCK REPAIRERS
PANEL-BEATERS
IMMEDIATELY

'I'll try that,' he said faintly. 'What's the pay?'
The man began to fill in a form at once.
'Take this', he said, 'to their employment manager. Ask

for Mr Mason and he'll fix you up. They are offering £7 per week with Saturdays off.'

Brazill took the slip, thanked the man, and left.

Old Bert worked the shredding machine in a small annexe or stall abutting on the stores. His was the most monotonous and lonely job in the whole factory. The 'shredder' was an electrically driven, hand-fed machine which resembled an old-fashioned farm mangle. Instead of pulping turnips for livestock, however, it ground down the coarse grain packing material fed indifferently into its maw by Old Bert, smoking the same endless cigarette, until the shreds could be reassimilated by the Dispatch Department. Crags and company were there, giant humourless stationary men, packing so tenderly the consignments of cold cream and vanishing cream, so that without interruption the cosmetic produce could go out to Mogul Street, Bombay, to Lyssiatis of Larnaca, and to all the world. At the hub of all this international commerce sat Old Bert, feeding his machine, grey of face, chain-smoking, farting. He had grown withered in the service of the company. Years before he had been presented with a silver watch and chain for fifty years of blameless service to the company. He could remember when the production manager Mr Lambert – a gentleman – had worked in his shirt-sleeves with the men in the stores.

Old Bert did all the dirty jobs about the place. He emptied the rejected jars from the tin trays beneath the conveyor belt into his handcart, oblivious to the spectacle of so many agitated female knees. He burnt the refuse from the laboratory and Lipstick Room in the big incinerator near the bicycle sheds – going head first into the very barrels and skips themselves and bearing dirt smelling to high heaven towards the fire. Evil-smelling matter the livid colour of intestines hung from his hands and fell into the flames. Rotted beauty preparations went up in smoke – glycol and pink face powder, spoilt slabs of lipstick, clots of over-sweet beeswax and jar upon jar of ruined cream – fifteen and sixteen barrelfuls at a time. Old Bert's own smell, from long attendance at the incinerator, was devastating. He could be recognised from all the other employees by this alone – he stank as though dipped in brimstone. He was manpower – personnel – at the end of its tether – both the decrepit gatekeeper who ushered the newcomer into the factory yard and also the superannuated wreck that Industry discarded after he had served his time: Bert Pollard, the phantom behind the Pension Scheme.

Old Bert was not dispirited, not wholly. A calendar hung on a nail behind him, a coloured photograph of a castle in Scotland, taken in the autumn. Sometimes he sang a stave:

> 'When the sun is in the sky (caesura)
> Storm-ee weather . . .'

That was his song. Meanwhile Brazill went about the factory with Bert's handcart looking for rejects and scraps.

That had been his beginning. He had gone up a dusty road on a day in June, with the Labour Exchange slip in his pocket, wearing his last shirt inside out because of the frayed collar, with $1\frac{1}{2}$d. between himself and perdition. Mr Mason had said to Mr Brogan, pointing dramatically at the 'promising aspirant':

'Mr Brogan, can we use this man?'

Whereupon Brazill threw out his chest and looked ready for anything. Mr Brogan looked him up and down, and said yes indeed they could. Brazill was then given a brown boilersuit and told to report himself to Bert Pollard at the shredding machine.

When nine months had drifted by he could begin to think with the rest, *For a period longer than I care to remember I have been in the employment of the Blackford Cosmetic Company, Middlesex . . . Am I ever going to leave?* After the initial 'soft time' with Old Bert, Brazill served time in the Packing Department, and then in the Dispatch Department, before he was moved finally into the stores ('You'll be laughing,' his mates said), where he worked longest and with least distress under the easygoing Mr Heavens.

Ted Heavens, a portly man with a sluggish nature and Roman nose, had lost his false teeth during the company outing to Southend, in a sand dune. ('Old Ted's a caution,' his mates said.) He walked slowly with a rolling gait, dragging his feet at the same time as though in a quagmire, and occupied most of his eight-hour stint making entries and counter-entries in his small office in the loading yard, leaving the donkeywork to the assiduous Mr Brogan. A messenger would arrive with a note from another department: 'Mr Heavens – please return six hacking knives to the tool supplies.' Five minutes later this neat entry would appear in his day-book: 'Six hacking knives returned to tool supplies.'

After a fortnight in the stores, Mr Mason came upon Brazill parading up and down, and asked him:

'Well Brazill, are you quite happy with Mr Heavens or shall we move you?'

Brazill said he was quite happy where he was, thank you Mr Mason. Only after months of experience had he mastered factory work – or had at least made himself efficient enough to be unobtrusive – but what he could not master was its more difficult corollary: factory idleness. When the time came for his mates to disappear, they melted imperceptibly from sight. One minute they were there, Jeffries and Tom Davies; the next minute both

were gone. To detect them in the act of going was impossible. ('Use your loaf,' they said.)

Mr Brogan was the charge-hand; he wore a white coat
and had authority to distribute the labour pool as he saw
fit – roving far and wide in search of malingerers. Time
and again he surprised Brazill manifestly idle, and put
him onto the conveyor belt where he had no time even
to blow his nose. Sometimes, seeing him loitering about
with half an hour to kill before he could punch his card
and leave, Ted Heavens would approach and say in confidence:

'You get lost upstairs, Eddy. Don't let Brogan catch
you.'

Then Brazill would retire, carrying some object as if
executing an order, stepping from the lift into the first
floor stores overflow, a long clean room above the
machine shop, and disappear from sight, hang-dog,
between the bales and boxes. He attempted this subter-
fuge during the slack part of the day, smoking half a
cigarette in hiding, and then would be lured out to the
loading bay. There he stood, plain for all to see, staring
down as though mesmerised at the chippers in the yard
below who worked at a piece rate and as a consequence
took their own time. They had been in the process of
breaking up the cement ramp for the best part of seven
weeks. Here was a company of elderly grizzled workers
who spat on their hands and raised their crowbars with a
measured ponderousness, and slowly, utterly slowly, the
earth came irregularly through. On Friday afternoon
the demolition squad were given their pay envelopes by
Mr Brogan. Resting on the handles of their crowbars they
opened the packets and suspiciously examined the long
scrolls of the days, the man hours, the overtime, the net
and the gross, hanging from their hands. Sometimes they

struck down with their crowbars in a blind fury, then carried on as slowly as before, as if nothing had happened.

But more often Brazill ignored the chippers and their grievances and stared instead over the Davall clock factory, the cider factory and the Enna Infants' Bath factory, at the high hill and the last green fields of England, bathed in a pale sourceless light neither of morning nor of evening, which came neither from the earth nor from the sky. Until Mr Brogan on his ceaseless rounds of inspection shot into sight, saw Brazill's white disengaged face, and without even abating his pace shouted up:

'Eddy! Eddy! Minnie wants a hand in the factory. Come down!'

The early shift began at six o'clock in the morning.

Brazill was forced from his bed at 4.45 by the uproar of no fewer than three alarm clocks going off simultaneously. He flung back the bedclothes and hurried to and fro in the dark silencing them. Then he struck a match and applied it to the crumbling asbestos face of the gas fire. Dragging his clothes from the back of a chair, he scattered them before the fire and began to dress in haste, girding himself as best he could for the rigours of Industry, puffing out his cheeks like an athlete. He pulled on a pair of stiff corduroys, a clammy shirt, numerous pullovers that had seen better days, a pair of hob-nailed boots. The kitchen was just across the landing; there he prepared and ate a rapid breakfast of tea and Quaker Oats. He crammed sandwiches wrapped in oilpaper into his jacket pocket, wound a woollen muffler several times around his neck, shovelled himself into an army great-coat. He put off the kitchen light and re-entered the bedroom, turning down the gas until it popped and went out. Then he descended into the hall, took his cap from the rack, turned the Yale lock and let himself out into the pitch blackness of Fordhook Road. Twelve minutes had elapsed since the alarms had gone off.

Walking fast he turned into the long drag of Uxbridge Road. A numb wind fastened its teeth into him. The morning was fouled with countless impurities, the air thick and lichenous, full of ice and soot. A rank-smelling pillar of cloud extended into the atmosphere for a mile above Greater London. A dead night wind was blowing from Acton Town – a colder stream of air into which he went blindly – intermingled with the reek coming from the open mouth of Ealing Common tube station opposite. Five o'clock began to strike from some windy steeple as he started across the common.

With lowered head he advanced down an avenue of black stricken timber, the wind whipping at his coat-tails. Half a mile away lay the Broadway; a furtive spill of orange light from the Belisha beacons flushing and ebbing on the columns of the Midland Bank; and beyond that the steps and grime of the station. He went on. All the within swirled together like an addled egg, the lights, the kidney and the spleen jolting with every step he took. In the leafless trees rainwater streamed down, dropping bough by bough to the saturated ground; on every side the liquid stir and fall, shaken loose from the trees and from the sagging trolley bus lines overhead – hesitating and then falling. A sound mingled with the inconsolable dirge of the telegraph wires, through which went the stray erratic clatter of his boots, going ahead of him only to be thrown back by the wet press of leaves, until it seemed that not one but several Brazills were heading for the Mall. The thaw had begun. Heavy lorries were starting on Hanger Lane. The wheels of Industry were turning already.

Walking down the Uxbridge Road before light he sometimes recalled fishing expeditions with his father when he was a boy. Ned leading him through the fields before daybreak to where the clay-coloured river flowed casually by, with the clouds which belonged neither to day nor to night in rout above its surface. His father drew in the line, his face a patient mask discoloured by river and sky, drawing in the catch, the last couple of feet coming in fast. The eel coiled itself about the claspknife as Ned dug at its neck; then bones and tendons were cut and blood splattered on the grass. The catch was gutted and beheaded; the river went straight on over the weir. In the rhythm of near lightless calm, something passed out from the earth. The sweat of its passage lay on objects, human and inanimate, as one by one they emerged out of the surrounding dark. A sweat not even born of the craven human fear of extinction, but the matter which life in convulsion ejects – relinquishes – when life is no longer there. The river that vanished, cut short in mid-stride, the fish deprived of stomachs and heads, both released a steam, an exhalation from scale and surface, of which the ending of life seemed only part.

After a year's service he felt he could no longer bear the cosmetic factory, and left with £20 in his pocket for higher wages elsewhere.

He found the higher wages in an extrusion moulding plant in Burnt Oak. Punfield & Barstow (Mouldings) had a high diverse output, produced by the minimum of man-power in the maximum of hours. The day shift started at 7 a.m. and ended at 6 p.m., and the night shift started at 7 p.m. and ended at 7 a.m. Diehards were prepared to work the extra hour overtime, so that the presses were never cold, never still. The bigger semi-automatic presses thundered away on their cement beds twenty-four hours a day. One operator controlled each machine, loading it with polythene and keeping the pressure constant. A chart was made out each day by the production foreman and hung outside his office. This chart allocated specific presses to individual operators and indicated also the pressure and time cycle they were expected to follow. The fastest was a fifteen-second cycle producing four articles per minute. However, it was possible, even in the day shift under the eagle eye of Di Palmo, to force the pressure up a little and extrude two seconds prematurely. In order to achieve a four-a-minute cycle, it was necessary to allow, say, two seconds for opening, one second for extruding, two seconds for closing – opening on the tenth second, extruding on the twelfth, closing on the fifteenth and repeating this ratio four times every minute. But by opening on the eighth second, extruding and closing as per instructions, it was possible to close on the thirteenth instead of on the fifteenth second, opening again on the twenty-first, to close on the twenty-sixth instead of on the thirtieth, and so on, gaining two seconds on every quarter of a cycle. This was common practice.

On the night shift a charge-hand took over for an hour during the staggered tea break, working a legitimate cycle and keeping his produce (for which he was paid) separate. But for the rest of the night Brazill and his mates slaved away at an eleven-hour stint, opening, extruding and closing 28,000 times a night instead of the regulation 24,000, recklessly forcing up individual outputs. Fifteen machines rattled away day and night while a one-handed clock on the wall counted off the seconds. Two amplifiers connected to an unseen radio were rigged overhead and deluged the workers with a prolonged instrumental and vocal uproar. 'The Yellow Rose of Texas' alternated with another favourite which began:

> 'Beeee my life's companion
> And you'll never grow old,

Never grow old,
Never grow old.'

And beyond that cries of anger and dismay, seldom abating, wrung from the operators who felt themselves dropping behind schedule. And beyond that again the relentless concussion of the hand presses, echoing down from the skylights. It was in this uproarious company that Brazill spent seven months. On the night shift he preferred to stand rather than sit, as he was at liberty to do, lest in a doze he should fall into one of the presses and have his head crushed.

Monk the Jew, Blizzard the Jamaican, beautiful Basket the Pakistani, Doody the moody Corkman, a fellow-countryman, and Brazill emerged alike at the end of twelve hours, grey of face, endurance drained to the last drop, to punch their cards and depart into the slush and fog of Burnt Oak. Brazill had a hovel in West Ealing and went home to sleep all day.

For seven months Brazill was a link in the noisy chain-gang, a prey to the most wretched fancies in the long troubled night shifts, during which he was torn apart by wild black horses. In the long watches lustful reverie too had its place. Then he left once again for employment offering less exacting hours.

A small firm of woollen distributors in the City next hired him as their office factotum. The firm consisted of a Scotsman who had stomach ulcers and a Swiss Jew who did the book-keeping. A distinguished-looking gentleman sometimes called, fingering the bales with Mr Hogarth and taking away samples; this was their traveller. The duties that fell to Brazill were not exacting. He was required to dust the office in the morning, deposit cheques in the Bank of Canada, look smart, collect odd bales of cloth from Baker Street and Euston, travelling to and fro in a taxi. Most of the day he spent wrapping tartan rugs in cellophane bags, staring into the ladies' corsetry department of Liberty's.

Other employments came and went, other rituals, other faces. The money he had saved dwindled and then disappeared; the periods between employments grew longer and longer. Not that he was reluctant to work, indeed no; but by dint of walking through London he had contrived to put himself outside labour altogether. In the end he stood aloof, aghast at its possibilities. Not labour's possibilities (from it he had suffered nothing but hardship and vexation), but London's. This was a perilous state to arrive at and led inevitably to a period of decline and semi-starvation.

Two more years passed, and by that time Brazill was reduced to a beggarly condition. The diet of the down-trodden and the unfortunate is tea, bread and dripping; he had fallen below even that – below subsistence level into the limbo of unemployment and health benefits. As in a dream his time in Industry came back to him. He heard the girl screaming in the Lipstick Room with her hand impaled in the carding machine.

He watched the white froth from the cider factory next door falling in the yard like midsummer snow. A group of girls dressed in purple overalls stared through smoked glass at an eclipse of the sun on 30 July 1952, and Milly Ashebrook said:

'The next time, Eddy, you won't be alive.'

Eddy Brazill saw the face of the man who had a stroke in the canteen, struck down on the floor. He had begun to swallow his own tongue.

During that summer Ebbie Cook's brassière burst under the acacia tree in Kew Old Deer Park. In Shepherd's Bush the elderly whore with the complexion of an Easter Islander paraded up and down opposite the mouth of Rockery Road. He lay down on the flat of his back in the sun on Haven Green. Full of apprehension he slunk along Pentonville Road, stepping over the threshold of the King's Cross Labour Exchange. A stout tweed-clad man with a watch-chain spanning his paunch offered him a Player cigarette. The man questioned him about his previous employment. The cant expression he used was:

'Put me in the picture.'

As best he could Brazill did so. The man said 'Hmmm', and looked down at his papers, as if all Brazill's past and future were there exposed. It seemed a phantom of himself that had entered months, yes and years before, telling the same tale, his stomach a void; the meek no more shall inherit the earth.

It was during this period that he lived in an upper room in Abbey Road. Too disheartened even to claim unemployment benefit (which would have meant presenting himself twice a week at the Labour Exchange in Camden Town), he lay on his bed all day listening to the cries on the road and the activities of the milkman. Wholefart and Angel were his co-tenants, running endless baths, fat decayed women in bathrobes on the floor above. Which was Wholefart and which Angel?

Once in a while, to pay the rent, he dug up black shale and cinders in Swiss Cottage gardens or rolled the lawns, at three shillings an hour. Half a pint of milk a day, a small loaf, a tin of Tate and Lyle's Golden Syrup kept him alive, barely alive. He seldom went out. The air too full of brutal purpose assaulted him. As he passed by the saloon bar by the circus a beery woman's voice said in confidence:

– 'That's right, sittin' indoors I could 'ear Nelly's chest wheezin' . . . I could 'ear it whistlin' . . .'

A well-known siren leant forward from the Kilburn

newsboards eyeing Brazill. She wore a skin-tight sheath dress with a generous cut into the bust, into which the passing eye travelled irresistibly. ANYA, BRITAIN'S SINGING BOMBSHELL!

All that lay behind.

His time in Industry dropped away. The false snow falling into the factory yard, the girl screaming and screaming, her hand nailed to the belt; the Bristol lorry driver's tattooed arm with a crucifixion among the hairs, and FATHER, MOTHER, CHRIST, FORGET ME NOT inscribed about the Cross – all gone.

Alone and miserable beyond words, Brazill walked out along a high parapet of hunger. In his decline he had rejected both logic and hope; logic which demanded that he take a grip on himself before his condition got out of hand; hope which spoke incorrigibly of better days. When not grinding his teeth with fury, he enjoyed a very elevated humour, combined with great vivacity of spirits. Capable of the wildest pranks, he seldom failed to disgrace himself in one way or another. Indistinguishable from the sober press of passers-by, he could commute in the West End without too much adverse comment – just one among many in pinched circumstances this side of outright begging. Until, seized by the demon, his shoulders would begin to shake and uncommon expressions fly across his features, until the whole face started to crack and break up, and out came anarchy. Once he showed that face his condition deteriorated rapidly. Sniggering and shaking he was then obliged to stand with his nose pressed to a convenient shop window, laughing away to himself until the tears streamed down his cheeks. But this behaviour inevitably created a disturbance within. Before long assistant managers and floor walkers would converge, and then come flying out to drive him off. Shabby, threadbare, down-at-heel, he went guffawing away. The demon tickled his pleurae and would not leave off until Brazill was roaring. The slender chance he had of becoming a swimming-pool attendant in Seymour Place public baths ended in rout. Brazill had to leave the building at a smart trot, waving his hands before his face as if attacked by wasps, and hold onto the pointed railings in front, laughing until he wept. Behind his back an eccentric paused, dressed in a Macleod kilt, plimsolls, a skean-dhu projecting from his Highland stocking, an outsize packet of Corn Flakes under his arm. He watched Brazill for a while, then went on towards Marylebone Road, gaily whistling.

One fine day Brazill went as far afield as Fulham, to offer his services as a stoker in the gas works. He was not taken on. Then he began wandering about as usual, without purpose or destination, in the purlieus of Earls Court and Hammersmith. He walked on and on until it turned three o'clock and he could walk no further. Famished, he remembered that some scraps still remained over from his ordinary (a pudding of bread and syrup) in far-off Abbey Road. He found eightpence in his jacket pocket. It was sufficient for a bun and coffee but nothing else; it would mean footing it all the way to Kilburn – and that was beyond him. He decided to walk as far as Notting Hill Gate and take the tube from there to Swiss Cottage. Weak in the legs he tottered on up Campden Hill.

At last he reached the high street and crossed over to the station. He bought a ticket and took up a position by the lift gates. After a while he heard the gates close below and the whine of the lift ascending. A group of people gathered silently about him. Muggy air rushed up from the shaft. Now fainting with real hunger and fatigue he felt the whole weight of his hot oppressive flesh hanging down. He fastened his eyes on the neck of the

person before him. It seemed to him that if he were to
fall no hands could hold him up. For the second time in
his life he stood on the edge of the pit; another minute
or two and he would collapse among them. For certain
he would carry the fellow heavily through the gates and
down into the shaft with him; his exhaustion was such
that it could burst its way through iron gates, carrying all
before it. There at the bottom of the earth, among the
used tickets and grease, he and the labourer would stir a
little, broken up, beyond hope, mutilated.

There among bystanders, in the short space of time
that it took the lift to rise into sight, the revelation
occurred once more. The pressure of the moment had
burst something asunder. His own past, with its absurd
pretensions intact, blew before; the body of Brazill
dropped downwards like a stone between them. Infused
with superhuman strength, it seemed that he could stand
there for ever. A dead wind blew patiently into his eyes
from its damp origin below the earth. *Oh dear God,* he
thought, *Oh dear God, am I not even going to faint?* It seemed
to him that he was carried headlong into a damp black
morning of the past. The avenue of chestnuts were out.
It was summer. Everywhere water was dripping. The
green-blue circles of street lights strayed among the
leaves. Behind the dark trunks, sunken in an opaque
light, he saw the outline of a seat. There, under overcoats
and sacks, a down-and-out slept his thin troubled sleep.
As Brazill drew close to this mound, the sleeper rose up
in a terrifying manner, still sleeping, struggling with a
nightmare and the damp coverings, then fell back again.
An indescribable feeling of loss took hold of Brazill. To
the end of his life that scene, that helpless gesture, would
be repeated. It seemed then that the only acknowledge-
ment one could offer to another human being, once life

was over, would be in the form of an embrace. He would have to lie under the sacks himself to be at peace.

At that moment, close by, he heard the sounds of staples parting. The gates opened then and he was driven foremost into the lift.

Stye

The Bouchers had lived for ages immemorial in their towered ancestral mansion near the Lucan spa. Mr Alexander Gill Boucher was a man of stern principles and even sterner prejudices, whose wife had paid her debt to nature long before and had departed to the Pale Kingdoms. He lived alone with his son and four retainers. Alcohol and Roman Catholicism were anathema to him. He had an aristocrat's contempt for the incapable multitude and a feeling little short of revulsion for those whom he regarded as their mouthpiece: the Roman clergy. He lived in the midst of poor Catholic farm labourers and tenants. Both he and his late wife had inherited wealth. The local poor referred to him as 'Lord Boucher'. He in his turn despised them. 'No truck with Catholics' was one of his dogmas. Christian Brothers, curates, novice priests out from Maynooth and Clongowes, parish priests on the prowl – these were perpetually cycling past the front gate with dazed expressions – black divisions on the move. Lord Boucher glared at them or looked elsewhere. His attitude to 'the little scoundrels in the black cassocks' was known throughout Kildare. The priests were a curse; the common people had their place, and were expected to stay in it.

His son Ben Boucher, aged forty, was paunched, high complexioned and deaf as a post. He wore a hearing-aid and carried its clumsy battery under his arm. Of a sportful and Bacchic nature, Ben was the self-appointed destroyer of his papa's composure. He was a keen golfer and an even keener drinker. Lager in the morning, a fourball in the afternoon, Scotch in the evening, confusion at night – that was Ben Boucher's way. He knew no curb to his drinking, and even treated artisan golfers at the club bar. His father once surprised him in a drunken state with the blacksmith's assistant in the snug at Hermitage. He had no snobbishness or pettiness in his nature. The smith's assistant wore cheap shirts with frayed collars which stood on end, and was referred to in scathing tones as 'the surly papist in point ruff'.

'A *deplorable* fellow,' Mr Alex Boucher confided to another member's ear; 'risen from the gutters and most likely a pure blood descendant of Sinn Fein gunmen . . .'

The old man had not long to live and possibly knew it. When he sat down to draw up his will he saw to it that all his prejudices outlived him. He left everything to his buffoon of a son – everything. The Lucan home, property in Armagh (a boot factory), stocks and shares in South America and £66,000 in ready cash. The money was willed on condition that the legatee stayed not only sober but strictly TT for a whole calendar year. Shortly afterwards he died.

On that day the club flag hung at half-mast and the members vied with each other in recalling, almost with charity, the foibles of the cantankerous elder Gill Boucher. The bar remained closed until noon and the course all day. The son was nowhere to be seen.

A year passed. Ben Boucher showed no great determination in his few attempts to inherit his fortune. All attempts to stay 'on the wagon' had ended in acrimonious disorder and long bouts of drunkenness. 'All the

damnable degrees of drinking have I staggered through,'
he confessed almost with pride.

After two years of such carousing it came to him one
sober hour that the £66,000 was withdrawing itself almost
casually from his grasp. That remained the position until
one day he discovered his salvation in a book. The author
– a qualified doctor and naturopathic practitioner named
Vergiff – ran a smart sanatorium for incurables at a
watering-place on the English east coast. Ben Boucher
discovered *The Fallacy of the Hopeless Case* in the Marylebone public library, and read it in a sitting, round the
corner in a Baker Street winehouse.

The photograph on the frontispiece showed a well set-
up Henry Jamesian figure in his early fifties. A massive
head and shoulders were presented three-quarter face.
The lips were pressed firmly together. A thick neck rose
from the stiff upward-mounting professional collar. The
face was of a resolute if somewhat brutal cast of expression
which had tried but failed to be benign. Across the chest
a mute line of unidentified ribbons was suspended. Dr
M. A. Vergiff was so well endowed with titles and degrees,
real and honorary, that the printer was obliged to affix
'Etc.' at the end of a double column of qualifications (as
a prelate on fire with the Word of God will tag on 'Amen'
at the end of a lengthy sermon, which in the nature of
things can have no ending, as a provisional halt, stamping
down from the pulpit, leaving the congregation gaping).
The pose and obdurate bulk, tense and gross, stuffed into
a Savile Row suit, suggested a theatrical impresario, or a
ringmaster, rather than a doctor, at all events a veritable
Nero of the consulting room.

It was to this faith healer that Ben Boucher came to
entrust his predicament, and to none other. He wrote a
cautious letter, care of the publishers, asking not to be
cured or even treated for the terms of an inflexible will

(and, by implication, the ill-disguised or now no longer disguised contempt of a strong-willed deceased father), but asked instead, in bolder terms, to be treated for obesity and incipient alcoholism.

Dr Vergiff wrote by reply from Stye. He could fit Mr Boucher into his sanatorium with pleasure. The treatment lasted ten weeks. He would be under his personal care at Fortune's Gate. The fee was £100 with 50 per cent deposit there and then. Dr Vergiff himself was looking forward to their better acquaintanceship.

According to the Automobile Association handbook there were no less than three golf links in Stye, and one three-star hotel. Only one matter remained to be settled: the Companion, *fidus Achates* or Conscience. The *golfing* companion – for in his deafness Ben Boucher was alone and found it almost impossible to make new friends. A day later, like an act of God, he ran into his old opponent from Hermitage days – 'the surly papist in point ruff' in person. Brazill, the artisan champion golfer, had altered greatly in five years. It was some time since he had ceased to work for anybody. Mr Ben Boucher, looking very rubicund, had come parading out of the West End in a new hat. Brazill had not eaten a square meal for over two months. The meeting occurred outside the Irish Tourist Agency in Regent Street.

'Why, Brazill,' Mr Boucher said in high good humour, 'what brings you out of the fields? You look awful. Have you been in the stocks? Come and have a drink!'

Brazill feared that in his condition a drink might finish him, but did not refuse. They began to walk in the direction of Piccadilly Circus.

'Down here,' Mr Boucher directed, pointing.

They turned into Beak Street. Some way down the narrow gorge Brazill saw the modest sign of the Cumberland Stores Saloon.

'Here we are!' Mr Boucher said gaily, pushing Brazill before him.

Brazill stumbled into a small semicircular bar. Plates of hamburgers of a delicate and nutritious brown were piled at casual intervals along the counter. A gentleman in narrow check trousers sat on a high stool drinking beer. Another gentleman in a bowler hat a shade too small for his head leant over the seated gentleman, murmuring confidences in his ear. Both had the pointed features of good English thoroughbreds.

The knotted intestines in Brazill's stomach constricted even tighter when he smelt food again, after so long. A hard fist seemed to stir and poke in his stomach, which tried to withdraw itself further in order to protect its persistent nagging hunger. Saliva dropped from his mouth into his interior as into a retort – sluggish and poisonous drops falling into himself, leaving his parched mouth drier than before.

'Shall we eat something as well?' Ben Boucher asked, laying his hearing-aid before him on the bar.

Brazill nodded his head as though in a coma, indicating the hamburgers.

'Right!' said Mr Boucher, slapping the counter. 'Two bitters and two hamburgers here!' he called out.

Now a third gentleman entered, sweeping off his hat (another bowler) as he did so. A stout flushed fellow in tweeds, also of the boot and spur confraternity. Grinning inanely he joined the others.

The food and mugs of bitter were placed before Brazill. Mr Boucher took a fistful of silver from his pocket and spread it before him on the wood saying 'How much?'

The barman rang up the amount on the till. The gentleman in check trousers rose and greeted the flushed newcomer.

'Leon! Well I never! Wonders never cease!'

The two gentlemen shook hands warmly. Smiling and shaking his head the first gentleman made the introductions:

'Larry Courtney, I want you to meet Leon Fabricius, of stormy South Africa.'

'Fab,' the flushed one said, out of breath as though he had come running all the way. 'Call me Fab!'

Ben Boucher saw broken and not over-clean nails close on a still-warm hamburger and the hand, trembling, carry the food carefully to Brazill's mouth, and saw the other shaken by some strange emotion, close his eyes as his jaws fastened on the food, as though he would never let go.

Four days later Mr Boucher and Brazill had moved, bag and baggage, to the Bon Accord Hotel at sunny Stye-by-the-Sea, Playground of the Industrial North. It was the first week in December and the place lay deserted.

All Brazill's arrears in rent were paid up, as well as some small debts he had incurred. To earn his salary he was expected to play eighteen holes a day against Mr Boucher, try to keep him amused and resolutely bar his way to the Buttery Hatch.

'Until I get the hang of it,' his new employer said. 'The cure is to take ten weeks. Perhaps by then I'll have developed a taste for tomato juice.'

On arrival, Mr Boucher went directly to report himself at Fortune's Gate sanatorium. A liveried waiter lifted up Brazill's dilapidated holdall as if it were a dead dog and, posing at the foot of the stairs, said 'This way, sir . . . this way.'

Brazill followed him to number 55. It was a clean airy room under the mansard. A feather mattress, a deep quilt, mahogany furniture, a wardrobe in which to hang his few possessions, a long window with a cramped view of the Braddan Hills – and all for Brazill. He had never been inside a hotel room before in his life. A glass-topped table stood by the bed, with a reading light, for him who never read. A white basin with constant hot and cold running water was built into one wall, near it a towel rack holding two clean towels. A single oil painting graced the walls, above his bed, higher than eye level, obscured by glass. Brazill did not care for the look of it. The waiter withdrew, scowling. Brazill studied the painting.

A small lady with pinched features and alabaster brow, evidently the denizen of a bygone century, reclined on blue satin in a bedchamber full of drooping stuffs, all velvet, which gave a suggestion of the 'continuous event' to what was happening in the foreground – as a wall of water falling sheer from a reservoir will lead the eye, out of mere exhaustion, forward into the spillover. The lady wore a pair of tightly fitted pantaloons out of which compact hips bulged over the cushions. She sat upright with knees drawn together, her spine curved back like a bow. From the waist up she was as unadorned as the town of Trim – not a stitch anywhere to spare her blushes. Her eyes were partly closed and a belt bit into the flesh at her midriff. The long curve of an arm rested on the back of her accomplice, whose hand in turn rested on her knee. A riding-stock hung limp from her fingers.

The accomplice was a blazing turkeycock, big as a buzzard, blue-black, its scarlet comb tumescent, its claw fastened on the lady's thigh. The bird had assumed sinister proportions in the privacy of the boudoir. Its feathers were ruffled erect in a ferocious display of rage or lust or both: a creature part mythology and part fact. The classical feminine languor was finely contrasted to the vigour of the bird. The dark swollen blood colour of the comb mocked the tinge of shame on the cheeks of the blushing bride. Over the room hung the smoke of an uncheckable human appetite for the forbidden, for outrage and depravity. Even though the painting was explicit, indeed over-explicit, in what it portrayed, yet its dauntless protagonists (perhaps because of their very outrageousness) still defied curiosity. The picture had by no means surrendered all its secrets. Ludicrous and inappropriate, the bird and woman sailed on a dark tide of other more unspeakable practices. The props and costuming were unfortunate and had tended to make the event accessible to public ridicule, had at least shifted the focus down to suit public taste (as the stain of ash on the forehead at Passiontide tends to disguise or mitigate what it is the ceremony wishes to evoke – the mind and the gross heart appeased for the time being with a fraction of the truth); so it was with the painting. The ingredients may have been obvious enough, but the intentions behind it were not. Something lurked in the background of this absurdity, casting its shadow over the lady's flesh and making the claw bite deeper. The screens seemed to shake; something truly beyond all decency, satanic, was moving there. The signature and the date were alike indecipherable. It had no title. Some forgotten dauber in the past had laboured to bring this horror forth. It hung aloft to one side of Brazill's bed as prominent as a skull and crossbones.

Brazill ran hot water into the basin. With a stiff nail-brush he began to clean the faces of his iron clubs. When he had cleaned and dried them all he sandpapered the faces of his woods. He ran more hot water and began to wash a pair of thick woollen socks.

The ritual of 'a round on Braddan' was to continue from that first day, no matter what weather confronted them. Mr Boucher's full cheeks glowed a duller red as he went trudging up the slopes (with which the place abounded) after his high drives. The curvature of his spine became more pronounced, rounding into a positive hump. As he struck the ball he grunted, leaving behind on the tee the smell of tobacco, good-quality cloth and that other rank yet proper odour which seemed to Brazill the very epitome of good living. Everything about Mr Boucher was rounded. The toes of his shoes turned up, his spine curved towards his head, his skull curved over into an inflamed face. The very strokes he made were curved, struck with a half-swing from rounded shoulders, and curved the parabola of the ball itself.

High over the sea on the exposed Braddan Hills Mr Boucher and he pursued their respective drives. The days were wretchedly cold. Brazill wore earmuffs and his eyes watered. Seabirds crouching on the fairways flung themselves wailing into the air at their approach and were swept skyward.

After a week they moved to a boarding house on Woodbourne Road which was more convenient to the sanatorium. Beverley Mount was run by a Mrs Crowe, a woman with a beaked nose and trampled-down slippers. The roast beef of old England became their staple diet.

Mr Crowe was in Public Transport. He drove a double-decker bus on the Ongar route. A pinch-featured and dispirited consumptive was Tom Crowe, who strayed about his house in slippers and braces as though a veritable stranger in his own home. Into his conversation he introduced the intolerable tedium of his profession, going up and down over the same subject or 'route' until his listeners dropped off exhausted. This was the ghostly shade on the landing who mumbled 'Hullo' to Brazill. He did the same to Mr Boucher, coming upon him without deaf-aid from the bathroom, and was affronted because Mr Boucher did not answer him, could not answer him because he had not heard him.

When the supper had been cleared away they sat on

either side of the fire, Mr Boucher reading and Brazill dozing. It was at such times that Mr Boucher liked to open his mind to Brazill. Defying one of his late-lamented father's strictures (the impossibility of 'drumming anything' into the heads of the poor), he spoke at considerable length to him, sitting opposite with a poker in his hand hoping he did not look as stupid and uncomfortable as he felt, of other generations even more scandalous than their own. Night after night Mr Boucher foraged about in his memory for the refuse of previous centuries, depositing all he could find at Brazill's feet.

On a black freezing evening they went to church. Due to a misunderstood notice before the church door, they expected Negro spirituals and a dark revivalist bawling hell and damnation. They heard no such thing. The Right Reverend Shafto turned out to be nothing worse than an effete gentleman of the Methodist persuasion, who stood in the pulpit and demanded of his flock:

'Were you there, Brethren! Were you there when they nailed Him on the Tree? Were you there when they laid Him in the tomb?'

While at his back, in a low choir loft, an angelic line of local virgins sang 'Coming over Jordan' out of key.

The round a day ('to reduce obesity'), went on over the frozen and detested links. After lunch Brazill was at liberty to continue his roaming about the port. A discoloured nose and watery eyes was all that remained visible between the upturned collar of his greatcoat and the downturned peak of a cloth cap. Peering through this visor he made himself familiar with Stye and with what was happening in it. Before supper he liked to take a turn on the Esplanade. He went stamping up and down in the cutting east wind, sensible of the dark tumult about him in the air, and the prolonged tearing sound of the surf.

Sometimes he entered the Peveril bar, ordered a tot of rum, swallowed it at a gulp and went out coughing. In deference to Mr Boucher's weakness he sucked a peppermint on the way home, opening and shutting his mouth so that all his bad teeth raged together.

In the mild days the sky over Stye turned the flesh-pink of yew bark, a roseate island light. On a giant hoarding facing the sea the Firmin Futura orchestra was boldly advertised, the fatuous grin of the public entertainer spreading itself with unction over a generous area. A mimic bandsman serenaded him from below with a terrifically angled saxophone, a loyal but virtually impossible flash of teeth bisected by the mouthpiece of his instrument. Both performers displayed an uninhibited abandon that was truly Nubian in character; fingers outflung, they wooed their public with rolling eyeball and dynamic stance.

The entire conception was splashed onto its ground in alternating mauve and vermilion. A concentrated howl of black, BLACKER print demanded that it should be seen. On closer inspection Brazill found that rain and wind and even worse – admonitory seagulls – had succeeded in reducing some of the splendour of this parade. The paper had begun to peel along its boundary. Lines of text ballooned together in parts, and the stock-in-trade leer of the star was off true. A wearing, patient and more persistent than the more obvious day-in-day-out wear and tear of performance had laid waste some of the Futura glory. Brazill looked closer. The titles at the foot of the page showed that some months had elapsed since opening night (Brazill's shadow passed humpbacked across the foot of the hoarding): Futura's orchestra had come and gone.

Further along the Esplanade a white tiled super-cinema stood foursquare in acres of ground, revelling in its vacancy. A semicircular sweep of gravel led to the steps and façade. High above coal-black fasces triumphed at cornice and pediment. The shocked spectacular frontage climbed into the winter sky, an immense public convenience rearing up – this too closed for the off-season. At the far end of the Esplanade, set on a plateau overhanging the sea, Brazill found a deserted fun-fair: the White City. All the booths were padlocked and a car on the Ferris wheel had been halted in mid-air at the summit of its sweep, a dark and cumbersome object straddling the void.

One morning early in January, cold enough to repel even the stout Mr Boucher, he said: 'Well, I think we can forget golf for today, Brazill. Do as you please. I must finish some letters.'

Brazill went down the hill through the fumes of the brewery. As he approached the front an odd cortège, turning by the monument, came towards him. Two men were holding some object between them, surrounded by four or five weeping women. As they passed Brazill noticed the men's eyes starting from their sockets, and great veins stood out prominently on their necks, as though they were repressing shouts. The long-haired dripping object in their arms was a dead child – a scarcely human rictus of small clothes and clenched fists. Some time that morning she had been drowned in an ornamental fountain under three feet of water. The basin itself did not exceed four feet in depth. No one had seen her climb up or slip; as she fell she broke the ice and lay face down in the water as it froze again above her.

As they drew near Brazill gave way. Panting and struggling, the group passed below the monument. The outstretched shadow of the soldier fell on them briefly below the bayonet and blank eyes. They gained the main road, shuffled across it, passing from sight down one of the narrow lanes. Brazill walked slowly after them. In the warren of lanes leading to and from the quayside he had come across a decayed little cinema squeezed between near-derelict timber buildings. Now he found it once more by accident. Its façade, yellow and peeling, displayed old-style billboards announcing Chaplin in *Tilly's Punctured Romance*. It was ten o'clock in the morning, a freezing day of wind and bright sun. A charwoman was scrubbing the foyer. Her rear end faced the street, with a hobble-skirt furled recklessly about her middle; at a compelling eye level above the steps he saw garters, stockinet drawers gripping a cramped expanse of white blubbery thigh. Further down the lane a sullen-faced young woman sat by an open window composing a letter. As he drew opposite below her, muffled up like a wanted man, she brought the envelope casually to her mouth. He stopped in the gutter below the window. But her eyes travelled indifferently over him and over the lane as she licked the envelope hinge. When he moved on she brought the heel of her fist down fiercely on the letter. Brazill made an inarticulate noise in his throat.

The whole day lay before him and he was free to do as he pleased. In the course of a month he had visited all the empty churches in the town. The muted interiors free of worshippers pleased him. He had climbed into the pulpits and read from all the bibles, turning aside heavy Anglican and Lutheran bookmarks, long and richly embroidered as a priest's stole. When he had visited what he imagined were all the churches of every denomination in Stye, he suddenly missed his own – the Roman Catholic.

He found it in a poor district on the outskirts of town, a squat building with an awkward belfry crouching below the derricks which were visible over the nearby rooftops.

A noticeboard faced the street, black with white Gothic script:

St Kyran's Roman Catholic Church,
Stye.
Mass and Holy Communion: 8 a.m.
Daily.

Leaflets and manuals were stacked on a display stand in the porch. Most were devoted to the Little Flower. The door sighed shut and street noises abated. A band of diffused coloured light filtered through the stained-glass windows above the fourth and fifth Stations of the Cross. Near at hand, balanced lopsided on a pedestal, stood the Virgin Mary, sky-blue for fortitude and compassion for the dead. The holy light burned feebly before the altar. He went under it slowly down the centre aisle. In one of the transepts a dark confessional crouched alone with its plush curtains drawn apart. Air holes were drilled along the top of the penitent's box, as though the blast of sin and repentance required an actual physical outlet. On either side of the confessional frescoes of angels were painted on the wall. The angel on the left hand had sly eyes and a prudish O for a mouth. Its elbows were held stiffly by its sides and the palms of the hands extended outwards below shoulder level in a frozen cataleptic attitude of Solace-for-the-Sinner. In graphic capitals below on a scroll blowing in the free winds of heaven was printed a single word: MISERICORDIA.

The angel on the opposite side held a formidable key diagonally across its chest, its brows drawn together in a severe manner. On a companion scroll was printed: ABSOLUTIO. On the half-door of the confessional a white card hung at an angle: *Rev. A. Croker, P. P.* His box. The wind was humming in the apertures of the windows above the altar. The noises of the street and the port had sunk

to an innuendo. It was the first week following Epiphany.
Cap in hand, Brazill wandered towards the altar.

A Night at the Empress Theatre

Addressing covetous glances at the numerous attractive
women who had appeared out of nowhere, Brazill followed Mr Boucher down the aisle of the Empress Theatre
on the night of 10 January.

The entrance of the gaunt scratch golfer with blazing
hair and heavy tread (a month in the fresh air and regular
meals had given him a scorched complexion and quite
dispersed his harvest of acne), preceded by his deaf
humpbacked mentor, with spavined racked gait and cumbersome hearing apparatus – this caused a stir and the
names of several little-known celebrities were bandied
about. An usherette came running from a side aisle with
programmes to show them to their seats.

No sooner were they seated when the pianist entered
through the auditorium. He strode forward dressed in a
shiny purple jacket with tails and silk-seamed trousers,
with a lighted cigar in his hand. Selecting a sheet of music
from the collection on the stand he began to play the
opening bars of the National Anthem. The man had
the relentlessly clean-shaven look common to his profession and hit the keys as though he detested them all.
As the audience rose to its feet he disappeared from sight.
When they were seated again he commenced to play the
overture with a bland composed air, while cigar smoke
rose languidly from the piano lid. Just before the
curtain rose an unseen orchestra of violins and horns
overtook and finally overwhelmed him. Throughout the
show, whenever the volume of the orchestra permitted,

the piano's obstinate diminuendo could again be distinguished, the pianist puffing away at his cigar, not even condescending to look at the stage.

The curtain rose.

A line of stamping near-nude chorus girls danced, flashing bewitching smiles, against a cobalt and white backdrop of a spectral Riviera. Rotating their hips they drew together, kneeling. Overt, demonstrative, they pointed all their hands at a midget queen sheathed in a scarlet twill silk ball dress and nodding ostrich plumes who had appeared on a mock castle balcony to sing a sentimental love song, with lapidary hand movements, absently touching her flanks.

In a later number only the back of the stage was lit: a shallow dais waited there, whitely, in a flux of light. In hushed tones the compère directed the attention of all towards it. The light was then extinguished and the piano struck up a popular air. The light flooded on again. A girl with a green parasol and green high-heeled shoes, carrying a green handbag, stood on the dais, surprised with one leg forward, wearing nothing but a G-string. The compère began his patter, seconded by the gallant piano.

'Here we see her once again,' the voice intoned, 'our modern Miss. *This* time, on her way to the office . . .'

The same girl appeared in a series of *tableaux vivants*, and was very popular. Mr Boucher kept up a running flow of ejaculations:

'Spontaneous or nothing! . . . Good girl, good girl! . . . We never closed! . . . Pure gold!'

The show was very undressed throughout, notwithstanding the cold, and the curtain fell at the interval on prolonged applause. Mr Boucher paced to and fro in the frozen street by the monument, expressing surprise at such a wealth of out-of-the-way talent.

The second half of the programme opened in dense

fumes of cigarette and cigar smoke. Immediately in front of Brazill a bald toad-like man kept stroking his head, shifting about and laughing indulgently.

The show's progress was shown in neon lights on a small box screen to one side of the stage. The screen went blank as 15 was withdrawn. Light flooded in once more: 16. The screen went blank again, then wobbling 16 held steady: *16*. The lights began to dim out; the orchestra leader furtively raised his baton. The microphone sank slowly from sight.

A girl attired in tights, black whalebone bodice and fishnet stockings came forward to the footlights. She stood close above the front row of seats, exposing the battery of her charms without any show of embarrassment. The stage lights sank further. She stood in a bright shaft of light directed from somewhere beneath the whorled stucco and the Titian cherubs clustered about the boxes. In their dark interiors, suspended precariously here and there above the parterre, programmes rustled. The fancy were stirring at last.

Now the orchestra, invisible but alert in their pit, emitted a single long-drawn-out woodwind quaver. As though with heads bent over their instruments, the oboes and saxophones began to play a brown air, mercifully free from its lyric aphesis, which recalled to mind abandoned lofts and barns of a long-lost decayed grandeur.

The engaging creature stood waiting for her cue, implacable hips braced in a white disc of light, the heavily made-up eyes inscrutable, her face a bright majolica mask. Brazill peered narrowly into his programme but could decipher nothing. At that moment a gentleman struck a match in the row behind. In the brief glare, sucked into the bowl of a pipe rapidly and then extinguished, his eyes flew along the printed text and found:

16. Feuilles Mortes . . . Elizabeth Sted.

The lights went out and a clear inconsolable voice began its lament. A cold blast went through Brazill and his scalp began to rise. All was dark around her. She delivered the doleful lines as if trying to remember something else. Standing with one leg somewhat advanced, straddling a pool of light, she seemed both knowing and innocent: garbed as the conventional tantaliser of the common dream, the precocious harlot born of celluloid and strip cartoon. Between verses she stood lost in contemplation before a captive audience. She might have just strode through the stage door, through all the painted wings and fake doors, arriving hotfoot from quite a different theatre where quite a different audience had applauded. Despite her preposterous garb, she retained a personal dignity and even mystery. The throaty contralto sang out and beyond herself, beyond Stye, beyond any audience it could muster. She sang to the end over and through the audience as if it were not there – singing to herself in an empty auditorium. The song ended and the lights went up.

The curtains dashed together and the audience vigorously applauded a vision of shot silk butterflies and elaborate grottoes of purple fungus. Then she was admitted through the curtains and stood there bowing, not smiling, her shoulders and bodice reflecting light. After a while the applause abated and then ceased. The curtains flew apart once more and the pantomime went on.

The clown Sevi advanced indomitable towards his lost audience. In one hand he held a maroon outsize corset, padlocked, and in the other an enamel chamber-pot. Thirty years before he could have done what he liked with them. But a generation or two had been swallowed up by the Granada circuit and 'live' acts such as his had gone out of fashion. Mr Boucher was delighted with Sevi. He bent forward, spluttering and coughing:

'Farce must survive, Brazill!' the well-bred voice declared. 'Farce must survive!'

The whole row bent forward to have a look. Mr Boucher contorted himself still further, shaken with merriment. But Brazill had neither eyes nor ears for anything but the absent *chanteuse*. He examined the programme again.

Notes on the Cast!

Elizabeth is well-known to our local – Principal Boy in 1951 panto – but prefers dramatic roles – Catherine Earnshaw in Wuthering Heights *– memorable performance –* Elizabeth Lady of Lea *– in this theatre last summer.*

Every day after lunch Mr Boucher walked to Fortune's Gate for his infra-ray treatment. After that he liked to remain 'quietly at home' in Beverley Mount, meditating and reading. What had once been a stray volume or two on a casual table became in time a fine auxiliary collection. After dinner he began to talk and would not leave off talking until he went to bed. Laying a book across his knee and looking into the fire Mr Boucher would resume where he had left off the preceding night:

'Six bishops were on calling terms with her before she turned twenty. She had more in that little bird's head of hers than all the fine liberal females of today put together. Greek and Roman history, Platonic and Epicurean philosophy, the errors of Hobbes, physics and anatomy, perhaps some Latin, French certainly . . . if one is to believe Swift. When she was four-and-twenty she shot and killed an armed intruder with one of those dangerous cap-and-ball affairs. A band of them had come to the house and she was alone there but for the servants. They could do anything they liked – those marvellous ladies of the eighteenth century, before Women's Emancipation overturned the cart and we were overrun by all the opinionated bitches who abound today. Brazill, have you the faintest conception what those ladies were like? No, of course not. You must read history, Brazill. Madame de Pompadour had a way with Louis XV and virtually ruled France for a decade. That is, until the Lisbon earthquake brought down her spirit a trifle and she had his private entrance into her apartment sealed up. That unfortunate creature Madame de Warens had a way with Rousseau. The Marquise du Châtelet had hers, up to a point, with Voltaire. Juliette Récamier conquered Chateaubriand and Benjamin Constant, as is well known. And then there was Lady Montagu and Madame de Sévigné – reading her letters, according to Emperor Napoleon, was like eating snowballs. We have nothing to compare with them today – not even remotely, neither the style nor the intelligence. It's our misfortune that we are offered women MPs instead. The proprieties of our accursed century have bred the "professional" woman. The professional woman athlete, professional woman politician, professional woman this, that and the other – artist, poetess and actress – something that is neither woman, invert nor jennet, but a creature quite outside nature. It comes as a surprise to us that they can even bear children. In Proust we are offered the last of woman's dignity and aloofness. It's a terrible pity. Nothing is left to us now but American film stars. International celebrities, if you please. If Voltaire were alive today what would he do for woman's company? You tell me. What would he do for that communion with idle, charming and cultivated women which Balzac calls "the chief consolation" of genius? The great writer-philosophers today are obliged to marry nonentities whom one

never hears of again – supposing there are any great
writer-philosophers today, which we may be pardoned for
doubting. Where are the queens and prize bulls of the
past? The wits and courtesans – girls who had plunging
necklines *and* forty-inch busts *and* could hold their own
with talkers like Montesquieu? Who have we now?'

Dazed by this interminable monologue, Brazill reclined
far back in his armchair, his head fallen forward on his
chest, his legs stretched out. There was no means of
shaking Mr Boucher off his subject, once fairly given the
scent. If it was not Esther Johnson or Emily Brontë or
Emile du Châtelet, it would be somebody else. Mr Boucher's penetrating accent sawed into Brazill's ignorant
head . . .

A steep escarpment overlooked the rear of the Empress
Theatre. A row of dingy brick cottages stood on the
summit, faced by near-derelict vegetable patches, a belt
of stunted trees growing among thorn and bramble.
Wooden steps led up from the road.

For three successive nights Brazill hid himself among
the bushes and watched the cast going home. And on
three successive nights Elizabeth Sted went home alone.
It was then that he resolved to write to her. He composed
and posted a dramatic letter which attempted to touch
her vanity and interest, appealing to the actress, to the
proud citizen of Stye, to the inquisitive person behind
both, offering the Beverley Mount telephone number.
But no sooner had he posted it than he began to regret
ever having written it. He went once again to the pantomime. This time alone. He took a seat three rows from
the front. She came on in the second half of the programme, but he wanted to sit through it all. Early on
the scenery had already become her scenery and when the
time came the rest of the cast would part and she would

emerge. Brazill wanted it all to happen exactly as it happened before. And he himself to indulge in the feelings he had experienced, all over again. Like a dog who will lift his leg to the food he cannot devour rather than release it to another ravenous brute, he knew that he would resent everyone else's applause but his own.

Once again the lights dimmed and the arresting figure strode to the prompter's box. Once more the music veered around towards her and the solitary woodwind blew its sourly expiring note. Nothing had altered. Ten times more desirable, the singer filled him with disquiet and longing.

In despair he could see his pathetic letter on the board by the stage door, first overlooked, then opened and passed round, an object of common ridicule. She knows I am an upstart, Brazill thought miserably.

On the following day – Sunday – while window-gazing on the main street, he turned and came face to face with her. She was accompanied by another girl and did not seem to notice him. Brazill, not knowing where to look, turned abruptly to the window and watched both girls pass ghost-like through an array of frantic staring dummies. He saw them vanish out of sight into the up-ended reflection of the main street. Resting his hand on the glass he looked intently at the dummies, his heart pounding in his chest. She is virtuous, was his first reaction, virtuous and has received the letter, considers it impertinent and will do nothing ... After all, she is an actress and has been subjected to this before. She dislikes the implication and will have nothing to do with me. After a while he thought: 'She has received my letter, is not disposed to grant her favours to all and sundry, thinks I am another stage-door Johnny and will in due course send a polite refusal.' This seemed incredible, until other alternatives as plausible presented themselves to him. 'She is certainly not virtuous,' Brazill thought, 'has received the letter, knows everybody in Stye, consequently knows it was Brazill she saw and none other, did not like the look of me and will do nothing.' That satisfied him until he thought, 'No, she has *not* received the letter, is herself virtuous, will see I am an honest fellow and will phone this evening.' Then he thought, 'She has the letter, is or is not virtuous as the case may be, has seen me but does not yet know it is me, and is thinking it over.' And lastly he thought, 'She has received the letter, is not herself as virtuous as she might be, has now realised it is me, and is reconsidering it.' He turned suddenly, but the street was empty save for a stray citizen far away and patrols of loitering dogs. A blank Sunday afternoon.

Mr Boucher's penetrating accent sawed into Brazill's head:

'Devoted to the metaphysics of Christianus Wolffius and the physics of Newton, that woman never did anything in moderation in her life. One night in October of 1747 at Fontainebleau she lost over 80,000 francs gambling at the queen's table. She competed against Voltaire for an essay prize offered by the Academy, working at night for secrecy. Sleeping two hours in eight nights, putting her hands into iced water to keep awake, she completed it within a month. I cannot recall whether she defeated him or not. She proved that different rays of coloured light do not have an equal degree of heat. Was it to Marmontel he lost her finally? . . . I forget.'

A coal fell in the fire and Brazill was wide awake.

'Questions, questions,' Mr Boucher's voice said distinctly, 'what are they but our memory of what we have forgotten? I do seem to remember Voltaire – who was in any case by that time an old man – surprising a gentleman in undress on the staircase at Ferney, and Emilie screeching abuse from her bed. Well the abuse rebounded, for she died giving birth to the bastard. Frederick the Great wrote her epitaph, "*Here lies one who lost her life giving birth to an unfortunate infant and a treatise on philosophy.*" Now then, by the time de Cléry had begun to put together...'

But Brazill had begun to slip again. Faintly, too faintly, the words gushed and poured into his failing eardrums:

'Marc Calas... the Bishop of Castille... the forest of Montmorency... the siren voices... La Barre's shoe... the five executioners... ichuria, the pox... Chambéry ... the *Confessions*... General Lalley... Crébillon... Swift... the salt tax... d'Alembert... the Irish Jacobite ... Boswell... the Whigs... the Yahoos... the *Pucelle*... the Brontës...'

On the day following, shortly after darkness had fallen, while Brazill and Mr Boucher sat thawing out before the fire, the telephone in the hall rang. As certainly as if a hand had been laid on his shoulder, Brazill knew it was for him. After some delay a door opened down the passage and Mrs Crowe made her slovenly way past the door. The telephone rang still. The sound of the receiver being unhooked from its cradle came faintly to Brazill's ears, followed by the landlady's rancorous tones:

'Yais... Yais, death's rite. Whew? Yais, certainly. Hold on.'

Brazill heard the sound of the receiver being put down. Then the door opened of its own accord and from without, like a stage direction, a relentless voice announced:

'Foremaster Brazill!'

Brazill rose in consternation and made blindly for the door. He waited with the instrument in his hand until the sound of Mrs Crowe's retreat ended with the banging of the kitchen door; then he lifted the instrument to his ear. He had not said a dozen words when her voice said: 'You're Irish, aren't you?'

Brazill admitted it. She sounded composed, approachable, even amiable, even apologising for the delay in answering his letter – and went so far as to admit herself 'intrigued' with it. Extra rehearsals for some new number in the show had allowed her no free time for the past week and a half, but from the day following she expected to be free, more or less, once again. Yes, she would like to meet him. Where? The calm unfamiliar voice spoke against his ear. The museum – did he know where it was? Brazill said yes. He kept his eyes fixed on the glass of the front door. Behind the mullioned panes shadows of palm fronds moved before the light and then were still, moved and were still. Would next day at 2.30 suit, at the museum? Brazill said yes.

Mr Boucher spoke that night of even earlier centuries and their dark times, urging that calamities were not exclusively confined to the twentieth century. He spoke of the tipping-houses and stews of London in 1665 emptied of their custom by the Great Plague. The dead carts going about and the pit dug in the parish of Aldgate into which in a fortnight more than a thousand bodies were thrown. He told of the plague houses marked with a red cross and 'Lord, have mercy upon us' scrawled on the doors; and of the poor infected wretches who ran demented through the streets in their nightshirts, with the hard plague boils upon them which would not break so that they knew they were done for, in any case more dead than alive after the attentions of the physicians. The fires were burning in the open streets throughout the city and along the embankment by order of the Lord Mayor, for the alleged purifying qualities of sulphur and smoke. And all of this a premonition of the Great Fire that followed the year after, reducing all that the plague had not already destroyed to ashes; one catastrophe following another, until the people had begun to fear that Almighty God had resolved to treat London as previously he had treated the Cities of the Plain, and destroy the place utterly, and all who were in it.

'So that was London in the middle of the seventeenth century,' said Mr Boucher, 'the fires choking anybody who in spite of everything still had managed to stay alive. And as for the dead, why they went into the pit by the cartload. The names of London thoroughfares even to this day have a ring of affliction about them. Cripplegate, Morden, Houndsditch, Fulwell, Pitshanger. Orphanages, mental homes, gas and sewage works, cemeteries for Gentile and Jew – yes, all that; but the hollow rumble of the death cart still goes through them all.'

To these tirades Brazill inclined a polite ear, while awake; hearing the gist of it in a pleasant torpid state that was neither sleeping nor waking.

Brazill, on tenterhooks, stood in the museum hall. About him were Crimean uniforms, medals for valour from all the fronts of the world, a relief map of a settlement in the Stone Age. The antlers and mournful elongated head of an elk cast troubled shadows on the ceiling. He walked to the swing doors and pressed his face close to the glass. Clouds in a weak evening light, scarred by the dark silhouette of the forecourt walls, fled over Stye housetops. Brazill felt as though he were standing at the bottom of the world.

From the corner of his eye he saw a movement in the gateway and stepped back smartly. A person coming up the steps would be visible from the waist up but, seeing the light was against the glass, the person inside would very likely be invisible. But nothing happened. Brazill stepped up to the door again and looked out. Two mongrel dogs had entered the yard and were moving about and jostling each other, in turn stealthily wetting the walls. Idly he watched them engaged in their peripatetic reading of atmosphere and light. One was a type of whippet, spindle-legged, with the starved anxious features of its kind. The other, an intractable-looking brute, a leader, was examining the premises with that bossy officious air which even the mangiest cur can sometimes assume. The whippet had in the meantime reached the steps and stood there, smelling the tethering post. A leisurely leg was already half raised against this when it noticed the face watching in a luminous rectangle of glass. All set with lolling tongue the whippet stared unabashed at Brazill; but it had made up its mind, and by God it would go through with it. In quick succession the whippet let fly twice at the stone. It had turned about to study the result when, in a rage, Brazill threw open the door and launched himself from the top step. Howling already, the whippet saw the furious dark shape storming down upon it. But as Brazill strove to recover his balance on the ground, both dogs fled from the yard.

Brazill paced to and fro before the museum, uncomfortable in his finery; somewhere in the town a clock struck the half-hour. He approached the wicket gate, pushed it open and looked down. A steep flight of steps overhung by skeletal boughs, from which the last leaves were falling, slowly and aimlessly drifting in the air, led out to the road below. The steps were deserted. Brazill closed the gate, crossed the gravel and passed out through the main gates.

Turning left he walked about eighty yards to the cross-roads, and stood staring about him. No one that could conceivably be Elizabeth Sted was abroad there. After a while he began to walk back again. Far away the raucous rising note of a bugle made its challenge.

In the distance he saw a girl approaching from the opposite direction on the same pavement, bound for the museum. Brazill immediately increased his pace. He reached the gate well ahead of her and turned in without once looking in her direction. He hurried across the yard, up the steps and into the museum again. It was darker there and he fancied that he could acquit himself better. A few minutes later he heard steps crossing the gravel and saw a head pass below the window. Brazill put his hand on each side of a showcase and looked in. A card which read, *A relief map of a Stone Age encampment on the Isle of Man*, neatly typed, was laid amongst the petrified figures. That was Manx pre-history. Brazill saw, with a start, the reflection of his own gob and furtive eyes, darting this way and that among the little brown Plasticine men, and wished at that moment from the very depths of his heart that he had never seen, much less heard, the engaging *chanteuse* Elizabeth Sted.

Unknown to him, the door had opened and closed silently. Someone was standing opposite the Manx showcase, breathing quietly.

Coupling in Old Stye

During the black frost of that winter, too cold at night for even a dog to venture out, Brazill began his courtship of Elizabeth Demeter Sted, the pantomime girl.

Night after night they walked out from Stye, heading for the high land about Braddan Hills. The country road stretched calmly before them, quartz glittering on its surface, the low-cropped hedges, enamelled by the evening frost, still on either side. The road rose and fell following the contour of the land; in a field a dazed piebald horse was subsiding. The girl was dressed in a beige hood, sand-coloured overcoat and snowboots. She pointed out the scattered houses where her friends lived.

Peaceful in the moonlight, a huddle of buildings lay below, a miniature harbour. A vessel, preparing to be off with the tide, was drawn up against the jetty; its cargo being offloaded under arc lamps. The sound of the cranes came faintly. In the distance, across pasture land, prominent against the sea as if moored there, a rectangular building stood with all its lights blazing.

'And that,' said Brazill, pointing, 'is it the Academy?'

'It is not,' she said. 'It's Lamona Asylum.'

From the pavilion roof she pointed out the docks with the Liverpool boat clearing the harbour. They walked under the skeleton grandstand on the motorcycle circuit. The headlights of a car crossing a frozen field lit up her face for an instant and then veered away. Brazill heard subdued voices in the air and the crunch of tyres passing over stiffened grass.

'Rabbit killers,' Elizabeth said. '*Most* illegal.'

The term she used most frequently was 'like a bomb'; most things went like a bomb. As they turned down towards the town again, the shotgun reports came, flat, one upon another.

Miss Sted lived a hermetically sealed-off home life, with her martinet mother on the slopes of Hillcrest Drive. Mrs Sted – a widow – spent her declining years resting and praying for the suffering souls in Purgatory and for the sins of the world. A voluminous sexagenarian of strict and narrow principles, she was regarded as the prop and stay of the local Catholic church.

She waddled out, weighed down in sombre brown, rosary beads and holy scapulars disposed freely about her person ('ten years' indulgence'), a cameo at the throat her sole concession to human frailty. The floral decorations on the high altar were left to Mrs Sted. She was a covetous puffy-faced woman with a sour, vindictive look in her eye. The unfavourably disposed mouth ('not *another* word shall pass my lips') was pinched shut in a cast of expression not generally associated with kindness or generosity. An immense head of upstanding white hair recalled, uneasily, the coif; but the coif in recoil or rout. It seemed incongruous, or indecent, that this barren-tempered woman should ever have borne children (the nun with the scandalous past), but she had; there was a daughter on the stage and a Jesuit son in a Uganda mission station to prove it. Her clothes were stifling and dark, overflowing as the penitent and all-enclosing habit of a nun, even a Reverend Mother (so strict her demeanour): the nun who must forgo the woman, bedded in temptation and outright sin, in order to come even within hailing distance of God's Providence. No elderly fowl come to a late moulting, with one wing gone over sideways, with nothing much left to look forward to, and precious little to look back upon, could have appeared more mournful.

She was of an unsociable disposition and had barricaded the house against all intrusion. In the Sted home heavy draperies of a monastic strain were much in evidence. The rooms were crowded out with dark and oppressive furniture. Yellow lace permitted in only a guarded daylight. High-backed chairs were drawn up to the dining-room table for the guests who would never arrive. A thin-runged rocking-chair piled high with cushions was drawn against the french windows in such a way that no one from outside – should they be so inclined – could see past it. Newman, Thackeray, *Essays of Elia*, Mary Russell Mitford, Smollett, tattered illustrated editions of the Bard, all were trapped behind glass. Similarly with the fire, coldly set in the frame of its firescreen.

No chances were being taken. A dismal wallpaper design was overlaid with Victorian miniatures and a mezzotint of the Pope. Every room had a fusty odour. Domestic holy water fonts of enamel fitted with sponges invited comment at front and back door. Tradespeople were not invited in. A photograph of the deceased, Arthur Sted, Esquire, hung over a china display cabinet. The goatee, wing collar and frosty unbeholden features, shot against a smoky background of uncertain content, resembled to a striking degree the Boer hero General Smuts.

When the widow was not visiting the church she liked to take her ease in the conservatory, for there she could observe without being seen. For a woman who disliked her contemporaries and notoriously did not 'mix', May Sted had a remarkable grasp of Stye gossip and scandal, which she sometimes liked to reassemble with some malice for her daughter's edification. She spent a great deal of time behind glass in summer, with not a button undone or a layer discarded, smothering among the tomato plants, perhaps atoning for her sins – the huge white head nodding behind creepers.

Meanwhile her daughter occupied the time entertaining Mr Brazill in the rug-infested drawing room.

At first they sat, all decorum, well apart on separate chairs; but presently they were on the same sofa, and soon after that Mr Brazill made so bold as to take her on his knee. It was in those edifying surroundings, amid proliferating plants extensive enough to do credit to a botanic garden, that he lost his heart.

Had he been blessed with the gift of language, he might have said: 'My desires, my hopes, have taken root, are flowering in thee.'

Or something to that effect; but, there, he was not so blessed. Oral exchanges were indeed few and far between for his love was not a great talker either. She was somewhat melancholy in disposition; one of their first expeditions was to her youngest brother's grave. She played 'Feuilles Mortes' for him on the gramophone. By playing it over scores of times she had learnt the song by heart. Mr Brazill was *intrigued.*

Elizabeth Sted was not a lewd girl. Quite the contrary. Brazill had to hang his cap many times on the antlers in the hall before she would consent to sit on his knee. With his fingertip he touched her lips and throat saying: 'Only this far?'

And she said yes. Only after a week of such restraint would she consent to show him her bedroom. A squat oaken wardrobe reached to the low ceiling. A couple of dressing tables with powder puffs and a small crinolined doll with a hatpin stuck in her shirt stood against one wall. A double bed took up most of the room. A bedside table with a fringed cloth held three brushes and as many combs, a Norwegian trinket jar, a rosary. Everything was very tidy. A low window looked down a vista of trees. This was where Elizabeth slept – as if on the bright scalloped bottom of a coral sea. Only after much persuasion would she consent to sit with him on the bed saying:

'Only here – only my mouth. Now do you hear?'

So that phase passed. Then, unable to curb Mr Brazill, she consented to remove her stockings and skirt and lay in the semi-darkness in her girdle, saying:

'Only this far.'

Calm as fishes they lay side by side, watching the reflections of the boughs thrown on the low ceiling – a pale susurration of agitated light.

Once she complained:

'Your hand is like an old claw . . .'

And once she said:

'I am the most ignorant person alive.'

And once:

'Oh for the love of God get out and leave me alone!' But by that time, reduced to less than her shift, she was already fighting a losing battle. For, after she had said that, she consented, some weeks after the original Only-this-far, to the removal of the last impediment, the girdle, saying:

'Oh fig!'

But this was to happen on a night full of unseemly behaviour and in Beverley Mount in Mr Brazill's arms, in the latter's dark brown bed. Moreover, that night was to see the end of more than one oppressive dream. Brazill, in his pursuit of the siren Sted, had not been paying too much attention to Mr Boucher's nightly discourses, a continual paying out of the line which by its monotony and regularity had long ceased to hold his attention; so that he failed to notice the point at which the strike was made, failed to notice that the line was coming in now, fast, hand over hand – so profound was his ignorance, his unbelief. So perfect was his non-participation that, when it all came out, he could not even comprehend that the other had used him as bait all along, no, he could not even fathom that. On the last day in the church on his knees when he had prayed: 'Dear God, let my ignorance be less complete' – not even an articulated prayer at that, but merely the motion of fear in his heart, blood turning over as it were in a flurry, the feeling that the survivor must have as he stands by the fatal accident – even then he could not fathom it or tell when it began.

Brazill did not realise that anything was wrong, or that behind the Christlike parables used by his employer something was stirring; and even when all his talk was of worms and disease, Brazill was impervious still, and with an almost total blankness in the face of the other's suffering – such being the birthright of the poor in heart. Brazill had never come into contact with the insane. So that to the end he sat on cushions of fatigue and despair and watched, almost with equanimity, Mr Boucher's mind giving way.

One evening during Brazill's 'coorting days', Mr Boucher sank down in his chair with a cold pipe in his mouth and opened his mouth to say this:

'You are the man who stands in the door of life, scraping his boots on the mat. Never mind, Brazill. Wait until the tying of a bootlace costs you a great effort and regret that. No; regret nothing. Don't regret failure, the failure of the body least of all. With what brutish obstinacy we persist in claiming our due! Oh it's sickening, sickening. But the established failure who in his rashness or wisdom has put himself outside the beneficial scheme of things – he is the happy man. Nothing is more disgusting than the sight of the conformable citizen striding forward to his just reward – surrounded by wife, issue, dependants – with the light that comes from a difficult task well performed shining in his eye. No pride in bounden duty, be it performed well or be it performed ill, can offer a satisfactory answer to the pain we feel sometimes, here and here, in the sacrum and the joints, in the wretched hang of the limbs ... The remorse, in a word, of the entire organism's unwillingness to continue with the farce much longer. Don't we feel it already in our faces, across the bridge of the nose and in the sockets of the eyes – there it is for you, the posthumous pressure of the bone. Then we die and, marvellous to relate, the coffin is exactly right for us.'

Brazill found he could offer no satisfactory answer to this austere philosophy and contented himself with saying nothing.

'Sooner or later,' said Mr Boucher, 'we all come to rest

in the ruins of ourselves. So we should try to get there with the least presumption. Now you pretend not to understand – but you do, better than myself. The world's full of cranks. Think of the woman who wanted to be buried, wearing her blue underwear, in her own fowl-run; or the other who laid a wreath every year at Valentino's grave and began her own death there. To be all day, first dressing one's body, then dragging it abroad, then stuffing the guts, then washing them with tea, then wagging one's . . . no, it's gone on too long. Have you, or has anyone for that matter, determined that point in time ahead where the bludgeon waits for each one of us? Perhaps the weapon has been chosen, the time and site selected. Well, that lies before us. As a Christian you must believe it, Brazill. Look here, in the 1820s a young poet, unknown to himself, was dying inchmeal in Rome. He feared to visit the Opera because he had been there once and got the fright of his life. He imagined the sentinels who stood aloof from the action holding spears were visible to him alone. They were the Powers, infernal or divine, come to claim his immortal soul. Ah, you may smile boy, you may smile, but let me tell you this: he was dead within a month. So are we, perhaps unknown to ourselves, walking under the shadow of an upraised arm. One good *dunt* will finish the job. So much for us. Do what we can our progress in the end will be just another bit of time pushed to the side. We must be suspicious of everybody – everybody. Those who feel they are in a position to call themselves our close friends and who believe themselves indispensable to us – avoid them! You hear? Unless we stand out alone without encumbrances we may be struck down with our mouths open, and a pretty sight that will be for the survivors.'

Here Brazill crossed his legs and grunted.

Lifting up La Rochefoucauld's *Maxims*, Mr Boucher,

who was a professed atheist and enjoyed private means, continued reading. The books that Brazill let fall from his grasp as he dozed had titles like *Clubfoot the Avenger, Oh Daughter of Babylon* by Francis Dale, and an illustrated serial which ran wild with italics – *Sheena Ran Sobbing: 'I won't go home again!' (Will the 220 lb. policeman bring his daughter back by force?)*

Brazill had relapsed back into his sleep again. The clock hands stood at 9.20, as they had stood every day since the new lodgers' arrival. Twin forked stains stretched across the carpet where, on successive nights, first Brazill and then Mr Boucher had accidentally spilled Indian ink. The dry sounds of the palms came, fidgeting, from outside the window. Stye lay sleeping.

Outside the door, Mr Crowe, admitting that the entertainment was over for the night, straightened up and passed silently by.

Vis-à-vis with that same keyhole he had seen and heard some strange things in his time. The recurring drone of information issuing from Mr Boucher was an improvement, in his opinion, on the Home Service. Sometimes Mr Boucher emitted a high-pitched humourless laugh to which Mr Brazill, dead silent until then, obligingly added his unhinged whinny. One evening when he was alone Mr Boucher had walked to and fro for the best part of an hour from the fire to the window, counting in French. Another evening, which had not been such a success, he had remarked to Brazill:

'The shadows on the wall seem longer by comparison to the furniture placed against the mantelpiece.'

A silence. And then:

'When the unclean spirit is gone out of a man, he walketh through dry places, seeking rest and finding none.'

'I think so,' Brazill's voice said, as though out of a bin.

'Our Mr Crowe seems a very dampened man,' Mr Boucher's voice said coolly. 'Who was it said the notion of liberty amuses the English, because it helps to keep off the *taedium vitae?* It's a damned lie.'

It was not, let it be said in all fairness, this backhander which finally altered Mr Tom Crowe's attitude in respect of Mr Boucher's inspired monologues, but something else, hatching its cuckoo's egg of doubt, gave him some reason to suppose that the voice and antics he was listening to belonged to no sane man, but were the voice and antics of an unfortunate lunatic – or something precious near it – in the relentless grip of his dementia.

Mr Boucher had to amuse himself alone in the month during which Brazill sported with Elizabeth Sted. Brazill would retire upstairs to brush his clothes, to appear presently at the door, standing on one leg, greeted by Mr Boucher's unvarying sally:

'Well Brazill, off again?'

And Brazill would say yes, look sheepish and depart. Then Mr Boucher stripped himself of his deaf-aid and traversed the carpet for hours at a stretch, formulating damning questions, grinding his teeth, staring on tiptoe at himself in the mirror, shaking all over like a retriever; while poor Mr Tom Crowe crept all trembling to the door again and applied his eye to the keyhole. There was something wrong: the voice speaking to itself alone there; the imperative tones which demanded respect uttering nonsensical phrases or worse, as Mr Boucher turned sour and morose and began to empty his pisspot in the spectator's face. But always the obsessions came back to the father, as a whipped dog will circle round its home.

'Shite . . . shite Dadda . . . Do you hear?'

Eventually he was moving at a high trot, hard pressed, the talons of remorse goading him on and the well-bred voice calling his father by every opprobrious name in the gutter vocabulary, and much else that was meaningless.

'Hair-like worm Man or swine or rat – '

Tearing something in his hands and groaning to himself: 'Shreds and fragments, shreds and fragments!'

Enough to move the bowels of compassion. And Tom Crowe, that good-hearted man, crouched down on the other side of the door with a frightened face, muttering to himself, *Holy Virgin, what are we to do? . . . Holy Mary what are we to do?* While inside Mr Boucher's voice was grinding:

'Whips, chains, dark chambers, straw – '

Until he stopped still, looked at his watch and bade himself sternly:

'Time to turn in.'

And with that Tom Crowe crept away into the fastness of the kitchen, absolved from all responsibility.

Brazill slept one evening by himself a deep uneasy sleep by the Beverley Mount fire. In his dream he was back again in the days of his misfortune. The day before Mr Crowe had come to him and asked: 'Your friend – is he all right?'

Brazill answered that he had been peculiar as long as he knew him. Mr Crowe said 'He counts to himself in French,' and went away. In the dream he was travelling from somewhere to Swiss Cottage. He had not eaten properly for a long time and was fiercely hungry. The compartment was empty save for himself. At St John's Wood he noticed for the first time a brown crumpled object on the seat opposite. As he picked it up it fell apart. It was a pair of lady's leather gloves. Underneath the gloves was a purse full of money. As the train slowed along Swiss Cottage platform he saw a porter standing by the door. He walked up to the man as soon as the doors opened. They stood face to face. Brazill opened his mouth but no words came. He saw the expression of politeness leave the other's face. The faded blue eyes under the hat brim stared into his own. Brazill heard the doors begin to close behind him and wheeled around, pointing to the gloves. The man looked to where Brazill was pointing, but by then the doors had closed and the lost property was out of sight. The train began to draw out of the station and the porter left Brazill standing as if he had never tried to address him. It was a dream from the days when both food and normal behaviour were denied to him, before he had met Mr Boucher and lived in peace and plenty.

Then, as though sleep had disgorged all its phantoms, he found himself fully awake. The slow reeling, burdensome step of Mr Boucher was coming up the flagged path from the gate.

On the way out of sleep he had heard the gate shake to its hinges as it was flung to, followed by the sweeping and clashing of the palms, then the heavy uncertain steps again. He began to tremble, *I shouldn't have – Now there'll be trouble;* then wind broke into the house itself. All the pictures in the hall shook; the door was flung to and a heavy stick was either thrown into or withdrawn from the stand. The steps advanced along the short corridor, stopping outside the door. It was no dream. Brazill recognised the predictable noises of old: Mr Boucher was drunk.

He heard the blood pounding in his head. *Now I'll know,* he thought. He heard the other's shoulder hit the door frame as the handle was turned. The door swung open quite peacefully and Mr Boucher stood astride the mat, red of eye, breathing heavily. Below in the bowels of the kitchen Brazill heard the Crowes complaining together at this violence. He rose in alarm.

Water dripped from Mr Boucher's overcoat onto the carpet, its black hair glistening like an animal's hide. Perspiration or rain shone on his wild face. He advanced until they stood breast to breast. On the point of speaking he turned suddenly and, lowering his head he removed his deaf-aid equipment with a whirling motion. He turned again on Brazill and said:

'I can hear!'

'You mean you – ' Brazill stopped.

'Say something, Brazill.'

'What am I to say?' Brazill said unhappily.

'Say something, will you?'

Brazill put his mouth close to Mr Boucher's ear and said distinctly, as into the mouthpiece of a telephone: 'Can you hear me, Ben?'

He watched the blood vessels swell up about the other's moist eyes and the black hairs curling from his nostrils and smelt the viscid whiskey fumes from his breath. He saw the eyes slowly close as though Mr Boucher were listening to some miraculous transformation taking place within him. Then the eyes flew open; a sly disdainful stare bored into him, down-pointed and dangerous. He had not heard a word. He said:

'Then spit on me.'

Brazill made to recoil a step but found he had frozen in his tracks. The voice said again, as if coming from a long way off:

'Here – here – spit on me here, Brazill' (indicating his cheek).

Brazill said in a voice unfamiliar to himself: 'Jesus Christ! I can't do that.'

Breathing rich whiskey fumes and smelling of something explosive as cordite, Mr Boucher said flatly: 'I'm asking you.'

'Ah no,' Brazill said.

As they stood face to face on the worn carpet across which two black stains had spread, Brazill felt as though his limbs were being drawn out. Sweat broke out on his forehead and on the palms of his hands. Mr Boucher's whole face was drenched. He glared at Brazill and slowly turned his face, inviting outrage. A timid splatter propelled from Brazill's dry mouth adhered to the other's dark jowl.

'Again! That's not good enough,' Mr Boucher said. 'Again!'

Anything, anything, Brazill thought, trembling with fear and indignity, anything to end it. He spat violently into his employer's face. This time the sword went home all right. Mr Boucher closed his eyes. His expression had not altered. With studied indifference he turned away. He collected his deaf-aid without saying another word. Brazill stood as if paralysed. As Mr Boucher left the room he said:

'Late tonight . . .'

As if a friendly discussion had to be reluctantly broken up. Brazill heard him labouring up the stairs, and after a while the bathroom door closed.

Asylum

It was the seventh week of Mr Boucher's treatment. Dr Vergiff had distributed a circular to all his patients; the great naturopath would give a talk – a *Rosicrucian* talk – on 20 January, in the pavilion, entitled 'Out of this World to Soft Lights and Music'. It was to be an evening of snow and craziness; Brazill was invited.

As soon as daylight went on the 20th the snow began

to fall. Mr Boucher had booked a table for four at the Bon Accord. He said:

'Tell your Miss Sted to find Ben Boucher a pretty partner – a dazzling Centre Court personality – preferably one who drinks' (here he laughed boisterously).

The partner turned out to be a calm and easy young woman with amber hair. This was Pat Ellen. The party introduced themselves to each other in the foyer. The dinner passed off pleasantly enough. Mr Boucher, mellowed by 'a few stiff whiskeys' which he had taken the precaution of swallowing before sitting down, ordered gin all round for the ladies, and narrated a whole series of witty anecdotes and incomprehensible jokes with inflexible gravity of countenance. Applying himself to his soup, he made a loud blustery noise which Pat Ellen affected not to notice. As they were finishing coffee a waiter spoke into Mr Boucher's ear. He began folding his napkin and said patiently:

'Louder. I am slightly deaf' – pointing to his ear – 'on this side.'

The taxi had arrived. Mr Boucher stood in the hall calling for the ladies' coats. Then, with much shouting and merriment, Mr Boucher's party embarked for Fortune's Gate and an evening of prestidigitation and occult lore.

The sanatorium was surrounded by a high glass-topped wall and a plantation of elm and oak. That night Brazill passed in under the Latin gate (*Fortiter et Recte*) for the first and last time. Halfway up the front drive Mr Boucher told the taximan to stop. The party got out, still laughing, and the driver was paid off. The taxi went on ahead, backed into one of the rides, reversed, and passed them on the way out. They called out goodnight before they went in among the trees. The pavilion stood some way from the main building, enclosed by shrubbery in the wooded grounds. Mr Boucher led the way unerringly. The ladies walked behind in a thin layer of snow without complaining. The snow was still falling. Presently they came to a clearing. Crowding thickly around the pavilion door white ghostly figures were struggling to gain entry. Snow fell impartially on the Vergiff patients and on the town trulls who had been invited, dropping slowly and steadily from a dark sky into the light. Mr Boucher flashed his credentials at the door and with much bowing and scraping his party was admitted. Brazill entered last and looked around in amazement.

The place was almost full. Muted but resonant music came from concealed amplifiers. The floor was carpeted and raked. Five-pointed stars hung in profusion from the walls. The dimensions, seating accommodation and overall decorations were a baffling mixture of Art Cinema and sheikh's tent. The five-pointed stars winked down from every cornice: the sign of the Scythian grand mufti himself. The stage curtains were open and the stage itself was empty save for a small card table covered in blue cloth. Nothing was lacking save incense and perhaps vestal virgins.

'Come, Brazill,' Mr Boucher said.

They were directed to four seats halfway down the aisle. Pat Ellen was invited to enter the row first; Elizabeth followed, then after a struggle, Brazill; Mr Boucher sat on the outside of the row. No sooner was he seated when he rose up saying: 'No, no, this won't do at all.'

He got into the aisle and stood looking at Brazill. Brazill rose and invited Elizabeth to do the same. Both edged out into the aisle. Pat Ellen followed. When Mr Boucher saw this he waved his hands and said: 'No. God's death, where are you going? . . . Very well then.'

All stood in the aisle. Then Elizabeth entered the row again and sat down in Pat Ellen's seat; Brazill sat next to her; Pat Ellen sat next to Brazill and Mr Boucher sat down again on the outside. Brazill continued to gape about.

A great up-ended pile of props filled one whole side of the stage as if the roof had given way at that point and the contents of a lumber room emptied itself pell-mell onto the boards. A small space had been cleared for the performer's little card table. Brazill saw, or thought he saw, the following objects: an old tripod camera with a hood, a distorting mirror, a wax nude with some fingers missing, a brass funnel, a child's crib with ribbons, a prie-dieu, an *épée* and a mandolin, a copper coal scuttle, a shield and coat of arms, a stuffed animal (marmoset? mink?), a pair of Prussian boots, a truss, a brass bedstead on which were piled clerical vestments, plumes, a double-barrelled shotgun, a pair of candlesticks, a whip, a shako, an old-fashioned HMV gramophone with loudspeaker, trick boxes with coloured sides, and beside the bed a crimson sofa with black and white striped epaulettes on its shoulders. As well as a fishing rod and a dinner bell, a white *papier mâché* castle with a flag flying, an ormolu clock, a hunting horn, a dummy in a nightdress, a cock on a weathervane, a road sign, Chinese lanterns, a shocked lady's leg in brown stockings, a blackboard with magician's signs, a trellis with artificial roses and a closed carriage in the background. Prominent in the midst of this a single picture stood. The head of a young man, in oils – painted in such a way that the eyes were always staring at the beholder. The background was dark and the oval features peered forward out of it, the complexion deathly pale and the eyes set in a fixed stare.

Mr Boucher gaily pointed out the Vergiff incurables – the girl who came from India every year, with a fractured spine following the birth of her first lost child, and the others known to him. After an hour's delay the music abruptly ended. From the back of the pavilion a deep sonorous voice began speaking through a microphone. It was unmistakably Dr Vergiff. After formal greetings to all, including his non-patients, he began to read extracts from newspapers, the great thumping lies of the world's great thumping press. Mr Boucher and party had by this time sobered up somewhat. Before each extract, Dr Vergiff quoted the title, authority and date. Some of the references went as far back as ten years. The subject-matter seemed wholly concerned with humans-in-the-shape-of-monsters, cures-when-all-hope-had-failed, perfidious women and blackguard men, flabbergasting cases from the police files, the more revolting the better, odd-behaviour-of-lovely-girl-in-Lent; in a word, the black incorrigible backside of Lourdes, *Basses-Pyrenées*.

The precise relevance of what was being read escaped Brazill and after a while he ceased to listen. The face of the damned soul stared at him from the picture on the stage. Outside he heard the sigh of trees and almost organ music. The snow was falling patiently on the roof, dropping out of space, thicker and thicker, swirling down on the chimneyless, windowless house of Ahriman. Beside him Elizabeth never moved or altered her position once. He could hear Mr Boucher's stertorous breathing beyond, evidently greatly excited. Unfathomable depths of banality calculated to rouse the dead were narrated in a truly flattening manner by the Doctor. Until, exactly one hour after he had uttered his first word, he stopped. In the silence Brazill fancied he could hear the snow falling.

In the silence, Dr Vergiff himself, a figure of para-ecclesiastical splendour, swept towards the stage in a voluminous opera cloak. The audience wheeled around at his approach. All the faces and eyes stared in his direction like so many thirsty flowers opening towards the sun; and then, as he passed, there was nothing but the blank backs of the heads again, which tell so little, so many wilting flowers closing quietly again, in a great displacement of air and scent. Dr Vergiff mounted the stage with an athletic bound that was an example to all his patients.

He was carrying in one hand a colossal top hat. This object he dealt a single blow and deflated, laying it aside. He swung about to face his audience, simultaneously unbuckling the opera cloak. Down it went, covering the hat, silk lining out. Dr Vergiff wore underneath a smoking jacket of purple cord, gold-fringed at cuff and lapel. A dazzling white shirt with an old-fashioned wing collar spanned his chest, erupting again at the sleeves where eight heavy inches of cuff was held in place by moonstone studs the size of walnuts. The trousers were dark with a satin seam, ending in pointed patent leather shoes. The weight of oppressive flesh about the hips was suggestive of cruppers, docked tails; the ponderous dignity and the heavy bones had about them something of the horse that has been 'broken in' – or so, obscurely, it seemed to Brazill. To Mr Boucher, on the other hand, the whole solemn dumbfounding presence recalled to mind the old school of divines. To Pat Ellen and Elizabeth this was the owner of Fortune's Gate, the impresario on the Esplanade who invited the better-looking local girls to join his 'Magic Circle'. A bamboozler and a very rich man whom one had better avoid.

Without saying another word Dr Vergiff commenced to perform conjuring tricks. The obliging ladies in the audience were offering him their handkerchiefs and calling out the names of various scents. The Doctor made the magic passes and the handkerchiefs were returned scented appropriately – lilac, verbena, lily of the valley.

After not more than half an hour of this the Doctor wished all his kind ladies and gentlemen goodnight and vanished through a door at the back of the stage. The amplifiers blared out the Anthem and the dazed audience filed out into a snowstorm.

On the frozen path Mr Boucher drew Brazill aside and confided to him that he intended to spend the night at the hotel.

'You see the girls home,' he said. 'I'm going back to Beverley Mount now to pack an overnight bag. Perhaps you can move the rest of my things tomorrow?'

He walked away as if he were blind. The indecisive gait and tight-clamped mouth seemed a parody of those so afflicted. His face was cocked to the sky and the snow fell peacefully down.

Mr Boucher removed his hearing-aid and laid it on the hotel bedroom table. Then he drew up a chair and sat down. Bringing his hands together in a gesture almost of prayer he closed his eyes, trying to prepare himself.

About the same time Brazill glided upstairs ahead of his paramour and both passed safely into the Beverley Mount bedroom.

'The Crowes rise about seven,' Brazill said *sotto voce.* 'You must be out by 6.30.'

He began to set the alarm for 6.10.

Mr Boucher opened the missal he had taken from Brazill and found a passage at random. He read: 'I am the true vine, and my father is the husbandman. Every branch in me that beareth not fruit, he will take away; and every one that beareth fruit he will purge . . .' He read down to: 'Now you are clean.'

Brazill and Elizabeth Sted undressed themselves and got into bed.

Mr Boucher turned pages at random and read: 'If any man come to me, and hate not his father . . . and his own life also, he cannot be my disciple. Which of you having a mind to build a tower, doth not first sit down and reckon the charges . . .' He read down to, 'and is able to finish it, and all that see it begin to mock him.'

He turned a few pages, breathing fast, and read: 'The angels shall go out, and shall separate the wicked from among the just, and shall cast them into the furnace . . .' He felt the perspiration trickle down his side. 'And so shall it be at the end of the world.'

Mr Boucher closed the missal and laid it aside. Now at last he understood what he was required to do. He rose, removed his jacket and went to the window. Putting his finger into the hook he pulled it up, his distorted reflection appearing to rise up with it. He did the same with the second window. The subdued sounds of the port filled the room. He struck a match and set fire to the long curtains. They took immediately with the draught. Mr Boucher began to pitch all that he could lay his hands on out of the windows.

Four hours later Brazill left the Bon Accord, moving in a daze, his hair on end. He found a Catholic church overgrown with ivy which he had never noticed before; doffing his cap he entered.

Row upon row of candles were burning by the porch and about the high altar among white flowers. Early Mass was in progress, and all the devout parishioners of Stye were kneeling there. Two altar boys in red were kneeling before the altar and the priest was praying and genuflecting, and the little bell was rung twice by one altar boy as the priest elevated the blessed host and all the congregation with their heads bowed were praying. And then the priest genuflected once more and the bell rang again and it was over.

He lit a candle for Mr Boucher who was not a believer and knelt again, clasping his hands as his late employer had done not so long before and tried to pray. But he could find no words of prayer; all he could say in wonder was, *He has gone to the madhouse, I have come from the poor home*, over and over again.

Then the priest was coming down from the high altar and all the people were rising.

II

During the eight constipated years of its composition Balcony of
Europe *gave me endless trouble; I have since withdrawn it from
circulation as a failure. It presumes too much. For a year or two
during the writing no recognisable human figures appeared; they
seemed reluctant to emerge from wherever they were skulking.*

*Instead, nebulous pseudo-characters began to appear, hybrids
pale as mushrooms. But only so far; they grew only so high,
approached only so near before fading away again in a most
tiresome and vexing manner. I could not grasp them, to draw
them into life. Their common fate – doomed for ever to be stunted
beings – worried them, and me. They began to retire again whence
they had come, still hardly human, apparitions frowning with
displeasure, not speaking much. They were my despair.*

*As characters in a 'real' novel they were useless but still carry
about with them some faint authentic whiff of that time and
place: Andalucía in the year of the Bay of Pigs when the world
seemed about to come to an end, with Kennedy's vigilantes in
orbit twenty-four hours a day, overflying Spain from their base
in Moron de la Frontera.*

*Enough is enough: I decided to call it a day and handed over
the much corrected and amended typescript to my publisher
Calder, himself as inspired an editor as Boswell, that other canny
Scot, to do with it as he saw fit. We wrestled with it for a year,*

reducing it from over a thousand pages – the length of Vasari's Lives – to a more manageable 463 pages, including four pages of Rejected Epigraphs stuck in as misleading signposts.

Some of this intractable material has since been revulcanised and put to work again as radio texts for BBC commissions. Re-adapted once more, they have come full circle as wayward prose pieces, now mere mood music for the good times gone.

My late philosophical friend Arland Ussher liked to argue that Germans couldn't write novels because they could not stop explaining (Mann); this was before Herr Grass arrived to dumbfound one and all. Certainly an all-knowing narrator clogs up the action and inhibits other characters, who then all begin to speak in the same voice – witness Dostoevsky's Father Zossima and Faulkner's garrulous Southern lawyer Gavin Stevens, two of the great bores of literature.

The Nerja of that time no longer exists; that Spain under that Generalissimo. The population that doubled in the decade from 1960, has since quadrupled; gone the way of Torremolinos, gone the way of the world.

Catchpole

The Spoils of Exeter

You do a thing, you do a thing, you do another
thing. You say a guy: 'Hey, I need this,' and he says:
'Hey, okay.' And then he goes and does it. So, you
use him once, and he comes through, you call him
up again. You say: 'Now I need this other thing.' So
he goes: 'When?' You say: 'Tamarra.' He says: 'I can't
do it then. Gimme Thursday. I'll be there.' You say:
'Thursday. You got it.' Thursday he is there. And he
has got the thing.

George V. Higgins

An actor reaches out a hand, the sun is there, a cloud
moves, and the whole story is changed.

Orson Welles

He was a mythical beast come alive. Hornsetter the
Awful Queer Dun Beast, the tail-end of the panto
horse, a fellow fit for all seasons. His name
sounded as if it belonged to a rare language unknown to
all, summoning initiates – de Vigny's sad horn awinding
in the depths of the wood. 'The name's J. J. Catchpole
but you may call me Josh. Let's not stand on ceremony
here. Put it there.'

Reluctantly I shook a limp, clammy hand moist as a

fish. 'A bit of a tongue-twister I'll grant you but common as Rinso in Rutland, or do I mean Romford?'

He rambled on with awful twiddle-twaddle involving some nuns, serene Vincentians, to which I listened with half an ear. He was edgy and liked to inflict himself on one. And wouldn't it make you puke, just to look at him! He had the red-rimmed eyelids of a white rabbit or a smelly yellow ferret or a sore anus, that hot abused look. Even his height – six feet, six inches, egad – the same height as Peter the Great of far-from-sainted memory, seemed another aberration, gratuitously excessive.

'Call me whatever you wish, fly-by-night or bashful frequenter of underground comfort stations. In a strange country be prepared for surprises. A ham actor with awful halitosis and painted eyebrows, a trapdoor opening into a void, someone playing the fiddle, the wrong hair clippings in the teeth of a comb. Stuff like that.

'Melancholy sensitive chaps like us tend to get very wound up in ourselves. Dark introspective brooding laden with dire forebodings has ever been our staple since *The Sorrows of Young Werther* produced a perfect surfeit of suicides.'

He moved in a smokescreen of indiscretions and intimate confessions, permanently horny, late of Romford, dragging wife and child behind him, whispering, 'Pish, pish!' He was a pathological bullshitter. The murk of intense feelings, expiring hopes, were his, both plausible and very implausible. How sadly winds the horn in the depths of the wood!

For him, ever eager for nooky, it would always be rutting time. Amorous play made him simmer; and narrow the gap betwixt and between the savoury and the decidedly *un*savoury. 'Achilles was a man's man.' He was seen in the stalls for *The Changing Room*, a David Storey play running in the West End, eyeing an all-male cast that wore only jockstraps, applying bandages and lint. He had been spotted naked and sobbing in the changing room of a gym at the University of British Columbia. But was it Catchpole weeping? Who else could it be in the wide world?

His was a most capricious lewdness. He was wont to start into scandalous anecdotes, indiscretions, secrets, as a hound flushing out a hare, then burst into scalding tears.

He was a London pansy with all the vanity and fussiness and *unreality* peculiar to the breed, a faded flower of the city; with strong Dominican affinities, spoke feelingly of Savonarola and Thomas Aquinas. A Catholic convert, he was a daily Mass man, took the Sacraments, referred to confessors in Farm Street and the Brompton Oratory.

He said he 'sort of arranged kids' programmes' for the BBC, contributed to the *Cornhill Magazine*, was married (a blind?) to a lady called Sybil Steptoe by whom he had a dearly beloved daughter, Megan (Megs to you), the apple of his eye.

They lived down Friern Barnet way in the outer London suburbs, almost into Hertfordshire.

We ran into him during the August *feria*. Or rather *he* ran into us, hounding us down, for in his estimation we 'looked interesting'. We were sitting eating *pinchitos* that had been cooked over a charcoal fire by an Arab in a fez behind the church on the Plaza de los Martires. There was a strong smell of marijuana. We had round after round of good *pinchitos* skewered on wire and were drinking chilled Victoria beer, minding our own business when he arrived in a rush at our table – tall, impetuous, spotty and sweaty, tow-coloured hair standing on end.

'My wife wonders what you do.'

The oblique approach was his crafty feminine side, the

question addressed evasively to me. What he intended to convey was: 'Are you queerer than little me?'

My spouse, ever polite, invited him to join us. It was a mistake. I bought a bottle of Cognac for the table, another mistake generating unwanted confidences. And an hour later my *esposa* excused herself and left the field to Catchpole, cracksman and faithless husband to Sybil who had yet to put in an appearance.

With a preliminary iron rumble the clock in the church tower began to sound the quarter-hour, while the local band played jiggy music in the *paseo*. All about us were the stalls, tombola prizes of plastic tubs and buckets for the beach, hideous mauve dolls with chubby legs wide apart, little bulls and bottles of Montilla, cheap cigars. The Arab continued to smoke ganja as he stirred the garnished meat over the red-hot brazier and somewhere a high female voice was calling out '*¡Otra muñeca!*' as the band played on and pink plastic dolls were passed from hand to hand, and mothers said they were '*Muy linda*' and J. J. Catchpole made inroads into the Cognac and took up the discontinued tale that was to be the story of his life.

He was not the type of queer that you would expect to encounter; nor wish to meet, being a great buttonholer and most indiscreet. He spoke in *italics*, confessing everything, took off. How strange the homo-fire!

J. J. said it was rather noisy here amid all the tombola stalls and the continuing cries of '*¡Otra muñeca!*' and the band thundering away, so what about going back to his place for a bit of peace and quiet, and I could meet his nice wife, if she was awake. This suggestion was offered with a sidelong look. So we broke camp, with the last third of a bottle of woody Fundador, not the best of brandies.

The ground-floor apartment was near the Hotel Pepe

Rico. The weak wattage gave a feeble glow in a sepia-tinted living room replete with plastic fittings. The wife was nowhere to be seen. J. J. Catchpole brought forth a bottle of Gordon's gin and began filling me in on the story of his life.

He was most indiscreet, for he would have me know everything about himself, no holes barred. His complexion was bad; his skin gave off an aroma of spoilt meat, his voice was unpleasant and high-pitched. He croaked when excited. I had hardly met him and yet had to listen to impassioned anti-feminist diatribes. His wife's flesh and womanly odours repelled him. When he was drunk he slept with her, to satisfy her natural needs – lest she become more intolerable – though it gave him little pleasure, none at all in fact. Have another gin. We smoked like paddle steamers. Time passed. The feeble wattage became ever more feeble, the noise of distant merry-making and the band drifted up from the *paseo*. Then someone coughed in another room and a soft appeasing voice called his name. Jerome!

I heard the voices murmuring, a tap ran, then the clink of a glass, then a door gently closed and he was back again, wiping his brow. He had gone to her on tiptoe like the giant with his club. She could not sleep, had asked for a glass of water. It was her way of intimating that she had heard every word he uttered and could he not modify his indiscretions? But it did not seem to concern him; on he raged. The unseen Mrs C. was a stuffed doll. I was to met her the next day.

Her tall husband had decided to latch onto us, we were definitely his type. Sybil seemed immune to his insults, his barbs; and he could be caustic, with a mixture of the greyhound and the ferret in his nature – the red-rimmed eyes, the fidgety sniffing, never easy, seldom sober, too eager by far. As with Oscar Wilde, though for a different reason, he had done time, sewn mailbags, walked the exercise yard, searched for love in a flowery dell.

It came about in this fashion. He coveted jewellery and precious stones, wore rings on his long fingers; with another quick-fingered like-minded lad he had planned and executed a daring night robbery at Exeter; drove with the spoils to Leamington Spa – £800 worth of stuff lifted from the display window. Masked and gloved at dead of night they had approached the jeweller's shop, lifted the stuff; laughing immoderately they had driven off at speed. Then they had trouble disposing of the spoils, their profit was marginal. Rashly, unable to leave well alone, they had decided to try again on a bigger scale. They would rob on a grand scale, empty a big window. They had cased the joint, a display at Exeter all lit up, there to be taken.

Again they donned their masks and gloves, laughing immoderately; but this time they were caught. Halted at traffic lights waiting for orange to change to green and go in empty Exeter, when another car drew up alongside and Catchpole lost his head, laughing hysterically, pointing to the other (sober) night driver. '*Do* something. We're splutched.'

The other driver gave them a sour look, memorised their number, drove away. At the next town – it might have been Lyme Bay – the police were waiting. Grim-faced country constabulary stood at the barrier, threw up their hands; Catchpole (the world's worst driver) swore and swerved away, accelerating, crashed through a picket fence. He was sentenced to twelve months inside.

Inside was like outside for him. In the nick he performed fellatio on an Irish gypsy, a handsome if greasy lad, most unwashed. 'It was like sucking off a dirty steam engine.'

Later they shared a flowery dell, but the dirty one would

not let Catchpole as much as lay a hand on him, cursing him as a fairy, a poof.

When he came out he was conscripted into the British Army, 'from one grand English institution into another', out of the frying pan (the sadistic screws) into the fire (the sadistic officers); of the twain he preferred prison, and decided to spring himself. He had a friend in Prague mail him seditious literature and this he planted in the officers' mess when he was cleaning there. Soon he was summoned before his commanding officer and failed to make a good impression; his manner was hysterical and shifty. Eyebrows were raised and a month later he was safely back in civvy street. He decided to go straight; he was not cut out for crime.

All this and more he told me that night, pouring out indiscretions into my ear like one of Conrad's narrators. Jittery, a thirsty talker, at first a plausible and then a most implausible liar – he could embellish his stories too well to bother about the literal truth – six foot six inches of queer aggressiveness and spite, he prized, coveted what others had, according to the value they had set upon them, itched to steal what others owned (was this also true of homosexual loves?).

He drank gin, the preferred tipple of sad neurotics the world over, to calm his nerves; smoked long cigars, to convey authority, for he liked to impress. He lied until he was blue in the face. He was ambitious, tall as a giraffe, seldom calm, with a considerable feminine streak in his make-up, slapping on warpaint with a liberal hand, cruising the *calles* and bars like one afflicted with jaundice.

The hidden and abused wife stayed out of sight in the dark bedroom and let him rage on. Somewhere in the stuffy ground-floor apartment the little daughter slept, a violet in the Catchpole garden of love.

When Sybil appeared she was behind a pushchair; the

soul of calmness, never losing her even temper or raising her voice, ever consistent in the even tenure of her ways; her colour never changed. Whereas her husband was yellow as a leper when he wasn't purple with apoplexy, in another tizzy, frothing at the mouth. He was very high-handed with her. She wore spectacles, patiently endured his frequent outbursts and tantrums. Sybil concentrated on her knitting and translations, her little pet, kept the apartment spotless, cooked for them, changed nappies, consoled. Her knowledge of the ways of the wicked world was limited. Coming down onto Burriana beach in an unbecoming bathing costume and robe, her pale thighs quivered and wobbled in a meek yet purposeful womanly way and brought to mind a line from Herrick about 'the thighs of the engulfing bride'. The pale child peered nervously from the pushchair. Fierce gulls squawked overhead. Then came tall Daddy grimacing, looking around for rough trade, tittering.

They had met at the Pushkin Club in London. Sybil Steptoe undertook translations from the Russian and her publisher sent cheques. She cycled about the city, the very reincarnation of a Bloomsbury bluestocking.

Together they visited the grave of Karl Marx in High-gate cemetery. J. J. discovered that she would inherit a not inconsiderable fortune. She was perfect. He was proud of her. Inordinately proud of her; for his own origins were lowly, in fact working class, which he attempted to conceal (not that he had ever worked manually except for that stint in prison); but betrayed by dirty diphthongs.

Despite his tallness he picked up trade around London: homesick Paddies in Kilburn, lonesome inverts in Kentish Town, lost souls around the Craven A factory beyond Tottenham Court Road, exotic gents in South Ken, rough trade off the Edgware Road, black men in Willesden Green. All were grist to his mill, and his mill ground small. He had a rapacious appetite for one-night stands, alarming one of Mrs Fury's male tenants in Bedford Park when, boldly knocking, he asked for a match at four o'clock in the morning. He wanted it *all* the time.

Holding his breath J. J. pulled the chain as a signal, following an exchange of notes in a comfort station deep under Belsize Park, the deepest and dirtiest tube station in London, carefully (all aflutter now) half-opened the half-door of his stall and in disarray confronted an old fellow short-taken, who attempted to force an entry, with the noise of a veritable waterfall (flushing) cascading. While, with the most perfect sang-froid, an elusive and lovely youth waved, smiled and departed. The grandest catches always escaped downstream.

Ah, love with its boundless opportunities and inevitable setbacks, flowering here and there amid the rank reek of chlorine and male piss, such tender feelings flowering in ordure. Love had indeed 'pitched its mansion in the place of excrement'; but were they tender feelings, or the longing to be abused, abased, brought to one's knees, brought low?

He took daily Mass; twice or thrice weekly he confessed all into the hot hairy ear of a priest; confessing hastily, sometimes turned away by Iberian priests astute enough to guess that this tall penitent was not repenting but boasting. He liked to speak of sin and redemption, carried his missal about with him, attended *Missa* at Nerja in the Church of San Salvador near the bordello, confessed to handsome Padre Paco the handsomest priest in Andalucía and attended *Missa* again in Málaga Cathedral near the port.

'It means so much to you, then?'

A soft, appeasing, slithery smile.

'It means everything to me, my love' (eyes downcast coyly).

'A little less of that if you *don't* mind, Catchpole.'

'Sometimes I don't go, on purpose, to punish myself.'

He spoke with warmth of Pius XII, Eugenio Pacelli, the profile on the medal, the Italian cardinal become Pope in the little satin skullcap who had levitated about the Vatican Gardens as six million Jews went up in smoke.

His Oiliness had washed His hands of the whole affair as white puffs of smoke ascended from St Peter's roof, conveying the good news to the vast multitude packed into the square below, sending them into transports of joy. It had happened when I was but a lad in the County Kildare, stunned by the pollen-infested summers of long ago.

'*Habemus Papam!*' The thin hands were raised above their heads in a magnificently slow papal blessing. '*Caelo supinas manus!*'

'When Orson Welles – himself a sort of Pope – was granted a solo audience with this singular cleric, He held onto Orson's pudgy, sweaty hand for forty-five minutes and wouldn't let go,' I said.

'Bizarre.'

'He enquired of Tyrone Power's marriage prospects and the imminent divorce of Irene Dunne. He was *au fait* with all the hot Hollywood gossip. His hot dry hands were as hard as a lizard's skin, Welles said, and He gave off palpable vibrations.'

'How about that,' breathed Catchpole, widening his nostrils.

'He has an Allee named after Him in Berlin. Pacelli Allee near a beer kiosk where I used to drink. Albert Speer lived nearby at Wannsee and noticed crowds of Jews packing Nikolassee S-Bahn, awaiting trains to remove them to the incinerators. It was my local station.'

*

J. J. really *used* the confessional.

Some of his accounts of sins committed were as ripe with buggery as pages torn from *The Decameron*. Once he had made a trip to Moscow; once attended a film festival at Pula, all buggery; he certainly got around. Strange indeed is the homo-fire, the fire of the cat on heat, the thin and anxious thread of need stretched to the limit, the membrane wrung. Something there of the blind bloodlust of ferret, that blind animal with eyes as red as rubies that hunts and kills underground in darkness, taking victims from behind against the end wall of the burrow. All stretched to the very limit of need; the victim's abject terror, the killer's lust for the kill, as in my boyhood days of ferreting with Josey Darlington the blacksmith's son who owned a white ferret named Nazi, a great little killer who did much slaughter down in the burrows.

Or the highly strung edginess of greyhound or whippet chronically constipated, sensing more than seeing the lure, the false hares careering down the track ahead. He had qualities of those creatures in him, both predator and sportful blood; and something in the eyes, moistly appealing, myopic behind heavy-rim spectacles, recalled the novice in the seminary, the saint in the sentimental print, and behind them, smiling a tight, *contained* smile, Pacelli.

He tittered. An uneasy tittering that hardly cleared the breast and lungs, the most innocent of all diuretics. With Brill-pad mop of dry and dusty hair, sideburns and bad complexion (Lenten far in the seminary refectory), the pockmarked face, he stank worse than Colfer of old. Was it the salve applied so liberally under the make-up, the infected flesh, or a sorry mixture of all three?

Those nervous hands, veined as Pacelli's, blue-veined and moist (sins past and to come) were never still; hands

that never tired of probing and never gave up, that urged:
'Feel, you fool! Feel and escape!'

Catchpole had seated himself outside the Marisol and
stared about him with affected composure. In fact he was
far from composed; rather say he was on fire. He looked
flushed with that unmistakable queer aura of need which
Saul Bellow, referring to a mobster, has wickedly identified as 'the cynosure flush'. Catchpole was blushing
prettily because he found himself the focus of attention
from someone whom he fancied, pirouetting by on the
paseo. Presently he would take his courage in both hands,
re-arrange the bait (cigars fit for plutocrats, new-minted
peseta notes of high denomination, coffee and a good
Cognac) about him and leer winningly back at the
Mariposa.

Oh yes, giving his cream a swirl and tipping some of
the brandy in, presently he would make his move. But
not quite yet; the readyness was all, the pleasure lay in
the waiting, the fixing of the bait.

In the meantime Señor Hatchplan sat there blushing
like a peony, cheeks filled with shy blood and a piteous
beseeching and open supplication in his meek gooseberry-coloured eyes that were always somewhat bloodshot,
hence the shades, the Panama hat with fancy band of
blue. Oh but wasn't he the sly one! Wasn't he just!

Catchpole spread his spiderweb carefully. Notecase
abulge with clean hundred and new-minted 1,000-
denomination peseta notes and a 5,000 note laid on the
table with the continental *Daily Mail* and an invitingly
open cigar box suggestive of endless liberality, bait for
the local unsophisticates, the handsome young men who
sauntered by from Marisol to Bastion (the Big Cheese or
heliport at the end of the *paseo*) and back again, up

and down, Butterfly Corelli and the stout queer with the soprano voice. With *gitano* and even Moorish blood coursing through their veins, they held themselves like toreros tight-arsed in their *trajes de luz*, their suits of light, shooting glances his way, affecting indifference for the tall spider artfully suspended in the centre of his web. Feel, you fuckers, feel and escape!

His Spanish was just about adequate (*¡Entiendo MUUCHO!*), his ways devious (King Spider motionless in taut web), fast with the chairs, quick with offers of Cognac and coffee, reckless where his frustrated passions were involved (and that was most of the time; for he thought of little else), as a sudden wind scattered 1,000-denomination notes and pages of the continental *Daily Mail* across the *paseo*. And then some honest fellow would give chase, catch and bring it all back to him there rising and perspiring and with profuse apologies, blushing with pleasure (for they were all remarkably handsome and well hung), knocking over his cold coffee and gesticulating mutely at his table, the invitingly empty chair. Care for a *copita*?

He loved them all.

Many anxious and pleasurable hours did Catchpole spend alone outside the Marisol, dangling spider in carefully constructed web stuck together with spittle and semen; it required much patience to go on sitting there alone, pretending to read the newspaper as if he hadn't a care in the world or a dirty thought in his Brillo-pad head.

A few times I sat with him there or again outside the Balcón de Europa bar and watched the youths pass by; they whom on previous occasions he had inveigled into the Cine Olimpia, bought them popcorn and pawed them in the dark, laughing at Laurel and Hardy. Now they were parading up and down before him, nudging each other and laughing openly at him. I marvelled at such persistence; he really lived for it. A warmly inviting breeze, warm as the Terral, always blows on the true pansy.

So that was inversion, perversity, a willed daydream that occupied the whole day from dawn to dusk, a potent dream. He lost his unstable heart at least once a month, this voracious and insatiable lover of men; for him it was the rutting season all summer and winter long. Would the ancient Greeks have sympathised with such a state of mind? Would they have approved? And the ancient Romans?

The local *mariposas* laughed but went with him into the dark. He had found a small beach beyond Burriana where the Swedish nudists went sunbathing, and took to spending the day there when free of buck-naked Swedes, waiting for some intrepid gallant to jump around the rocks and surprise him there.

Of course there were always Málaga and Torremolinos, the Sodom and Gomorrah of the Costa del Sol. The soft evenings were for Mass in the Cathedral with Christian Baude at the organ, running through a repertoire that was sure to include *Sinfonia Sevillana* and *Ars Antigua*. Passing the great leather windbreak guarding the western doorway was like penetrating into the depths of a wood: from stained-glass windows high above shafts of sunlight shone down on polychrome saints. Whereas the dark interior of the Cine Olimpia was a hell of ghastly stinks among which featured Sotol and farting; the walls were decorated with what appeared to be a mixture of porridge and pubic hair. Midway down the centre aisle sat Catchpole pink as a rose with the dreamboy Pepito Corelli languishing by his side; he was the perfect *mariposa* (I'd seen her sitting on a boulder in horseshoe-shaped Playa de Carabeo, trim as a mermaid with long hair, lighting up a Bisonte *con filtro*, a presence part-female and disturbing).

Impatient Catchpole sat outside the Marisol, complaining of the slow service. I advised him to try Miguel's bar next door where coffee was cheaper and service faster.

'Oh, but you quite misunderstand me. It's not the poor service I object to – I quite enjoy waiting. I only want to be *serviced.*'

He looked googoo at me with his gooseberry eyes, the pockmarked face made up, green porkpie hat with sporty pheasant feather on the table by the sunglasses and box of cigars. He sat amid his props and frustrations as the lovely boys strolled by, tittering and whispering, giving him the eye. He sighed, donned his dark glasses.

'Love will find a way. Where there's a will there's a way. We'll manage somehow. Amn't I small as a mouse's earhole? Tiny,' he squeaked. 'Absolutely tiny!'

The palm fronds were trussed up along the *paseo*, above the poverty and squalor of Calahonda beach and its cats and dogs. The *paseo* was deserted. The Peninsular War cannons recovered from the seabed were aimed at Maro up in the hills where a window winked brightly, a semaphore.

'I'm a regular gal really,' he tittered into his coffee. 'I lost my cherry young. But look, here comes my dull little wife.' And sure enough Sybil was pushing her daughter down the incline of Puerto del Mar, heading our way and already smiling sweetly. The pushchair was decorated with pink plastic windmills all aflutter in the breeze.

Catchpole gave English lessons for nominal fees. The blond ephebe employed as courier in the Maro caves was his first student. Catchpole called him his Cave Man; both tensed calf, curly hair and manifest virilia, both the curved bow and the butterfly wings, Cupid and Psyche. Catchpole 'rotated' him with the pale-faced *Guardia Civil* who was anxious to better himself by learning some English. He was the Young Officer, a bleak type not much given to levity or high spirits.

The Cave Man had a tricky smile and used it a lot; whereas the Young Officer never smiled at all. The former favoured tight Levis and had a blond quiff like a bow-wave; the latter was *muy serioso* with crewcut.

All that long wet winter in Andalucía, and all over Spain, which is no more part of Europe than Ireland is part of England, during the worst winter in living memory, the lights failed with predictable regularity and in tempests of wind and rain the village (10,000 *habitantes* as Guernica before the bombing) vanished into Stygian darkness. The bars laid in stocks of candles. The effects were ghastly and eerie as a painting by de Chirico, shadowy faces lining the counter.

Catchpole sat with the winged messenger of Love from the Underworld, perspiring with desire and embarrassment as the lights dipped their wattage and failed once more. When they went down again, preparatory to going out for good, he suffered agonies. Real agonies.

'I was blushing like a traffic light. It was a wonder he didn't notice me, glowing in the dark. It was a room absolutely made for love.'

I asked him what was homosexual love.

He gave me a considered stare but did not answer.

'Was it', I suggested, 'going to bed with draymen and coal heavers, backstreet barbers?'

'Not exactly,' he said. He was attracted only to boys, and handsome ones at that.

'In Mother Russia I was hot all the time.'

He laughed with his bad teeth, laughter wrung out of him. 'It never stopped snowing. Can you imagine? I travelled into Russia by train. Russian trains are wonderful. The Ost–West gallops through Köln half asleep, then Hamm, Halmstedt, Marienborn to the Saxon accents of the Vopos studying passports, then Berlin.'

'Ah.'

'Poznan, Kutno, Warsaw in Central European Time, Brest, Minsk, Orsza in Moscow Time. Then Smolensk, Moscow in the afternoon, 1,880 miles in twenty-nine hours of travelling.

'The gauge changes at Brest-Litovsk over the border with a different set of wheels under you and the ride through Warsaw to Moscow is fast and smooth. Pure joy. Lemon tea available at all hours; a decent man sits by a brazier dispensing it, the atmosphere is friendly. All types travel and you never know whom you'll meet. I shared a carriage with two Nigerian girls studying medicine on Russian scholarships, buying textbooks in London and giving cheek to the Vopos. There were six different nationalities travelling with me. One worried English schoolteacher and family bound for Japan via Siberia.

'The approaches to Moscow are poor – wooden chalets, most of them abandoned and lousy, set back among trees. The skies over the capital very high, limitless grey. I stayed at the Hotel Moskja or Wockba on Marx Prospect just opposite the Kremlin. They said that the Moscow summers are very close and hot, so they said, but when I was there the water gushed from the taps just above freezing. Maybe that's the Russian sense of humour. The citizens have slug-white faces, the sort of complexion that goes peony pink in summer. And mountains of snow on the streets. Moscow summers are said to be hotter than Nigerian summers but I wouldn't know about that. Sufficient to say that the carriages stank of lioness and we talked all the way.

'The people, by and large, I found very suspicious; they

watch you. During the day the houses are deserted, I dare
say the owners are all out at work. A disciplined people,
though many drunks are seen at night, staggering about.
The old ones like going for walks in the daytime. You see
them in the big stores and markets, babushkas wandering
about, fingering the goods, not buying, keeping warm I
dare say, until it's time to go home. They like playing
"Moscow Nights".'

The great axles groaned over the frozen tracks. The
snow flew by in an agreeable manner. All the carriages
were heated and the windows coated with ice. He was
there, where he wanted most to be, travelling alone,
sitting upright, staring ahead. And yet, and yet (*pero, pero*),
he felt like a child, the tears came welling from his inmost
heart, such scalding tears, while thinking of him of whom
he would always think with the most tender love.

And a good name for a brute, too: Jürgen Endell of
the Westerwald. The spotty art student whom he had
accosted late one wet afternoon in the National Gallery
in Trafalgar Square, standing stock still midway between
Veronese's *Unfaithfulness* and *Scorn.*

Well, what can you do in the National Gallery on any
wet afternoon, coming up to closing time? What do you
make of the *Mona Lisa*'s smirk? What is she hiding? What
do you think of our English School? What do you say to
a pot of coffee in the Strand? Will you be Kallmann to my
Auden?

Loathsome Jürgen of Mainz smiled an enigmatic smile
and allowed himself to be picked up by the tall *Engländer.*
They set up house together in Maida Vale, shopping in
John Barnes, drinking in Hampstead. Jürgen was Alcibiades.

When J. J. Catchpole married Sybil Steptoe, Jürgen was
best man. The nuptials were high comedy, a sofa farce by
Labiche. J. J. told me about it, the great day, as though it

were another's affair and not his, laughing immoderately. Before the ceremony the prospective father-in-law surprised best man and groom making up their faces like actors preparing to go on, the latter stark naked and the former in a manifest state of tumescence, wearing dear Sybil's pink Celanese panties with lacy edges. Both were drunk as skunks.

The wedding itself went off without a hitch.

Well primed with Navy rum the nervous bridegroom kissed the composed bride. The reception was rather grand, the house full of the most proper people spilling out into a rented marquee in the garden. Later that night the mother-in-law unexpectedly came upon the best man under the groom on the grassy verge of the front drive. Eyebrows were raised but nothing was said; the day had not been unfree of incident. No doubt it would all work out for the best. Sybil has her head screwed on.

He told his new wife that he 'wanted to go away somewhere' in order to be quiet and write '*seriously*'. She believed him; they found a country seat in County Monaghan set between two small loughs. It had possibilities. From tall elms the crows squirted their white loads against the long windows, smearing the glass. Perfect, he said, and his wife agreed; they rented it, moved in. There was no catch. It was just perfect.

A log fire was kept burning all day in the big grate of the Round Room where J. J. worked up his notes with his feet up, smoking cigars and drinking gin, formulating theories, reading Schopenhauer and meditating on this and that.

His stories, when he began to show them, were thinly disguised homosexual exploits of his own. Credulous Sybil praised his inventiveness to the skies. He would go far, she said, if he kept at it. Tell the truth, but tell it slant.

The Round Room with its Veronese-green walls was like
a Beaton set for a Wilde play. The house was extensive
and old; it would take time and work to knock it into
shape, not having been lived in for years, but they were
relatively young. The owner was dead. A local woman, a
Methodist with a cleft palate and straw-coloured hair in
a bun, Mrs Mac, looked after the upkeep. She lived in a
room off the kitchen, feeding the pigs that wandered
through the plantation.

Catchpole was not a great cook; doubtless he had things
other than sauces and recipes to occupy him. Once he
had served up a disgusting repast of sheeps' eyes that
even he couldn't stomach but was obliged to pitch the
contents of the pot out the window into the shrubbery,
alarming Mrs Mac who was as usual beating the bushes
in search of lost pigs.

After that mishap Sybil took over the cooking. Her
husband had the palate of a dog.

'Love means "I want to be" according to St Augustine,
and who am I to contradict him? We were as well matched
as a couple of hot mince pies, as close as arse and shirt-
tail, but my love was slippery as an eel, even if he looked
more like a lynx or do I mean lammergaier the devourer
of bones, or Möllberg with the pointed ears and the cruel
view of history? When Jürgen sang alto I sang contralto,
then *I* sang alto and he sang contralto turn and turn
about. Bill Neate biffs the Gasman who biffs Bill back
again. As septic wounds refuse to heal, an old love cannot
rest.'

In velveteen smoking jacket and slippers, puffing a long
cigar to keep the midges at bay, Catchpole strolled about
his estate in the long summer evenings, a sulky country
squire overseeing his property quite in the manner of
Flaubert at Croisset. Playing the gentleman farmer

immersed in the land and its crops, seasonal rotations, wrapped up in creation, don't you know.

The grimly taciturn Monaghan farmers had nothing much to offer Squire Catchpole of Green Gables, known to the postman as Ard na Greine, similar in name to thousands of others throughout the land. The crabby neighbours were judged 'impossible' and no contact attempted.

The crows befouled the long Georgian windows, a nest fell into the fire, nobody called, Squire Catchpole stared up at the moulding of the off-white ceiling now grey with threadings of spiderwebs. He lived for the post but few letters arrived. They were getting out of touch. Catchpole was bored. And when he was bored he was bored.

When Sybil became pregnant she still worked at her Russian translations. Her husband praised her to the skies, genuinely proud of her; publishers wrote to her, sent her cheques, copies of good reviews. She met all the deadlines, she was wonderful. They had kept in touch with the Pushkin Club but rarely visited London. The shit-brown Plymouth took a beating, for Catchpole was an atrocious driver. Once he had collided with a tractor, twice he ran into a wall, thrice into a ditch; every outing left a mark, a bent bumper, a shattered windscreen, a dented door. The crows used it as a latrine. Sybil's translation fees kept the nervous husband in petrol, cigars, alcohol and newspapers. He spent a certain amount of each day poring over his papers and giving vent to heartfelt sighs and groans. The in-laws were kept informed as to his prospects and plans; he was thought to be steadying himself for a major creative effort, a spring offensive. Meanwhile a little stranger was on the way.

A stand of old beech trees kept out the sunlight of which there was a paucity in the wintertime. Bending and groaning in persistent downpours of rain day and night they were covered with moss and ivy; a raucous assembly of crows arrived at dusk to empty their bowels noisily before dark. Fledglings were blown about in the wind-whipped wood in May, made miserable by squalls of gusting rain. In the daytime a few bedraggled unhappy-looking wood pigeons balanced on a swaying branch, cooing faintly, limp as rags. And Catchpole found himself to be bored out of his wits. Life in the country did not suit him, after all; he didn't hit it off with the neighbours, needed stimulating company, and where would you find that in bloody Monaghan?

Then lo and behold, the bad angel found the good angel out. Phoning from London to say he was destitute, could he pay a short visit, he would not be in the way.

Jürgen arrived looking wan and ill, yellower than ever. Sybil was instructed to feed him up. She was a mother now. In the rambling old house baby Megan (Megs) bawled in a great echoing room. The proud new father took her in his arms, crooned to her, showed her the perfect view, the elms crowded with cawcaws, the glittering lake full of fish and Mrs Mac beating the undergrowth for her missing pigs.

The woodland was flooded with an odd clarity of opaline light and the leaves were drifting down and pools left by a recent rain sparkled on the paths made vivid as anv landscape by Palmer or Corot or as seen in some previous existence. Casement windows gave onto a thoroughly drenched shrubbery of glistening rhododendrons and beyond that the murky wood again sparkling after cascades of rain and beyond that again lay Monaghan proper, a doped land feculent with pig slurry.

Windows were thrown open to admit fresh air and a moderate amount of light into Jerome's lair or cubbyhole, presently to be fouled up by Jürgen and his filthy habits. The rooms were thoroughly aired and furniture waxed and varnished and freshened up by the ever-loving Sybil with chaste floral arrangements and the flowers regularly renewed, for Sybil Catchpole was a woman as quietly proud of her housekeeping as of her own purity. Then in marched the thoughtless squire with his muddy boots and fetid cigar.

The scrofulous Endell bathed rarely and then reluctantly, took echinacen drops twice daily, wore a little rouge, was sometimes the Ill-Wind-That-Bodes-No-Good, sometimes the Sullen Baggage, but always and ever reedy-voiced Jürgen the two-faced flirt and nasty idle little schemer. A neat disorder in the dress was ever Jürgen's way. Considerate Jerome ran a deep bath for the turbid one who lay motionless in it for three-quarters of an hour with eyes closed, fast asleep.

He of the dusty hue, the musty manner, had arrived in reach-me-down clothes, somebody's castoffs smelling of mothballs, looking looney, drained and old – deathly pale Werner Krauss emerging from the wall in *The Cabinet of Doctor Caligari*, a dirty faggot gone to seed, an ear of corn bent by the rain, though argumentative as ever – 'Don't tell me, arsehole, you don't like *Lubitsch*!' He was altogether an insufferable prick, though indispensable to the longsuffering and besotted Catchpole, *Wetter und Gewitter.*

A slurred address, the hint of a lisp, little pinched lips, ferrety blue eyes, rings on his fingers – stolen goods? – a rodent head darting crafty, rapacious glances hither and thither, all betrayed an inherent shiftiness. The husky voice of the seducer, the dandy's cane. Fish-face!

The man of little bottle sat nervously by the man of great bottle – he had enough bottle for two – on the green *chaise-longue*, slyly holding hands and exchanging butterfly and oyster kisses while Sybil was otherwise engaged at maternal chores.

The phlegmatic locals avoided Green Gables like the

plague. The word may have got around: here were practising sodomites. But Catchpole was not discountenanced,
not a whit.

'In the normal hurly-burly I came on as a womanly
man, another Bloom. Or a manly woman, I'm not sure
which. Some imbalance there, I fancy. No wonder I'm
odd. Goddammit I *feel* queer. Take me for what I am.'

Love must find a way.

He was jittery, always on the qui vive for a bit on the
side, a sweaty connection, to be banged up. Was that love?
Epithalamium or bordello; or just a craving, a hankering?
A pitiable state to be in, like a door swelling in a damp
winter, hard to close.

Soon stippled from head to toe with white emulsion
the frantic painters attacked an upper room with loaded
rollers dripping paint as a preparation for painting the
entire upper floor, after stripping off the old decayed
wallpaper that ballooned from the walls in uncoiling
swaths.

In worn denim cutoffs with artfully frayed edges,
stained about the crotch, and nothing more but espa-
drilles and sweatband about his forehead, double-jointed
and unhandy, Jürgen slapped on the first coat, singing
lustily, his ribs protruding as if he hadn't had a square
meal in months.

'You look like John the Baptist,' Catchpole tittered.

'Vee two look as if shat upon by crows,' sniggered
Jürgen.

Guffawing fit to bust, Squire Catchpole ran upstairs
and downstairs with chilled beer and sandwiches for the
manly painters stripped to the waist, in lathers of sweat.

And Jürgen succumbed again.

As a consequence the job did not progress too rapidly
or very far. The German wore gloves to protect his hands.
After supper they sat around the log fire in the Round

Room and smoked cigars, sipped Martell and vodka and drew up elaborate plans for the house, spoke of ambitious creative projects. Indiscretions came into play of course. When Megs was being fed, Catchpole confessed that he had been unfaithful himself, with a labourer in a ditch. 'With hairy chest the fellow's a regular Mellors.' Catchpole admitted to visiting the rustic cottage to invite Mellors to local pubs, got him well and truly tanked up. Jürgen digested this in silence, making a wry mouth.

Yesterday I met a dear farmer in a cornfield. Poor Monsieur Melmoth rode the lame horse Madrone. In the embrasures of the long windows flies were buzzing, fighting for their lives with the spider that came shinning up and down his web, wrapping them up; soon they were shells of insects picked clean. One of the straying pigs venturing too far choked itself to death in a gripe. The mangy yard cat was flattened by the milk van. Alas!

Sybil, again seated opposite, smiled and smiled and went on knitting an endless seamless garment. She felt well disposed towards the quiet-spoken *Freund*, so polite and serious, so German. So nervous, so nervous. Sickly and yellowish as quince and covered in eczema, with foul breath, ring piercing one ear, he was not Montgomery Clift; but then again Montgomery Clift had been no Alcibiades. Snickering at Catchpole's lame jokes when not sucking up to him or chewing Toblerone, Jürgen exuded a sour antiseptic stink, the very stink of perdition. His face was a dead sort of olive colour. Behind green tinted bottleglass spectacles wobbled froggy eyes enlarged by the lenses, venomous little balls of mercury wobbling in a spirit level.

In the much-battered shit-brown Plymouth, Catchpole drove like a maniac to rural pubs where the instantly inflamed Jürgen made eyes at the men, pressing himself up against them at the serving hatch, following them into the *retrete*. They drove back in a cold and murderous silence. Again the long windows besmeared and bespattered with crowshit, again the bawling babe. Wild and whirling words were bandied about and terrible accusations hurled.

'Get off my back!'

'Take the breeze, cocksucker!'

'Out of my sight for ever!'

'Sod off, tomcat!'

'Out with you, you cunt!'

'Shitface!'

'Poxbritches!'

'*Caca!*'

'You vomit!'

'Heap of manure!'

'Creampuff!'

'Dogturd!'

'Ponce!'

'Libertine!'

'Gobshite!'

'Minty manure!'

'Face-fucker!'

'Jerk!'

'Buffoon!'

'Wanker!'

'Get stuffed!'

'Baboon!'

'Crow-bait!'

'Fart-face!'

'Bag of shit!'

'Arsehole!'

Sybil, tilting little Megs over her shoulder to bring up wind, said they were both being very silly. It was all too dramatic. But Jerome said he wasn't having any of it. Jürgen was told in no uncertain terms to get onto his bike and push off, never to darken the door again. He could leave just as soon as he liked. Which he did sourly, cursing under his vile breath, with a flea in his earhole and a wild hair up his arse. He stole money and his host's herring-bone tweed suit, pissed in the playpen, scrawled abuse on the front door.

Sybil continued to knit a long green pullover with endless arms by the crackling wood fire, purl and plain, purl and plain, her husband stood to be measured, held the corded wool with hands shaking, praised the colour (olive green), the adroit cable stitch. Never more would he tolerate that fucking philanderer in his home. Green Gables had seen the last of him.

But soon he relented – how could he not? – with heart in mouth he flew to murky London town where a monstrous rebuff awaited. Jürgen was living with a woman whom he intended to marry! A *woman*! Lorna Lovaduck. But would not his oldest and truest *Freund* (here a merry twinkle in the moistful froggy eye) do him the honour to be their best man? And return the compliment, as it were; for had not Jürgen Endell been his? Here Catchpole hit the roof. Are you *serious*, you Westerwald cocksucker! Not on your fucking Nelly!

He gave a coarse raspberry and stormed out. The gifts were scattered on the floor, the woman nowhere to be seen. With high irrationality Love says, 'Out of all creation do I pick thee.' And had not Jerome chosen Jürgen whom he loved from the bottom of his giddy, faithless heart? Not rawboned Rabo Encendio nor dark-visaged Callos Vasco nor Father Caspar Juniparo the riproaring Franciscan monk, nor Staremburg, not Huntley nor Palmer, nor Salerio nor Solana, but Jürgen Endell with the fetid breath of a lynx and the shifty manner. Every sensualist possesses a voluminous tenderness. Vice has its own rules like everything else. They were made for each other. Catchpole said: 'But obviously in my life "love" has to be betrayed, and often. I don't know why this is so, I only know I am relieved to have finished with it. Yet in a perverse way I'm still the same and nothing has changed. Still the same old song: "For a Long Time Now I Have Not Seen the Prince of Change in My Dreams." What do you say to a brimming glass of Cuné to put us in the right frame of mind?'

Catchpole flew home in a state of shock. Back to the bawling babe, seemingly shrunken in his absence, to sour Mrs Mac in a vile humour calling the lost pigs; to beshatten windows, to the stink of absence. A forlorn west wind boomed through the empty rooms and a weak winter sun leaked into cold interiors 'like sanies into a bucket' (*Merci, Monsieur B.*!). A freezing winter wind howled 'Imbecile!' down the chimney and extinguished the fire.

Sybil, well muffled up, emerged wraithlike into the open air, pushing baby Megan in her little chair, the teething Megs bawling her little guts out. Diffident Mum advanced with a fixed and purposeful smile on a pale affronted face free of make-up. Jerome could be very trying at times. His late 'friend', the pisser in the playpen, had admitted to illegal badger-baiting in the Irish Republic and the Catchpoles were dreading a visitation from the Garda Síochána. It was time to break camp. Sybil was ordered to pack forthwith.

From Belfast they flew to Gatwick, then on to Málaga, into the Mediterranean sunshine. Soon they had discovered Nerja and moved there, bag and baggage. Antonio's dim bar became Catchpole's home from home, comfortable as a confession box, the Andalucían morgue.

It so happened to be my first and most favoured Nerja bar, a bar without music, generally deserted.

'That geezer really got on my tits,' Catchpole confessed.

Love, the imminence of love, and intolerable remembering.

Jürgen was very quick to take offence. That nasty man had daubed in white paint on the front door:

'SCUMBAGS
LIVE HERE!'

Moskja! Moskja! (When I First Saw You)

> A man who is not afraid of the sea will soon be drowned, for he will be going out on a day he shouldn't. But we do be afraid of the sea and we do only be drowned now and again.
>
> J. M. Synge, *The Aran Islands*

> Go through that meadow. Who the country is beautiful! Who the trees are thick! You hear the birds gurgling! Which pleasure! Which charm!
>
> Portuguese–English primer

> When a Russian finds himself in Tashkent, he thinks he is still in Russia.
>
> Ryszard Kapucinski, in conversation with Hans Magnus Enzensberger

'*¿Cuándo?*' whispers the priest behind the wire grille, moving his posterior uneasily, heavy as an animal in its lair.

'*¿Adónde?*'
'*¿Cuántas veces?*'

'The last kiss is given to the void,' said Catchpole.

He gave a smile soft, venal and fruity. He was 'Lucky' Lucan, the gambler and high-flyer, the missing seventh Earl, the enigma. Had he drowned himself or was he living incognito elsewhere, in another country?

'With my eyes closed,' said Catchpole (closing them the better to savour the fond memory), I'd recognise any country in the world where I'd ever been, by its smell. And with my eyes closed now, were he to enter this bar, I'd know it was he.'

Were he to enter; get him! Butterball!

A violin in a violin case was Jürgen Endell, Catchpole's doxy and four-flush heart-throb. To you and me he may have been oily as an eel, spry as a spider; he with the shop-soiled look of objects kept too long in the window, that have been long mouldering away out of the fresh air. Endell was a joke, and a bad joke at that. Who was it said that comedy depends on the female aspect of the male brought out and mocked – or do I mean the male aspect of the female – the Dame in panto, old Mother Riley, whaddyacaller? Something stiff as a scarecrow on the lit stage, an effigy bundled into a stale old corset exposing hairy legs and knock knees, an ancient wig, the nose of a habitual drinker. Capering about, got up fake as a dressmaker's dummy but full of obscene life, giddy and crotchety, croaking innuendoes in a disguised male voice.

The stage voice sounded hollowly from the throat, as the gobble-gobble of an enraged turkeycock with wattles inflamed, cruelly beaked and spurred killer and devourer of its own progeny, overlord of the farmyard.

Impotent Endell with a fancy ring in one ear adding a piratical touch, straw-coloured kinky hair in a ponytail, festering skin, was one slippery customer. He spoke in intense and compromising vagaries.

'I am called "Tiny-Huge" because I am everyone's,

everywhere, always. Every cock in the farmyard crows for me. Sometimes one meets a woman who is beast turning human, *nicht wahr*? Where did I read it?'

Here a supercilious curl of thin depraved lips that exuded venom.

At an AA centre in Brisbane, Australia, was he not introduced as 'Nigel', suffering from memory loss and acute depression? Admitting to housebreaking and burglary in Geelong in the back of beyond. In Berlin, Germany, he had passed himself off as Lord Lucan, the missing Earl or vanished English peer. Or again as Baron Ingo von Hintern of Val d'Isère, heir to millions. Or again, stretching fancy as far as it would go, he became his fantasy feminine alter egos, rough trade off the street: Ulrika ('Ulli') Wollfisch or Helen Horne.

Elsewhere he was Rough Ricky or Randy Roy, peerless cocksmen. It's a long way from Berlin to Uruguay and back again. As the distance from Cape Cod and Jaffa is terrible – and yet not so great.

'Am I sick of this manwoman thing,' the venomous lips pronounced. 'It's been going on for too long. Too much cape, not enough *muleta*. The murmur of nocturnal rain brings it all back to me.'

Inside every groaning mother always is another groaning mother dying to be let out. As inside every babushka is another slightly smaller babushka dying to be let out, and inside *her*, eenymeenyminymo another ever smaller. All those ever smaller babushkas begging in voices grown ever fainter, to be let out.

Who was it said that babes are assured salvation? It's a damned lie. Regard the grotesque ugliness of the Christ Child in Old Masters, the babe in the manger or cradled in the mother's arms – frequently a distorted manikin gnarled as an old root. And why is that? Mum must be an invention of necessity. Trapped in our mothers' wombs, those darksome gurgling bolt-holes, awaiting the summons to leave, deaf and half-formed babes sucking their thumbs can recognise those hammerblows as Mum's heartbeats, when laved in her amniotic fluids they await the word to go. In every heartbeat they sense changing worlds.

In every blessed heartbeat they sense changing worlds! Yes! Do you believe, *barin*, that the dead will rise again? People *say* they will, but maybe they won't.

Life teems with such quiet fun.

Watch those sausages! Which is more fattening – crisps or nuts? You tell me. Who was it said 'The wish to be good is the urge to be destroyed'? People are what they are; they have no other choice. Every man's opinions go in accordance with hidden permanent prejudices. Greta Garbo at sixty-five liked to dress up in the clothes of the handsome young Gore Vidal. She spoke English in a manly voice and always referred to herself as 'he', perceiving herself as a lad among lads with hooded ice-grey eyes. So says an old crotchety Vidal holed up in Ravello.

Jan Morris used to be a man. In Canada he was injected over 2,000 times with the hormones of gravid mares. In Wales 'she' wept womanlike when her first public book (*Conundrum*) was savaged by male critics.

Mary Quant trimmed her pubic hair heart-shaped to please her husband, sold tearproof mascara in the Quant range of toiletries, made a packet.

Credulous mariners believed that when a hand gesticulated from the waves it was a forecast of imminent shipwreck.

The tiny red spot on Jupiter indicates where it has been raining non-stop for 700 years over an area several thousand miles in diameter.

At 2 a.m. one wintry morning on Hungerford Bridge an actor hurrying to catch a train at Charing Cross Station had his throat cut from ear to ear and expired in hospital. Across the walkway on the bridge a despairing hand had painted in bold white capital letters

MRS ROBINSON CAN'T WE MEET JUST ONCE?
NATIONAL GALLERY 1PM THURSDAY

in a calligraphic howl of despair.

Genet wrote in *Pompes funèbres*: 'Apartments offer themselves to the burglar with painful immodesty.'

All imagined something – something incorrect.

The Russian chess grandmaster Tartower said, 'The blunders are all there, just waiting to be made.'

The American grandmaster Fischer boasted that he had known the moves before he learnt how to play the game.

I yawned into Catchpole's face as he opened wide his mole's eyes to find himself at mid-morn in winter standing within Antonio Cerezo Criado's mausoleum, morgue-like as the Bar Pombo in Málaga. It was deserted but for the three of us – Antonio was brewing himself some coffee in the kitchen but would presently join us.

Bored by J. J.'s persistence I said nothing. For surely he did go on about his *amours*, in particular his Annie Laurie. Catchpole's pockmarked face displayed avidity; tenacious memory could not let go. Although he had not specified anybody by name I guessed to whom he was referring: spotty Endell. Maintenance men crib and bellyache about job complications but love to boast of difficulties surmounted. Mountaineers boast of difficult peaks they have conquered or hope to conquer; Catchpole spoke of his great love, the loathsome Jürgen. Who was it contends that love melts only in pleasure, that there must be setbacks before the arrows and the fire? Old Burton? Jürgen had married an unknown Englishwoman and they were living in Crouch End, north London near the playing-fields. Relenting a little – how could he do otherwise? – hasty Catchpole bought an expensive wedding present and mailed it off express, wishing the faithless one a long and happy life, lots of *Glück*.

Jürgen, true to form, did not reply.

Catchpole would not see him again. But he could not forget him, that acne-blasted kraut with the bad complexion and the mouth made more for sauerkraut than 'the madness of kisses'.

I stood at the bar counter, sipping gin that tasted vaguely of mouse droppings, wishing I were elsewhere or alone. Catchpole, that long twisted string of licorice allsorts, had an importunate way of filling one up with unwanted confidences, a past teeming with protean male partners.

It was the day of his departure for London. Memory glowed off him, a true homo-glow. His face was lit from within like a Bellini angel. Bellini the Venetian, that strange Italian painter whose Saviours resembled women wearing false beards.

As I fumbled to light a Celtas Catchpole bent and kissed me quickly on the cheek. 'Take care,' he mumbled and stumbled backways out of the bar. Antonio batted his circumflex eyelashes and blew on his coffee.

Never strike a pansy, bully Hemingway counsels, they scream.

'Time passes,' I ventured in Spanish.

'No, you pass; time stands still,' Antonio responded robustly.

'*Un otro, por favor,*' I fluted in Spanish as idiotic as El Diminuto, alias Stan Laurel dubbed into blithering-idiot Spanish.

Antonio obligingly splashed in a generous libation. Never say when. I had hoped to have seen the last of

Catchpole but presently in he came all acne-blast and perfumed from the kiosk where he had bought four packets of Celtas, two of which he threw on the counter.

'I never told you of my trip to Moscow,' said he, lighting up and blowing a slow smoke-ring into the chill bar.

'Russia! A red duster on a pole down a narrow road in a green pine forest. Pure Chagall. The customs shed back a couple of kilometres on a plain of rich grass and wild strawberries. Picture the waiting room. On the table a game of chess is set out, indicative of monstrous bureaucratic delays to be expected. Above the desk where sit two po-faced Soviet officials hang matching pictures in fading monochrome depicting two bushy-bearded sombre-eyed mean-looking men of destiny in loose-fitting tunics – Messrs Marx and Engels. Mean *hombres*. But wait! There lies a land where time and space have a different scale to what we have grown accustomed. Leningrad in the rain – and what rain! – black bile discharged from the clouds dragging their bases on the broad Neva. A river like a sea.

'I visited the Winter Palace and Hermitage and left the others alone; they can wait – Summer Palace, Admiralty, Exchange, Academy, Stroganoff Palace, Smolny Convent, Portress – façades thousands of metres long of coloured colonnades and sculptures set against the sky and against walls coloured ochre and eau-de-Nil, maroon, cobalt. Architectural spaces to the scale of open landscape calling on an architecture of movement, scale, depth and relief, colour and sculpture to stand up to it, withstand its force.

'When I got back I could follow John Reed's blow-by-blow account step by step, so to speak. In the Hermitage Gallery I looked for the rarely seen Impressionists and very early Cubists and after about an hour found them up under the roof, in the servants' quarters. Monet water-lilies and rather uncertain Picassos straight from the

Bâteau Lavoir. Just in time . . . for looking down to the Place de Mars I got a blinding attack of migraine and was uncertain of what century I was in. One day was enough to shake *me*.

'Far away in the distance a white church with a golden onion dome. Well, the ruined churches with roofs gone in and vegetation springing up through the windows might have been expected, yet stop one short. The queue for Lenin's mausoleum is seen by some as an apotheosis, evidence of the necessity to take account of more than the passing. That queue certainly requires some explaining. A larger than life arrangement of a crowd by Eisenstein.

'Inside, no cameras or hands in pockets allowed, enhancing the illusion that one is in a kind of cathedral. One chap's hands dragged out of his pockets by irate guards producing the air of a holy place desecrated – but perhaps just coincidence, through fear of bombs, ever popular in Russia.

'It is a fine country, that's all one can say. In Soviet Russia the ways are still very long and things pleasingly distant and remote. The sun barely rises above the horizon during the Moscow winter. Even at noon it hangs low in the southern sky, casting a yellowish light and long shadows and the air is filled with fine white snow, a "real Moscow frost" as the natives say.

'In the evening rush-hour the tramcars rattle along with frosted windows, you cannot see in or out. Didn't your man Yeats write somewhere that there may be a landscape equivalent to certain spiritual conditions that awaken hunger such as cats feel for valerian? That was Holy Russia for me, Soviets or no Soviets. There is a strong sense of a limitless land and limitless time and I suppose the constant possibility of violence. My kind of place. But now I must pass water, if you'll excuse me. Shan't be long. Watch those drinks.'

Catchpole went plunging off into the back part of the bar where Carme was singing, swabbing with a mop. Brother Antonio, ex-footballer of Málaga with no word of English, stood at the door gazing out like a graven image as was his wont, playing pocket billiards.

The Bâteau Lavoir!

Impressionism – the lost dream, the one that took such a long time to get accepted. The lost Paradise, the unde-manding dream of oneness with nature, oneness with other people, oneness with oneself.

Monet's waterlilies, the 'lavendered limbs' of Madame Bonnard in the tub. Her husband wouldn't allow her to age, followed her into the bathroom. He painted rumpled bed-sheets as if they were clouds; painted massing clouds as if they were rumpled bed-sheets after a tempestuous night of love with Madame B.

The doorway darkened again, Antonio stood politely aside as gigantic Catchpole came grinning in, wiping his face with a paper tissue. I had ordered up another lethal round of Larios gin still tasting vaguely of mouse droppings.

'The coldness of hot countries is absolutely poignant. Think I may have pissed in a cupboard back there. It's a dark hole all right but what the hell, bums up!' He buried his nose in the long glass where ice cubes jostled lemon slices. The *servicio* was a convenient hole in the floor. The wattage was weak back there and the ammonia reek of male piss strong as if a pride of lions had staked out their territory.

'Strange times. One must cross the wide square by subway; the surface is only for traffic, as I soon discovered. The population practically *lives* underground – great hordes shambling along in subterranean walkways where black marketeers sell fashion journals from the West and you can buy the most delicious ice cream I've ever tasted.

The standard of clothing on sale is approximately that of the Age of Steam.'

'There's a fellow in Berlin who only paints rivers,' I said. 'He went to the north of Norway in places abandoned by the Lapps who had all left to work in the Oslo factories. He said it was like the Garden of Eden.'

'Gosh.'

'Met a Pole once, a refugee from the death camps, who only painted boats. Boats drawn up on the shore, with rotted ribs that could never again put to sea. They were sort of votive prayers for a brother gassed and incinerated in Auschwitz.'

In the rocking corridor of an express train hurtling towards Moscow, Catchpole stood with all his papers in order and roubles in his pocket, trying not to look too often at a handsome youth who was putting his fair head out the window with every chance of being decapitated by a viaduct or another train flashing by in the opposite direction.

J. J. Catchpole, all six and a half feet of him, was ripe for an affair.

Already in his mind's eye (the eye in the back of his head, ever alert for mischief) he could see many such young and handsome Soviet males walking about with much sang-froid in fur-lined boots, slapping gloved hands together, puffing out reddened cheeks and saluting each other in a language as difficult as it was melodious, a beautiful if incomprehensible tongue.

They would be tall as pine trees, neat as spruce, laughing into each other's flushed faces. Big glowing males hairy as polar bears would wrestle with him under fleecy eiderdowns. It would be a regular stud farm, a collective blood brotherhood of like-minded males.

Ah, the tongueless vigil, the foreign faces, and all the pain!

'You must live with the pine, try and make good sense of it,' gobbled Catchpole in his eager, shifty way, swallowing his dirty diphthongs and rolling dishonest gooseberry eyes swimming in used dishwater, chapped lips all wet with saliva.

'Make your life a circle. A circle of pine.'

'What's all this pine, Catchpole?'

'Why, the pine of living.'

I remembered the cramped apartments of Copenhagen queers, full of flowers, roses mainly. Stolen roses. A summer moon shone on Dyrehaven where Baroness Blixen walked alone to the hermitage on the hill. Nanna cycled to Østersøgade in the gloaming, admired the starry sky, heard the frogs, the whisper of leaves.

A lilac wood on Rørvig was full of trulls, full of *Schniksal*. In the woman who overwhelms us there must be nothing familiar (Salter).

Avid for new love, he threw caution to the winds, casting anxious glances through blue-tinged shades at the lovely lad moving his weight from one foot to the other and blowing out his cheeks as if he had pins and needles or was walking on ice. Meanwhile he was darting the most pleading looks in the direction of the tall pale foreigner who was perhaps Clint Eastwood, pockmarks and all.

J. J. Catchpole for his part was fervently praying for an endless tunnel to come and swallow up the speeding express and the lights to fail and the onrushing train never to emerge from the tunnel and the lights never to come on again and the journey never to end. Passion is a wheel going faster and faster.

Oh and ah, the furtive hot unambiguous stares!

Love, Slav-style, was an onrushing express, the sound

of huge greased wheels grinding over the frozen railbed, the shuddering windows all latticed with ice; a blindingly white horizon with onion-shaped domes racing towards them, madness howling in the redhot belly of the locomotive and an unknown destination risen apparition-like before their astonished eyes in a screen of blown snow.

The utmost grace the old Greeks (buggers to a man) could show would scarce compare to this. They were entering Moscow hand in hand; the frozen city beloved of arsonists and pyromaniacs lay before them like a huge wedding cake.

The great wheels were pounding onward, expelling sparks, the brake mechanism giving sudden spurts of smoke and boiling steam, and in the overheated corridor the long madness of hot returned stares, preceded by uncertain glances, sighs, fidgeting. In ancient Greece, in days of yore . . . ho, hum.

Love, awaiting him in Moscow, had sent forth this pretty knight-errant, this comely page. Fucksters (you that would be happy), for standing tarses we kind nature thank. The young man standing in the corridor was bony, fair complexioned, with an intelligent face and slitty eyes.

'I could have jagged myself to death on him,' Catchpole admitted candidly, 'and candidly he wouldn't have minded, by the engaging look of him. Not he.'

This candour was engaging; the dalliance in the train was tricky as the obscure and seldom seen love-dance of tropical insects caught in a shaft of sunlight deep in an equatorial forest far from women's eyes.

Then the long train started into the curve, blowing its whistle, running wild. The faun, mesmerised, was still staring out the window at the white domes dancing far away and minarets in a pearl sky out of which snow was swirling down like falling gems, brilliants.

Moscow! Mother Russia!

Land of horses, land of sleighs, tinkling bells and bass voices, land of limitlessness. Of jiggery-pokery.

'I wanted to offer him roubles, wanted to grope him, offer him all I had in the world,' Catchpole confessed. 'But I kept my hands to myself and behaved. I was a good boy. Then by God I got my reward. For as the floor of the train began curving into the gradient he was carried across into my arms as if on a slide, and I lifted him off his feet and kissed him, got the whiff of garlic and vodka and fur and the sweat of love. At least I think it was. Do you suppose it was love at first sight or just pity because he saw I was an outsize freak? What do you suppose?'

I looked at Antonio, who batted his circumflex eyelashes at me.

'Love at first sight,' I pronounced. 'Undoubtedly.'

'Oh, you are sweet,' said Catchpole, touching my glass with the tilted rim of his own and blushing rose-red before sinking his nose into bubbling gin and tonic that still retained the musty and discreet flavour of mouse droppings.

With much shuddering down all its purposeful length the train began drawing into the terminus and a stout station guard appeared at the window, as if bolted into a stiff uniform, to rap smartly on the glass and blow a mighty blast on his whistle and call out something incomprehensible, pointing imperiously, before disappearing again, as if a moving platform had carried him away.

The express was letting off a great urgent spew of brake smoke and slowly pulling up alongside the main platform and the carriage doors were springing open down the whole length of the train and the faun stepped lightly down, his breath steaming in the freezing air. He waved, seemed to blow a kiss or was merely wiping his nose, and began striding quickly away out of Moscow Central and hence out of Catchpole's life.

He was glowing now, no two ways about it, a lambent homo-glow and it wasn't just the mouse droppings. Indeed he looked quite beautiful, become faun-like himself, transformed by love. Even the plainest ones can become radiant and glow betimes when beastly circumstance allows, when times bode well and not ill, for even Cellini himself must have often glowed in this way, with the lineaments of gratified desire.

But to tell the sober truth I was sick and tired of Catchpole's false boys and faithless ones sucking their thumbs. Love has a spider's eye, to find out each particular pain.

Now all the carriage doors were flung open down all the long Ost–West Express and loud umpettythump martial music blared from loudspeakers and a name in Cyrillic loomed up with some of the letters inverted like circus acrobats and an urgent whistle blew lustily all over the station. And then and only then did J. J. Catchpole rise up, much rumpled by hours of travel, to gather together his baggage and prepare to step down onto Soviet Russian soil.

'Moscow was like nothing on earth. Come here till I tell you. Soviet sailors walked about hand in hand with the names of their ships emblazoned on the front of their caps, which had coquettish tassels at the side, singing and shouting to each other, wearing the *tightest* pants imaginable.'

Snow fell light as confetti on furry earflaps. All the church bells were madly ringing when huge hairy fellows tumbled him in vast beds as big as fields and he could neither repent nor confess and be shriven and absolved, due to the variety of temptations on offer, and the language barrier.

'Russia of the heavy buttocks,' said Catchpole with relish. 'They have gratuitously gross behinds.'

The young enlisted men were angels playing dirty games. Felled by cross-buttock throws not seen in the ring since the heyday of bare-knuckle champions such as Cribb and Crabb, unless I confuse them with Sprigg and Spring, he had the stuffing knocked out of him regularly.

The Soviet Russian earth was frozen ten foot deep under a blanket of snow fourteen feet high and his English reserve (of which he had very little, fair dues to him) melted as snow under a hot sun. He was shown all that was most beautiful and best by kind-hearted Soviet he-men. All the angels played games between his feet and were always there and most obliging and all of them most beautiful and well hung.

In sign language he addressed them, showed them the tube map of London and photos of his wife Sybil and little Megs and he told them he was a pansy and these the small flowers of his garden. Briefly, he made a holy show of himself in the bars, fired up by vodka and hot looks, to which he was most adaptive.

Moscow was teeming with temptation. He just couldn't resist. Airmen, sailors and soldiers strolled about in the snow making pretty arabesques, waved to him, or seemed to, smiling, steaming.

When he left his hotel in the morning the hoar-frost formed on his eyebrows. The walls of the Kremlin faced a square where nobody walked. The bones of Gorky were immured there. J. J. Catchpole stood at the crossroads of his life, breathing deeply, all frosted up, simmering.

'You once asked me what is homosexual love. Well, I

suppose it's the same as any other love – a strange place where you've never been before, whose language you don't at first understand. The air and the customs seem a little strange, at first, somewhat peculiar until you begin to get the hang of it. Anyway, that was Moscow for me, the *terra incognita.*'

His voice trembled with the eternal chronic anxiety that sounds so querulously in the voices of all queers. I thought of Stendhal in Milan and the odour of love in the air; it was the honest tang of horse manure.

'If I was expecting a museum, as I was, I found a zoo with all the exuberance of a real forest where the animals actually kill each other. A dangerous place to find yourself in, *amigo*. Darkish with shafts of sunlight spearing down. A huge enclosed area devoted to prankish carryings-on; such goings-on you cannot imagine. You simply cannot conceive of such salvos of happenings, of repleteness. Is it too much to say "exaltation"? No.'

He was hot on 'the occasions of sin', the allure of it.

'Stalin's preferred tipple was Georgian vodka, which "cuts your legs and makes you feel sparks bursting from your stomach", according to Aldo Buzzi,' I said.

'Soviet samovarandvodkawithsparks-style love can be very heating on the system. Maybe it was just as well that I left when I did. I was like an athlete overdoing it.'

At night, alone or not as the case may be, he heard the trains departing, screeching like huge bats as they left the seven great terminals for destinations beyond the Urals, penetrating far into Siberia and Asia.

He looked out of his hotel bedroom one morning to see a ruddy-faced Red Army major dressing down a squad of privates, all of them heavy as tuns, with small little suspicious piggy eyes, their breath steaming in the air, hot as ridden horses.

The Major was in a towering rage.

Their tracks in the snow made pretty patterns across the otherwise empty square.

The sluggish Soviet sun rose late above the honey-coloured churches and guards with sullen manners presented arms and admitted a large automobile with pennants flying into the Kremlin. Perhaps it was Khrushchev.

A strapping young fellow marched up and down, goose-stepping to keep warm. Full of vodka and bonhomie, J. J. Catchpole attempted to board him but was coldly repulsed.

'I was really philandering. Hardly knew which way my sitting parts hung.'

The big studs knocked the stuffing out of him all right. They seemed to enjoy themselves; language barriers were surmountable, with much else. He was kissed and wrestled to the bed by brawny muscle-men who came puffing in, giving off a heady reek of barracks and gym, swallowed shots of vodka in quick time, began discarding enough clothes to cover the backs of four or five needy British families.

'I'll not conceal it from you, dear friend, I was fucked silly.'

'And Pula?' I asked smoothly, attempting to distract him from his hot fancies.

'Pula was different.'

He brought back to London 'a terrific suntan, a holy icon and a dose of the clap' contracted from a casual pick-up on his cruising grounds; the blond or brunette might have been either Soviet or Slav. It was 'inconvenient' when he returned home to Sybil. He attended a VD clinic in London to be painfully cured of his affliction. It was humiliating.

'The intern stuck something up my arse that opened out like a little umbrella, and when he pulled it out I screamed with pain. I could barely walk – as if I'd been fucked by a bull elephant a number of times.'

'Now try and stay clean,' the jowly intern had said, wiping his instrument. 'Be a good boy.'

The holy icon was something to see.

'May we see it?'

'Unfortunately not.'

He had grown tired of it and sold it to a dealer at a considerable loss. Sybil forgave him his recklessness. She never reproached him for anything he did. When accused of misdemeanours he flew into a tantrum and screamed like a hysterical woman; and then made the wildest counter-accusation (very Russian). So it was really advisable to remain calm and say nothing. This Sybil did to perfection, with long practice. What else could she do? A mother bird with no time to preen her feathers. All serene then, eh? Calmly does it.

I stared at Antonio Cerezo Criado's assembly of knick-knacks, oddments and artefacts that had long adorned the bar. Both parents had strokes and were out of circulation, rarely venturing downstairs. The daughter Carme looked after them, made fiery *tapas*, passed through the bar with her hair in curlers, the Gorgon Medusa personified, a resentful female force emptying chamber-pots. Young brother Rafael was built like a wrestler. Debt-collector and part-time potboy, he served behind the bar on Sunday nights when it was crowded and took over twice yearly when Antonio allowed himself a free day. Bull steaks at La Luna were the extent of his dissipation; for he was a lonely man. Rafael strode from one end of Burriana beach to the other in generously cut bathing drawers that enhanced a mighty lingam-bulge worthy of the Lord Siva himself. The great mahogany-brown face and trunk were seen above the low wall overlooking Carabeo beach or presently down below wallowing in the shallows attempting a sedate breaststroke; emerging dripping to astonish the ladies with an alarming display of damp virilia and the slanted nipples of a gorilla. It was the summer when Faulkner died in distant Jackson, Mississippi; the summer when the *extranjero* wives ran in bras and panties on Playa de Torrecillas. Good Faulkner gets better with time, whereas bad Faulkner gets worse.

The bell of San Salvador began to strike the half-hour from the church belfry in the Plaza de la Iglesia behind the Cine Olimpia and the Plaza José Antonio Primo de Rivera. Catchpole heaved a mighty sigh.

From the dim recesses of the bar the rheumy-eyed Ancient of Days on the Fundador poster caught and held my eye. He grasped a shot of Fundador in one wormy-veined hand, squatted patiently there, more like an advertisement for coronary thrombosis than a brand of Cognac. What was the free hand doing with the beard? His monumental aspect was so fixed and graven he might have been cast in stone; Moses, lifting up the Tablets of the Law, when in fact he was only raising a glass of mediocre brandy. An up-ended dummy iguana clung to the wall behind Antonio.

'Just the day for ordering up a carriage for a jaunt to the woods,' Catchpole murmured. 'Paris in the autumn and a fiacre to the Bois! Antonia, *chéri*, *tiene* Ricard or Pernod or better still absinthe that makes the heart grow fonder? Goodness' (this to me) 'those Valentino eyelashes slay me.'

Antonio shrugged his beefy shoulders quite in the Gallic way to show that he didn't give a toss one way or another as he splashed out more lethal doses of Larios gin rough as ammonia into our glasses, thrust out his chin at the street to indicate that a passer-by known to us was passing by.

'*Tu amigo.*'

From the narrow portage came the demented call, followed by an all-too-familiar whinny.

'Cocksuckers!'

Poole.

The remittance man had us spotted at the bar counter with mid-morn drinks in our fists, topers after his own drinksodden heart. The demented laughter faded away down the Puerto del Mar, merrily as Dixieland jazz or the snows of yesteryear. Merrily. Merrily.

III

Helsingør Station

Matterly Light

In Denmark every day is different; so say the old books. It's made up of islands, every island different, and a witch on each. There are over 300 of them. I knew one of them once. She lived in Copenhagen, that port up there on Kattegat. We were fire and water, like Kafka and Milena, a daring combination only for people who believe in transformations, or like boiling water. You were Mathilda de la Mole.

No, you were you to the end of your days. Why should I complain? The other day I was thinking of you.

The pale Swedish dramatist who lives over on Sortedam Dossering with a distinguished Danish theatrical lady claims that he has learnt Danish in bed. Across the long wall of the Kommune Hospital a solicitous female hand had inscribed a proclamation to the effect that many of the nurses there are lesbian, too. Ten years ago the nurses of this city were regarded as being no better than common whores.

Down there in a basement you had lived like a rat with good old Psycho, in a lice-ridden hole below street level

229

in a kind of cellar, the walls green with mould. Water dripped from above, you suffered, Petrusjka was but a babe. The place was full of furnace fumes by day, rats ran about at night, chewed up your stockings. Drunks fell down into the area. You lived there then. I didn't know you. Where was I?

This Danish capital is a tidy well-run place. The little grey city is relatively free of the subversive aerosol squirt and graffiti-smeared walls of West Berlin; though the pedestrian underpass near Bar Lustig is marked with a daring axiom to the effect that *Kusse er godt for hodet* or cunt is good for the head, with a crude heart pierced by an arrow.

You wrapped newspapers inside your clothes, crouched behind Psycho Kaare, your arms about him, bound for Sweden. That was your life then. All the associations with your lovers seem to have been pre-ordained, moving rapidly towards consummation. He was the third man in your life. Blind in one eye, 192 centimetres tall, a failed dramatist turned carpenter, transvestite, father-to-be of little Petrusjka Kaare.

You lied to the shop-girls. The outsize dresses were not for 'a big mum', but for Psycho, wanting the impossible, garbed in female attire, ill, unshaven, chain-smoking, drinking Luksus beer, looking out the window into the street of whores. There was a strange smell off his breath. Both of you were undernourished, half starving. You left him, lived with an alcoholic pianist for three weeks. Then you couldn't stand it any more – there was an even worse smell off *him*. Empty turps bottles crowded the WC. You swallowed your pride and approached your mother for a loan. Mrs Edith Olsen gave it grudgingly. You returned to Psycho, the tall unshaven figure in the chair, dressed as a woman, looking out the window.

Then you were standing for an endless time with your

hand on the red Polish kettle that was getting warmer and warmer; knowing that an important moment had arrived for you. You would go to bed with him. He would be the father of your only child. So nothing is ever entirely wasted, nothing ever entirely spent. Something always remains. What? Shall I tell you?

Oh he was a young man once, and very thin. He knew Sweden, had been there before. He arranged the papers for renting a house. It was cheap there then. He was writing one-act plays, a mixture of Dada and Monty Python. They were funny. He sat cross-legged on a chair, typing away, laughing. As a child he had done homework with frozen feet stuck to the cold floor. The Royal Theatre rejected the plays. You loved him. Light came from his face. He was young once; not any more. In his early forties he had begun to grow old. Now he is a dead man.

The motorbike, covered in sacks, hid under snow. All the boards in the hut creaked. Winter pressed down on the roof. In the *dacha*, you and Psycho began starving again. A plump partridge strutted up and down in the garden every evening. Each evening it returned. Armed with a stick Psycho waited behind a tree. You watched from the window. The bird was too clever, Psycho too weak with hunger, the cooking pot stayed empty. You wept.

Then Psycho couldn't stand it any longer and left for Copenhagen, the cellar and the rats. He couldn't take it any longer. You couldn't bear to return and stayed on. You were alone for weeks, made a fire at night, to keep off the living men, and the dead men too. The dead were full of guile and slippery as eels.

Going into Sweden on the back of Psycho's motorbike you had almost died of cold. Motorcyclists are known to experience a sense of detachment, and *may not even recall arriving at their destination*. St Brendan the Navigator saw

Judas chained to an iceberg in the middle of the Atlantic. It happened once a year, by God's mercy, a day's relief for the betrayer from his prison in the everlasting fires of Hell.

But you accepted all the buffetings of fate. You walked into the forest. You said: 'It's difficult to think in a forest. I am thinking *av karse*, but the thought never finds its end, as near the mountains or by the sea. It's heavy in there, the wall of trees keeps out the sun. There is absolute silence in a Swedish forest, no singing birds there. Even the *uuuls* are silent. Oh that was a miss for me.'

In the forest you came face to face with an elk. The great prehistoric head was suddenly there, the mighty span of horns, the mossy tines, set like an ancient plough into the weighty head. You glared, separated by only the breadth of a bedroom. The great beast was grey all over, like a certain type of small Spanish wild flower found in the hills. The dead flower in the jar of the Cómpeta bedroom.

Then, without a sound, without breaking a twig, the elk faded away into the forest. It was very quiet there. Heavy too, like the Swedes themselves. They worked all day, raced home in identical Volvos in the evening, closed their doors. It was a *Shakespearean* forest, you thought, with no dead leaves, no undergrowth, but mossy underfoot. The light there was very dim, angled in, then draining away. *Matterly light*, you thought. Elks moved always in 'matterly light', fading back into the silence out of which they had come. The Swedish-Shakespearean wilderness.

Perhaps the best idea is to imagine a country, never going there. Otherwise you end up writing impressionistic letters from abroad, while feeling superior to those who stayed at home.

We were in Spain, in a *pueblo* in the sierras. It was raining. Outside, a narrow wet street of glistening umbrellas. We sat in a window annexe, waited an hour for a poor meal. You didn't mind, drinking *vino*, telling me about your flat, where I had never been. You described it. The Russian icon with the bullet-hole. It had been torn from a Moscow wall during the Revolution. You described the delicate colours of a Chinese scroll. The pewter candlestick of 1840 with a lump of lead soldered into it, making it less valuable. Your apartment overlooked the lake. Your landlady was unhinged. From a ground-floor window she watched you come and go, wanted to get you out. You rode a tall old bike. Psycho worked as a self-employed carpenter above the brothel quarter.

'I always talk in showers,' you said, 'and then I am sad.' Your green eyes, as if never seeing clearly what they looked at, looked at me, took me in. Who was this? You seemed to be chewing on memories of other times, places, situations, other loves. You travelled about, to Venice, the Scilly Isles, Greece, finally Spain, where I was to meet you. At Naxos you saw the seabed of the most delicate character, and 'there the finest sands I have ever seen'. In Tripoli, of all places, you found timelessness. You felt at home there in its endless evenings, far from the Western mess.

Pastel was your favourite shade. The long evenings on Naxos, where you had mourned a lost love, were pastel coloured. Not mauve, not lilac, nor scarlet as on the Algarve. You, Misery's Mistress, grown beautiful, in sunglasses, walked through pastel shades. The 'Greekish' men chased scantily clad foreign women into the sea or through the pine woods. Hippies copulated in the most public places. On the beach, in the backs of crowded buses.

You told me of your first love. It wasn't really love. His name had been Olsen too, a married man. You went to bed with him in Olsen's Hotel because he had spoken lovingly to you of his wife, then in childbed. You were on a cycling trip with your plain friend Alice. You were sixteen, become attractive after endless puberty. It was Easter 1958 at Holbæk, sixty kilometres from Copenhagen. Hymns were relayed from a loudspeaker into the square. You ordered Tuborg, an orange juice for Alice. You wore jeans and an anorak, a late developer, flat-chested. You entered the men's toilet by mistake after the Tuborg and came out whistling to hide your embarrassment. 'I thought it were a boy,' remarked a rustic.

Bjørn Olsen was a commercial traveller in perfumes. He was kind. At first you said no and then yes. You were shocked by the size of his prick. This was serious stuff. But it wasn't love.

You were nineteen in the country, the plainness of puberty gone. You spent a weekend with a couple of friends and ended up in bed with them. Andersen the painter was 'insatiable and fucked all the good-looking girls'. He wanted you in bed with his beautiful redheaded wife. First her and then you. Andersen would not take no. The whole house creaked.

You tried to take your life by opening a vein in your wrist with the point of a pencil. It had nothing to do with Andersen, you didn't want to live, had nothing to live for, you opened the vein, closed your eyes, covering yourself with your overcoat.

'But, as you see, I recovered. Afterwards you feel worse than before. I felt so ashamed. You are still alive and the bed soaked with blood.'

Things will never be the same again. No, things are the

same as they always were, only you're the same too, so
things will never be the same again. I say things but I may
mean times and places. Times with you. Is the memory
of things better than the things themselves? We will never
know. But no matter what happens I still love you very
much, though obviously in my life 'love' has to be
betrayed, and many times. I do not know why this is so. I
only know I am relieved to have finished, yet in a perverse
way I'm still the same, and nothing has changed.

In a stand of oak a leaf falls. Queen Caroline Mathilde,
dressed as a man, goes out riding. She is on the lookout
for the son of the German cobbler Struensee with whom
she is besotted. He enjoys her favours, in between advising
the king – and who is himself insane and knows full well
that the queen's condition is incurable.

We stayed in a hotel in Málaga, coming and going like
marine creatures in a grotto of transparent water, in the
depths of the fine old mirrors set into the doors of two
hanging cupboards in room *número* 37 on the fourth floor
of Hotel Residencia Cataluña on Plaza del Obispo facing
the cathedral. The gonging bell galvanised us at every
stroke. At the corner some stonemasons were chipping
away tirelessly at tombstones, covered in fine white dust.

You told me of Diana's mirrors, Nero's sunken brothel-
ship. We went out. You found it was cold and returned for
your poncho. The lift attendant asked were you married. I
bought a small hand mirror for Petrusjka, whom I had
never seen. I told you about the red spot on Jupiter. When
daylight struck the bevelled edges, the mirrors threw out
rainbow hues. We came and went in them, nude as newts,
as in a deep-focus medium shot thrown on the black-and-
white screen by Toland. They were fine old-fashioned
mirrors such as you do not come across today. Whatever
has happened to those far-off happy days? Were they

happy days? Was being with you happiness for me? And
with me for you? Were we happy then?

One morning you said it was beginning to end, you
could feel it. You had to go away again. The return flight
was booked. The stonemasons continued chipping away,
covered in fine dust, as we went past for the last time.
Málaga was Yo-Yo mad. It was the day of the *Subnormales*.
A child dressed up as a bride was being photographed in
the Alameda Gardens as we passed through, climbing up
though the levels of the Alcazaba, past the cruising gays
anxious as whippets. Below appeared the bullring, the
sanded oval, tiers of empty seats; beyond it the port. A
long rusty Soviet oil tanker lay to in the dazzling bay.
Covered in sweat we climbed to the Hotel Gibralfaro,
which belongs to another European time. Maids in black
taffeta were waiting at table. I was charged 400 pesetas
for a half-bottle of chilled Valdepeñas. Over by the bar
stood von Stroheim, the great director of *Greed*, with his
back to us, in riding-breeches, whip under one arm, a
monocle screwed into one eye-socket, throwing back
double Scotch. We returned to our room late.

A seal-like hooded statue of Rasmussen in stone stands
on the Strandvej promenade, a memorial to the hero of
Thule. We walked hand in hand down the promenade,
which was the length of your own childhood. To our left
the seal-like hooded figure stared out towards Kattegat.
An ever-alert eye peered out under bushy eyebrows stiff
with hoar-frost. We took a number 1 bus to Central
Station, and walked out from there. You said you wanted
to show me places from your past. We presently found
one and went in. It was full of Danes. A pianist crouched
over the keyboard and sang like a woman, high and
mocking. Then a burly friend from the past came in,
embraced you. He sat at the piano, began to play. It was

part of the past when you had lived like a rat with good old Psycho. Someone had tried to cook their semen in a frying-pan. Perhaps the pianist?

Danish was very much a language of the stomach, you told me. *Mave* had a 'stomach-sound', as Mogens Glistrup was a most Danish name, Danish as Trudholm. 'Everything is dangerous to a Dane.' By Thulevej a signpost above a small cliff, more chine than cliff, warns wanderers of *livsfare jordskred*, unsteady earth.

Your apartment did not disappoint. It was the sort of nest you would find to live in, irregular in shape, with windows overlooking the lake. Your abode. I was there with you. The last swallows flew over the yacht basin and a skiff with two active oarsmen went skimming by. It was a bright September Sunday. Light scudded off the water, the clouds drifted high up.

You had read Walter Schubart's *Religion og Erotik* in translation and were full of it, spoke slightingly of St Paul, convert and martyr. He whom you called Paulus of Tarsus had 'fucked up' the teachings of Christ and changed Christendom.

And then? The wind threshing the hedges at Melby. A blue crossing over Kattegat (for we were *en route* for Rørvig). Six passengers sat silently in the narrow cabin as we crossed a thoroughly Danish sea to Skanse Hage. In the *fiskhus* the flounders caught that morning at Isefjord were breathing their last.

In the *bodega* at Hundested, that Place of Dogs, the recorded voice of Kathleen Ferrier sang 'Jesu, Joy of Man's Desiring' on the muted transistor. You had sung this at the top of your voice as a child, standing on a chair, to the astonishment of Papa Olsen, who played a cornet from the back of a truck with his group on Labour Day. In the yard an outsize dog frisked about our table. From another table an unsober Dane asked you:

'Why don't you come over and sit with us, and tell that fellow to go back to wherever he came from?'

And now we are approaching the Rasmussenhus. The signs have become vague and weathered; we are nearing the homestead of the hero of Thule. The dormer windows overlook Kattegat. He had built the house with his own hands. Before entering these hallowed precincts I enter you near the cliff face in the long grass, removing the minimum of clothes. We hear Danish voices passing amicably through the hidden paths.

He died in hospital outside Copenhagen in 1934, when I was seven years old and you not yet born. He died of flu and eating rotten seal-meat. He was fifty-four. His rare windswept spirit abides at Thulevej, in the Rasmussenhus set back among fir trees, protected from the elements. It looks out always at Kattegat's tides, sails, gulls, swans, the air and peace. His kayak hangs from a beam. His hunting-spears are there. A great pot-bellied stove occupies the study where he wrote up his diary, where a large white cat followed us silently from room to room.

LEV LESBISK is painted prominently athwart the bridge approaches at Peblingessen. For fine young women live husbandless today in Denmark, with single children secure in carriers, cycling home from Klampenborg. The young mothers are turning their backs on menfolk, or marriage. Venus (Lesbia) rules hereabouts.

In the little red train that takes us to Hundested from Hillerød, a woman no longer young is immersed in her book. The deliberating eyes are fixed steadfastly on the text, her slow right hand turns another page, as we move through this ordered countryside. A lynx-faced cat mews miserably in a basket. A drunk raises a Hof beer on a passing platform. The head of the cat is pushed out of sight by an abstracted female hand. Single dogs go prowling in the fields so bare of livestock or any living thing. Even bird life is missing. The wheat stubble is burning, scarring the fields with long black lines. The windbreaks are odd-looking things, if they are windbreaks. What else could they be?

Last spring we passed Kokkedal's cut hayfields. The dry hay was lying in neat swaths. Mown wheat. Cyclists drifted alongside the train, waving, thoroughly Danish, as the train traversed a region of lilac woods.

Now Vedbæk, Rungstedlund where Baroness Blixen lies buried under her favourite tree; the Danish poets give Sunday readings there. We sat at a table under a tree at Humlebæk, coffee and Cognac before us, looked across at the white Swedish shore: a nuclear plant.

Thobin Thimm

It is an early September day in Copenhagen, sunny after yesterday's rain. Over Øster Søgade the mews make their cries of secateurs cutting. It's seventeen feet deep in the middle and thus cannot be man-made, says the Swedish dramatist. Trust a Swede to notice that.

Handsome jogging couples pass in jogging outfits. Drained with fever I sleep. You nurse me. Plain yoghurt, purple grapes, chilled Rioja. For review comes *Wise Blood*. Sandra Holm arrives late and covers the bed in flowers. She is a little bull. I have some kind of virus. My temperature is 'midway between normal and where you die', the nurse tells me, studying the thermometer. I spend three days in bed.

Then, after washing off the death-sweat, I sally forth, feeling frail, unshaven. Into the thin sunlight, the *Kondilovers* go by, one attached to a dog on a lead. Muddy carp-like fish hang comatose in the shallow brown waters by the footpaths. The bomb shelters are overgrown. In the middle of the lake a small islet is covered in vegetation. In the garden of Bar Lustig a boy sells us grapes. It is autumn now in Denmark, the air cold and bracing. The foliage hangs stiffly. I feel unwell. Cyclists drift by. A crab-red sun sinks over the pseudo-bridge, a causeway for ingoing and outgoing traffic. The sky is clear as yesterday. Music drifts over the water. Though unwell, I feel irrationally happy, *feverishly* so. Green neon from the Finansbanken spills into Øster Søgade lake. Ambulance sirens sound off incessantly between the two hospitals. Danish dead are being hustled in and out.

Four white dray horses pull a Carlsberg wagon over the 'bridge', out of the past. A municipal cleaner in orange Day-Glo sweeps the path. The rush of air from fast cars – angelic wings. I start into a second American title: *Everything That Rises Must Converge*. Feeble things. My fever returns.

It has all come back: coughing, lemon drinks, bed-sweats, dry throat. The nude nurse is in bed with the feverish patient clasped in her arms. An enlarged harvest moon sinks over the pseudo-bridge. Traffic lights wink and blink like mooring lights lost in the trees. Tiny Bodini has no peace because of the magnitude of his task. You told me that your grandmother's name had been Lemm, which signifies Prick. She was Pomeranian, made good soups. So you had Hungarian-Pomeranian blood coursing in your veins.

You sat on the sofa, crossed your long stylish legs, stared at me. No one could have guessed what was in that grey-green look, even I did not know. You dialled a number, listened, replaced the receiver. Your transistor played low. Now you are stalking about before the long mirror, dressed only in Italian shoes with five-inch stiletto heels. You are 'paying the world a gleaming lie'.

Italians applaud at the end of every movement, I tell you. Danes slow-clap to show their appreciation. If the English do it it means the opposite, censure. The Chinese are fond of noise and find silence oppressive. Similarly Greeks and Spaniards. Not so the Danes, you say, rolling your hips at me.

Then, lo and behold, I am well again. An old flame arrives from Jutland. Thobin Thimm is a painter, he and his sister run a rose farm in Jutland. He invites us to dine with him at a new Italian place. Shape of the frog in the sauce. Grapy flavour of Italian wine, tang of the cheese. Petrusjka sits with us, a lady.

I stood you a haircut at Frisør Kirsten's near the Gyldne And or Golden Duck. Kirsten herself cut our hair; she dressed in black leather trousers, her hips bulged seductively as she snipped away with small scissors, and your slanted eyes watched me in the mirror. Thimm had gone to bed with Kirsten Arboll. She had lived in Johannesburg, thought that the blacks had not much to complain about. The sun shone through the glass annexe of the Gyldne. And where we drank gin. A numbing wind from Østersøen was sweeping the streets clean. Lutheran bells rang grudgingly in their belfries.

Dyrehaven was a woody place where few people went, with mole-casts between the trees and in the open, where there were low mounds. Baroness Blixen used to walk there. 'A life of sniffing and sleeping and fear,' you said, of the moles. 'What sort of existence was that?' Thobin had departed to Jutland.

Then, one evening, the 'handsome painter chap' Thimm appeared again. He had loved you once, perhaps loved you still. I was just stepping up out of the Chinese takeaway when he emerged out of the snow-mist. His overcoat worn as a cloak, arms outstretched after the manner of Count Dracula, his breath steaming. The three of us went to a candlelit bar below street level and drank double Jameson.

One night we (you and I) drank in the *bodega* opposite the Gyldne And until four in the morning and were presented with an almost Swedish bill. You downfaced the rude barman. Your eyes flashed; the cheeky fellow muttered something indistinct; you called out something devastating. The barman wiped his hands on a dirty apron tied about his waist.

There sat Old Fröde the mythical one, a sad man searching for some security and not finding it. You spoke to him.

On the way home I addressed a quiet man who sat on a doorstep with a bottle of beer by him, staring out at the lake. He answered by addressing you in Danish. What had he said? Why not tell your friend to go home.

The days were freezing now. The city prepared for winter. We bought fresh vegetables in the market and fish at the fishmongers, going down a few steps off the street. If a certain window was open in a certain square it meant that an elderly male friend was at home. But the window always remained closed.

Young rollerbladers on roller-skates, dressed in combat fatigues and leg-warmers, shot through Jorcks Passage.

That time, that place, was it all your own invention, that you shared with me? And I too perhaps was your invention, and the goings-on in that oddly shaped apartment, the patent-leather black court shoes, the Greek–English dictionary – *Zina Skarum 20 Lektioner* – a bowl of Greek pebbles, a narrow bottle containing stones from the Naxos foreshore, a book on Crete (*Kreta: Tegninger og Madstage*), a vase of white tulips, strangely shaped Israeli oranges. The muted telephone whispering, the mews flying over Øster Søgade, the icy air outside, the grey lake. Petrolio was 30 kroner for ten litres, and a northern winter coming on, Fimbal and Old Fröde went limping through the snow.

You ordered up a double mattress, trade name Sultan, and argued hotly with the manufacturers over delivery. Then one freezing morning the pantechnicon appeared below, the driver calling up for help. It took three of us to get Sultan into place.

Another morning and another fellow arrived with a bottle of some herbal concoction, good for the digestion. Witch-piss you said it was. The stove went cold again for the second time in one week. We drank the witch-piss under duvet covers, listening to the gull-squall and mew-cry outside. The stove was out, the nights bitterly cold. Every day was different. One Saturday, *Politiken* published a poem of yours that began 'Erotisk... lethed', with a photograph of you in a Phrygian wool cap, looking sultry.

Clouds drifted through the September sky as we walked again through Dyrehaven to the hermitage on the hill. The unwalled, unguarded mansion amid a copse of beech was where the widows of dead Danish kings lived out their retirement. No moat or castle keep separated it from citizens who passed on foot, or horse-riders and pony-trekkers.

A stag was bellowing to its herd of wives near Tre Pile Stedet, or The Three Twigs, where a dumpy sweet-faced woman served you coffee and me red wine, calling out for 'Matthew' in an accent that you swore was Bornholm. We sat at a table outside. There you had come as a child with your parents. There you had sat as a child, heard the warning bell at the level crossing, saw the little red train rush through. Heard the hoarse stage-bellow at rutting time, felt the air move. There you were young once, an 'innocent'.

In the flower shop run by your stepfather-in-law, a retired sea-captain now working as a pimp for male prostitutes, you told a long witty story in Danish, and the pimp shook all over, wiping his eyes.

Copenhagen is a city of uneasy old people, who stay indoors, live on cat food and dog food, rarely venture out, hesitating at street corners, fearful of the wild young, the nudist park, the drug scene. The young are not much in evidence except by night in Central Station, bumming kroner for more beer, collapsing across loaded tables.

City of phantoms, of tired faces, of sailors on shore leave. Or German students returning from a trip around the harbour. The Master Race, you said, were still after the little Danish butter-hole. Granite port of *Belge brote, somner platte, frikadeller.* Sing-song musical voices.

The sleepy Danes are modest in a reserved way; reserve with them being a form of arrogance. Public displays of anger only amuse them. The music in the bars is muted. In the San Miguel Bar the flamenco music was turned down. There is not too much laughter or high spirits in evidence. These drably dressed citizens of the north are warmly bundled into their lives. Babes with chronically disgruntled old faces peer critically from hooded prams. Headscarves are favoured by the young mothers who move about on high antiquated bikes. The long *allées* open like yawns.

Elderly couples walk soberly in lime-green *Lodens* through the King's Gardens. The males wear pork-pie hats and puff cigars, the tubby wives go sedately in warm little hats with feathers, and a dog on a lead as like as not. The feeling is of sedate bourgeois Germans in a German provincial town, but don't tell that to a Dane.

Flagstaffs are a feature of the island of Rørvig. Narrow Danish house-flags get entangled in the firs. The cellar under your far-sighted father's floorboards yielded up

good home-made schnapps made from herbs, very
potent. We dismantled two single beds and spread mat-
tresses on the floor. And then went cycling on high old
bikes – pedal backwards to stop – from Helleveg, the way
to the sea. A three-masted schooner appeared out of the
haze, and a swan flew overhead, sawing the air creakily,
as I took you in the dunes, in the cold, still feverish.

One day I went by train on my own to Kronborg, to
see the castle where Hamlet had 'run around after the
ghost of his father'. There is nothing much to see at
Elsinore. Shakespeare had heard about it from his friend
John Dowland. A Swedish passenger craft big as a street
seemed to be dragging the houses down along the
harbour. Minute passengers crossed over by a glassed-in
overpass to Helsingør Station.

An ashen-faced invalid in a belted raincoat, moving
with pain on two arm-crutches, his mouth set in a grim
line, closed the window. So much for fresh air. Now all
the windows were sealed tight, an Airedale stinking, no
air all the way to Østerport!

I had some words of German, some words of Spanish,
but of Danish nothing but *Skaak!* and felt a right Charley
in the shops where no English was spoken, going out in
the cold morning, skinned alive at the corner by the
North Sea wind, leaving you and little Petrusjka together
on Sultan under the duvet, two pairs of brown eyes
watching me from the warmth, I descending steps into
the bakery, tore a ticket from the dispenser, waited for
my number to be called. But what did '17' sound like in
Danish?

Your language sounds more far-off than it is, its pronun-
ciation being far removed from any known thing, to my
ears at least. Your misnomers were charming: 'artist's
cocks' (artichokes); 'corny cobs' (corncobs); 'upflung
waters' (fountains); 'downburnt buildings' (blitzed

London); 'ox' (braised beef); 'outsplashed ladies' (the nude models of Delacroix, with their 'fleshful thighs').

'I am uproared,' you said, meaning miffed. 'Moistful,' you said. 'I'd jump into bed with Olaf Palme.' You left *postillons d'amour* lying around. 'Sweetheart – gone for a little walk. The lunch is set for tomorrow instead of today. Kisses – home again soon. Nanna.'

'I look into the mirror sometimes and don't believe what I see' (watching yourself narrowly in the glass). 'I think it's funny to pay the world a gleaming lie' (applying make-up but no lipstick, no scent, no earrings; the scentless perfume was 'Ancient Moose'). Much will have more.

Do you know why witches fly?

You prepared the 'squints' (squids) Bilbao style in their own ink, following the instructions. Pull the heads off the squids from the bodies and remove and discard the spines and all the internal organs except the ink sacs, which must be put into a cup and reserved. Cut off the testicles just below the eyes and discard the heads. Wash thoroughly. *Calamares en su tinta a la bilbaína.*

Conkers split on the cobbles under the chestnut trees near the yacht basin where the 'damned' Little Mermaid poses so coyly naked on her bronze seat on a boulder there, and a plain girl in a loose-fitting blue T-shirt displays big wobbly breasts as she goes laughing by with her pretty friend, and a company of Danish soldiers in sharp uniforms, with long hair and rifles at the port position, go marching by the Lutheran church where your model friend Sweet Anna was wedded to Strong Sven, the translator of Marquez. It was snowing then. Mr Fimbal the Danish god of hard winters stumbled by with his single arm.

We passed again by a group of stone women all stark naked in stone, tending one who appeared to be injured or in the toils of childbirth.

'What is this?' I asked.
'The Jewish Memorial.'

Professor Tribini, top-hatted and villainously musta-
chioed, sporting a red carnation in his buttonhole,
flashed his gallant ringmaster's eyes at you, all fire and
sexual push, at Peter Liep's in Beaulieu, where the railway
tracks lead back to Centrum.

Bakken had come before the Tivoli Gardens, you told
me. Here was the real rough stuff – sailors on the spree,
big strong girls wrestling stark naked in mud. It was
slightly before your time.

You had been at a Gyldendal party there, had trouble
opening a sealed pat of butter, your dinner partner did
it for you. You took him home with you on condition that
you rode his tall new bicycle. With skirt rolled about your
hips and 'brown all over' and at your most attractive after
Naxos, you took him home. It was a time I would never
know. You rode slowly home, his hand on the small of
your back, through the pre-dawn at Bakken, down the
long avenue of trees where we had walked, watched by
Professor Tribini, abusing himself behind an oak.

'Oh, I am over-lewd!'
'I was somewhat exalterated,' you said.

You served up an excellent Hungarian soup with sour
cream and told me your radio story of Satan in the wood,
based on a real lecher, my successor after the time in
Spain. You sat opposite me, giving me the eye. You'd
certainly been at the Cognac again, a couple of snorters
before setting out.

We were in Spain again. You had been going on about
'Paulus of Tarsus'. We were in an olive grove below the
logging trail and heard the damnedest noise rising up
out of the valley, a strange inconstant murmurous belling,
bleating and baaing.

Some time later, over a drink at Viento de Palmas, a herd of over a thousand shorn sheep and lambs went tripping past, with active dogs as outriders and rough-looking shepherds bringing up the rear. The din was stirring – bells, barking, baaing. The shepherds did not stop for drinks, heading on for new pastures.

Now freezing air leaks into the kitchen and you turn the gas low, open the oven door, light candles. The water in the lavatory bowl becomes agitated, as if we were at sea. Sudden gusts of winter air strike through the interstices of the cramped toilet and the floor seems to shift underfoot. The Danes were all secret sailors, you said.

The spiritual suffering of the Swedes (which knows no bounds) is said to be unmatched in any other European country, their suicide rate the highest in the world. By the end of the first quarter of the next century all Sweden would be in the custody of a few large companies, the sameness of Swedish life then complete.

We passed the Jewish Memorial again, the naked women bound together in lumpish humanitarianism. And once your dotty landlady Mrs Andersen passed us on her witch's black bike, sending a hostile look our way.

I write down the magic names:

ØSTERPORT	ØSTER SØGADE	ORDRUP
HUMBLEBÆK	HELLERUP	HUNDESTED
KLAMPENBORG	KOKKEDAL	KASTRUP
KRONBORG	SKODSBORG	VEDBÆK
BEAULIEU	RØRVIG	BAKKEN
NIVÅ	ESPERGÆRDE	RUNGSTEDLUND
DYREHAVEN	HELSINGØR	MELBY

In Denmark every day is different; so the old books say. Blow out the light.

Sodden Fields

1927
Earliest Misgiving; the March of the Cadavers

Is it the sole, that strange denizen of the deep, a lurker on seabeds, that (out of curiosity about the hook) *catches itself?* Unless I am confusing sole with plaice, or monk, or flounder.

Be that as it may, I was born on the third day of March in the year 1927 in the old Barony of Salt in the County Kildare in the Province of Leinster, of lapsed Catholic parents since deceased, under the watery astrological sign of Pisces.

A fresh westerly airstream covered most areas while a frontal trough of low pressure remained stationary over Ireland but seemed about ready to move eastward.

Conceived at the tail-end of an early June day, in the Year of Grace 1926, I was expelled the following 3 March, passing over into 1927 puffing and choking with mouth half open, the cold without being so intense, well nigh irresistible the compulsion to sink back into the warmer uterine depths with a bubbling groan.

Hearing faraway music, moody themes from the good-times-gone: Albinoni's now-famous *Adagio* or a Debussy *Arabesque* played on the harp. Not yet the wild nocturnal bagpipe music and the night wind tipping the pans of the weighing-scales as they filled with rainwater on the bedroom windowsill of a bungalow in Emor Street just off the South Circular Road in the so-called Liberties in the city of Dublin. This would be in the late seventies when I was the ill-dressed recipient of a most welcome cheque for $7,000 from the American-Irish Foundation – Kennedy bad-conscience money paid out on sole condition that I reside for ten months in my erstwhile homeland, which I had not been in a position to afford since leaving it twenty-five years before.

A group of young lady harpists from New York, all of surpassing comeliness, were entertaining the American ambassador, Mr Shannon, and his lovely wife and their selected guests after lunch in the US representative's fine residence in the Phoenix Park. A herd of grazing deer was visible through the elegant long windows as Ambassador Shannon, bald as a coot though a decade younger than the shabby recipient, handed over a sealed envelope. Held in close-up for Irish television viewers to admire, it was seen to be clearly addressed to Seamus Heaney, the previous year's winner.

· I had just turned fifty.

All this by way of preamble. Nothing is too clear, of its nature, least of all the limpidities of language, the particles of which must be 'clear as sand'. The strange phosphorus of life, nameless under the old misappellation.

I tell you a thing. I could tell it otherwise. A few pictures emerge into the light from the shadows within me. I consider them. Quite often they fail to please me. I call them 'pictures' but you, kind readers, ideal readers suffering from an ideal insomnia, must know otherwise. What I mean to convey is: *movements from the past.*

So, putting as bold a face on it as I could under the circumstances, out I crawled yelling blue bloody murder, roughly handled by a wet-nurse from Cavan.

Why, there are days when we do not know ourselves, when we do not properly belong to ourselves, as children know to their cost. Assailed by mysterious sundowns and gory red endings of days: the extraordinary clarity of the nocturnal firmament burning above the little pier on Annaghvaughan and the unmilked cattle bawling in descant. Then out went the candle and we were left darkling. Breathe in, breathe out. In the memory of old men it's always June. But were the summers of my childhood as sunny as I seem to recall?

In that Year of Our Lord nineteen hundred and twenty-seven, Coole Park was taken over by the Land and Forestry Commission in County Galway. In America, at Bridgewater Penitentiary, Sacco and Vanzetti walked to the electric chair. Flying out over the Atlantic in the dark, the intrepid Colonel Lindbergh landed near Paris in the dark. In Berlin the ageing lecher Frank Harris was lecturing on Shakespeare. Kevin O'Higgins, our first diplomat, returning home from Mass, was murdered outside his own front gate. In a public ward of St Patrick Dun's Hospital in Dublin, the Countess Markiewicz died of peritonitis. Long insane and widowed sixty years, the Empress Carlotta passed away quietly in Belgium.

The lost *mediodesorientado* Hugo von Hofmannsthal would soon die in Vienna. In Paris the long-demented Baroness Elsa von Freytag-Loringhoven gassed herself, the Baron having taken his own life just before the outbreak of the Great War. In Paris the American novelist Djuna Barnes with her lover Thelma Wood, the silverpoint artist from Missouri, were looking after the richly left Natalie Clifford Barney's garden in the rue Jacob, a patch of earth that had formerly belonged to Racine. Tea and special little cakes were served up there in the temple dating from just before the French Revolution; tall Thelma the infected carrier of the past, the born *somnambule*, the bitch of all time, turning up as 'Robin Vote' in the 1936 novel *Nightwood*; Djuna Barnes was 'Nora Flood'. Their anguished avatars were quarrelling in the apartment with the wooden horse and heavy liturgical decorations, the ill-fitting purple dress and shapeless Napoleonic hat, on the fifth floor of number 9 rue St-Romain, going out to get thoroughly pickled at the Flore.

It was the year that Alice Prin (Kiki of Montparnasse), the mistress of Man Ray the Dada artist and photographer, had an exhibition of her paintings at Galerie du Sacre du Printemps.

While from Kenosha, a town on Lake Michigan on the Wisconsin shore, Richard Ives Welles was committed by his father into Kankakee State Hospital. Stuttering Dick had been the laughing-stock of the Kenosha cornerboys. In Cuba that summer his precociously gifted younger brother George Orson was on vacation with his guardian, the shifty Dr Bernstein.

All this occurred in 1927, the year of the long count in the Dempsey–Tunney world heavyweight fight, the year when de Valera began the even longer *völkisch* reign of Fianna Fáil. Hand in glove with the cultural nationalism proper to those peerless warriors of yore: our own elite dead long gone to their reward, the Fianna Eireann.

In 1927, a year after the first staging of Sean O'Casey's play *The Plough and the Stars*, the playwright married Eileen Reynolds, a pretty actress twenty-three years younger than himself.

Do you hear me now?

Are we not all somebody's rearing in the wretched bric-à-brac and rigmarole of history, of which our life may be assigned some part, however minor, if only as passive bystander?

In that Year of Grace 1927, Sylvia Townsend Warner's novel *Mr Fortune's Maggot* came out in London. Vipers appear, earthworms engender, forward turnips rot and toads crawl forth every year in March. 'It is the period *just before oneself*, the period of which in earliest days one knew the actual survivors, that really lays a strong hand upon one's heart.' I must have read it somewhere.

In 1927 young Clarence Malcolm Lowry was homeward bound aboard the SS *Pyrrhus* from the Far East with a mixed cargo of wild beasts and crawling reptiles, an elephant, five black panthers, ten snakes, a wild boar, all trapped in the Straits Settlements and now consigned to lifelong captivity in the Dublin Zoo, to be cared for by Superintendent Flood. Where presently, shivering all over like a dog, I would be lifted up by my nanny, in order to offer a banana to Lowry's elephant, or rather to a long, feeling, prehensile trunk that blew on me a gust of wildness, unknown terrain, swamps, a scorching sun. Taken by Nanny to see the wild animals, I was struck by the untamed sulphurous stink of the lion house, hardly less by the rude monkey house, the elephant house, the giraffe house. Cracked semi-human voices spoke out from the fidgety macaws in the parrot house, their plumage the colour of fire and blood, of red rage trapped in a hothouse, humming, lurid, obscene. These fraught excursions to the grey city with its own peculiar and (for me) disturbing smells would always end with a spell of vomiting.

'The lad's overexcited,' my parents agreed.

Henry Williamson's *Tarka the Otter* was published in

1927, to be read aloud to me by my mother some years later. Joseph-Napoléon Primoli died that year. Between receiving the Nobel Prize in 1925 and publishing *The Intelligent Woman's Guide to Socialism and Capitalism*, the spry septuagenerian and vegetarian George Bernard Shaw, social reformer and patron of the Life Force, dogmatic busybody and former vestryman and borough councillor who had several times raised the question of women's toilets for St Pancras and tried to organise a crematorium there, had turned seventy-one. Instantly recognisable everywhere thanks to his tweedy knickerbockers and long argumentative beard, he had been around since 1856, seemingly the same frail Elderly Protestant Irish Gent all his natural life. He had twenty-three more useful years of postcard-writing to total strangers, when not pottering about the garden at Ayot St Lawrence. Captious, he had an answer for everything, liked to put philosophers in their place, dined on raw vegetables, milk, hardboiled eggs. He wanted to dazzle, to confound.

In the same year America drew up secret military plans for war against Great Britain. Against Winter, chess grandmaster Capa made insolent moves standing up, hardly bothering to sit down and think.

Legend had it that grandmaster Paul Morphy died in his bath surrounded by women's shoes. It was not long before Alekhine gave up alcohol, switched to milk and trounced Dr Max Euwe (1901–81) to hold the world chess title for the next two years, a decade before *Guernica*. In Trinity College, Dublin, a Bachelor of Arts degree was conferred upon Samuel Barclay Beckett.

In 1927 King Ferdinand I of Romania, the second Hohenzollern king, died of cancer of the bowel in Bucharest. Abel Gance's epic movie *Napoléon* was released; the talkies began in Hollywood. Mícheál MacLiammóir left the Slade and joined the touring company of his brother-in-law, Anew MacMaster. In Dublin the O'Nolan family, formerly of Tyrone, moved from Herbert Place to Black-rock. Virginia Woolf's novel *To the Lighthouse* was published by the Hogarth Press. Hammond of Gloucester-shire scored a thousand runs in May, at Southampton against Hampshire.

On 6 August a London insurance clerk called Edward Harry ('Ed') Temme swam the freezing English Channel from Cap Grisnez to Lydden Spout, using the trudgeon stroke. Helen Wills Moody won the ladies' singles in the first of her record eight victories at Wimbledon. Anne Yeats, W. B.'s little daughter, put a squeaky cushion on a chair for Lady Gregory to sit upon; her ladyship was not amused.

It was the year of *la generación de 1927* in Madrid, with Lorca, Alberti, Altolaguirre, Cernude, José Bergamin and Pedro Garfias meeting to talk and foment dissension in the Café Gijon, the Granje del Henar, the Café Castilla, the Fornos, Kutz, Café de la Montaña, Café Pombo where Raymon de la Serna held court every Saturday night; Buñuel, Dali and Pepín Bello were in the Casa de Leonor, a brothel on the Calle de la Reine.

In the spring of that year, V. S. Pritchett had set out from London to walk across western Spain from Badajoz to León, a hundred-mile hike in heavy winter tweeds, on foot and alone. In Berlin the shifty Brecht, a lifelong womaniser, parted company with Marianne Brecht, née Zoll, to take up with his future wife Helene Weigel. Günter Grass was born in Danzig, hereinafter Gdansk, Poland.

In 1927 T. S. Eliot was received into the Anglo-Catholic faith at St Stephen's church opposite the Russian Orthodox Church in Exile, not far from the Round Pond in Kensington where W. B. Yeats as a boy had sailed his fancy toy yacht.

In June of that year the Woolfs had witnessed an eclipse of the sun from a moor in north Yorkshire ('The earth was dead,' Virginia recorded in her diary). The next eclipse would be in 1999.

In that year Buckminster Fuller, the Harvard man who had invented the geodesic dome, gave up earning a living, stopped talking for two years. Ernst Lubitsch made *In Old Heidelberg*, a silent movie version of Romberg's operetta *The Student Prince*. Hollywood films were shown in the stables off the cobbled courtyard at Oakley Park. My younger brother and I sucked bull's-eyes and marvelled at the G-men. The villagers craned forward on kitchen chairs, guffawed at Leon Errol.

In 1933, when I would have turned six, the Liffey flooded the village up as far as Marley Abbey. The flood came out through the open forge door and the houses seemed all set to sail away.

March 3rd in Basho's day was the Festival of the Dolls in sixteenth-century Japan: *hina matsuri*, sometimes called the Festival of Pearl Blossoms. Or simply Girls' Festival, which would suit me fine, backing into the strange withdrawn world of the fish. The Piscean twilight world of the deep fish lost, or just gone astray in the head. Is this why the light still enchants me, the hidden observer remaining a prey to the most giddy kind of guilt? But now, classic-lovers, it's diddley-diddley time once again.

Fifty was Basho's age when with failing health he began that long last marathon hike into south Japan in 1694. He was six years junior to Jane Bowles – if you'd kindly be good enough to move on three centuries – when she died in a hospital in Málaga, capital of sorrow. In a snail-bar near the brothel quarter the shabby ghost of Terry Butler of Shanganagh, never so shabby in life, failed to recognise me, darkened by tramping in the Sierra Almijara.

Who am I? Am I or am I not the same person I have always taken myself to be? In that case, who am I? Is the silence significant or just lack of something to say? Is that significant? Speak up, but kindly confine yourself to essentials; write on one side of the paper only.

Where am I? Where was I then? What do you do when memory begins to go? I spend much of the time looking back into the past. It is no longer there. It has moved. Where to?

The city certainly had changed. The Grafton Picture House was closed, turned into a bingo arcade, the ghosts in the toilet departed, the commissionaire Mr Shakespear dead. It was still raining in that most mournful thorough-fare called Aungier Street, on the offices of Fanagan the undertaker, the busiest man in Dublin.

Meanwhile, then, up in his fine new residence in Rathfarnham, Senator William Butler Yeats, impaled upon a fine idea, was just looking at his yellow canaries and saw symbols streaming. Moving to his writing-desk in a dream he seated himself, drew out his day-book, wrote in his distinguished calligraphy: 'I am a crowd. I am a lonely man. I am nothing.' Whereupon all the canaries started singing.

He did not care to name his enemies as such when corresponding with fine ladies, Irish and English, but designated them thus: The Wolf Dog, The Harp, The Shamrock, The Tower. And (rather finely) Verdis-Green Sectaries.

Senator Willie was his father's son and no two ways about it. The correspondence with his father is nothing less than heart-warming, and not something you expect in such close blood connections. James Joyce was still working on the scaffolding of the *Wake* in sinful Paris. Mr Beckett had just written: 'The sun shone, having no alternative, on the nothing new.' The sharp-faced student Brian Ó Nuallain was refusing to learn bad Irish from his professor, Douglas Hyde, later to be President of Ireland; he whom David Thomson saw crawling on all fours across a drawing room with a bar of chocolate protruding from his mouth below the walrus moustache, challenging some well-brought-up little colleens to take a bite; he too perhaps impaled upon a dream.

In Kinsale great hauls of mackerel were taken; three fish-girls sea-salting and packing per barrel, cutting and stowing the catch for the cooper to come and tack down the barrels which were then rolled along the pier.

The Wall Street Crash was imminent.

1987
Battle and Aftermath; the Beast of Ballynagrumoolia

If the wholesale slaughter that was the Battle of Kinsale finished off the rough princely world of Latinists and gallowglasses in three hours in the Ballinamona bog, had it not been lost already when McMahon sold out O'Neill in return for a bottle of the hard stuff on that miserable wet late December day 387 years ago? No?

Neap tides flooded 9,288 times into Ballymacus Creek where as a difficult young thing you liked to retire, to sulk. Our independence won with jigs and reels God knows how many church collections later, and the national flag raised jerkily aloft in mismatching shades of dandelion orange (leaves, stalk and root containing a bitter milky juice) and septic green, divided by neutral white, and complemented by a National Anthem that was never any great shakes, 'composed' by a north Dublin house painter, a bowsy by the name of Carney reputedly related to the roistering Behans.

Years later, out walking with you on another soft December day beyond the ramparts, we spotted the Beast of Ballynagrumoolia beyond a denuded winter hedge. Pale and plump, the deep-set piggish eyes red-rimmed like an anus, the flaccid cheeks soiled with mud, immemorial slobber, shit and tears. The Beast's stiff yellow hair was erupting from under nodding headgear, fore-hooves rooting in the driveway, the twin enraged nostrils aflare; while from the deep barrel chest stormily rising and subsiding came grievous sighs and the most heartfelt groans. Great sods of earth were being hurled about; an apparition as alarming as a she-gorilla enraged – the very stuff of nightmares.

Scavengers, looters and pillagers, the extreme poor of Munster arrived with the wild dogs and birds of prey to cover the battlefields now become graveyards, a thousand of O'Neill's and O'Donnell's men become shades, in an unforgettable day that would be for Ireland what Kossovo would be for Hungary. But the poison was already being prepared and the wild geese scattered, soon to become extinct. Something was broken so that something else could begin.

And sure enough, scarcely had a year passed than there came yet another in the long roster of our betrayal; this one by the name of Jamsey Blake, turncoat and native of Galway who was said to be in the pay of Sir George Carew the Lord High President of Munster. It was he who arranged that poison be laid out for Red Hugh at a dinner in Simancas, watched him sample wine of the Palomino grapes, swig and swallow; take *percebes*, which are goose barnacles, now stuffed with death, take his portion with a slow easy hand. Blake, hidden, watched, and so did some ruffed and bearded Spanish grandees, not comprehending; saw him swallow it in a place now outside of time, wiped out by time, frozen within time.

As the Scots troops crouched miserably all night in corn-stooks in freezing rain, their powder damp, their spirits low, awaiting Cromwell's fearful attack at sunup, time stopped. At daybreak the Scots troops began shuffling into line.

Elsewhere in other times and places in different darkness St Elmo's fire was glinting on damp Irish lances (not to be used much that day) and Panzer tank engines coughing into life at sunup were rolling toward Kusk. These fields, Kossovo and its crows, the tank battle of Kusk, the graveyard of Kinsale, a drenched cornfield in Scotland. *Jamais deux sans trois*; never four without more.

Shrapnel tore through the grey insentient air, bees with their hives knocked over. From the enemy lines the machine-gun fire was reaching out, stuttering, probing, stitching the air. Somewhere in the murk ahead lay the pierced barbed-wire entanglements. Juss trod on something soft and yielding – flayed human flesh not yet dead, himself dragged along by the current of time. His face felt stiff as a death mask, from generous tots of three-star Hennessy. The thought flew unsoberly through his head: *Schicksal* had become *Schnicksal*, both British and Germanic destiny become ridiculous and dirty, become piercing red-hot. The ordinary expection of suffering was one thing; this was something else again.

The Beast of Ballynagrumoolia had come via Ballinspittle through all the intervening gardens of Munster, breaking down clapboard fences, trampling vegetable patches, grunting and sweating, to Kippagh.

The Battle of Kinsale was fought and lost one vile wet Sunday on 24 December 1601 and over in barely three hours. Within a period so brief a large force was destroyed by a smaller one, the English horse under Wingfield pursued the fleeing Irish as far as Innishannon five miles distant, killing at will. The Spanish presence within the town had been more a hindrance than a help. Trust not foreign friends; the old adage had a cruel ethnic twist to it. The River Bandon snaked about the small port, a walled town of 200 houses, as duodenum and colon, lower bowel and anus. Spared the shame of defeat, the Spanish were flushed down the river and out to sea. Don Juan del Aquila was in command. The Armada had sunk only thirteen years before. For the Irish, crippling defeats at the Yellow Ford and Benburb, and now Kinsale, the final setback. The ancestors had begun to seem strange. *Kolkrabe the Raven greets you!* Shaking out sodden feathers, stropping its beak on the bars of the cage. Hiding its food, first under this stone, then under that. Swearing profusely, e'er all be over and done with. Ever since the sixteen century the wind had been blowing against European Catholicism.

Our Jamesie O'Connor, a fifth- or sixth-generation bachelor, on the dole, impoverished and half mad, was as a lost creature struggling in a mangrove swamp. Still believing that his dead brother had been converted into a crow and Jamsie out after him in all weathers in a long unchanged greasy overcoat in one pocket of which he kept his silent gun – a catapult.

He dwelt bachelor-style in a cramped and fetid one-room Assumption Terrace cottage hard by the charitable fishmongers who fed him, opposite the health centre

('Pregnant? We can help') and the Garda station out of which at any moment the opera-loving but ill-tempered Guard Con Concannon might purposefully stride, demanding a licence for the silent gun, make him eat crow.

Insects too have their hour.

Jamesie's window overlooked the end of the ancient Celtic world. He whittled at odds and ends to make a fire, kept a mangy cat, preferred candles to newfangled notions such as electric light, drank in the Harp and Shamrock, where he was known as 'Whackers'. As with Wagner before him, he suffered agonies from skin disease, piles and rotten bladder, his memory shot to pieces. Irish to the core, his temper uncertain, he wanted to kill the crow that was his brother. The same old dingdong.

Out walking in winter, one memorable evening, we encountered the Beast of Ballynagrumoolia at close quarters, in all her glory. A dinted and holed aluminium chamber-pot was clamped down on the pointed skull and fastened with a demi-veil of fishing net knotted about the throat in a loose fashion with brown scapulars contesting with an Immaculate Conception badge on a faded crimson thread; the white paint cracked on the chamber, the blue rim chipped, and strapped about it (a daring touch) welder's goggles. A scarf of pale green fruit-netting the colour of a well-weathered copper church dome bisected the neck. And from neck to ankle a kimono-like vestment of a nondescript dull colour, a swaggered double skirt like a priest's cassock or Franciscan's habit, at midriff a double length of hairy twine, of the same colour as the hair erupting from under the cracked chamber. This mottled black shapeless bolt of cloth ended in battered brogans. Mad blue periwinkle eyes were set in the middle of the 'face' implanted with an iron-hard snout, for rooting in nameless filth. The deep-set eyes were hidden and furtive, wedged into their sockets below the fuzzy eyebrows; the corrugations of the narrow forehead signalling God knows what itch, what fury, puzzlement betraying softly mimed buffoonery with a tug to tow-coloured hair, absented finger up one nostril, a quick tug at the hair wiry as tow, the snot examined and tasted, swallowed. And then stock still, ears cocked, listening hard, then relaxed, whereupon a deep rumbling fart to end this evening's performance. It was a she-beast assuredly to judge from the nauseating vegetable smell that wafted its way across the narrow roadway as we slunk by. Not our Queen Maeve as represented on the one-punt denomination note looking as woebegone as if she had a crippling pain in the hole, nor yet *Verfremdungseffekt* nor Bubba nor Maggie Humm, nor Banba nor Foohla the Flighty, nor Puckoon, nor the Old-Sow-That-Eats-Her-Farrow, nor yet again Emanrehsihtstahw, the lowly form of an immortal always encountered at that mystical hour 'twixt gloaming and dusk, as now. On all fours, face on fire, grovelling in the dirt.

We passed down the mossy boreen until we came to the main road leading in one direction to nowhere in particular, in the other by the house of hidden Jago and the otter path, then past the flowering cherry at the Carraigin corner and by the blind-factory to the marsh and its assembly of wild birds with their diverse cries, curlews and oystercatchers and plover and mallard, the heavenliness of birdsong that so enraptured W. H. Hudson on the pampas in Argentina in the nineteenth century, as the birds of Hampshire had delighted Gilbert White the Selborne divine in the century before.

The trawler *Girl Fiona* was tied up at the World's End

wharf near where the Cornishman 'mad' Mark Trick lived under a thatched roof with his ever-loving wife Lucinda (née Minogue) of the knockers. Her lord and master was playing loud *Magic Flute* music all night long on the transistor, having brought his dead mother safely from distant Cornwall in a coffin, set out upon the Harbour Bar counter, Mad Mark calling loudly for drinks on the house. And then the casket up-ended in a corner like a cello, then more drinks before burial in Courtaparteen cemetery, that old disused place near the deserted village.

Only dead fish swim with the tide. Our past is most certainly dead. More than that, much more; it's unimaginable. Unthinkable as the legendary but extinct horseflesh Twohelochroo, or Boggeragh, or flighty Firbolg, or the Pooka, or Babh, or the mighty thundering hooves of the Morrigu herself.

Jackdaws nest in the limes of Friary Hill, tear twigs, lay eggs, raise young, drop eggshells and whiten with their squirted lime-shit the newly washed limousines lined up for Mass, strut about on the road. A robin calls 'Swing low, sweet chariot!' over by the French Prison and from near the slaughterhouse on Chairman's Lane a blackbird answers *'Aujourd'hui! Aujourd'hui!'* as the legless man is pushed in his wheelchair into a waiting car, and the Buck goes bounding down the narrow stairs and out into the freshness of Cork Street, jacket hooked over one finger, humming 'The Mountains of Mourne', released from rearranging that evergreen lament for his male voice choir.

Daybreak comes early in June to the port, with a bantam cock crowing lustily twenty-nine times, mongrels in the morning, the canoodling of pigeons, the tide coming into the town of ghosts (population 2,000); 1601 was but yesterday, and spooks abound. Joy-bells ring for living and drowned (the Irish life underneath the waves); when the tide goes out and the wind drops there'll be a couple of jumps.

A bitch on heat is being chased through the flat of town by six mongrels anxious to cover her, despite newly enacted by-laws for the control of wandering pets; but ours was ever a country notoriously difficult to control. Windblown pines, surging ambient darkness.

Monsignor Cosimo Bumperini, SJ, Th.D., Ph.D., rotund and benign, a well-pleased ecclesiastical pumpkin, confidant to His Eminence the Cardinal Primate, the Papal Nuncio, having left Ardcarrig guest-house on Compass Hill (perhaps the most expensive B & B in Munster), strolled by Dr FitzGerald's ivy-covered wall, heading for the friary, murmuring his Nones.

Monsignor Bumperini's belly extended a good eighteen or twenty centimetres in advance of the rest of him, the gooseberry-coloured eyes fairly starting from their sockets. Capillaries had erupted on his purple cheeks and small veins ruptured on his nose, testifying to liberal intake of more than just altar wine. His bulgy eyes looked craftily out behind the glint of spectacles. A seemingly kind man; not exactly a man of God, a self-promoting party who held himself in the highest esteem. The smile was misleadingly benevolent, more smirk than smile.

Gravely he saluted a bearded fellow in blue, Peter Storm, out walking with his darksome fancy-woman, now heading back to the Dutch House, a third-storey apartment under the eaves loud with the croodles and canoodling of amorous pigeons, hard by the French Prison.

The Jesuit father was over from Turin on an Irish visit and would dine that evening with Canon Norman Prior of St Multose in the Blue Haven, a favoured meeting-place of Protestants. Now he came upon a strange sight, to be sure.

A little hunchback friar with crooked teeth was ringing the Angelus. Light as a leaf in his brown habit he was lifted a good two or three feet off *terra firma* in his sandals at each energetic pull at the rope, to be followed presently by the resonant clang of the big bell on its stanchion firm as a guillotine, grim as a gallows; the friar ascending and descending with eely agility, grinning from ear to ear. Monsignor Bumperini thought of Quasimodo. Passing he gravely blessed the small unearthly airborne friar again rising on his rope.

'Such delightful serenity,' breathed the monsignor to himself, nodding to the again ascending diminutive friar at the end of his rope. The monsignor quickened his pace. At that moment all the lights sprang on in the Tap Tavern.

On the main dock before the Trident Hotel (long closed for repairs) the filthy German coaster *Eugen Rothenhoefer* out of Hamburg was offloading maize for Henry Good, and there a pair of far from polished peas-ants saluted us affably. Sick and tired of cooling their heels outside the Temperance Hall, Garr and his mate Paddy Locke had set out for a breath of fresh air by the river at the Archdeacon Duggan bridge. Not 'peasants of the cuntree' but fine upstanding fishermen of Kinsale and they lifelong buddies as inseparable as curds and whey. To ward off carnal desire they swore mighty oaths all the time, spitting, Paddy advancing crabwise in an indirect and shifty manner that had grown habitual with him when in his cups.

Paddy Locke devoured ox hearts, sheeps' lights, eels and pike from the Bandon, calves' livers, pigs' crubeens, hedgehog and pigeon, saddle of hare, curlew breasts,

Carrigaline duck, buck rabbit, salmon in and out of season from the drift nets, herring and crab, chanterelle and ceps from the damp Garrettstown bluebell woods, free-range eggs, skate from the seabed off the Old Head, mussels from under seaweed on the rocks below the Dutch flats. All this to his heart's content, when he could keep it down. For his appetite for food as such was not great, his staple and preferred diet being draught Guinness in pint tumblers.

He perjured himself as the other fishermen did in the District Court on the ticklish subject of monofilament nets drifting for salmon out of season, a double illegality, contradicting stoutly all the water bailiff had seen or thought he had seen on the rocks, in the sea, pulling in, the coming and going, the dimmed lights, the covering and uncovering, who was carrying what where, all impossible to prove in a court of law. But, as is well known, fishermen from St Peter on were all notorious liars.

The lights were springing up all over Kinsale and evening drinkers gathering at the Cuckoo's Nest and the Grey Hound and the Armada, formerly the Blue Shark. The Fish was leaving his council house on St John's Terrace, passing the candle factory. Snug in Mother Hubbard's café about a coal fire four phlegmatic Yorkshiremen fell to discussing Nostradamus, that seer of doom. The tide was flooding in past the Bulman Bar where the great O'Leary was downing a dark potion of draught Guinness as daylight faded from the western windows.

It was you and I who walked out of town, the fancy-woman and her rake going by the old ramparts, the site of the Blind Gate, the ground of the old battlefield, not shooting pool in the Dunderrow Bar, you all in grey and the rake in handwoven Donegal tweed jacket, hardly appropriate but purchased in Kildare Street, Dublin, to attend luncheon at Iveagh House upon the invitation of Dr FitzGerald, to honour the King and Queen of Spain – handsome Don Juan Carlos and his lovely consort over on their first state visit.

Paddy Locke and Garr dived into the Lobster Pot.

Monsignor Cosimo Bumperini, SJ, was lavishly entertaining Canon Norman Prior at the Blue Haven in Kinsale, pouring Muscadet with a steady and liberal hand.

'A glass of wine, Canon?'

Canon Prior graciously inclined his head.

'*Ecco, two* glasses of new wine. *Et on mange des asperges . . .*'

Canon Prior, a tall grey Anglican, amused his convivial Italian host with an anecdote involving his only son Peregrine who had attended a fancy-dress ball at Acton's Hotel, got up as a dustbin.

'*Basta!*' cried the mellow monsignor, laughing indulgently. '*Audaces fortuna iuvat*, if I recall my Horace correctly.'

'And does not Strabo say – '

'Ah, *Strabo!*'

Their choice of fish was sole for the canon, turbot for the monsignor; their preferred tipple Muscadet, to be followed by sherbet and three-star brandy with the coffee.

Nipping the end off a Dutch corona with a gold clippers taken from a fob pocket Monsignor Bumperini was regaling the canon with a first-hand account of his audience with the Pope at the Vatican the previous summer, together with an assembly of bishops from Rome.

A majestic tubular figure vested in shimmering white received them, took his hand in both of his, smiled without condescension, or so it seemed, looking into his eyes as if he could see into his heart. Pope John Paul

II, Karol Wojtyła, the former Bishop of Kraków, was an aristocratic figure with a great domed forehead.

From a capacious inside pocket the Pope drew out a thick bunch of keys but seemed uncertain of which key fitted which lock, indeed seemed unfamiliar with the topography of the Vatican, its labyrinthine ways. He waited smiling before the door of the Pontifical Antechamber. On the other side stood Swiss Guards, tall and upright, barely breathing, still as statues. His Holiness stood smiling, key in hand, not uttering a word in the gorgeous room covered in red damask.

The Vatican doors were invisible once they were closed, no lock or doorknob to be seen, covered in *boiseries*, all sealed mysterious chambers. The smiling Polish Presence was lost, had not been long in office; his composure was absolute, a figure cast in bronze.

Canon Prior was moderately intrigued, sniffing his Hennessy, keeping his thoughts to himself. The monsignor was positively twinkling, now puffing a thumping big King Edward corona.

Staggering from the Lobster Pot, Paddy Locke now full to the gills made his way on foot and alone past the scum on the Scilly dam, smelling (Paddy, not the dam) even more powerfully than before of creosote (an odour similar to smoked meat), damp rope and stale Guinness, stole up the hill by the Spaniard and in with him to the Spinnaker, of all places, where presently in an indistinct rapid manner, like a priest muttering Latin Mass, he recited swiftly 'The Ballad of the Crossbarry Queer' for the benefit of the two foreign nancy-boys got up in fine expensive clothes:

> Now wimmendowimmen
> an' mendomen . . .

[The Ballad of the Crossbarry Queer:
In the town of Crossbarry
Where I was born,
A fine strapping lad,
And they called me John Curran.
  Now women do women
  And men do men;
But best of all was when John did a hen!
And when John passed away and went down to Hell
He did have a go at Satan as well.
Satan stood up and asked 'Whom have we here?'
And John answered back 'It's the Crossbarry Queer!']

The ethnic air has a cruel country twist to it, its intent to belittle and begrudge all strangeness, all non-Irishness; death and dishonour to all deviants.

'*Progettare è un poco sognare . . .?*' one polite Italian queen questioned the other. 'Do we not detect a certain foul smell?'

'Willy singyouse anudder?'

'I scarcely think so, no thank you.' Does he not see his snot's dripping into his drink? he asked the other in Italian.

Paddy could not help it, snot the colour of eau-de-Nil was depending from each nostril, every now and again hastily snuffled back, like mercury rising and falling in a pipette.

'Hoose rownn?' he asked truculently, wiping snot with the back of his hand. 'Hoosa rownn nowah?'

The two foreign gentleman finished their whiskey without undue haste, donned mufflers and street clothes and quietly departed, bidding adieu in dumb show.

Heaving a heavy sigh Paddy Locke sank into a stupefied reverie.

Time passed. Others came and went. Paddy slept, standing like a horse at the bar.

Canvas cap askew, Lanky Locke was smoking a roll-up and dribbling, racked by storms of coughing, his head down, the spent roll-up between his fingers so stained with nicotine they might have been dipped in cowdung.

He heaved and groaned, resting his raging temple on the cool bar counter (as if he had removed his head from a sack), staring down at twin boots the colour of diseased brass, side by side an immense distance below, stapled to the floor.

'Ah no,' groaned Paddy, 'fuck me, no.'

The floor came up at him then sank away again.

'*Buenos tardes, amigo!*' came a loud convivial hail from somewhere in the mist and who was it but Steamboat himself up from the loading dock and coming through now, four sheets to the wind, having had a few in the Fishermen's Wharf Bar. A hard fraternal fist smote Paddy between the shoulderblades and Steamboat's whiskery voice breathed hotly into one ear.

'Get this down you.'

Opening one eye Paddy Locke perceived a glass of the *hard stuff* not six inches away from his nose, levitating along the bar counter, where in the far distance the hazy shape of Steamboat was gesticulating, glass in hand.

The cast of Paddy's eye was watery, all mucus and tears, the eyes opaque and out of alignment, muddy as the gaze of a carp or bream.

'Down with her, Paddy.'

Paddy Locke rested his head against the counter and backed away, holding onto an invisible rail, like a bullock in a pen, and made a low rumbling fart in his breeches not dissimilar to distant summer thunder, but mercifully odourless.

'Do youse wanna anudder?'

This time, by Jove, he broke wind almost soundlessly, a summery zephyr surging and soughing through swaying boscage, setting all astir and asway in its path and releasing the delicate aromas of pollen and blossom and sap-crammed leaf, though the stench now released into the bar was another matter.

'A wettan windy May fillsda barn with corn an' hay,' said Paddy, upright and teetering, straightening his cap. He was five feet four inches and rarely sober if he could help it, *if* he could afford it. At times he ate a block of ice cream, the only food he could hold down. He screwed his old soiled canvas cap into alignment with his nose, swivelling it about his overheated skull as if adjusting the lid of a pot.

'Two moons in May means no money an' no tay.'

'The hard Paddy,' said Steamboat.

'I'm fullassa tick,' said Paddy thickly. 'Fuller *nor* a tick. A wet ass an' a hungry gut.'

'The hard Paddy.'

'No, no,' said Paddy darkly, now thoroughly cross-eyed in drink with whiskey raging through him. 'Am drunker nora cunt.'

Paddy Locke convulsed his features and seemed to concentrate himself intensely as he shrank to the size of a low, bandy-legged basset, unearther of foxes and badgers. After some deliberation, with head invisible between his shoulders and both hands gripping the bar counter, he released one concluding mighty obbligato.

On the roadstead the rusty coaster *Paz*, out from the Gold Coast with a cargo of soya pellets for livestock, long in service, long as a street in Valparaíso, was pushing slowly upstream on the flooding tide. At other times and other tides it would be maize or sunflower or rape-seed from Amsterdam and Hamburg, but today on this tide it was soya pellets from the Gold Coast for the tranquillised pigs and heavily injected heifers of Munster with a long wet winter behind them and they in need of protein to ready them for suburban tables throughout the land. Out from Kinsale went malting barley for the continent, and in came this.

One of the deckhands was walking on his hands along the hold covered in blue tarpaulin stretched tight as a drum. Some others leant upon the taffrail, smoking, ears pricked for the banshee wail of '*Cabo de velho*', the famous Irish death-cry. A mile ahead the warps were readied, the Fish and Steamboat standing by, spitting on their hands.

The Polish herring fleet was in, a dozen dirty factory ships, some moored out in the bay, others up and down the river as far as the new bridge, one a Soviet spy ship, the stink of fish-guts pervasive, the ravening gulls thick on the tide. No Poles set foot onshore. If any crewman defected the captain would be shot on return to port, where life was hard, a man had to hold down two jobs, for Poland was poor. Work began on the factory ships at seven in the morning, the winches groaning. Rowing boats pulled out after dark for trade in poteen and Polish vodka.

Summercove was to starboard, the slip, the Bulman Bar, a warm fire, the *habitués*, had the frozen observers on the taffrail been free to avail themselves of it, the bar with smoke rising from its chimney.

Ensconced as usual in the left chimneybreast and roasted on one side by the coal fire burning in the grate, Trapper Revatta, lean as a leprechaun, dozed by his half-consumed pint of Guinness and glass of port, as down the chimney floated the voice of his late brother Fred, a murmur hardly distinguishable from the low noise of the fire, whispering confidentially that the hereafter was savage altogether. *Brutal,* said the unseen one.

Not that the sleeping Trapper minded, for he had no

belief in an afterlife; life here on earth was enough and more than enough.

Shocken, breathed the disembodied voice down the flue. *This place is pure hell, Joe boy.*

Steam rose from the Trapper's mucky boots. He had been labouring long hours in the freezing Fort Charles.

Tell us, the dead brother whispered in a coaxy voice, *what goes up the chimney down and down the chimney up?* Ofttimes the mood was on him for levity, but when in God's name would you find levity in a dump the like of this? The stacked fire made a gentle sibilant sound as if calling to bats and the Trapper, awakened by the voices of spooks, stared wildly about him with eyes that had the whey-blue sheen found inside mussel shells, the left eye blind. But only O'Leary, enormously elongated, was perched on his stool by the door, immersed in a crossword puzzle.

Breathing thinly the Trapper sipped port the colour of blood which brought back a little life into him. He felt thinly alert again, there by the good fire set by Willie.

A stud, answered the voice in the chimney with low laughter. *A stud in a man's boot.*

The voice came laughing down the chimney. The Trapper dozed off, hands plunged in trouser pockets, his breathing soft as a hare in a mountain form.

When he surfaced again the bar was flooded with an agreeable amber afterlight, an old amber bottle in which the newcomers (a young Australian couple from the youth hostel) moved sluggish as fish in a tinted glass tank. Their voices rose and fell, coming from the antipodes.

'Me head is leppen,' muttered the Trapper, and the gnarled hands wormy with old veins clasped themselves convulsively about his knees.

Willie's ingle was a wobby kind of a place frequented by spooks. Casting a squinty look about him the Trapper reached up with a trembling hand for the pint three-quarters emptied on the low mantel.

'Illin,' Joe murmured coaxingly. 'Givesa nudder pint, Illin. Me head do be leppen.'

Transfixed, Helen Fair was staring out the window. The Trapper hung his head and glared at his hands as if at strange appendages that did not belong to him.

The finest day that ivver came outa de hivens! the whispery disembodied voice breathed down the flue.

'Lave us now,' mumbled Joe, bowed as a pair of callipers, cross, fuming.

A gust of smoke blew back down the chimney.

'He do,' the Trapper said to the smouldering fire in the narrow grate, 'he do.'

Helen Fair began absently polishing a pint glass.

'Illin,' murmured Joe patiently. 'Givesa port here, Illin. Me head do be *leppen!*'

'Oh God my legs are killing me,' sighed Helen Fair.

Pollard pellets and locust beans came in on all the tides for Good's mills, for the rats on the roadside and the hungry birds of the air, for the cattle in the drenched fields. A high-pitched grinding sound from the swivelling crane working on the dock carried on the wind to Summercove and was heard in the Bulman when the door was open, heard by Trapper Revatta in the ingle, the great *auriculae* pricked up and attentive. He knew from what quarter the wind blew, where the tide was, without consulting the papers.

'Are you trying to give me a hard time, Joe?'

'No, no, Illin, no,' the Trapper said, rising awkwardly to his feet, blinking with smeary, blurred, frantic blue eyes.

'Well then, will you behave yourself?'

Trapper Revatta's home was a cosy place down the Bulman lane. Reclusive brother Tom had converted it

from a lofty pig-shed into a narrow L-shaped abode similar
to a railway carriage, if somewhat damp; and there Joe
lived alone, within hailing distance of the brother. There
was little communication between them. Brother Tom
lived in the main house, not drinking alcohol nor
smoking tobacco, disapproving of Joe's wayward ways.

Since his fishing days ended the Trapper had been an
employee of the Office of Public Works, and carried with
him the foul weather from Fort Charles; for up there on
the eminence a cold wind blew winter and summer, from
time immemorial. The Trapper worked with a long-
handled shovel, leaning on it as on a crutch, his mouth
ajar, wisps of hair escaping from under his cap. He was
sixty-two years old but might have passed for a man much
older; his moods varied. He drank pints of draught Guinness with shots of port, a strange mixture. He was his own
man.

The great O'Leary was absently trimming and manicu-
ring his broken black fingernails with the edge of a Yale
key on a bunch that included penknife and corkscrew
with an instrument for removing stones from hooves,
sourly observed by Helen Fair who was bored out of her
wits, having pulled pints on and off since midday when
she came on duty, when not selling sweets to children
over the counter. The great O'Leary had mentioned
trouble with his passport, stamped UDA by the Israeli
authorities, and how he, the undesirable alien, had hopes
of employment in, Reykjavik, gutting fish, or work in
Algeria, or maybe Australia, work of an unspecified but
lucrative nature.

A pugnacious bachelor with missing front teeth to
prove it, he had been sent packing from a kibbutz,
deported from Israel. Taking offence at words let drop
he had stuck the prongs of a dining-fork into a man's
throat with a quick lunge across the refectory table.

All day long he drank draught Guinness, going through the *Mirror* and *Cork Examiner,* laughing his head off, analysing world news, local scandal, calling for refills. Gossip and hot scandal were his style. The long hours spent in the bar, always on the same high stool or standing by, had become a *Missa pro defunctis* celebrated alone, just as if he were dead to the world and ready for the grave. He had a rough tongue but a good heart. The fuckers had it made, he said, all bets covered. The best possibilities were always out of reach. The fix was in.

His manner was to make a mockery of everything. He had teeth missing, was held by indolence. Looking out now he saw the ghostly vessel passing by and dark faces aft peering across the taffrail where the Panamanian flag hung limp.

'Nignogs,' said the great O'Leary, 'floating by.'

The tide continued up the sea wall. The wake of *Paz* slapped against the rocks, ran up the slip. The acrobat on the hold was upright now, hosing down the tarpaulin. From the transistor behind the bar counter the voice of Paul McCartney sang of all the lonely people.

'Oh God am I *bored,*' groaned Helen Fair, yawning, delicate as a cat. 'I need to be kept humoured.'

But the great O'Leary was again lost in a crossword.

The best single of all time, averred the imbecile on Radio 2. 'Of all, *all* time.' Radio Dublin was always blathering away near the serving hatch, in the best of times, the worst of times. The great O'Leary, the Bulman's most reliable customer, lived alone in a caravan parked rent-free in a field owned by Billy O'Brien to windward of a hedge of ash and beech near a gate into the property not one Irish mile from Ballymacus Creek where you swam nude near two swans that had flown in from Oysterhaven Bay.

The great O'Leary owned few personal possessions

beyond the clothes on his back, a two-stroke made way for the Suzuki GSX 250, second-hand, before that he had footed it the six miles to and from the Bulman Bar and the uncertain humours of its owner, to the caravan parked to windward of a hedge as if it had come down out of the sky.

Above the field, the rich grass ravelled by the wind, the larks sang in spring, spiralling up into the clouds. Unseen corncrakes *kraak-krakked* in summer, the pale Brindley beauty alighted on the hedgerows amid wild garlic. In winter it was a different story. Then the caravan trembled and took a pounding from a freezing south-easterly blowing over Oysterhaven Bay and the flatlands of east Cork. Out at Ballymacus Point the red-haired Daw Harding took ill again.

The undesirable alien was five feet ten inches in height, weighed eight stone six ounces which put him in the welterweight class, was thirty-three years old and could let down pints until the cows came home. The great O'Leary was a deep reader of newspapers, addicted to crosswords in the *Cork Examiner*, the London *Mirror*, Philip Elting's *Herald Tribune*. He read through them all in his free time, of which he seemed to have an inordinate amount. As with the booze and roll-up tobacco, newsprint and press photos of the world's calamities were meat and drink to Tomás, forms of sedation, forgetfulness.

The rich Beatle sang of the moribund northern city, the once great port, its factories closed and its docks dead, sang of Eleanor Rigby, of Liverpool, of all the lonely people.

'This kind of weather gives me the pip,' said Helen Fair, cross as a rat.

The great O'Leary said nothing, standing as if turned to stone at the end of the bar, lost to the *Cork Examiner* ('Oxx has the form').

'Mind you . . .' said Helen Fair, but did not pursue the matter further, staring abstracted out the window like Rapunzel locked up in her tower.

'Nice an' gloomy in here,' murmured Joe Revatta to the fire.

The great O'Leary was lost in a Cork fog. The absented right hand felt for the print, found it, he drank with his eyes still fixed on newsprint ('Bishop's plea sparks walkout'), inhaling Old Holborn roll-ups. He turned a page to the crossword puzzle and Joe Revatta continued to stare into the fire, while Helen Fair gazed out the window.

'*Apiarist!*' suddenly cried out the great O'Leary, briskly shuffling his dirty great combat boots, and marked it down in rude capitals.

An enigmatic (all Munster) caption raged across the opposite page: 'REIGN OF TERROR BY BRUTE DAD.'

A reprise of the opening toccata.

Now, swelling as if it meant business, the tide came flooding in from beyond the Bulman buoy. The fire was dying in the hearth and the last rounds called. It was closing time in the bar and the great O'Leary at last feeling the drag and pull of an immense fatigue mixed with a nameless sadness, having stood a good twelve hours and swallowed fourteen pints, as he had put away sixteen the day before and maybe nineteen the day before that again in a week where all the days had run together to this moment in an endless time of unemployment, during which he had run up a colossal tab with Willie O'Brien, not always the most patient of publicans.

Crouched at the other end of the counter under the old faded sepia photographs now turning up at the edges, the faces of dead fishermen and the great fishes caught, seated at *his* place and grave as an owl in a tod of ivy, under twitching eyebrows his enemy watched, heard the high intemperate speech, the loud guffaws, noted the flushed visage, the sign language for the tab, wished him ill.

But now it was closing time and Willie with his high cries was driving them all out into the night. *Thou shalt not*, his enemy thought, wiping his mouth, moving last. *You O'Leary.*

The tide had finally crept up the sea wall and over the slip where oystercatchers took wing. The gulls were calling out sadly over the river at Summercove where everybody gets up everybody else's nose all the time.

'Night, Dick.'

A bad-sign sickle moon was riding high above Kinsale, dragging the evening star on her back. It would rain tomorrow. And in the air, stronger than ozone or seaweed, the stench of herring guts was stronger than ammonia.

Then one day I'd come upon Paddy Locke lurching about the place with his eyes crooked under the soiled cloth cap a size or two too small for the heated head; with a yaw to the left and then to the right, once even seen teetering up Friary Lane under the fine stand of elms by the grotto to the Virgin, and then swallowed up by the dark open door of the friary, perhaps gone to whisper his sins into the sympathetic ear of a Carmelite friar.

Or again standing on one leg outside the Lobster Pot, the Oyster Inn or the Harp and Shamrock, low in funds and uncertain whether to enter or not. Or doing sentry duty outside the Temperance Hall, or lurching and tacking with some other inshore fishermen by the Scilly dam, come from the Spaniard, squinting at the girls' legs. On those rare occasions he would address me quite civilly as 'Killer'; I never knew why.

Paddy sometimes gave the impression of being a sleep-walker in broad daylight. The cloth cap stuck on casually at an unusual angle or pressed awry on the pointed skull, and from under it the wandering cock-eyed stare askew, and Paddy advancing crabwise in a series of somnambulistic staggers alongside the tidal shifts of the Scilly dam, bound for the Spaniard or tottering by the Temperance Hall and the Methodist church (a total of five active parishioners) and up the lane by Jim Edwards's gorgeous handpainted sign for Restaurant and Bar on a blue ground executed by Paula's da; and so to the Harp and Shamrock or the Glen, where a pint would be started at the pumps the moment Paddy sidled in.

One late December afternoon at close of day we were walking the ring road, heading for drinks at the Bulman, when we saw the Trapper Revatta and a stout co-worker from the Office of Public Works knocking off for the day. The long-handled shovels on their shoulders might have been pikes. They were the very image of the defeated stragglers of 1601 heading home with pikes shouldered, silhouetted against the pale stone of Fort Charles and the steely dying light on the Bandon beyond, around about the 387th anniversary of the defeat, 'defiantly conceding the battle'. Chased over all the fields and ditches of Belgooly and Ballyshannon by Carew's shouting troopers, Wingfield's horse; beshitting their breeches and calling for protection to the Virgin. Two gallant figures on a windswept hill, going home.

Trooper Revatta. His only luxury a warming-stone in the cold bachelor's bed; not the last man in Ireland to try warming his bed with a stone (*cloch*).

An English captain wrote home by rushlight in a damp Godforsaken place: 'Quite a number of our Foe whom I hath Personally Dispatched in the act of scaling walls or retreating but still menacing with Catcalls, Jeers, etcetera not infrequently hath I seen again, still alive and jeering, and *must kill again.* Come to parley or surrender, hurling down abuse and Offensive Matter (faecal) from breached Castle walls.

'That is ever the way with Winter Campaigns, of which this must be the Foremost and engaged in the fowlest Weather. It seems the Enemy is everywhere, lying low to spring at us – a Hydra-headed monster that has to be slaughtered not once but many times. Or else every Irishman hath ten brothers.

'Ye will scarce credit this, but yesterday at a plashy place called Ballymakkus did see a flock of white-breasted birds flying *backwards and upside-down* over a low hill by the Creek, with high cheeping cries as the *picho ichos* in Spain. The Irish have a name for these. They fly fast in flocks and seem to lay their eggs in thickets.'

'They do come in March,' said Billy O'Brien, screwing up his eyes and nodding his head. 'They hatches on the rocks.' He didn't know their name, a name in Irish.

Two fishermen in yellow oilskins were chopping off fish-heads on the deck of the *Sovereign Dawn* moored out on a bobbing orange buoy off Summercove. The men worked methodically, spilling the guts one way, tossing the headless fish into barrels. Seagulls squabbled over the remains as it was carried out by the tide.

The great O'Leary came in by the back door bringing with him a powerful gust of freezing air.

'Begod,' he said amiably, 'it's snowing in the jakes.'

'Yesterday was the holy fly altogether,' the Trapper said. Helen Fair said nothing.

Next morning the river was all grey and nothing moving on it but a motor launch with a party of men in drab suiting – perhaps mourners – setting off to drop ashes, human remains of some citizen departed this life who didn't wish to be buried in St Multose or St Eltin's six feet under, being taken out to the fishing grounds beyond the Bulman buoy.

The cat's narrow head, a skull covered in fur, with whiskers, pushed into my hand, began purring. The heating system was on but the cat's purring was louder, I could feel it running up my arm. The motor launch had disappeared around the corner. The area once half grass was now all cement, the Bulman car park. The professional gambler who was married to the female professional psychiatrist, a disciple of Jung, drove up from Cork in his beaten-up old Ford to park in the car park by the Bulman slip and gaze for hours at a stretch at his old home, now owned by an American belly-dancer and her computer husband.

Matty Maunsell was just stepping into the Bulman, having removed his swanky pork-pie hat and scratched his head as if his brains were boiling and then replacing the hat and going into the deserted bar. And then came a couple of tourists with backpacks to gaze in stupefaction at the slip, the tidal river, the fort across the way, the Bulman sign, as if these prodigies of nature had just come into existence before their astonished eyes. The sightseers stood bemused in the middle of the road, reading the signs and portents.

Within the Bulman now a neat fire had been set and all the table-tops given a wipe by Willie O'Brien the publican.

'I'd be in the *horrors* of drink!' cried Willie to no one in particular, throwing a fierce challenging look about.

'He was in this morning trying to sell me a *blast* of glasses!' Willie was flitting to and fro on the catwalk behind the counter, checking up, poring over the *Cork Examiner*, keeping always a weather eye on the great O'Leary.

He was a shortish broad man with a somewhat waspish nature, a high intelligent cranium and short-cropped

black hair going grey about the ears; hair which on
occasion could *stand on end.* He had the threatening stare
of a little auk ('high, shrill laughing chatter') and early
in October flew out with his nice wife Kay to the Canaries
and Portugal, for a change of air.

'He'd try to sell you *anything!*'

The great O'Leary studied the tricky crossword puzzle
like a graphologist confronted by a bogus signature.

'I couldn't believe anybody would sink so low!'

Nobody said a word.

'He's too exuberant, isn't he?'

Little auks breed on broken rocky cliffs. They have a
basilisk glare in the eye sometimes, for life is very hard
and unyielding for auks, who are ever anxious, rightly or
wrongly feeling themselves to be a threatened species;
although Willie O'Brien as a publican did all right for
himself. And publicans are by no means a threatened
species in County Cork, quite the contrary. All competition was removed a mile away at the Spaniard, or three
miles in another direction at fabled Belgooly, a haunt of
Provos, fervent if misguided nationalists who had blown
up a couple of tracking stations atop Mount Gabriel,
mistakenly supposed to be British Army surveillance
plants on Munster soil. With bombs, sectarian killing,
hunger strikes, protection rackets and their own excrement, the Belgooly boys would free old Ireland once
again of the Sassenach yoke.

This little auk was grey about the ears and spoke, in
intense and compromising vagaries, between clenched
teeth. He was a proper bridge fiend.

The 'nameless' Irish bird had three names in English,
on the word of no less an authority than the great
English ornithologist Sir William Jardine, who called
them fallow-smith, whitear, white-tail or white-rump. It
can be easily identified by the white rump as it flits from

stone to stone, appearing to fall, then resuming its erratic flight. It *appears* white-breasted because it flies backwards and you are looking at its rump, not its chest. The whitear arrives in Ireland in March or April, always alone, flying swiftly over the east coast to her high nesting grounds.

Billy O'Brien of Ballymacus was a dapper (does not Milton refer to 'dapper elves'?) little man with glazy eyes in a wrinkled weatherbeaten face made distinctive by the arched, truculent nose of Punch. He was not related to bossy Willie O'Brien of Ardbrack, bridge-player, setter of fires, good husband of Kay, father of Peter and Patricia, vacationer in the Canaries and Portugal. This arbitrator of arguments would sometimes bar O'Leary or Maunsell from his licensed premises for periods of probation, turn and turn about. Billy O'Brien was the kind landlord of O'Leary who paid no rent. Blinking his eyes and nodding his head, his eyes reduced to mere slits, Billy moved his shoulders inside his jacket like a small disgruntled bird ruffling its features.

Billy referred to 'a fierce quiet man in a hat' (in the sense that horses are 'fierce cute', or highly intelligent); meaning the man rarely spoke, never removed his hat. Then the nod, the blink, the fluffing up of feathers, the look of keen perplexity.

Matty Maunsell had worked as a driver and rigger in Fosset's Circus, erecting and taking down the marquee. Once he had 'lost' a lion in Inchicore. He was a great reader of books, pulp literature, a persistent cadger; there was the remnants of a natty dresser. He wore a posh pork-pie hat in order to doff it to the ladies, tilting it, the lid of a kettle on the boil, an archaic and charming gesture. He did not go as far as to hold the pork-pie like a begging bowl, but the gesture had in it something of a begging of charity invoked in silence. Matty was sixty-three years of age, but could have passed for seventy-two; a Protestant, his memory going, or gone.

While Matty's acrylic mottled grey pork-pie suggested old gentility, Paddy Locke's cap had a vaguely seafaring appearance, a longshoreman's headgear. He did not conform to one's notion of fisherman, nor had I ever seen him rowing a boat or letting down a lobster pot or pulling in a net; he looked more like a superannuated boxer, with the bow-legged appearance and battered face of a bantamweight.

I had seen him unsoberly hang over the riverwall to call out abuse and encouragement to those below on the rocks, at the back-breaking labour of pulling in nets, fishing for salmon in the ebb tide.

Guard Concannon the opera buff sang a deep bass, had a smattering of Italian and learnt some French from the Basque fishermen, drove an expensive car, the property of his brother-in-law Ned, and 'had it in' for you, over some parking dispute. He was a strict law-enforcement officer of the stamp of 'Bow-Wow', 'Ball Tyres' and the peerless 'Book and Pencil'.

Guard Con Concannon sang like a bull in the choirloft, boomed away in his big bass in *Ruddigore* under the Buck's uplifted baton, tore into *La Traviata*: *Tra-la-LAA! Thummm. Tum-te-tum-te-TUAM!*' So sang big Con, all lower jaw, taciturnity forgotten, the serious face awash in sweat: a *singing* bull, by God!

Willie O'Brien spoke in exclamation marks.

'Whackers' was to be seen tying up his green front door with a length of frayed rope and sallying forth to collect odds and ends of timber for his fire. The fishmonger Murphy looked after him, saw that he did not want. Mackerel were down again, praise be to God: three medium-sized for 75p were laid out on the slab like survivors from the Ark.

Whackers clung to the hand-rail at the foot of Friary Lane under the stand of elms, with jackdaws and cats, addressed a listless lady down from her prayers at the friary, telling her of the destructive habits of the grey crows, prone to pick out the eyes of newborn lambs.

'Is that *so* now?'

Stout young Finn hired two ethnic groups on a pro rata basis and they played in the front Armada bar on alternate weeks, one week the ruddy-cheeked Firbolgs and the next the ranting and roaring Tuatha de Danaan. Their music sounded identical.

With the darkness would arrive bodhrán player, fiddler, maybe a penny-whistler, a conceited vocalist with stunned female groupie in tow; an excrescence of folkish fancy, promised a fair fee in advance. Stereotypes are never good.

On a high bar stool sat the Farting Farmer with plump right fist clamped to his pint of draught Guiness, perspiring like a pig. The Firbolgs were the right boyos!

The songs came gustily as the west wind blowing over boglands, flattening grass and up-ending swans in tarns the colour of lapis lazuli, whistling through the crannies of a remote cottage perched somewhere in the back of beyond, entering a death-room and pushing aside a curtain to discover an inert corpse laid out, looking down its nose at the bare upturned feet, the waxen hands manacled with rosary beads. The surly brutes were never at a loss when spouting out ripe runic wisdom, frothing a little at the mouth betimes, chaunting with the drone of the warpipes, glottal stops in the throat, droning away for form's sake. 'The Town I Loved So Well' was from the ever-expanding repertoire of the peerless Furey Brothers, a twosome matchless in their invocation of the Irish *Schicksal* (destiny) whistling down a hollow tube. They played in the long front bar where the atmosphere was presently sauna-like.

This chaunting folk music (diddley-diddley shit) went down very well. Finn told me that there was *mighty history* about the Old Head, the McCarthy lands and castles plundered by the Norman de Courceys.

'That place is rotten with McCarthys. Beyond Summercove they're all either McCarthys or Hurleys.'

The whole place was rotten with history; Summercove itself a haunt of suicides.

Your grandmother was buried in the little cemetery hard by Fort Charles, where you took me on our first walk. The Foleys lay for all eternity with their toes to the tides, your granny with her two children; one had died at eight months and the other not much older, of diphtheria.

In October the little port began to stink of fish; if you were walking down the Cork road, the smell of herring came to meet you. Three Polish factory ships were moored upriver between the Trident Hotel and the new bridge. Trawlers followed the herring shoals around the coast, coming from as far as Killybegs.

At other times the town smelt of brewery; from the malty stock-feed transported from the holds of foreign coasters into Good's mills opposite the Pier Cinema and the dead railway station on Knocknabohinny.

A bearded worker was letting down a plumbline from the ramparts of the French Prison in the rain, the corrugated roof having been removed, as also the slate roof of the friary, pending renovations by the Office of Public Works and E & T Builders respectively.

A young worker got out of his pick-up truck and pressed the chiming bell of a house called Deas Mumhan near the postbox let into the wall, the red initials VR were now painted green, and someone had cut 'SEX' with a penknife. The worker threw pebbles against an upstairs window. Presently there the curtains were drawn a little apart and a hand signalled.

Two little girls were passing below Friary Lane, one blessed herself in mid-leap as they skipped on down the hill past the French Prison where scaffolding had been erected against the window embrasures. The little girls skipped on past Deas Mumhan and its neighbour Mel Teog, where dwelt lace-curtain Irish. SEAN O'NEILL, ESTATE AGENT, a sign said sadly.

Miley Murphy was plucking a cock pheasant in the middle of his bicycle shop and two large dogs with tongues lolling were stuck together at Boland's corner.

The tide was almost fully out around the batteries of Fort Charles where half a dozen bored English soldiers had done themselves in at the turn of the century; there as a child you had played around the battlements.

From southern Europe in May, flying over the Brenner, came the red admirals to breed in the nettles.

The Bird I Fancied

In the Summer of Imran Khan

He was alone at the end of the bar, staring out of the window above my head, with a pint of Harry's indifferent bitter a third depleted before him, his thoughts miles away. A dead ringer for William Trevor. There were just the two of us in the small bar half an hour after opening time, and Harry eating an apple, minding his own business.

'Excuse me,' said I.

Odd ale-coloured eyes stared at me in astonishment and the gingery hair stood on end.

'You are not William Trevor?'

A slow hand reached out for the dying pint and in a low but distinctly Irish voice he said no he wasn't but not offering to say who he was.

'Pardon the intrusion.'

He did not answer. Vaguely vinegary Irish. This happened in the Coach and Hound, down from Jack Straw's Castle, patronised by queers and queer-bashers, not to be confused with the Coach and Horses, a Young's house near Hampstead tube station, patronised by the fancy.

Jack Trevor Story the thrice-bankrupt one was some-

times to be seen there, firing down double brandies in
the company of adoring young floozies. An ex-vaudeville
dancer, now well on in years, stood at the horseshoe-
shaped bar, gossiping with Harry. The White Russian
Lenski, a landscape painter in oils, and his inseparable
Estonian friend Malik, refugees from a pogrom, introduced an exotic foreign note to that corner of the bar,
to the right as you enter. Jack Trevor Story preferred to
sit at the counter with his floozies around him. He had a
deep brandy voice.

When old Megs was tippling at the sherry you could
wait half an hour to be served. It was a nice quiet bar.
The brother and sister drove to the opera in Harry's
vintage Overland. The sign of the window read

DNUOH DNA HCAOC

A month or two later, with a pint of Directors' set before
me, whom did I see but the same Gingery Man once
again materialising at the end of the bar, empty at that
time; squinting askance into the *Times* crossword. I sidled
near.

'You are William Trevor?'

He snorted a short barking laugh and across his
freckled features there spread an expression that can only
be described as damned shifty. Seen close to he looked a
different man.

'Indeed to goodness I am not,' he answered mildly. 'I
seem to remember that you asked me that once before.'

Nonplussed I did not reply. It was just after opening
time at the Coach and Hound. The Gingery Man looked
narrowly at me. His manner was such that did not invite
familiarity.

'You don't happen to have been at C— yourself?' he
asked, naming the very dump.

Now I was flabbergasted. Amused ale-coloured eyes studied me over the rim of his pint.

'Recognised you at once from a photo in the school mag,' he volunteered in a fruity voice fairly exuding privilege.

I said nothing. He looked uneasily at me as though he had made a social gaffe.

'No offence meant, I'm sure.'

'You evidently are not he,' I said.

'No. Unfortunately not. You know him?'

'No.'

He drew a deep breath and his strange eyes bulged out of their sockets. Then, with a nod, he resumed his intense deliberations with the *Times* crossword. In a while I passed behind him into the Gents. When I returned he was tapping his teeth thoughtfully with a biro. It was a quarter of an hour after opening time and the regulars had begun to trickle in, braying.

Some weeks later I recognised him at the Woodman and later again at the Prince of Wales, not alone now but in the company of a statuesque brunette with flashing eyes and an excitable manner; the pair of them with a powerful sandy Labrador in tow.

Then one evening at the Prince of Wales this happened. The William Trevor *doppelgänger* passed me *en route* to the Gents with eyes bulging and gingery hair again up-standing. He gave the impression of advancing always against a headwind, the eyes in his head swivelling. He had what my dear late mother used to call a 'consequential' air about him – meaning up to no good. He was always up to something, being a born plotter. On his way back he greeted me cordially.

'You again,' he said. 'There is someone here whom I'd like you to meet, if you have a moment to spare.' He beckoned me around the corner to where the brunette stood sipping her drink at the curve of the bar, surrounded by admirers.

'Mitzi,' said the Gingery Man masterfully laying a hand on her bare arm. 'Mitzi, here's a fellow countryman of mine who keeps insisting that I am William Trevor.'

'He is not William Trevor,' said Mitzi, drawing back a step to stare at me, high on the social occasion, high on life.

'My name, what is my name?' said the GM, just like Captain Fluellen.

'I shouldn't be a bit surprised if he *wasn't* William Trevor,' spoke up a non-reader, guffawing into his drink, joined in by Mitzi with her high silvery laugh.

'Perceptive of you, I'm sure,' sneered the GM.

'Perhaps he's *Jack* Trevor Story,' sniggered another.

'*Au contraire,*' replied the GM suavely. Sensing that something momentous had been concluded above his head, the powerful champagne-coloured Labrador seized this opportunity to thrust his damp muzzle into my crotch in a forceful and familiar way, the first but by no means the last of such frontal goosings, amid the general merriment.

'Down, Riley!' they cried. '*Manners!*'

Groaningly Riley subsided. The GM man extended his hand, saying: 'I'm Rory Beamish, of whom you would not have heard, and this lovely lady is Mitzi Kilkelly.'

'Brian,' I said.

They both looked at me, as did Riley from below.

'Anything else?' asked Mitzi.

'Brian Borumna, King of Munster?' Beamish tittered into his pint.

'Not a bit like him,' said Mitzi.

'Brian Mallord de Courcey Burke at your service.'

'What a nice name,' said Mitzi brightly.

'Thorpe?' the GM suggested.

'Burke,' I said rather loudly. 'As in Burke and Hare, you know.'

'Oh, *Burke!*' the GM cried. 'Now I get you. What will you have, er, Brian?'

'A White Shield, thank you,' I said.

'*Could* we just have some rapid service here!' Beamish rapping on the counter with the heel of his glass.

The great blond Labrador put down his head and commenced slobbering over his gruesomely distended far-from-private parts.

'*Riley!*' they shouted together, 'be*have!*'

It was through this hedonistic couple that I first met you, on an outing to the George Washington in Belsize village. It was to be a repeat performance of an afternoon when all, as so rarely, had gone well. Beamish picked me up at the Prince, his eyes popping; for he was ever a lover of conspiracy, full of 'sly iniquitee' as Chaucer's fox, very often sodden towards sundown.

'We're going to collect a friend.'

You were Mitzi Kilkelly's friend. Rory's too until I would take you away from him, make you his enemy. We drove to Belsize village in a company car with Wagner blasting from the stereo system and Riley attempting to sing along with his head and shoulders out the window. Beamish had been made redundant but still held onto the car, had gone on the dole. You sat behind me with Mitzi; I had not looked at you as you had come through the gate, feeling my *Schicksal* approaching. I could not place your accent, I could not remember your name. Beamish and Mitzi were laughing their heads off. I remained quiet, feeling you close to me.

Gatting was slow approaching his first test century or

'ton'. Prodding on the 'off', cutting on the 'leg', pulling to the boundary when he could. All the members were pushing into the Warner's Stand with gin and tonics in hand. Gatting wore a rural sun hat with a floppy brim as if haymaking, not batting for England, and was only thirty short of his hundred. But he never made it that day, for Imran was bowling like a man possessed.

Many were of the opinion that the Pakistani captain was a greater 'all-rounder' than bully-boy Botham of Somerset, who (said the silly commentator gentleman in the 'box') had been bowling *well within himself.*

Somerset Settle Bed

Her cat sat by the stove. Her hessian dress, as heavy as a cassock, was tied with a belt of blue. She hooked a plastic bucket over her arm. She held a skinned rabbit by its hind legs.

The goodnight kiss could lead to more than that. In their double bed, in your single bed, on the sofa or the settle bed in the kitchen, on a picnic, in the dunes, how long and how ardently when it happened and how often? The old man was a crotch-sniffer, a panty panter, with his sleeves rolled up soaping you in the bath. In your petticoat, in your chemise, in your gymslip. Observing you with his green eyes, lusting after his own flesh and blood, and you reduced to lower than the hired slut, the loose woman, the half-witted slattern in Glastonbury. 'Don't breathe a word of this to your mum.' He should have been castrated with Buddizzo pincers, a remarkable invention by an Italian doctor of genius. Groaning and whispering, 'Not a word of this to your mother, do you hear? Put on your nightie now.'

A crusty bachelor kept savage dogs. One of them flew at you and hung onto your arse growling tenaciously, until Old Parr broke his stick upon its back and off it ran howling.

As a young girl you hung upside down by your legs from a certain tree near Glastonbury, quondam centre of British Christianity, showing off your thighs and knickers, and made a wish. Any wish made while hanging upside down from that tree was sure to come true.

You rode the stallion Jupiter unshod and without bridle in the fields below the Tor. Then you were sixteen years old and working in a coffee shop in Glastonbury, with a half-hour walk home through a park. You were walking home one winter afternoon when the rapist suddenly emerged from ambush and joined you uninvited. 'You are the girl who works in the coffee shop.'

He threw you on the ground and raped you; you struggled and marked his face. You couldn't tell your parents. Mum had known about Dad's carryings-on when you were eight or nine. She had said nothing.

At the age of eighteen you had a pet jackdaw and were in love with David Attenborough.

At the age of nineteen or twenty years you left Glastonbury as a fully fledged *femme fatale* and took a train to London where in no time at all you were being offered drinks on the house by the legendary Compton brothers, Leslie and Denis, lords of the Prince of Wales in Highgate village, being put to bed upstairs, tearing off long strips of wallpaper with your bare fingernails. Of a frolicsome and easy disposition when not down in the dumps, you were frequently high as a kite.

Then, after many adventures, you were Carmencita the hot Spanish or Italian maid visited regularly in your poor attic at night by sweaty Bert the Express Dairy milk-roundsman in blue overalls and peaked cap, climbing through the skylight. On the cheap bedside table a packet of Celtas or Disque Bleu, a bottle of Diamante, two tumblers, a tattered copy of *Oggi*, a small purse with a few pounds in it, a hairclip. I came disguised as the randy roundsman whispering '*Carmen! Je chante pour moi-même!*' I was Fernando and you Martina, the steamed-up lovers in the *fotonovela*. I was the lion roaring in the pear tree.

'I don't play games,' the not yet familiar voice said coolly down the line. At the end of the saloon bar in the Angel I had kept two doors under observation and now kept the door of the phone booth ajar and one door under observation. You had promised to come at midday and now it was 1.30. I had bought two Scandinavian glasses in a hardware shop in Highgate near where I had embraced and bussed you the night before, while Beamish and his lady waited with glasses of brandy in the coffee shop. The heath was five minutes away, the sun was shining, my hopes were high, and now this.

'You can't come out?'

'I *won't* come out,' the voice said calmly. 'As I told you: I don't play games.'

'Who is playing games?'

She had nothing to say to that.

'I am being punished,' I said. 'Is that it?'

'You are being impertinent. And presuming a little, sir. I hardly know you.'

'Who is playing games now?'

She had nothing to say to that. I heard her breathing, listening, the indistinct sounds of her house not five miles away. The silence prolonged itself.

'Well, I suppose I'll see you around,' the voice said airily. As I had nothing to say to that she replaced the receiver and the line went dead.

*

You said to Moose, 'You want to kill me.' Moose said no, not you; it was evident whom he meant. Sometimes you had to sleep with him; it was no good. You made up your own room upstairs; he followed you up. You crept down, slept alone in his room; he followed you down. He was 100 per cent physical, a Haringey second-row forward, the heavy in the boilerhouse. He began to break things up. You and he could neither part nor live amicably together. It was the classic situation – the Marital Impasse. All concerned were having a bad time. The three children suffered: Saxon, Titus and Liza. The eldest son was twenty-two; Liza had been molested at the age of eight by an artist with a studio in Kentish Town. You knew him. You told me what would happen when you caught him.

You left Moose and went to stay with a redheaded businesswoman who had three redheaded daughters, having left her Jewish husband, a dentist in Golders Green. It is quite rare to meet interesting people in the Golders Green area. Beth Brocklehurst, breathing fire, followed you into her bathroom, sat smoking on the edge of the tub, praised your figure, enquired of your love-life, begged a goodnight kiss. She was attracted to lesbians and ladies with leanings. Her living room was decorated with posters of sinewy masculine-looking females who had legs long and sinewy as Fanny Blankers Koen's.

We were 'married' by the middle daughter Trixie, aged six, in the kitchen. Sixteen rings from a broken white necklace ringed our fingers, our names were repeated. Sally-and-Brian joined and sworn sixteen times; well and truly joined in wedlock by this innocent.

You were generous; when your dying mother gave you her own mother's jewellery, you handed it on to Liza. You looked after your mother, slept with her despite the terrible smell, washed her, put her on the pot. She was 'going down like a balloon', shrunken. 'My death comes in a direct line through her.' The old man had moved into the spare room, protesting that he was shy. Your mother had grown sharp; the old man didn't want to watch her dying. She had always been pretty, and now was pretty again; 'making sense at last'. She whispered to you: 'Your children are grown up now . . . Save yourself while you can.'

The long, long delays and then nothing any more; and then, out of the blue, a phone call. You never said your name, nor mine neither. So you would phone and if one of my sons took the call they would say 'It's Sally.' If Margaret took it she would say sourly 'An admirer.'

We walked down the hill and into Highgate Wood, and up the hill by the Woodman to the Flask and by a shortcut to the ponds. I watched you feeding the ducks on Highgate ponds, dropping grass into the water.

'You don't see me.'

'Of course I see you . . . feeding the ducks.'

No, you insisted, I didn't see you. I protested that I did, not being blind, but you were not mollified.

'I'm watching you,' you said, 'all the time.'

What was one to make of that? With you, I seemed to be further away from you. I could hardly call you my woman, much less my mistress. On good evenings we walked to the top of the hill past the police station, or I waited by the Woodman and you came off the bus when you were working for the deaf.

'I'm shattered,' you said.

You were frequently shattered.

'I won't live long. I'll die soon. I'm old.'

You remarked on the shortness of my nails. Yours grew and grew, your hair too. Two years ago you told me that you loved me. Me too, I said.

You glared at me.

'Oh no, I won't take that.'

I looked at your hands, fine feminine hands wrinkled at the knuckles, determined hands. You asked me to hold both your hands when you crouched over a narrow trench cut by road workers; this was at night behind Fortis Green police station, and I was supposed to whistle. You wore a sort of moss-green-grey T-shirt over the usual loose black fatigues, with Oxfam shoes of a crushed strawberry colour, which you managed to piss over.

I saw the form of a hedgehog run over many times on the dust of the track, and you mentioned cattle-traps of Somerset with hedgehog runs below them. I had to hold both your hands as you leant back, and I was supposed to whistle, in the dry lane behind the Clissold Arms, a dull, airless very English pub that was like an ocean liner *en route* to India in the 1930s. The lounge was crowded with the undead and their stale cigarette smoke. 'They're not worth saving,' you said, dismissing them.

You spent a wet winter's night in the ruins of Alexandra Palace, a foolish thing to do; arrived home with chattering teeth for Moose to throw open the door. He asked no questions, had murder on his mind. We had nowhere to go.

For Moose the footer season opened with fractured ribs, ended with broken teeth. At a rowdy party for rugger friends, all drinking their heads off, he forced you to sit on a hot and hairy lap, the only woman there. A part-time barman 'chatted you up' at the Baird, became aggressive, asked where was the Brain of Britain, demanded attention, kissed you in Beth's kitchen.

'I don't take no from a bird I fancy.'

You told him to go home, that he was pushing his luck. He slunk away, cursing. You took chances, thinking yourself safe in minicabs, asked the coloured driver to kiss you, you were kissing me. He said he was gay; you said it didn't matter, he kissed you. A kerb-crawler drove you home. You changed, were driven to Highgate Golf Club. You asked the fare, but it wasn't even a minicab. You might have been raped. You were moving fast in several directions at once, lost, 'shattered'. Your skin aroma: geranium. Your hair: meadowsweet.

It was around that time that your electricity supply was cut off, and the Falklands débâcle ended. 'The antipodes really grate on me,' a morose drinker admitted at the Gate House. You chased a peeping Tom out of Highgate Wood as if chasing a goose, not a flasher, a flustered biker carrying a white crash helmet into which he had been masturbating.

CHRIST IS COMING, went the graffiti on a wall; below it a wit had finely amended, WHEN? and below that another hand had written, SO IS TOM (PERRIER).

The endless beginning with you; the interminable endings.

One morning in June I received a mysterious phone call. An unknown voice spoke in my ear: 'Hallo,' said the male voice. 'This is Liam Kelly.'

'Yes, what can I do for you.'

'What can I do for *you?* I'm on the Grace Gate.'

Darkish clouds covered Trent Bridge. I showed you pictures of Imran Khan in action, the handsome Pathan all-rounder, the Pakistani captain. Never in your life had you seen such a handsome man.

'Easy, easy, easy,' chanted the louts before the Lord's Tavern, pints of lager in hand, as Imran Khan moved in to bowl, panther-like.

*

I was the one who used you and who would abandon you; I was the very worst. 'Wish you could shoot me with your gun,' you said, touching it. 'My breasts are enlarged, now that it's useless.' Where are the charming variations? Where would we be without our atmospherics? One day when we were in the kitchen, drinking white wine on opposite sides of the long refectory table, Buzz came downstairs looking for a comb; came wet from the shower with a small towel about her waist like a sarong, very black and gleaming. Buzz was your best friend; she came from the Windward Islands. She was going out with a West End chef who was half her age, having decided to ditch her husband, who was a relatively wealthy man. He had discovered Buzz on a beach at Barbados.

Now the urge took hold of us to be away from the habitat of Moose and his henchmen and informers (Freddy the Scouse), going by bus into the country, the hinterland where I had never set foot before. We boarded a bus that turned away from the Barnet route and ended up half an hour later near a police station and a huge pub with a garden at the back; it would have been one of the coach stops on the great north road out of London, a haunt of highwaymen. We stepped into a great echoing beery pub with food counters and desperate boozers hunched on seats, one fellow in a dirty raincoat taking a pile of old newspapers into the Gents, and in a corner a big throbbing jukebox flashing orange lights and out of it a bull voice bellowing. It brought to mind Pabst's movie *Kameradschaft*, the pandemonium with scores of coal-blackened naked miners in the showers, the steam rising up to the roof and the bundles of clothes that resembled hanged men being hauled up and down on chains. Now and again we went there, where I felt relatively unthreatened by Moose and his minions. It was the end of the line.

In Buzz's place now 'Black Sally' from St Kitts was laughing and shaking all over like a jolly black blancmange, all powerful eighteen stone of her balanced on your lap, crushing you. While busy Buzz Deering was cooking something hot and spicy on the stove we sent out for more white wine.

'Galway Sally', a small beaky-faced woman from Connemara, worked behind the food counter at the Green Man. And no doubt there were other versions of you walking about north London. You were multiplying (or subdividing) yourself. Reality was withdrawing from you, or you from reality.

Once, recovering from a hangover in the afternoon when the Prince had closed, you took me to a friend's place. She was out, the children in the kitchen said, but due back shortly. Molly Gentle came into the bedroom to find us washing each other in the sunken bath. We dressed and went downstairs to the kitchen where she was cooking pancakes. You told of the day when you and she had gone sheep-shearing in the estranged husband's Devon farm, nonplussed the natives who were inclined to sneer at city folk, and fine ladies at that. I walked into Highgate for more Rioja.

This was the good friend who told you later: Any man will do, those with no money who are drunk all the time won't do. After two years apart she returned to her husband.

We went naked to a lower room at Brocklehurst's place, dragged a double mattress from a spare bed. You asked or rather ordered me to strike you, but I would not. Going downstairs in a sheet, I returned with a tumbler of water and two pears from the garden, where a lion roared in the pear tree each time I had you; but I would not hit you. I was the milkman climbing through the skylight and you the French maid in her poor attic bed.

You had suggested, perhaps frivolously, a honeymoon in Bath, where we would drink at the Hat and Feathers, but we never went to Bath, we never made it. Instead I went to Wandsworth, to keep an eye on the house of friends who had gone to Tuscany (or was it Greece?) on vacation; and to feed their cat, Cecil. It was our ten-day honeymoon there, in Honeywell Road, the whole house seemed to float over the common, over the railway bridge out over the river, only to come floating back again over the County Arms and the Hope, back to its rightful place, and you and I in it, certainly not in our rightful place.

I went there alone, half hoping you would follow. The whole house took to creaking and groaning in the August heatwave, the woodwork continuing to contract and expand, to the accompaniment of a Rastafarian uproar in a house down the way. Next door an irate mother's voice spoke to a child: 'Come on, *sit up* and eat properly!' This into my ear. In the heat the walls had become paper-thin. I heard the child complain. 'You're going to get a *smack on the bottom!*' cried the mother, her patience sorely tried. Then the phone rang. It was midnight, maybe later. Then came the smack and the screams of the child.

'Sally is that you?'

'Dieter here,' said an alert unsober foreign male voice.

'Who?'

'Dieter,' the brisk foreign voice said, 'from Hamburg, you know. How are you *meek*? Happy birthday!'

'Who are you? Is this your idea of a joke?'

'Dieter,' the unsober foreign voice said. 'Dieter here *meek*. You are not *meek*?'

'No,' I said. 'I am *not* meek, damn you, whoever you are!'

I heard a buzzing and babble of confused voices and then the Dieter voice came clear.

'Who is this please?'

I thought about this. It was 2.10 a.m.

'Baron Hubert von Bechtolsheim,' I said, replacing the receiver.

The hot sun shone all next day but you did not come. I bought drink and provisions. The cat Cecil was infested with fleas, bluebottles hummed above the cat-dish. Rasta music started up as darkness fell. I did not venture out, thinking that you might arrive and find the house empty. At six you phoned. I gave you the address and directions how to get there. You were noncommittal. 'I *miss* you.'

I retired to bed at midnight, having drunk half a bottle of gin and one bottle of chilled Muscadet, dining lightly on corncobs. The house continued creaking and groaning. In the middle of the night the bell chimed briefly below and I was awake at once and heard you call my name through the letterbox, heard the engine throb of a minicab outside. I descended three flights of stairs, opened the front door, and there you were, with a minicab behind you and a West Indian driver rolling down the window.

'That's it then, miss?'

'That's him,' you said. 'Goodnight. Thanks.' He let in the clutch and drove away as you came into the hall to be embraced.

'I have arrived,' you said, 'so to speak.'

'Come in,' I said.

Juggernauts were weakening Hammersmith Bridge. Suspension chains had been slackened and iron studs collapsed in one of the towers. The bridge had slipped

two and a half inches and no more traffic was allowed
over.

The body of an unidentified man had been found
wrapped in curtain material in an East End rubbish tip.

We went again to Athene's, that Ali Baba's cave, and
Stavros the owner gave us drinks on the house because
his wife Mary was pregnant, and he wanted a son.

'A glass of wine then, to put us in the proper frame of
mind.'

Stavros insisted that it had to be Greek brandy.

'Go on, have a little taste.'

We said we would. The sexual assistant came and lit the
candle on our table and you told me of Sam and Annie
Loveridge, aged one hundred and two and ninety-nine
respectively, who lived with their eldest boy Jack aged
seventy-seven in a mobile home in a field near the village
of Curry Rivel, adjacent to Langport in Somerset. Everybody lived to a ripe old age in Somerset. The signs in
nature were for a good summer. Stavros came and sat
with us.

'What do you pair do in the daytime?'

He worked long hours, worked hard, intended to
return to Greece and buy property. London was 'unreal'.
He ordered more Greek brandy. You looked at me with
your lynx-green eyes under the bang of hair like a strange
animal in the mouth of its burrow – *stilly crouches she*.
Stavros said we must come to his place on Thursday nights
when all the Greeks were there.

'What happens?'

'Belly-dancing.'

'I made a complete horlicks of it,' you said. Your stories
tended to be on the grim side; was this the famous city
edge? You came breezily into the sitting room off the

kitchen where Beamish and Mitzi 'relaxed', and told how Brixton police had ganged up on one black man, and you wouldn't have it, you stuck up for him, gave cheek to the police. 'Oh so you are one of them too?' the copper sneered, perhaps mistaking you for a darkie. You were dark as an Ethiopian beauty with esoteric green eyes, the dark hair combed down over the eyes; and on your face tribal markings, a sign of caste and valour. Mitzi slammed the car door in your face, so you had a healed scar on the bridge of your nose, and would presently require five stitches in your chin, from an unsober accident in Buzz's garden. Testimony to the bottle.

You came wet and naked out of the sea at night and some Spanish fishermen were watching you dressing behind a wall and going into a *merendero* and ordering coffee and *anis seco* as the sun came up and you lit a Celtas.

You told of the fellow from Yorkshire who liked girls three in a bed, with *Playboy* centrefold nudes tacked on the wall. Nava wanted you to join her in a sauna and 'Mrs Bracegirdle' rather fancied you. We smoked your hash in the kitchen and I was dismembering a chicken and cutting it up on the breadboard and you were watching me and called out '*I can't stand it any more!*' and we went to bed and I had you twice. And then you told me that Mary Queen of Scots had her favourite Skye terrier hidden under her crinoline as she knelt at the block and when her head dropped into the basket the terrier flew out, at Fotheringhay, at Fotheringhay.

Contradictions abounded.

Beamish was a master of circumlocution. He had written a thriller, now he was writing a book about the gold standard, and it would 'make a mint'. He mixed lethal Silver Bullets in the kitchen, studied the *Economist* and

Financial Times in the living room, where several cats glided in and out or stared through the window at Riley slumped on the floor. We drank on either side of the round table. The picture above us framed behind glass was an illustration torn from the Bible: '*The great fish vomiting out Jonah upon the dry land*'. We sat there, drinking and talking, waiting for Mitzi to return from work.

'The Eskimos have thirty-eight different words for snow,' Beamish said.

'I wonder how many different words for sand the Arabs have.'

Life at number 64 continued on its own sweet way.

Technically you had lost your virginity at the age of four when you took a tumble off your tricycle. Your marriage was not a success. Your women friends were all divorced and all had gentle names of women one could trust: Molly Gentle, Sue Ainsley, Cheryl Bailey of the Caribbean, the Russian Nava Jahans, Geraldine Quinn, and a desperate Polish woman whom we had met one day in the Rose and Crown.

When let off the leash Riley became demented; freedom went to his head. At the cricket pitches in Highgate Wood he began quartering the ground, muzzle down and powerful shoulders working, backtracking and then disappearing among the trees, followed by Beamish in a highly exasperated mood. '*Rile-eeeee!*'

Riley went coursing through the wood, depositing steaming hot stools at every gate. Rushing down the hill he came upon a frail old woman out exercising her aged golden retriever, an animal as old and frail as the mistress. But soon Riley was gambolling about this pair, sniffing and canoodling, instantly aroused and attempting to mount the aged retriever dog, made dizzy by these avid attentions.

Love Goes A-riding (Your Well-deserved Garter)

A pregnant schoolgirl goes missing from a Cornish fishing village. A body is recovered, but not the right one. Are these two incidents connected?

We love what is imperishable, that other body perceived as being imperishable (the old lie). The reflection of your face in the window at Grand Avenue opening on the garden, with the children at the bonfire. Your dear face amid the children.

Later, making do, and no wiser, we love what is perishable; the other body rising and sinking like a corpse in the sea. But you would always remain the same age for me: a good-looking thirty-nine that could pass for six years younger. So you would never grow any older, provided I left you, provided we parted, preserving each other in aspic.

You were The-Tart-Over-the-Hill, The-Easy-Lay, The Flibbertigibbet, The Good-Fuck, The Woolworth's Girl, in Margaret's considered terms of opprobrium.

'I have an arts degree,' you said tartly, 'more than she has – the stuck-up bitch!' Margaret Burke, A Stuck-Up Bitch.

All for a bit of slap-and-tickle. All for a bit of fun; for my girl's a Somerset girl, tiddleybum, tiddleybum. We having begun our half-life together in others' gardens, terraces and kitchens, living rooms and spare bedrooms;

over an area that grew progressively wider to embrace not only Hampstead but Finsbury Park and the fringes of Crouch End and Barnet, covering say a twenty-mile radius. And when you lay down in the sun in bra and panties the peeping Toms crept forth, holding their breath, to tiptoe past; the eager voyeurs alertly observant on the slopes of the hill in Ken Wood or Hampstead Heath overlooking the ponds.

You had gone home for warmer clothes. Moose saw you in the bath with enlarged breasts, tufts of shameless hair under your arms, and dared to question you. He gave you penetrating looks and said *you* looked younger and prettier, must have been with a hundred men. You said nothing to that, spoke to your children, collected some clothes, phoned a minicab and again departed, leaving poor Moose speechless.

Nick Ridley at the Prince was 'into bondage', had strung up a Chinese girl, cut her down before she choked. He was not 'into verbals', but loved to hear the Monday night band play 'Georgia'.

Riddled with Silver Bullets one night Beamish asked Mitzi to dress up in fishnet stockings and red garters, black patent leathers with six-inch stiletto heels, a wet-look plastic mackintosh, and awoke sober next morning to find this apparition sleeping by his side. The dark eyeliner had run, the false eyelashes were awry, the stilettos had penetrated the wet-look mac. Beamish sprang out of bed, demanding to know what the fucking hell was this supposed to mean.

Your fancy, dear heart. Only your fancy.

You were scandalised by the gyrations of the English belly-dancer in the candlelit basement at Athene's. You told

me so. I sat beside you among the Greeks and drank
Greek brandy. Stavros sang in a velvety voice and they all
laughed and applauded. Then the lights were turned off
and on came the belly-dancer. She was as wanton and
buxom as could be desired, showing off her bowspring
back, her tufted armpits, the sweat of her brow. Stavros
stuffed a fiver into her cleavage to encourage the rest,
and soon bra and panties were abulge with fivers and
tenners, and she gyrated in the candlelight like a Pict girl
festooned with pagan feathers.

You told me your dream. You were climbing a hill with
me. There was the sound of stones rattling; splashings
from above, gurglings from below, on this rain-sodden
mountain. We came upon a spring of water that gushed
out from under a thicket and then saw an elephant,
dripping wet, washing itself there, using its trunk as a
hose. As we approached the elephant turned itself into
an ape.

One day you said: 'I dreamt you turned into a tree.'
And another day: 'I dreamt you came in my hair.' And
another day again: 'I dreamt you were a tree between my
legs.'

'I had a dream too,' I said. We were wandering from
room to room in this curious house of interleading rooms
like *Berlinzimmer* all empty or oddly furnished. We went
down the wide stairs into a room with tall windows. Again
and again I had dreamed of this vaguely disturbing place,
called 'Bullsease', or 'Haus Herzentodt'. I was there as
usual, waiting for you, nervous and anxious. Then I am
outside, and coming towards me a sort of hay wagon of
Somerset packed with long-stemmed flowers splendid as
fountain spray. An oldish countrywoman with a bandana
knotted about her head is holding the reins, but there is

no horse between the shafts, the wagon packed with
flowers moves slowly and grandly over the stubble.

I saw your dear face to one side, leaning out; and then
I was again inside and you approached with a gift of
flowers, 'flowershod and swaying', breathless.

We found ourselves in a narrow corridor. You suggested:
'Best meet her.' We passed a group of people pressed to
the wall, smiling. We went into the kitchen and Margaret
was there with her friend Betsy Arbuckle. I walked around
the table, having forgotten Betsy's name, said 'Nancy',
and made a gesture of metaphysical liquidation. Margaret
was freezingly polite.

After a short and uncomfortable time, Margaret silent
and staring, Betsy gushing, you made an excuse to leave
the room. I followed you. In 'our' room we were instantly
undressed and I pulled you down by the window. 'There's
moisture down below,' you said. There was indeed. 'One
of Mother Nature's little secrets,' you said. I had you *a
tergo* under the window.

There were houses and flats opposite, but not of
Somerset; just uncomfortable-looking dream dwellings. It
was late evening and electric lights were shining. In a
dressing-gown and in a mood of *post coitum triste* I went
out to unplug or disconnect these lights that were shining
into the room. I unplugged a number of them, but one
persistent light remained, the source of which I could not
find. I came to a Spanish bar. The drinkers were all male,
with their back to me, watching some game on television.

Beamish was now frequently to be seen in the John Baird
drinking pints of Directors' and talking to Alec Diggs, a
former member of the Spanish International Brigade. An
ex-postman from Mayo, a Gaelic speaker and reader of
An Béal Bocht, drank with them. From him Rory earned
for himself the sobriquet *Eoghan Ruadh an Bheil Bhinn* or

Red-Rory-of-the-Sweet-Mouth. This was Liam who worked on the Grace Gate at Lord's during test matches.

'Outside Tralee one time . . .' I heard the great raconteur say as I sidled in. He invited me to join them and ordered up a drink.

'How am I?' he said. 'Absolutely bloody well fed up to the back teeth.'

'The pound sterling rock steady and Glaxo shares up,' said Mitzi, tossing her head like a golliwog.

'Back again all bright and bushy-eyed are we?' said the intolerably gregarious barman. 'Same again then?'

'Must dash,' Mitzi said rising up. 'Things to be done. *Byeeee!*'

'I shouldn't be in the least surprised if you weren't William Trevor at all,' I said to Beamish who was staring fixedly at the door through which Mitzi had passed.

'Well, you may set your mind at rest,' he said, 'because I'm not.'

'What's Madame doing?'

'Part-time kindergartening, to keep me in the style I have grown so accustomed to,' said Beamish, applying his lips to his foaming Directors'.

'And ever-loyal Riley?'

Beamish put down his depleted pint and threw himself back in his seat, extending his right arm.

'The good Riley is at home, since you are kind enough to enquire, guarding our possessions. He has pulled this arm right out of its socket.' The Plantigrade Shuffler veering wildly from side to side, dragged hither and thither by Riley, 'luffing' in the manner of the insane butcher in Buñuel's *El*. The powerful champagne-coloured Labrador dragging him off his feet.

I recalled the hens scratching about the Drunken Duck public house and sailing on Lake Windermere by night under a sickle moon, fishing for char, listening to Villa-Lobos on the car radio as we waited for the ferry, Bill Swainson and I, and the trout rising on the lake at night and phosphorescent bubbles from the wake of the little yacht and the sickle moon breaking up into several moons. And walking over the fells to come to the Bridge Inn that Sunday, and ineffable melancholy mixed with joy, rare as hot sun on an April day, rarer than radium, missing you, but also knowing you were somewhere (in Glastonbury) thinking of me. And drinking the good Thwaites draught ale at the Masons, and the hut by the lake.

You came like the wind from Glastonbury, driven at 95 m.p.h. on the M4 by Murchison. A pebble flew up to shatter the windscreen which turned opaque but Murchison thrust his gloved fist through it and drove on, a regular Stirling Moss. And you went from pub to pub trying to find me, pursued by a Dubliner from the Red Lion and Sun. You were in a minicab, were quite pleased that I was 'so hard to find'; until coming into the Alexandra you found me with Verschoyle.

'I *missed* you,' you said. It was a recurring refrain. And what was Murchison doing in Glastonbury?

'Say something nice.'

I had missed you on Lake Windermere by the boathouse in early August, a month of falling stars; naked in the stream at Calne in Wiltshire in the converted millhouse mentioned in the Domesday Book; and in a wheatfield at Battle in Sussex, all in one summer.

'I dreamt I was in Acapulco with a boring old woman. It was so green and warm.'

She had her bottom pinched by Chuck Berry at a party after a gig. 'Nice ass,' said Chuck gallantly.

'I dreamt I was made managing director of Irish Cement.'

Another dream: You were invited to Sandringham to meet Prince Charles. In a cottage somewhere on the estate the Queen approached in jodhpurs and an orange jersey and her first words were: 'I'm afraid we seem to have an enormous lot of dogs here.'

The place was full of dogs, chows, corgis. Prince Charles's face appeared behind a sofa; he struggled to his feet, stood up to shake your hand. 'I *knew* I was right. I thought it was you.'

'Seen close to he is better-looking than the photos suggest. The ears don't stick out quite as much and the jaw is less lantern. He is in fact quite a handsome man. His opening shot was most diplomatic. He took my arm and led me aside to ask: "*Do* I recognise you?"'

'Impeccable timing. Then we had tea with the Queen and all the royal dogs.'

Another dream: you dreamed that you had breakfast with Prince Charles. Or rather you watched him eating his breakfast. An enormous butler's tray was brought to him on a trolley, and plate after plate put down before him, cups of tea, two fillets of kipper nicely arranged, a couple of big bangers, marmalade and toast, a portion of kedgeree. He ate it all quite calmly and didn't think to offer you any. By this time he was formally dressed in a grey suit and highly polished black shoes, none of your casual dressing-gown and slippers for Charles, to whom all this was quite normal, something he did every morning, served by his butler, being watched by an admirer and it just never occurred to him to offer you anything, 'although I was starving'. The butler was 'just a hand serving the heir to the English throne. I was nothing.

'Then Wales took me for a stroll about the estate. The

Queen had gone off with her dogs and we were alone. Then he took my arm again and said: "There is something I must show you." We went indoors again and on his private projector he ran a film which he thought I might like – *Bahama Passage* with Sterling Hayden and Madeleine Carroll up to no good on an isle underneath the sea that was mysteriously flooded with perpetual sunlight. Before that they were in a city and she took off her stockings behind a screen.

'Then I was walking with my father along a path. He was smoking a Woodbine and said in a very sour way: "Well, *you*'ve earned your Garter." '

'You don't see me,' were your accusing words. I was standing on a knoll watching you feeding grass to the ducks on Highgate pond, the ducks ignoring this food, circling about, quacking.

'Certainly I see you,' I said, 'feeding ducks.'

'He's been a bad husband to me,' you said of Moose, adding as an afterthought: 'But then again I've been a bad wife to him.'

For months at a stretch you went underground, did not contact me, I could not phone you. Then one fine morning you came strolling over the brow of the hill by the Swiss Chalet, carrying a string bag with French bread and cucumber, a Penguin book (*Querelle of Brest*). We went down the hill into the Royal Oak. You had painted two white fishes head-to-head on your brown Russian boots, it was our astrological sign, Pisces, the furtive ones. I showed you my passport photo and you took it, hid it in one of the Russian boots. You had been to Dorset, chauffeur for your father Victor Nutt, stopping in the pretty village of Langton Herring. Victor Nutt was smoking a

Woodbine. He looked around, asked: 'Why have you taken me here?'

You repeated once again that we were finished. 'Find another,' you said.

I said nothing to that. You touched my knee.

'Find somebody else,' you said. 'Live with a man.'

You had been to a gathering of gays in a club near Marble Arch. They were all smoking pot, got up in black leather like shining beetles. A Harley Davidson was hung up on chains and they were raffling it. The winner had to sing a song. He came up to the platform waving his winning ticket and sang the old George Shearing number 'The Nearness of You'. All the black-clad gays cheered. Later one of them bit your arse, twice. Another goosed you.

'You are my one and only,' I said. 'Am I not yours?'

The gays were drinking from six-packs, Budweiser and Schlitz, behaving in a truculent manner adopted from their heroes, Brando, Bronson, Clint Eastwood. You sat behind a curtain with a friendly gay. The floodlit motorbike hung on chains. 'Bud?' a gay said. 'I'm stone mad for it.'

'I am turning into you.'

'Then I'll turn into you,' I said.

You told of a male friend who dressed in drag, went to parties got up as Shirley Bassey, called herself 'Shirley', mimed to Bassey songs, wanted to be her, would-be Bassey the torch-singer of Tiger Bay, bursting out of a sheath dress with shoulders bare.

Butterflies can alter their wing patterns to make themselves more like their beloved, by and by, in the by-and-by. That studied languor of the bared flesh, the dark eyes aglitter under the 1920s fringe, fitful gleams of rings and pendants in the spotlight that moved as she moved. No period for feeling lachrymose.

Deare, if you change, I'll never chuse againe,
Sweet; if you shrink . . .

'Having another go at staying off the bottle,' your voice
at the end of the line said confidentially. 'Then fell off
the wagon with the hell of a crash. Got so bad for a week
it's a wonder I didn't drown. No guts you see.' (Pause)
'What did you say?'

'Nothing,' I said.

'Feel so frantic and alone,' the voice at the end of the
line resumed. (Longish silence) 'Look for you everywhere.' (Low) 'Talk about you to everybody.' (Longer
pause, lower) 'What's that supposed to mean?' (Silence,
emphatic) 'I *miss* you.' (Long silence) 'What was that?'

Sound of receiver being replaced to muffled curse.
When we met again you told me you had drunk about
200 glasses of wine at the Railway Tavern in Finsbury Park
and 'broke the place up'.

'Get sorted out,' they said.

You drank until you were cleaned out, feeling 'knack-
ered', and again went to ground.

I had asked you not to leave it so long and you promised
you would not. If I cannot have you, can I at least have
your photograph? On Axminster Station one day in
August of the previous year, looking very brown and Mediterranean, not posing but staring at the photographer
(Moose?), returning from family outing to Lyme Regis.
You looked grave.

Now rain fell like hailstones, white drops falling out of
the sky, and Buzz was driving off with her kids as I
approached the flat.

Nothing since the first of February and now 25 June
and still nothing, four months' abstinence, not quite that
for you; Moose still fancies you, perhaps still loves you,

wants to murder me. Then I saw you twice in seven months, had you twice in seven months, and both drunk each time. Once you were 'infected', once 'pregnant', and always missing me. The sun enters Cancer on the 21st. For one reason or another it appears to be strained relationships and uncertainty about the future. This cycle must end. I phoned Buzz and asked for your Glastonbury number, which you had urged me never to use, phoned that number and found myself speaking to an affable lady in Loch Ness, in cold far-off Scotland.

'How's the monster?'

Brief guffaw.

'He is very seasonable.'

'Sorry to trouble you. I seem to have the wrong number.'

'No trouble at all,' Loch Ness said brightly and hung up. Glastonbury did not respond. Perhaps you were out at Chewton Mendip entertaining the Nutts. On television Sir Harry Secombe got up in a blazer stood before the Wells Choir and the ballsy guys in blue blazers sang lustily 'The Fires of Love Die'.

You did not write, phone, or walk in the Broadway. Buzz thought you were still in Somerset. Distance is the prerequisite of happiness, some German (Eich Ehrgeiz?) thought perversely. I went on waiting, unhappily.

'All he ever wanted of her was a large hot meal every night, back-rubs in the bath and his rugby gear washed every Friday,' Buzz said, laughing.

'And his jockstrap,' I suggested.

Buzz screeched.

'But it's *you* she loves. She can't stop talking about you.'

I saw a brute whom I took to be Moose head-butting a terrified drinker outside the Eastern Electricity showrooms on the Broadway one night. If not getting thoroughly pissed on vodka in the Railway Arms he was stepping into the Alexandra by one door as I left by the other, walking up and down East Finchley, and what if I met him? Felled by a pile-driver in the breadbasket and castrated with a breadknife.

You said we 'might as well pack it in'; for our 'lack of the readies' was chronic.

Where, then, was our cottage small by a waterfall? In a time of heart-scalding and promises denied.

You would settle into the driving seat, light up a cigarette, and drive off to Blandford Forum, or Chaldon Herring, or Maiden Newton, or Litton Cheney, or Cerne Abbas in Dorset or Slough's Despond or some small village in the Mendip Hills, haunt of adders.

You were giving me a long reflective stare, a horse-eyed look under your bangs, saying nothing, your tipped cigarette on the lip of the ashtray, your pint a third depleted.

'I dreamt you came in my hair.'

Not in Lyme Regis nor in Chuffnell Regis. There stood the empty cottage; behind it the beach with driftwood.

'Where did you get those lovely moleskin trousers?'

'There wasn't a day down there in Wiltshire when I didn't think of you,' I said.

The clatter of the millrace, a spider's web in the centre of the millwheel, the rattle of the wren every morning, the murmur of the Marden. I brought out a cast-iron garden chair, stuck it in the stream, sat in it naked, read Prescott's *Conquest of Mexico*, felt your absence. A minnow gulped down a wasp under the plum tree where water-logged snails lay on the clay bed and warble-flies traversed the stream a foot wide where the heron had left its careful tracks.

'What do you mean,' you said, 'a day? Why not every minute?'

The sweet pealing of the church bell in Bremhill where Margaret (a great mislayer of things) had lost her pocket-book with all her holiday money, later reclaimed from some honest person; the choked-off cry of the pheasant and the birds calling '*Refrain, refrain, refrain*' to the eddies in the pool. Sunlight on leaves reflecting water, a stand of Victoria plums: ecstatic awareness.

'Why not indeed.'

You wrote from Glastonbury, a postcard showing the famous Tor in moonlight, discreetly sealed within an envelope. 'Dear Brian, It's raining and cold and the wind blows and the journey was beastly full of delays. I shall either come back immediately or stay longer than I had intended. Otherwise the air is fresh and the people friendly. Your Sally.'

In great warehouses in Glastonbury and in the Mendips, farmhouse Cheddar is slowly getting older and riper and stronger, wrapped in film and packed in wooden cases stored on well-ventilated shelves with two-inch cheesecloth protecting the perimeter, looked after by old cheese-makers with cheese-bores in hand, gripped in yellow rubber gloves, testing and crumbling the cheese, inhaling it, something good to write home about all right.

Calne, Wilts (Absences)

She needs to humiliate herself in order to save him. There's no wind at all. A gorgeous full moon rises. The fishing boats return to their anchorage at sundown. He walks along the shore.

Ye Dumb Post Inn. 'Did get leg over last night, Seth?' 'Nay, but tell thee what though: I get a better ride off tractor than ah do off t'Missus.'

*

I went down there with Margaret on *her* invitation, for a long weekend at the beginning of August, in a month of falling stars. We were lucky with the weather.

Walked out the first morning onto the Nature Trail which commenced with a large fresh human turd steaming on the middle of the path, not long discharged and a-hum with frantic bluebottles. Ten minutes later I all but trod on a rabbit dying of cruel myxomatosis, its head down, shuddering in agony. The path followed the Marden stream as it flowed under an antique hump-backed bridge and then across a road, and I could smell the toxic land and presently heard the grinding and screeching of industrial machinery as acetylene sparks flew from a dark open door. A woman out walking her dog bade me the time of day as we passed.

Returning I found a pool deep and wide enough to dip in, dressed and saw the familiar herd of Jerseys crossing a field and on approaching Hazeland Mill thought or imagined I saw whom but Margaret walking to meet me and waving but a closer view revealed this as my washed white shirt flapping on the line.

A hairy-chested fellow in a string vest called out that it was his birthday and he was buying the bar drinks. He had a cleft palate and seemed a little half-witted, a Viking who had lost his way. Some drank from pewter mugs, a fellow with one finger on his right hand, all tattooed fellows in T-shirts, then a smiling Negro appeared in shorts. A big solid lump of a man worked the pumps, affable to regulars, and this was Brian Pitt the genial host. An old-timer carried in a hand-cranked gramophone and set it to play some old favourites. Margaret and I sat by the window and saw a harvest moon rise over a distant hill and sheep moved around in a misty field as Richard

Tauber sang '*O Bella Margherita*' as though he were singing under the sea.

'A trip down Memory Lane,' the old man said. He put it all together again and departed.

We left the pub in the Wiltshire dusk and went down a hill by a field of peaceful sheep grazing in moonlight.

By Drewett's Mill a signpost pointed towards BATH 5 MILES. Tourists gazed at objects on the abbey walls and a bare-shouldered lady who might as well have been in a museum, was being edified by what she saw.

'The faithless wandering about,' Margaret said, 'faithlessly.'

Don't look now. When love begins to sicken and decay it useth an enforced ceremony.

Across the bar a young father dandled a baby on his lap, put it in the crook of his arm, gave it the bottle, all to a song by Joan Armatrading, in the Angel, Islington, where Margaret and I had gone for one last drink on our return from Wiltshire. The infant made cooing sounds, jerking out its bootees. Beyond them a window seemed to open on a blue sky but I knew darkness had already fallen, and the blue sky was a colour television screen where presently a line of burnt-out double-decker buses appeared and then earnest demonstrators marching with banners through Belfast. Margaret sat silent with her gin and tonic, tired by the long drive home. The barman pushed small change towards me.

'You're away over the top, mate.'

'Blame it on travel fatigue,' I said, pocketing the coins.

Back from Wiltshire and the phone rang twice. I assumed it was Beamish on the razzle and answered the second call with circumspection. You said my name rather loudly.

'How are the eyes?'

'All right. It's the teeth now. I lost one in Bath.'

'In the *bath*!'

'No, in Bath.'

'What were you doing in Bath?'

'Oh passing through, you know.'

The shire once lauded by Camden now sunken in apathy and sloth, in the force of inertia as defined in mechanics. It was on the tip of my tongue to say: It all depends what you were doing in Glastonbury.

In a time of fresh breezes, with temperatures soaring into the high seventies, we took a picnic one day into Alexandra Park, and lay down in the long grass before the palace, the scaffolding still up before the View Bar, as it had been for fifteen years, and a fellow in blue overalls who appeared to be brushing the stone lion's mane, combing it out, as you sank into the long grass. Before us the greyness and high-rise blocks and gasometers and glass, the city was laid out.

'If you took out the plug it would all flow down the sink,' you said. 'Oh God am I *tired*! I could sleep for a week.'

'Where are you working now?'

'For your bunch.'

'Who they?'

'The Irish Tourist Board in New Bond Street.' You didn't hit it off with the boss nor the 'snooty' lady assistants, but you liked Ned the doorman who liked Jameson.

So I was waiting for you there, walking about Cork Street and into New Bond Street and seeing through plate glass the stuck-up bitches stalking about on their high heels, talking to customers and smiling their brittle smiles, and saw an old love passing by. Petra grown old with all her charms quite gone passed me by twice, window-shopping. A midget looked up smiling into my face.

'We don't have no Underwoods here,' Ned the Irish doorman said stoutly. 'None by the name of Sally neither.'

A taxi drew up at the kerbside and you stepped out, miming amazement to see me there.

'Madame Lauriol de Barney, I presume?'

'None other.'

Ned escorted you up the steps as if you were royalty. A pair of Mohawks were passing in bovver boots and one called up after you '*Gizzakiss*!'

Your moods were up and down now; oftener down than up.

'And what of that?'

For us all the graces of courtship were wanting, those nice preliminaries to intimacy, then intimacy itself, based on mutual trust and attraction, 'the charming variations': the bottle of Jameson on the table, avocados and Mus-cadet in the fridge, fresh sheets turned back, a window thrown open upon a place I had never been, possibly Middle Chinnock. The first sallies of passion in a village in south Somerset.

Spasms of furious lubricity were not 'on' at Grand Avenue on Sunday afternoons, in what Germans call 'the little shepherd hour', given the frosty manner that Beamish our host had seen fit to adopt towards you. Lethal Silver Bullets were still being prepared in the kitchen by the lord and master of the manse, while Riley groaned and slobbered, licking a cone-shaped prick red as a tulip damp with the morning's dew. But Beamish's heart was not in it, and a Mickey Finn or cyanide were uppermost in his thoughts, not stiff cocktails.

'The hunched vulture on its reeking branch,' I said. Beamish had a clever way of getting your dander up, opening wide his ale-coloured calculating eyes, letting you run on, getting you riled. Then he would cut in:

'Don't *shout* at me, Sally. You're shouting again.' Then you would fly off the handle, as he knew you would.

We sat on a public bench in Cherry Tree Park in East Finchley and saw the tube trains come and go overground and spread the good Italian cheese (Pon) you had found on baguettes bought from an Indian shop, and over us the span of leafless branches, with some crows, one of which shat copiously and accurately.

'Even the crows despise us,' you said.

'Why does the name Manzoni remind me of some soft Italian cheese?'

We discussed our future: we had none. About us lay the miasmic and spirit-ridden forest, groans of animal resignation leaking from it. Your jealousy had become fertile in its inventiveness. We had nowhere to go.

We lived in an area where marriages broke up. Couples were living with different partners, or were letting rooms, or pimping on the sly, or had moved away, the children suffering.

You were browned off; things were looking a bit dodgy. Meaning that more unpleasant experiences were yet in store. 'The amazed hushed burning of hope and dream two-and-two engendered,' as Mr Faulkner had most intemperately phrased it, would not be for us. We were the twin miseries from Grimm: Joringel and Jorinde dressed in black velvet, holding hands, gazing sorrowfully into each other's eyes. Or the feverish saints John and Theresa clinging to the bars to prevent themselves levitating; for to be permanently earthbound can be anathema to some stricken souls.

Sexual love is a form of madness. There is of course the well-known element of pursuit in sexual relationships, but with us it was carried to extremes; it was all flight and pursuit.

You discovered my *destino* in Buzz's tarot pack at her long refectory table. It said: 'Meeting the Lord in a narrow street; one sees the Wagon dragged back, the Oxen halted, a man's hair and nose cut off.'

Buzz was quite silent for a change, looking from one to the other, mystified.

To walk by a winding tributary, one of the winding tributaries of the Avon, not Ebble nor Nadder nor the Wylye, but the Marden that flows through Wiltshire, enclosed as it is permanently by Gloucestershire, Dorsetshire, Somerset, Berkshire and a part of Hampshire; ever renowned for the splendour of its country seats ('passing pleasant and delightsome,' Camden thought), and to come to the heron's careful tread in the mud

and arrive at close of day at a whitewashed cottage, the same mentioned once in the Domesday Book, to a long deal table for working at and eating from, a bedroom with a double bed by a window, always left open; to be under the same roof together, in the same bed at night, where we ought to be.

Nothing is ever left anywhere but in the mind; impermanence is the true state of nature, deterioration and decay of the human husks. We had to all intents and purposes stopped living. Love would be a burying of the other deep within oneself. And I would take you in with all your dark moods, your insecurity; mutual trust would have the security and permanence of the grave. Since I wouldn't be with you, nor see you, you would not age but would stay the same for ever: always thirty-nine. Absence fixes attention to these static moments (the centrefold model girl in panties on the kitchen table), all that memory (or longing) can fix upon. You there then doing that. There would be more and more of the talk and less and less of the reality to record, until in due course (as with a prisoner doing life), as the reality fades, so too the recounting of it; until only gibberish remains. A fellow attempting to erase his features with his own free hand. We shall have to watch out, shan't we?

Every Tuesday night the Prince was thronged for jazz. The Tuesday night crowd would turn up: Howard and Elsa, Nick Ridley of manslaughter fame and his hangers-on, Darcy Brewster who had a coffee house near the Gate House, Eoin Belton (O.C.) and the lovely Geraldine Quinn. Willie Edgecumbe the old queen who had kept his queerness secret through forty years of marriage, and drank whiskey on his doctor's orders 'because it eased the strain on his heart'. Willie Moulton the quiet accountant (an alcoholic despite outward rectitude, concealing extensive consumption of Stag and J & B by cashing large cheques several times weekly in the butcher's shop opposite the Prince, admitting to the largest meat bill in north London), tormented Angela Harris the vibraphone player, Freddy Byswater and his dark friend Lincoln the flautist who was very slowly consuming halves of draught Guinness with an abstracted aristocratic manner, befitting a great lord or a Persian cat. Freddy himself, the true Scouse, drunk as a skunk and twice as sly. Our Maudie the eighty-year-old retired nurse who lived in one of the almshouses behind High-gate School. Christine the opera-singer, an imbiber of sweet cider. Russell the accountant and Jeff the gardener, the Camden controller of plants, looking like a Guards officer and much given to rolling silences. Lady Vi ('Bitter Veronica') the Scots witch of coven fame.

Wally Fawkes played alto sax with his Welsh pianist Bleddyn wallowing in Methodist guilt. Wally had played with Sidney Bechet in Paris and could still blow a relaxed alto sax – Strayhorn's 'Take the A Train', Hodges's 'That's the Blues, Old Man', or his own bitter-sweet rendering of 'Autumn in Tufnell Park'. He drank little while playing, halves of Yorkshire bitter and the occasional Scotch. Liked more Scotch whilst chewing the fat with his admirers, and a large one on leaving.

Lincoln was smiling into his Guinness in an ecstasy of dark contemplation and Freddy (like some villain in a Graham Greene 'entertainment') pushed himself up close to me and said out of the corner of his mouth: 'Seen anything of our Sally lately?'

As you were rarely to be seen, I moved away from those haunts into other haunts. Different tribes frequented these parts, speaking a different argot. Muswell Hill was neither in the city nor in the country, but an interim place, on the way to Potters Bar ('Are you stuck for a bit of cement?'). Arabs in flowing robes stood on their balconies outside top-storey apartments overlooking the cricket ground, breathing in the polluted London air, rich as Croesus.

One chilly grey day towards the end of May, following one of fourteen hours' sunshine, the sky teeming with swifts returned from Africa, you came up the hill past the Green Man, dressed that day in weed-grey battle-fatigues with engineer's pockets let into the thigh, dressed to kill. First I had seen your face, *mit allen Wassern gewaschen,* as the Germans say, then your shoulders, then your hips and the rest of you, a ravaged face coming up the hill. You had 'wept buckets', because of me.

You had cried out in your sleep, waking Moose; and naturally that had once more aroused his suspicions. *The heart tormented and buried with no further guarantee of success or performance.*

'Ever abstained for any length of time from the carnal act?' I asked Margaret.

She attended her octogenarian lover on Wednesdays as regular as the four seasons passing or the seven cycles of change, sometimes letting herself in very quietly with the milk on Thursday mornings, before her bath and breakfast, and then departing to work in Kentish Town, pussyfooting out.

'No. Why? Have you?'

'Certainly,' I said.

'For how long?'

'Oh, two and a half years, once.'

Margaret gave me a deliberating look and crossed her long stylish legs.

'What are you looking at? Me or something behind me?' I asked.

'I'm looking at you,' Margaret said. 'It's a wonder it's not sticking out of your ears.'

Now she was preparing to leave the room.

'I would assume that you're still quite attractive to women,' was her parting shot.

'Shall we chance another Silver Bullet? What do you think? Would it be wise, so early in the day? What do you say?' Beamish enquired silkily.

'Excellent sack,' I said, 'let's give it a whirl.'

Beamish gave me a look under lowered lids and went into the kitchen to assemble the powerful ingredients. He sometimes gave the impression that even his eyelashes were freckled, which would naturally be impossible, but it would not have been the only impossible thing about this Duke of Guise.

The thriller had been rejected by two publishers. When the first rejected it, he kept this quiet from Mitzi, and said he was changing publishers. After more rejections he would begin researching his book on gold. Mitzi swallowed it all.

His former employers, who had made him redundant (or sacked him), sent a man round for the company car. Shortly before he released it he was charged with drunken driving. At the station he was offered a *Mirror* to read but refused to read it, demanded *The Times*. 'Oh so we are going to be like that?' the copper said, and led him to a cell to sober up.

On his release next morning bright and early he took a taxi to the Dorchester and breakfasted royally there. You get the best breakfast in London at the Dorchester.

One day in the Prince I chanced to fall into conversation with Shorland-Ball, DSO, whom Beamish had wickedly nicknamed Biggles, and he told me he had flown in Beaufighters at night during the London Blitz, and been awarded a 'gong' – self-deprecating, the gong was the DSO.

Anyway he and some brother officers were summoned to Buckingham Palace to receive their medals from the hand of King George VI. They had had a few vodkas in the Ritz to calm their nerves, climbed into a taxi and said 'To the Palace!' But they were no sooner into the reception line than all four of them wanted a leak. Biggles had a word with the major-domo. 'Impossible, gentlemen,' he said, 'that's quite impossible.' The King was expected any minute, and in any event the palace had no public toilets. They would just have to grin and bear it, the major-domo said.

Now they were in a fix. Biggles drew aside the velvet drapes of a tall window and they got into the embrasure, opening the window a foot or two. Then in turn all four of them pissed out onto the King's flowerbeds below. In great acrobatic arcs no doubt, all four being superb flyers. Biggles, the captain, went last. He began to piss and seemed to hear a great crowd cheering, and looking out, member in hand, whom did he see just leaving the fore-court in an open carriage but the old ex-Queen Mary in her tiara. As the stately carriage drawn by spanking greys swept out by the open palace gates she raised up her bright parasol, and bells rang out all over London town.

Ye Loste Lande (London Zoo)

Your dream: a large black limousine awaits outside the library. My seat slides back. You slip behind the wheel and touch a button. As we drive off a portable bar opens out and on the muted stereo Bryan Ferry begins 'These Foolish Things'. We swing away to the dream cottage called 'Bullsease' or 'La Casa Maganaria', far from London, in the depths of the country.

As I help myself to a gin and tonic with ice cubes and a slice of lemon you reach back with a good cigar. Trum-pets are thrust from under clouds as we roll along. Piercing silvery music accompanies us as we pass through the Vale of Kennet in Berkshire. A signpost points towards Pangbourne and Goring. We travel grandly on, you at the wheel.

'Bullsease' is all prepared. You show me the long working table, the Anglepoise, a window overlooking rolling countryside without any pylons. I smell roasting rabbit. In an old beamed bedroom the trusty fourposter stands by an open window. Once more we take passage into the realm of transparent bliss.

Framed daguerreotypes of Schumann and Wagner hang on either side of the fourposter, a wood fire burns in the grate, and the faces of cats are pressed to the window; the garden giving its last show in the evening light.

Neptune and Jupiter are now about to make their presence felt in a rather spectacular way. We are naked as salmon between the blue sheets that smell freshly of rosemary. 'There is no "Thou shalt not",' you say.

It was one of those evenings when all the bars of Highgate seemed packed with braying idiots and Beamish and I had decided to move back up the hill.

'The deepest despair is full of secret satisfactions,' I said. 'Learning comes with suffering – or so the old Greeks believed. In twenty years or so of tenure the headmaster of Eton flogged an average of ten boys a day, beating Latin and Greek into their bums.'

'No finer example of emollient irony.'

Mitzi told us how she came through a hole in the hedge, in her pyjamas, and was standing in her bare feet at the front door with the key turning in the lock when she heard a familiar breezy male American voice say 'Hi there, Mitzi, how about a quickie?' She waved at him. 'A blow-job then?' She pushed open the door. 'What about a hand-job?' the American persisted. The door was closing and Mitzi heard 'I suppose a ride would be out of the question?' And then the roar: 'Goddammit Mitzi, how about a rump-roast?' It was in the early hours of the morning.

Chance would be a fine thing. What was happening? Who was losing? Mitzi was playing the Tough Cookie,

'Dirty Gerty' or Matilda Makejoy. For six months she had had an affair with Moose when you were in hospital with a bad back; Beamish in those days being still married to Gerda the Norwegian, who could freeze a room at will by entering it, prior to their separation.

Riley was stretched out at our feet like a hound after the hunt. And then curled up with his nose into his anus, twitching and dreaming of the chase, whimpering, then a lingering breaking of wind.

'Manners,' said Mitzi mildly.

'This morning in Euston Station I felt I was in Hell,' Beamish said, prodding Riley with his toe. 'Mush, Riley, mush! Comb the woods.'

Riley in his slumber heaved a heavy sigh.

Small twittery birds still invisible in their roosting places had begun stirring and twittering preparatory to yet another *aubade* as we stepped onto the wrought-iron balcony above the fire escape and felt the air and saw London below us in the morning haze, the sight-screens on Crouch End playing-fields and the distant silhouette of St Paul's by the River Thames.

'Don't know how I'll get out of this one,' you said, looking up from the second step at me in dressing-gown and slippers, covering my hand with your warm hand.

'I'll have to find a pond.'

You looked down at the two sad sycamores growing together with their roots gone into the foundations of the garage next door, their fates sealed already.

'Poor things, they're dying for water.'

You began to descend the spiral fire escape.

'Go back to bed. Or have a bath.'

I walked down to the Prince, where I ordered a White Shield from Trudy, said I would be back in a minute, and

stepped into Barclays Bank two doors down, beyond the
betting shop. A heavy butcher was leaning up against
the counter in a striped apron smelling of blood,
depositing bloodstained wads of notes secured with
rubber bands. I stood behind him and tried not to
breathe.

I changed some money and went back to find my drink
poured out and Trudy warming her backside at one of
the two coal fires.

'If you want anything just call.'

Trudy had a pleasant Scots accent. In the times when I
did not see you, the name Glastonbury uttered in a bar,
or the merest suggestion of a Somerset burr, this name
and these murmurous sounds were sufficient to fill me
with an ineffable sadness. You brought to mind those
suffering females in early French cinema, Arletty nude in
a revolving tub of water, Lys like a stoat, Vivianne
Romance naked under a fur coat, Michèle Morgan in a
belted raincoat in *Quai des Brumes*, but closer still Madeleine Robinson as the maid in *Une Si Jolie Petite Plage* saving
Gérard Philippe from suicide at the seaside in winter;
those who willingly gave all for love and came to sticky
ends themselves, shimmering naked in a lake: Hedy
Lemarr in *Extase*. Such fitful gleams.

You are your most characteristic, sitting with bowed head
at the end of the line of out-patients in the casualty ward
of the Whittington Hospital. Then it was your turn. I held
your hand. Not a murmur escaped you as the lady doctor
threaded five slow stitches into your chin, even if the first
stitch had followed hard upon the quick injection.

We waited at the bus stop. The injection and stitches
were 'like a cold wind blowing off a snow mountain', you
told me. 'It's like being dipped in silver.'

A number 134 rounded the corner and drew up before us.

'Nip on,' I said.

'My nipping on days are over.'

We took the left-hand front seats on the upper deck as the bus started up the hill.

'My face?'

'Still intact.'

'My arm?'

'I can feel it. Still there.'

'My leg?'

'Still on you.'

'Good.'

It was a Sunday in the early afternoon when you had phoned to say you were with Buzz and could I come over. I bought two litres of Italian wine and rolling tobacco and papers and walked across. You met me in shorts at the door, embraced me, led me to the bathroom where you dashed water on my face and neck, my hands. Buzz was in the garden with the children. We drank wine in the sun and Buzz dozed off in a deckhair and at an upper window next door a fellow preparing food in a string vest was very interested in your movements, now circling the flowerbeds on a child's bike, in shorts, with brown legs, smiling at me. Then you applied the brakes and went in slow motion over the handlebars as the bike reared up, and head first into the stones of the rockery. You lay there stunned and pumping blood. The chin wound was deep. I helped you up, now pale and bleeding, hands and thighs covered in blood, and then you were throwing up into the begonia beds.

Buzz phoned your doctor but he was out. She drove us to the Whittington and waited in the Out-patients of the casualty wards. Dr Sue Ainsley said to come back in three days to have the stitches out. I said I would go with you.

Buzz said she had never seen anything like it. You preparing for a difficult delivery and the husband (Brian) holding your hand in the public ward.

'*Bee-bee!*' Buzz screeched, at her most Barbadian. She drove you home. You didn't want a drink.

As you went slowly over the handlebars you were smiling trustfully at me, and the fellow in the string vest was looking down in amazement, something burning on the pan, as you smashed head first into the sharp rocks.

Dr Hilary (out on a call) was another of your many admirers; something had gone on between you in Paris. Nava the Russian lady kept imploring you to join her in the sauna.

My earliest loves were your unknown rivals. You were most fertile in your jealousies; for it was not only jealousy but jealousy multiplying. The blonde with the ankle bracelet in the flower shop at Fortis Green across from the Alexandra; the bar girl with long hair at Athene's; the girl from Kent who cut my hair at Cut 'n' Dry near the off-licence, these were all said to be your 'rivals'. And before them, cohorts of unknown teasers; the sexy tax inspectress ('that little silky lady') being the latest in line. Ortega says that in loving we abandon the tranquillity and permanence within ourselves and virtually migrate towards the objects of our desire; this constant state of migration is what it is to be in love – a constant state of migration.

I waited for you in a heavy drizzle of rain, walking up and down outside Dirty Dick's on Tottenham Lane, with darkness falling and the rain pouring down. An absent-minded fellow with open umbrella brushed against one of two drenched black brothers, half turning and hostile.

'Wottcho fukken brolly, mite!'

The ancient Greeks on the pass before battle, combing out their tangled yellow hair. And then you came drifting, drenched, up the hill, and we passed into the warmth and din of Dirty Dick's.

One fresh day we alighted from a number 134 in Camden Town and paid out some money to be admitted through the turnstiles of the London Zoo.

In the apiary the caged ones stretched out their long arms and took flying leaps at the trapeze. They reached out slowly for the bars, lower jaw out, showing their teeth. Hurling hay about; one dark ape with a finger up his wide nostril. A small black monkey was using its finger to draw with its own excrement, like Genet in prison in *Notre Dame des Fleurs*. With languorous movements capuchins swung on the branches of rootless trees, moving about in the quasi-wilderness of the dungy cage, amid nuts, orange peel, a begging bowl, necessities for these 'lifers' perhaps born into captivity, ignorant of the great roaring jungle. Here all the ceremonies of an idle life.

We passed out of there and into the walled compound of the hippos. On the dusty back of one standing still below us I scratched our epigraph: B. AMAT S. *Können Tiere lügen?*

'Can animals lie?' I asked.

'Of course not, silly.'

The mighty she-baboon sat in straw. Her dry leathery paps, the tufted hair on the domed skull like fluff on a coconut, the deep-set eyes hidden and furtive in the concavity of their sockets, were things to behold. Above the troubled fuzzy eyebrows, those ridges, the corrugations of a narrow subhuman forehead were signalling God knows what itch, fury, perplexity, bafflement; twitchy and colicky, in slow motion in a softly mimed buffoonery. For here was a great creature who could kill with her embrace, had she a mind to kill.

One absented stubby finger probed up to the joint into

one wide nostril; then followed a concentrated study of
the findings, the snot studied, tasted with a flutter of blubbery lips, then swallowed. Quasimodo was leering, gone
female, gone bananas; the she-beast oh so uniquely self-
pervaded, existence behind bars for ever, in a strange
void. A coloured diagram on a reduced atlas showed
where the species sprang from; and in another cage the
gibbons were hooting and shrieking as if still in the rain
forests of remote Borneo. The Madagascar vari (whose
scream in the night is said to stop the heart, twice) held
its grim silence, staring downwards.

After the apiary the aquarium. In the darkness the
illuminated tanks glowed and huge-lunged turtles swam
underwater as though flying through the air. And I
thought (obscurely, in this happiness), with me walks part
of Bideford, Barnstaple, Lundy Island lost in mist, Apple-
dore, the Mendips, the Polden Hills and the Quantocks,
as I walked with you, sweet Sally.

Your warm hand felt for mine, took it. We walked
through a darkly illuminated place become 'Ye Loste
Lande'.

Black Napoleon in Drag

Already before mid-October it was cold. The attic received
no sun. I stayed away. At night you coughed, were staying
away from work, letting the deaf ones fend for themselves,
once more feeling 'peculiar'. Love first, then *farmacia*.

And once more the air began to nip and bite. You
spoke in a disparaging way of hairy male intelligence, but
did not specify anyone in particular.

One day you came up Muswell Hill, dressed all in black
Kerseymere like a crow but for the Russian calf boots of

ox-red from Oxfam, the selfsame boots wherein you hid my passport photo, like a dagger for Moose. We turned into the Swiss Chalet.

You had an *Evening Standard* in your net bag. I asked you to look up their astrologer Walker. Walker wrote of Pisces: 'Sun entering birth sign on the 19th. Leave behind all you know to be limiting and emotionally harmful. The way ahead clearly signposted. Avoid travel plans this weekend. Keep to the minimum. Avoid people and situations you know will make you nervous and insecure. A truly exciting phase lies ahead and you cannot be browbeaten or upset by anyone.'

These days in the middle of February had all the charm of extended daylight. The nights were foggy and freezing. You were being pursued by a barman from the Baird who wouldn't take no for an answer.

Emerging from Athene's one night we saw a black transvestite sprinting by in the rain and a while later came upon the same party waiting for a cruising taxi outside the church, and you spoke to him (or her). She responded in a deep bass voice, was gorgeous, was *it*, but dangerous; hot as hell in shoes with six-inch stiletto heels, the gloved hand in matching kid held a monogrammed pouch of soft red leather and a small red parasol that a geisha might own; flashing brilliant dentures.

'Call me Dolores, lika dey do in de storybooks!'

She sported a Napoleonic cocked hat and under it a shoulder-length blonde wig. A late bus came by and she sprang nimbly aboard, waved a pale palm at us from the swaying platform, laughing a high-pitched laugh, her eyes flashing. Wig and hat were now removed in one swift motion in order to make an obeisance from the stage, exposing a curly black head tufted and shorn like a ram. Soldier Othello, the wheeling stranger.

A black Napoleon in drag was being carried away in an empty bus bound for the terminus at London Bridge, the compelling stranger bending low to wave us adieu as *he* was carried off the hill and down into the sinful city below.

I had stood before the canopied bed in Longwood House on St Helena, touched the stiff valance, the yellowed sheet's fringe rigid as the collar about a dead neck, the bed itself reduced to the dimensions of a child's cot and in the billiard room below saw the cracked billiard balls on mildewed green baize now gone the bleached colour of grass in Sudan sun, the balls still in position haphazardly arranged about the baize, long-lost cannon shots and kisses, and one yellow cue laid down, as though no other hand had touched it since.

I thought of the unimaginably small determined body out of whom the will had been removed by death, a peaceful deathbed for one responsible for so much wholesale slaughter; the corpse still shrinking and now gone the dull green of *haricots verts* in the century and a half spent within the mouldering wood, the lead, the marble, in the monstrous sarcophagus on the Seine, the tomb much photographed by Japanese tourists all the year round, and every year round.

The same wary assured Corsican fixing the buttons of his tight waistcoat while critically examining his tongue (*le foie!*) in the convex mirror in the hall was keeping tabs on the gallant English sentries marching on and off duty outside; he was still the good soldier, stout and perspiring, spying on them through a spy-hole bored into the woodwork, going down to dine, his heart not in it. Walking over the field of Eylau where near 30,000 dead lay scattered, an open-air abattoir with many wounded, he turned one corpse over with the toe of his polished boot, and merely observed '*De la petite monnaie.*'

We were love's small change.

Heine had seen Bonaparte in his green uniform and little world-renowned cocked had inverted like a calming compress upon that fertile and boiling Corsican brain of his, when he sat like marble astride his high horse, one marble hand lazily stroking the neck and mane; the emperor's hand and face had the hue which can be seen in Greek and Roman busts. Heine remarked upon this, for he (of all people) had admired Napoleon, as had Chateaubriand and Beyle.

Bonaparte sat somberly astride La Flamme de Temps out of Ancienne Flamme by Fils de Vesuvius, bred of the great mare Cabine Incendie by the legendary Volcan.

On Borodino field 75,000 had perished in one day, soiling their spotless breeches, some departing heavenward in fragmented form to face their Maker. Perhaps not even Napoleon himself could stomach walking amid that stench of carnage, his face gone chalk-white, the smell of freshly killed soldiers an aphrodisiac.

Dancer dear, the mummies of your crushed passions breathe upon me their irredeemable poison! Hot in pursuit of you were as motley a crew as might assemble in one dirty bar. Flynn the Pimp, Freddy the Fink, Harvey Wallbanger, the Fool on the Hill, the Rum Cove, the Bloke in the Blazer, the Horny Greek, the Baird Barman, the Right Prick, the Froglike Man in the Boat, to mention but these.

'Riley seems a bit down in the mouth this morning,' I said. 'What ails him? Not getting his oats?'

'Never again,' Beamish said. 'Poor Riley had his progenitive parts fixed by Mickey the Vet yesterday. He's got every reason for feeling poorly.'

'Poor Riley,' said I, patting the noble head, and was

licked on the hand. 'Great sniffer dog, great putative father, alas!'

'What about a swift Silver Bullet?'

'Couldn't do us any harm,' I said.

'Oh, I'm not so sure about *that*,' beamed Beamish as he moved into the kitchen and began to prepare the lethal cocktails, humming. A number of cats outside the windows watched his every move. Murphy and Molloy and two others whose names I could not remember; Beamish called them Mitzi's children.

A sight as sad as sad can be: the garden giving its last show in the evening light and faces of cats pressed to the window. Permanence has forsaken our world and jeopardy taken its place. Age does us no favours. The past itself is probably the most potent and enduring of all known aphrodisiacs.

You had confessed that you had 'had it off' with someone I knew. I had suggested a number of names but it was not one of them, it was 'someone you know'. Pimping Flynn? Freddy Byswater? Alec the Copper? No. Stavros of all people, in a semi-rape upstairs in his premises, while you were waiting for me and I didn't come. And for all I know the nameless punker with the prick the size of a French *boulette*, observed covertly in his crutch, 'under wraps'; he too perhaps had carnal knowledge of you.

'Your cock,' you said sadly. As if speaking of some wretched farmyard full of muck and feathers and the depressing odour of wet fowl; and over in one corner, under a dripping pear tree, a dishevelled brown hen being trodden into the earth by the swelling cock, in the teeming rain.

Battle of Hastings

Charing Cross Station exists no longer. At Embankment a recorded male voice hollowly intoned 'Mind the gap!' over and over. And then I was away. An hour too early, missing you again, seeing love-bowers below, rolling corn-fields of Sussex, stands of beech buffeted by the breeze, ferny gripes.

Sitting in the tube train coming down from Finsbury Park I was admiring the new murals in Charing Cross Station and was carried on to Embankment and had to take a northbound connection back, but still found myself too early in Euston. As a train for Battle was just leaving I took it, and it pulled away at 8.35 a.m.

'This is your God speaking,' an indistinct male voice boomed over the InterCity tannoy system. The accent was distinctly working-class but from no known region. 'You are on the 8.35 train for Battle. If any passengers do *not* wish to go to Battle, it's too late now.'

God, and an English God at that, had a sense of humour. We hurtied on towards Battle.

Soon the sweet air of Sussex came through the open window, an odour of cut hay. Sussex was some eighty miles across, and I was travelling on into sunny country-side under the immense stratocumulus over the Weald, by Wadhurst and a fat smiling girl on a fat piebald pony following a pretty black-haired friend on a sorrel, off for a day's trekking. Stonegate ('England, Home and Beauty'), Etchingham, a heron flying over the stubblefields, and what I took to be the ghost of Douglas Bader, the air ace, stumping heavily up and down Tonbridge Station, waiting for the London train.

Cut wheatfields around Frant. Then Tunbridge Wells Central, the inevitable pottery, Sevenoaks. I counted only seven cabbage whites along the woody railway embankments between Petts Wood (lacking a possessive) and Battle. Pesticides destroy the butterflies, our world.

Then High Brooms, Grove Junction, Robertsbridge, and Brownies embarking at Battle Station for a day's outing to Hastings. A damp mess of used clothes thrown out under a tree near a caravan site at the end of the road leading to the station; the balmy air of High Street. I walked over the famous battlefield with Professor Burns, felt nothing much; history's pomps are toy-like.

A Mexican couple were studying the battle array mounted in a glass case; toy lead soldiers on a field of green, an arrow in King Harold's eye.

'Look up in the sky, Hal, and tell me what you see.'

'I see the moon.'

'Well, how much farther do you want to see?'

The attack had been made uphill, great foolishness, over undulating terrain. The hidden bowmen, releasing their flights from a distance, killed at will. Modern warfare as such had begun – odd that the phlegmatic and peace-loving English should have invented it. The armoured knights attacked splendidly uphill with battleaxes raised, leaving behind them only a pond of blood. The battle area was smaller than expected; as Lord Byron, riding over it, had remarked upon the smallness of the field of Waterloo. Great deeds, as murder, require little space. To kill a man there is required a bright, shining and clear light. No sooner had a blood-red sun set behind the hazy border hills of Sussex than a paper-thin, bone-white sickle moon appeared in the sky, shrouded in cloud, to shine obliquely down on disordered and ghostly battle-dead at Hastings.

Overhead, orbiting in space, fixed upon an undeviating course, a trajectory of aligned accuracy that had not changed since observed in 87 BC by the seventeen-year-old stripling Caius Julius – in a time that went backwards

– Halley's Comet had come around again, dragging a tail of luminous gas said to be a hundred million kilometres long; a monster of antiquity breeding in the upper air.

Ahead, unknown to Caesar, were the years on horseback, sanguinary campaigns, promotion, war in Gaul. Not to mention the Rubicon, the Ides of March, and a text to trouble future generations of ink-stained schoolboys baffled by *De Bello Gallico*.

Orbiting overhead, letting off steam, the *rara avis* went rocketing onward, dropping off gross tonnage of itself in its haste to get beyond the sun. Nothing would be clear from the crib, except gleams of half-extinguished light, diffuse illusions; increasing and decreasing, no sooner seen than gone. This manifestation not to be seen again by human eye for seventy-six years, our lifespan, passing by without leaving a trace – Heaven's gas, numinous rejectamenta, a will-o'-the-wisp in the night sky.

Jupiter's red spot indicates where it has been raining, not bleeding, non-stop for 700 years. There is always a sign, if you look for it. But William, Duke of Normandy was ignorant of all this as he dined with his army chiefs.

Celibate as an Abelite or the albatross that mates every three years – chastity springing from lack of choice and a fastidious mood (abstinence, as absence, makes the heart grow less fond, *au fond*, makes it weary, also distorts the reality of the absent one); and I'd been eighteen months in that sorry condition when I first set eyes on you. The range of the squonk is limited.

How came you in these parts? Where were you bred? To escape into nothingness, struggle upward out of the Nothing, struggle on. Expect few favours; we live in modern times, after all. Sometimes you got tight by evening. One day we had thirty-two 'jars' in the Nightingale, beginning with Bloody Mary and ending with bitter. All your projects were to come to nothing. Working for the Irish Tourist Board, for the deaf, designing sandals, sculpting, making paper funeral flowers for an undertaker; nothing came of all this. Another life was pacing alongside your own.

Then you were in Somerset when your mother was dying of cancer. You feared to stay in the house with your father. You said: 'I can't stand it.'

'We must have a child.' We'd call it Jarleth. You had such sweet fancies.

At first I couldn't even remember your name. Not even that most primitive courtesy. It was an odd name with a bucolic ring to it: Fairfax, Fielding, Rutland, Greenwood, Moormist, Mildwater, Thorneycroft, Atwood, Woodfall, Honeycombe, Summerbee, Oldfield, Loveridge. *Liebe*, Lord, how does that come in! Love, an accomplice between two ailing beings. Why, one must fear even to be *liked*.

We lived high up in the dim attic as man and wife, in a bedroom permeated with old sorrows. You dragged yourself out of bed and went to work in Gower Street, got up in fatigues and battledress, never a skirt, having some notion about your legs. In fact you had a very nice pair, for had you not danced on a table in the Prince of Wales with Dr Graham Chapman, later to become famous as one of the Monty Python jokers?

Your rig-out might be a mixture of English Lesbos and Italian *partigiani*: savanna boots, shore kit, jungle casual wear. You liked to garb yourself in the colours of autumn and winter, though I always associated you with summer and the things of summer. If summers would ever be like summer again, in England, they would be linked with you under the beech tree in Hadley Wood, dressed in savanna boots and earrings. Or in the reedy riverbed at Brickendon Green, with nothing on at all.

We were together on the Spice Islands, on Fisherman's Wharf, on Banana Bay, on the nudist beach called Saline on St Barthelemys, when we were alone in Buzz's flat in Coniston Road with the louvred blinds half closed and the light out and you came naked from the bathroom. Buzz had framed and hung up bright coloured materials cut in shapes of Caribbean things to make a sort of stitched collage, and naked on the sofa we might just as well have been under waving palms.

It was Sunday and we had come by train from Finsbury Park (no sign of Moose on the platform or prowling the waiting room, and thereabouts I felt most uneasy, for you walking there would lead him to me), travelling out into the country to Brickendon Green and into the Ploughboy just in time to hear the suddenly very active barman calling out 'Time, *please*, gents!' and see the regulars straggling out.

Twice in the dry riverbed, once in the wood, with sunlight pouring across a field, and opening time come around again, was not Brickendon Green a veritable *Garten der Lüste?*

In the ferny gripe you lay nude with an incandescent amber glow, axillary tufts drenched, pussy sopping, lips moistful, for me: I knew you again. You gave yourself to me. You were my Amaryllis. Then I kissed you avidly all over.

'Having kissed you avidly all over,' I said, 'I must drink your piss.'

You said nothing, looked at your watch, smiled.

'Would a pint of Directors' not do?'

We dressed, combed ourselves out, and were among the first into the reopened Ploughboy, as five hours before we had been among the last out. The interval whiled away like Adam and Eve without shame under a spreading beech, walking by the wheatfield and the green, marvelling at the parts of 'Hang-Down', the bull.

Weakened and dehydrated by long bouts of kissing I ordered up pints and halves of foaming Directors' and turkey breasts with good fresh bread, with which you wanted pickles. *Pickles!* I never knew where I was with you. You told me that you had seen a pencilled invitation in the public toilet in Fortis Green, asking for beaver shots.

'What are they?'

You told me. You said I was a badger, my youngest son a fox. You had felt yourself under observation on the Broadway and looking across the road saw Shangar watching, still as a fox. You had stared at him, and he at you; looking away you looked back, and he had vanished, fox-like, melted away. You rarely went onto the Broadway. You spoke again of your old man and his carryings-on; old Nutt sounded like old Karamazov. Paedophilia and incest were on the increase. 'I won't play games,' you said. Was it a threat or a promise?

We drank White Shields in Harry's Bar in Hampstead near the ponds. The river flooded the valley and the sea came in, while Wells Choir sang Vivaldi's *Gloria* as if Cromwell's hangman had never strung up the abbot. Our maternal grandmothers had the same Christian name: Lily. We were both Pisceans. The double of John Arlott drank Guinness in the Shepherds on Archway Road and you told me how as a young girl you had offered to go to bed with Test wicket-keeper Taylor in a hotel in Derby. The place was marbled. You wore your mother's dress, your hair up bouffant-style; virginity had become a burden. Then champagne was ordered and you let your hair down. You made it quite clear to the handsome wicket-keeper that virginity was a burden to you. He said 'You are too nice for this,' and sent you home in a taxi.

Then we were in the Shepherds and it was near Christmas and you came in and began reading my copy of the *New Statesman.* I saw across from you seated by the gas fire a middle-aged florid Tory gent reading his *Evening Standard* and to hand a pint of Guinness on an oval table.

'It's Denis Compton,' I said. You looked across at him. 'More like John Arlott.'

This strange hybrid, the Dashing Cavalier, the witty cricket commentator, seemed immune to his present surroundings, not lifting his eyes, reading the sports page. Contradictions *abounded.*

One morning in the Prince I spoke to Mick Minogue, late of Scariff in the County Clare. He told me he was doing a job in Cromwell's old town house in Pond Square across the way, and praised the ornate woodwork. His mother had called him from the Beyond. Mick had heard her distinctly, the old thin voice of his mammy, and his hair stood on end. He sat down and drank a bottle of Scotch 'as if it were water'.

He had a hot tip for White City that evening, the dog track, so we moved to the betting shop next door. The crabbed finger went down the list of runners, Mystical Hound and Peaceful Rouge were fancied.

And in you came, blown in by the morning, breathless.

'My trouble is – I can't say no and I can't say yes.'

The 'deafies' were foaming at the mouth with excitement on the stairs. When you left the Royal Institute for the Deaf at Gower Street the deaf and staff wept to see you go.

You sold the old house, which you yourself had cleaned from cellar to attic, found a buyer, got the right price, spent two days in bed. Then bought another house not ten miles from the old one, in a rougher area for exactly the same price. In the first four months it was broken into twice, the back door smashed in with a sledge-hammer. Moose began burying his bills in the garden. He drank vodka, came back footless from the Railway Tavern and the Finishing Post. His fury was just contained.

Sometimes you said your mother was dying down there, at other times you yourself were dying in Finsbury Park. The confusion was total. I didn't know whom to believe, nor who was dying.

One night Katie Deering phoned late, saying a friend wished to speak to me. The name? 'Patricia.' It was you unsober at Athene's. Buzz prayed to the Lord, referring to Him as The Man. The Hereafter would be as bad as this world, run by heavenly Mafia; prayer was a kind of bribe, payola. Katie sat mesmerised before the large colour TV; Torvill and Dean skated *Bolero*; the three kids clung to her, transfixed, thumbs in mouths, Lizzy, Dizzy and Whizzy, watched the skaters twirling.

You yourself had a tendency to bolt. One night after closing time outside Chicago 20 you abandoned me for the *third* time, fled weeping into the dark. You were feeling edgy, shattered, had gone mad again. If I was a badger, you were a hare, both Pisceans. You wrote me a postcard from Somerset: 'My dear Brian – Going down on the train now. Hawthorn blossom all over the hedges all the way. Snow-in-June. Sally.'

You liked the big city for the edge it gave you, but were 'shattered' once more by events in the country. The deaths of Uncle Gilbert and your grandfather, both in their nineties. You'd remembered the pleasant peaty aroma of old men, when as a child you had sat on their laps, the warmth and protection (more imaginary than real) it afforded.

You had not many years to live, you said sadly, showing me your palms. Yet in Glastonbury they lived to a ripe old age – Uncle Gilbert for one. Your moods went on and off like traffic lights. You belonged in spirit to the fast set of a previous time: Emily Coleman and Mary Pyne, the daring lost ones – Thelma Wood accelerating about the Étoile in a red Bugatti with the muffler removed. Stingos at the Dôme. Sipping tea laced with absinthe with McAlmon at the Berlin Adlon.

You, as Harbinger of Woe, went with your dose of bad news every morning to wake up the estranged husband, Moose. Your name, when I did recall it, seemed to suit you, it fitted: Sally Underwood.

You took jobs that were beneath you, worked for a minicab firm, the deaf, kept the family going, knew petty criminals. To the yobbos and geezers you were the witchy-looking bird with the tits. The burglar with revolver in bag had offered you fifty quid to show your breasts. You said you needed the money but not that badly. Moose threw up his job, went bankrupt again, buried his bills in the garden. The VAT man was after him. The Somerset rooks were building high in the trees that spring; but other creatures were on the wing about the rape-fields.

Howling like attacking dervishes, savages at tribal rites deep in the jungle, the damned in deepest Hell, some wildly excited coloured youths were engaging in burying an unconscious drunken comrade in an open drain outside the Green Man on Muswell Hill. 'Darkies,' your mother called them. Head-butters were in action between Oscar's and Chicago 20, and Flynn the drug-pusher slinking home.

The small red Bugatti buzzed into Juan-les-Pins with muffler removed, into a broad street with tramlines leading to the harbour, the glittering sea. In the Bar Basque a band was tuning up, before launching into 'I'm Looking for Sally'. The large smiling gent in beige suiting sprawled with legs apart, pulling on a thick cigar, watching us dance over the sanded dance-floor under the turning fairy lights. A sea breeze, smell of resin, cigar smoke, glittering lights.

You, only you; a chestful of breasts, a bird's ever-suspicious eye with permanently enlarged pupils, on the lookout for predators. Slightly knock-kneed, with the inturned toes of a wide-hipped breeder. A warmly sexual nature, the barest hint of a rural burr. Say 'lardy cake'. Say 'Beacon Hill'. Say 'Wells'. Say 'Mendips'. The dark gods of Somerset are listening.

Bugger my old boots, but of all the birds in the air that ever floated on dark water, twittered, hid in reeds, flew in the night, skidded on ice, sang from treetop, perched in impossible places, lamented, rose early, retired late, had young, choked on chicken, reappeared next morning, drank to excess, went on the wagon, regretted nothing, died on the wing, struck against lighthouses, were incapable of restraint, I surely fancied you.

A shadow passing, a female presence gone. As sure as God's in bleeding Gloucestershire, it's true, dear heart.

The Dying Hyacinths

Of your parents in Glastonbury you said sadly: 'They see nobody now. Nobody they know. All their real friends are dead. Not much life left in those little grey cells. In the dark wardrobe the hyacinths are not coming up any more.'

I tried to see them dying in Glastonbury, but found it hard to imagine them there.

You were seized with this strange caprice. You wouldn't show up. You just damn well wouldn't. *You'd stand me up.*

Overcast days make some people inventive. You didn't play games ('Don't get ideas!'). You were a strange cup of tea.

Love mixed with sexual desire is a game with secret rules. You have to play, learn as you go. Touches are messages in code.

A pick-up truck was pulling away from outside Buzz's new place in Coniston Road before I had cognisance of it and could slow up; for the dark shadowy figure who crouched over the wheel, seen through the small mud-splashed rear window, mashing the gears while grimly puffing a fag, might well have been Moose, as I walked slowly towards it, like filings pulled by a magnet. ('Her husband's arriving any minute now to connect up the fridge!' Buzz screeched down the line.)

Moose was rocketing down the M1 out of London in his pick-up truck, exceeding the speed limit, duffing up heavies in strange pubs, having his front teeth knocked out at rough rugger, cooking for the three who were missing you, marvelling at you in the bath, implanting a warm kiss on your warm groin. 'It's a long way from Uruguay to Berlin,' murmured Moose, lingering on the *beso*.

Usually he said nothing, just glared. Many jealous ones are silent. That is to say, those ravaged by jealousy can conceal it, by saying nothing.

'Mighty pretty country around 'ere,' murmured Moose, laying his hand on meat.

You removed his hand.

'Heaven's breath,' muttered the flustered Moose, 'Heaven's breath smells wooingly 'ere.'

You were silent, just breathing, aloof from rut.

'The breezy call of incense-breathing morn,' Moose said with a heavy sigh.

Silence, your freezing aloofness.

'The Chambers made of Amber that is clear,' murmured the Moose gone all poetic, 'doth give a fine sweet smell if fire be near.'

Prolonged silence. (You have left the room.)

You phoned me under a number of patently false names ('Patricia' of the BBC, 'Mary-Lou' of the Caledonian); none of these disguises deceived Margaret, who passed on the message sourly: 'Your flibbertigibbet wishes to speak to you.' Or, more sourly: 'The whore phoned yesterday.'

Tout va changer. Margaret knew how to unsettle me, suffering her rancour. A secret worm eats into a pear.

'He said I'd be more comfortable waiting upstairs, but we were hardly in the door when the trousers were off.'

False Stavros of Athene's.

The coarse Liverpudlian Freddy was winking and nodding by the service-hatch.

'I could never give up beer because I'd be terribly constipated,' said the boozy voice. 'I feel bad now, but I'd feel much worse if I didn't drink.'

Nettles love to grow near ruins, the contemplation of which (the ruins) is said to be a masculine speciality. But why?

Your courtship sounded most odd. As far as I could gather Moose took you straight to bed, after which he marched you into the nearest jeweller's and bought a ring, made you pregnant with Saxon; and hardly had you expelled your second, Titus, than little Liza was on the way. Before one could say coil or condom you were already the mother of three, and Moose had already begun burying his bills in the garden.

*

One afternoon on the balcony, looking down into the Patch, the cemented compound where the kids played, where the two sycamores had been cut down by Haringey Council, I saw a little girl walking alone there, shouting 'Fuck! . . . Fuck!'

Along a wall by Hyde Park tube someone had painted in white capital letters this high-flown sentiment: THERE IS NO HEAT GREATER THAN LUST, NO ILLUSION GREATER THAN LIES.

Moose had been a dancer, as his mother had been in Cape Town; but had put on too much weight and had to give it up. He went into the building (or was it demolition?) trade instead. He was not a man one would care to encounter when his dander was up; and by all accounts it was up most of the time. I was having a quiet drink by myself in the Rose and Crown one day and Freddy Byswater and his mate the architect were playing a game of darts, Freddy throwing the 'arrows' in an ill-tempered way, effing and blinding, bad-mouthing minority sects, cursing the Jewish orphan girl behind the bar in the Prince. He drank with Moose in the Railway Tavern and the Finishing Post, and now he came to stand beside me. He also fancied you. I asked him: 'What kind of chap is this Moose?' 'Moose Underwood?' said Freddy, giving me a leery look. 'Over six foot of meanness – I wouldn't care to cross old Moose.'

Your friend Fidelma had 'hardly eaten in six weeks', lovely as Audrey Hepburn.

'I don't think Audrey Hepburn is any way lovely,' I said. 'Is your friend anorexic?'

'She has cancer.'

On the Barnet bus a mad Negro was shouting out curses

and maledictions, threatening the end of the world, but no Barnet skinheads were abroad, setting out for a night of wog-bashing aggro.

You and Moose slept apart, in different rooms on different floors, or you slept with Liza, who was in trouble with the black kids at school for being the sister of Titus who had been beaten up by a black gang for going out with one of their sisters.

'Pussy,' they whispered creepily. 'You've got a nice pussy, missy!'

'My nipples are sore,' you said.

In a park where coloured people strolled about near Highbury Corner I saw a man with a civet on a lead. The civet came sniffing and crawled over my foot; I felt that strange quick furtive life down there. Two coloured girls stopped to admire the civet. The owner of the civet spoke to them in their own language.

'Come and get me,' the loved voice said on the line. 'Can I pop around for half an hour?' was another ploy. Sometimes I was working on something, sometimes it was late at night ('Come out for a walk'), once I was asked to join you around midnight in a French friend's house in Hampstead. Once you attempted to force an entrance past Margaret at the door.

Cloudy days make some people inventive. When a thing is shapen, wrote Chaucer, it shall be. You belonged to the misty lost world of Claude Autant-Lara and *Le Diable au Corps*, of fleshly pleasure and retribution and of joy. You were not very good, as you put it, at correcting your instincts. Glastonbury seemed to me a magical place. In the abbey there were buried St Patrick, St Benedict Biscop, Blessed Aidan and the Venerable Bede himself, immured with Henry of Blois and Adam of Sodbury.

Joseph had come bearing two cruets of the holy blood and sweat.

You too came from the country.

In the end you told me that it was Murky Murchison ('someone you know'), at the heel of the hunt, who had had you twice or more in your bedroom where I had never been and in a hotel in Glastonbury into which the be-blazered brandy-voiced cad had inveigled you (had it been all that difficult?). When he had copulated with you, no doubt whispering brandy endearments into your ear, you wept. The heart tormented and buried; unbroken pain receding under this grey sky? I tried to imagine it, but could not. I tried to 'forgive' your misdemeanour, if that be the correct term.

> *Fancy passed me by*
> *And nothing will remain . . .*

Fallen Leaves

'The leaves are turning,' you said on Barnet Common. All the wood was bronze and golden and 'it was ending'. You tried to catch a small jumping frog in your cupped hand but instead caught a grasshopper. I found a dappled glade under an old beech tree where previous lovers had cut their initials and entwined hearts and another hand had cut FUCK and CUNT the much-abused synecdoche. Scabby and sore-looking the cuts were closing up, the resin set hard as amber. I had you twice in Hadley Wood and afterwards we dozed near a path in a meadow. It was the first time in six months. You told me that Moose was suffering from pains in his left ball, and that a jadeite

axe from Scandinavia, 6,000 years old, from the Later
Bronze Age, had been dug up in a 'sweat-trench' near
Glastonbury. We slept in the warm meadow, out of sight,
and at opening time went into the cool of Ye Olde
Moncken Holt in Barnet village to drink foaming pints
of Directors' ale.

You told me that your friend had died of cancer, you
were 'disconsolate', you were thinking of going to Italy
for a short holiday. You had another friend there with a
place near the border.

'Which border?'

'The French.'

'Can I come?'

'Don't be silly.'

I did not want you to go. We had more Directors'.
Alternatively you thought of Somerset. There was a beach,
driftwood, a cottage.

When with you I seemed far removed from you. Not
seeing you for months at a time I felt closer to you. You
reproached me for my many shortcomings. I was 'not to
be trusted'; I 'threatened' you; you remembered 'all the
bad times'; you 'feared me'.

'You wouldn't put yourself on the line for me.'

'What we need is a dappled glade,' you said. Hadley
Wood was sparse in undergrowth but was infested with
clumps of briar mixed with tangles of fern and nettles.
The sun did not penetrate into any of the grassy places
and I seemed to walk in circles with you following as if
reluctantly until we broke through a stand of beech saplings and over a horse ride and there before us was an
old beech tree and under it grass and sun, where you at
once took off your shoes, began undressing, with sun
pouring through the foliage above onto the dead leaves
on the grassy place, the veritable 'dappled glade', where
I had you twice, after a long half-year of abstinence. We

were back in the land of the harmattan. I saw the projecting rim of the Djenne mosque with its multiplication of phallic parts standing out like up-ended shell cases as part of the roof, protecting us from the fierce sun in the country of the Dogon and Folani, given to inbreeding, pestered by tsetse-flies. We were again Walkers in the Dream, going naked, hand in hand through the cool granaries dug out of the Bandiagara cliffs, a natural fortress, and isolated there for 600 years or more, and a third time I enjoyed you on a hill of wheat. And you so beautiful below me with closed eyes and drenched armpits said my name over and over between clenched teeth: 'Bludgeon, Bludgeon, you *Dagana . . .*' and I came alive again. I could feel the fierce sun cracking the roof high above us, but the cave was cool, a whole series of great cool interleading caves with mountains of grain piled up and up in cavern after cavern going back into the deep recesses of the mountain.

As the change from childish innocence to traumatic adulthood had been rapid (overnight?), so the change from girlhood to womanhood (the rape in Glastonbury?); you still carried the taint with you and no boyfriend could cure you. Your dark good looks were a curse. You were addicted to *amour fou*, deliberately inflicting pain on the lover who never would be able to forget you. You had a sultry Italian look, strong feeling agitating your bosom. You were not a country nor a city girl but rather a party from some bygone time – Maria Casares hanging up washing on a line in *Les Enfants du Paradis* (a coded French film about the Nazi occupation), or Mary of Modena the consort of James II, twenty-five years his junior ('eyes which had wept but were black and beautiful'). You were *infected* with the past.

Moose again resigned from his job, began burying bills in the garden. Ten years of misunderstanding had elapsed in your marriage, and shared between you 'an inability to say what's wrong'. You spoke up but he wouldn't listen to you.

'Why separate?' Moose asked.

You went again to Glastonbury, where your mother was no better. She had taken up embroidery.

'Is there another? . . . I don't mean to pry.'

Not half.

'Leave 'im, the blightah,' Old Nutt advised.

You returned to London.

'It's not working out,' Saxon said.

'I know.'

'You don't see me,' you said. 'You don't look at me.' A wild dark-veiled ('the afterglow of spent beauty'?), distraught look. The dark hair combed down over the eyes: the Mata Hari look. You handed me a snapshot of Moose dripping wet in a shower stall, a strapping handsome fellow with the big semi-erection of Prehistoric Man.

'Who took the photo?'

You told me stories of Somerset, of the Mendip Hills, of the blue pools between the mining dumps, of the river flooding in winter, calm cats licking their fur on windowsills or stretched out on the lower branches of apple trees; it sounded like the Garden of Eden.

Ah Mendips! haunt of adders.

'I cannot keep track of my disappointments.'

Dreaming of me, of us together, you had shouted out in your sleep 'Suck me! Suck me!' and woken Moose, driving him crazy again. He was taking you four or five times a night, like Boswell with Louisa the actress; and you couldn't do anything, because it would only have made it worse.

From Moose's fiery gorge, like smoke, rushed upwards all the words he spoke . . .

Two photos were hidden under your clothes in a chest of drawers in your room where I had never been. One showed an unshaven fellow photographed in snow at Parc St-Maur on the outskirts of Paris; the other showed you brown as a sultana after your holiday at Lyme Regis. They were 'lying face to face' in the bottom drawer. You and I: Brian and Sultry Sally.

In the meantime we were meeting and mating surreptitiously as hares, those furtive and ungainly creatures so attached to out-of-the-way places, who run in circles, box on their hind legs, go mad in March, scream while being torn to bits by greyhounds. Our totem animal by rights should not have been the Fish but the Hare that lives precariously by flight and escape. We were camouflaged in rather similar two-tone outfits. Your tufted armpits my idea, for I liked your sweat; again a cause of suspicion with Moose, who preferred you shaven. We were secretive as hares, as fungal agents, the pair of us.

Was I attracted to you, as you sometimes liked to suggest, because you reminded me of somebody else, or did I want you because you belonged to somebody else? One night in bed in the West Wing I called you by another name. Your scream and the blow to the face were simultaneous. I caught hold of you, pinned your arms, otherwise you might have jumped out of your skin. Leaping out of bed you were struggling into your clothes, phoning a minicab, cursing me. I heard the murmurings of Beamish and his lady in the bedroom next to ours. It was bang in the middle of the Muswell Hill night.

'You don't see me,' your repeated accusation. You wouldn't search for me unless you'd already found me. If you don't remember me, then I can't exist.

'I'll come looking for you when you least desire me.'

'And when would that be?' I asked.

The dregs of the city's sad love comes to us in the whirlwind (*la hojarasca*). A face full of shocking desires. *En el reino del amor huesped extraño* – a strange guest in the kingdom of love. *Polvo enamorado.*

Then you went away again. And I was alone, standing by Biggles in the Prince of Wales one grey evening, Biggles with his tot of Teacher's casting a speculative brown eye at cirrocumulus massing over Pond Square and drifting on over Hampstead Heath, excellent cover for Sopwith Camels to hide in and emerge suddenly with machine-guns stuttering at intruding Fokkers, Huns.

'Gimme a Pils,' said a soft-voiced man.

'Cooney hit the canvas twice,' boomed another man down the bar.

'A touch of autumn out there I fancy,' Biggles said quietly to me.

Adieu, Annie Laurie!

The schooner docks alongside the little pier. On the sea a painted ship made of cardboard. The girl immediately prepares to leave for Vera Cruz. What rotten luck! The night is rife with peril.

You were devious, untrustworthy, bitchy and intractable, difficult (sometimes impossible) to get on with, wrapped in sadness and a compulsive liar, the one who can't or won't tell the truth. In other words, a true female.

I knew you as trustworthy and honest and believed you as much as I believed anybody. You were a lost thing, as the Irish sea eagle (extinct since 1898), the striped bass of the Hudson River, the flaming maple forests of Vermont.

You told Mitzi: 'We can't be friends. Because you make all my confidences public.' Sadly Mitzi agreed. She and Beamish were incurable gossips, never off the telephone, never tired of rehashing stories. They were both twittery, their spurious gaiety a form of hysteria, and much given to persiflage.

Adieu, adieu, my Sally, you will ever be my Annie Laurie and I'll never forget you, dear Hard-to-Find. *Warte nur; bald ruhest du auch.* Wait awhile; soon you too will rest.

Frère Jacques, Bruder Hans

Yes, suddenly I saw it all, the mists cleared and there it was before me. Inspiration means starting a new story. Or so say the Zen Gaels. To begin something is to leave off something else. Begin again. Do not look back.

Oh he was a young one once, and very thin. With so much changed, it hardly seems my life today. Unnatural child, unnatural son, sickly adolescent, mistrustful young man, unnatural lover, unnatural husband, unnatural father, as grandfather-to-be.

I went in mortal fear of my own dear da. *Vater, Padre,* that small bully with the mind of a lathe-turner; a sad cliché. I feared him, his waspish humours, his orders, until I'd made him a grandfather, turned the tables, cut him down to size. He passed away in a suburban Dublin nursing home fifteen years ago when we were in Berlin. It was May then, as now. We flew out from Dublin on a lovely blue day. It was a perfect day for flying, you said.

I recall two incidents, insignificant in themselves: as the single-decker bus pulled away from Killiney village the word NO appeared in white paint, hove into view on the wall opposite the Sylvan Café. On the towpath by Dun Laoghaire Station our small middle son, closing his eyes and opening his mouth like a pup, deposited two pukes. We were away.

My mother had died two years previously of a brain haemorrhage. My father was dying of cancer. They had cut him up. It did no good; he was going anyway. I believe he had grown tired of life, as the guest who goes out for cigarettes and forgets to come back. Reality was receding from him, or he from reality; it amounts to the same thing. The blood halted in the veins, the face turned to the wall, *Misserfolg*, senses thickening, leaving the physical behind, the marrowbones freezing. Then a sudden blaze of darkness into the dying face. Then it was all over. Or so I imagined it. By then we were in the *Landhaus* at Dahlem; settling in.

My mother had despised him. She rarely spoke well of her Batty. Perhaps she hated him? When she had departed in the night, taking her hard feelings with her, he had to follow. There was no other way.

He was the only son in a family of fifteen – was it? – horse-faced sisters, my aunts; which may have explained his furtiveness and evasiveness, fear of exposure; not exactly rowdy nor calm, not assured, but something hidden in between, a little craven. Fidgety, uxorious, a stater of platitudes, an anti-Semite, a great scuffler of gravel, a copious tea-imbiber, a starer-out-of-windows, a great gossip, poking into his earhole with a safety match. His toilet was extravagant: the brown suit, the fawn outfit with hacking-jacket; he took hours preparing for town – a regular pasha.

Kildare is a place of follies.

Satan was reputed to have dined at Castletown House, following phenomenal participation at a hunt. He was invited to dinner, and cards after; he dropped the ace of spades. Stooping, the maid saw the cloven feet. He disappeared up the chimney in a puff of smoke; the priest sweated seven shirts and died.

I knew *my* place – a thin-shanked papist child, permanently unwell, difficult to feed, fearful of everything, of most people. Priests and civic guards particularly; hidden behind the old cook's skirt, or in the shrubbery, or behind the kitchen mangle where the cats made their stinks. Or in the back-yard cowshed, with the cowshit, or in the plantation in the stench of suppuration.

I conceived myself to be permanently guilty, though of what I could not say ('unclean thoughts') and suffered the agonies of the damned before confession, the weekly ordeal in the dark, whispering sweet nothings into a priest's inclined ear, behind the grille. With nuns and priests I lost my nerve altogether, became even more furtive. They were unreal, scarcely human.

'He's getting red again! . . . LOOK, he's got the guilty look!' I had the guilty look and could do nothing about it.

For my father, the hardest thing to believe in, to credit, was his own existence, a very Irish trait. He frittered money away when he had it; it didn't interest him. This stranger to honest toil had never worked a day in his life. For the most of it he had lived on inherited money, a copper mine in Arizona; and when it was gone he lived on credit, loans. And when that was gone, on hope of winning the Irish Sweep, even the Malta Sweep. He lived on hope, long odds.

In summers he hid himself away in the long uncut grass of the orchard, braced himself for the Irish sun, covered like a wrestler in cod-liver oil. The long winters 'took it out of him': what winter could not remove was laziness, nothing could shift that.

We, his four shy sons, hid in trees or perched on garden walls, observing him. To all callers he was not at home. We were instructed to say that he was 'out', or 'not well', or (a last resort) 'gone away'. He wanted to add, 'for good', but feared to go too far. Foxy in his slyness he waited, hid. He invented a stubborn ailment; the old appendix was at him again. 'It has me crippled.'

We bore no malice towards him but we feared him, for he had bullying ways. To those he knew to be his social superiors he was all affability, brazening it out – the merest bravado. He shrank as he aged. Finally he became pathetic. He wanted to be left alone. He was my da.

The notion of paying taxes was repugnant to him. He owned three gatelodges. One stood empty, condemned by the Health Authority. One poor consumptive needy tenant paid no rent for years, passing away in Peamount Sanatorium.

Major Brookes hid in a bush on his own driveway when the tax inspector called, as he did once in five years. My father hid himself in the orchard, ferocious in appearance as a Pawnee on the warpath. He was the narrow fellow in the grass, Pawnee or Cree brave with thoughts of scalps on his mind, breathing deeply, the deep breathing of the Plains Indian. Or an Aztec roasting himself in the sun. Or the fearless fire-eater of Mexico City on Avenida Reforma, a waterway when Montezuma rode out in his feathers, anticipating stout Hernán Cortés, but dreading his arrival. He is eating the fire. Behind it all intense fear. This was my mulberry-coloured father scorched royal purple, the sun-worshipper who got so little of what he loved.

My three brothers and I, taciturn, well-spaced-out walkers, none on speaking terms, arrived at Hazelhatch Station with what my father termed 'a good two hours' to wait, following an early rise, ablutions, best clothes, a two-mile walk. My father and the stationmaster, a Mr Darlington, paced up and down the departure platform, stopping every now and then for my father to emphasise a point; the lugubrious man narrowly observed my father, nodded, sucked Zubes. They recommenced pacing and my brothers and I watched them in sullen silence.

A slow bemused sick goldfish rotated slowly in a tank of unchanged greenish water at the top of the stairs at number 11 Springhill Park, Killiney, a private nursing home for the dying. A stale spent smell permeated the place. The old were sunken into easy chairs in an over-heated room, their eyes fixed unsteadily on wavering images on the television screen. They were looked after by a brisk ruddy-faced ex-nurse, the Presbyterian Mrs Hill. She and my father had disliked each other on sight. He referred to her as 'the Presbyterian bitch', snuffling up his nose, ruffling his feathers.

The old man's unsteady mind was elsewhere now, going into senility, approaching that terminus called Final Insolvency; his muddled thoughts fitfully dwelling on the past, pushed about like drifting clouds. Not much strength was left in him, tilted forward from his bedroom chair, hands out to the glow of the single electric bar. His fingers clenched and re-clenched, an old tomcat feeling the fires.

His liquids had been 'cut down'. In the WC he knelt, flushed the toilet, drank from cupped hands.

The dying moved about in a daze, the stairs creaked, a door closed. The old ones assembled in the living room downstairs, read outdated magazines through quizzing glasses, dozed on their chairs, waiting for the next meal. Mrs Hill was rigorously cheerful.

My old man sat forward at a dangerous angle from the chintz-covered chair, sunken into a past that no longer belonged to him. Ireland was finished, he said. And so was he. The Presbyterian bitch watched his every move. She spoke to my brother and me at the foot of the stairs. Had any *arrangements* been made? She did not expect this patient to last much longer; one could not expect miracles.

My father examined the contents of his pocket, abulge with letters, newspaper clippings, a stub for the Malta Sweep. Dr Duff the kidney expert was in sporadic attendance. It was May with all the gardens in bloom.

Dr Duff, in passing, tapped the glass tank of unclean water and the sick goldfish turned slowly over, giddily dying.

Perhaps he was not a kidney expert but a cancer expert? But are there cancer experts? He descended the stairs, smiling.

We stayed over in Killiney near the Druids' Chair public house, put up by a couple called Harper. Mr Harper had red hair and was Irish. Young Mrs Harper was English. She wore hotpants, stood on a table to clean a window, walked alone near the monument. A donkey grazed in a field below with a jackdaw on its back. A lawnmower was being pushed back and forth, back and forth through thick scrub grass. A mist rolled in from the bay, covering all in a trice. With much squealing of brakes the number 59 red single-decker bus went into a tight turn by the Sylvan Café, past the stern injunction NO. A white fog of freezing air curled past the closed windows of Regan's airless lounge where a Mayoman with incipient jigs raised a double brandy to his lips. Out of the fog came a pony and trap carrying tinkers with their pots and pans, with redheaded children clinging on. This nomadic entourage out of the past swept by, the little fast-trotting donkey goaded on with stick and curses. The father stood, clutching the reins, flogging him; the lot vanishing into the whiteness, down the hill.

I walked across the park to Killiney Hill, looked down into the seaweed beds. In a grim snug in Dalkey village a betting man encircled Royal Braide in the list of afternoon runners at Leopardstown. My father held a hot toddy between his hands and stared at me with unsteady watery blue eyes.

'This isn't right, Aidan. I never thought I'd come to this.'

He moves inchmeal; the surgery has been too extreme. I feel my fingertips tingle. I beg a lift down the hill in a passing car. We end up in Fitzgerald's.

A white mist rolled in from the bay, covering Dalkey Island. In the clinging whiteness a lone blackbird sings sweetly. Above the low door of the sunken Gents a notice reads: MIND YOUR HEAD. My fingers still tingle. The face in the mirror tells me: One day you too will be old and helpless.

My father was drifting in his thoughts that wandered around in vaguely concentric circles, where choice seemed both endless and tiresomely circumscribed. That was the way out.

Near the bottom of the tank a sick goldfish was suspended upside down with its intestines hanging out.

May 27, 1969 was a bright sunny day, all blue sky, a perfect day for flying. We flew from Dublin Airport to Heathrow, stood among rude Germans for the Lufthansa flight via Bremen and Hanover to Tempelhof, Berlin. The Germans wore curious hats, pressed to the front of the queue.

A little time passed.

We were living in a rented mansion in Nikolassee, near Schlachtensee and Krumme Lanke. French divers were crawling around the bed of the Oxo-brown lake in search of parts of a Lancaster bomber shot down in the *Kriegs-jahre*. On a raft a diver set out wet darkened fragments. No bones. A woodpecker drilled into a tree above the path. The American Army drilled away in the woods near the border – a mailed fist knocking on a heavy door that will not open.

Sinister grey battle tanks rolled along the grand *Alleen*, their pointed gun barrels inscribed with the names of Berlin sectors: Dahlem, Friedenau, Schöneberg, Charlottenburg. In the postbox by number 52 Beskiden-Strasse a brief postcard from my brother: *Father died yesterday. Sunday.* Dated 29.6.69.

Muss es sein: es muss sein. The earth pulls towards it all living things.

The Gnostics believed that the angels put to every dead person the same question: Where do you come from?

I bought a bottle of Jameson, his preferred tipple, accepted change from mildewed fingers. *Danke, danke, mein Herr!* Yesterday there was three days past here. My father would be buried already in Dean's Grange cemetery.

I walked through the Joachim-Klepper-Weg, broke off a sprig of flowering shrub. The stately house was lit up like a liner going through a dark sea. I poured out three libations, for the Aztec, the Red Indian, the dead Irishman.

My three small sons were having agreeable hysterics in a hot bath upstairs. You were singing 'Frère Jacques' to them, in German. They were laughing their little heads off. Tracery of leaves, tracery of leaves. They looked so defenceless in the deep Berliner bath, wet as seals, laughing at the absurdity of the 'Bruder Hans', their Germanic antics.

That which we are must cease to be, that we may come to pass in the being of another. Exist anew! A page was turned, an old man sighed. Leaves fell from the linden tree. A link, a link!

The Other Day I Was Thinking of You

Nullgrab

The other day I was thinking of you. Or, rather, of Nullgrab, that quartered city you love so much. It amounts to the same thing. When I recall Berlin I remember you, or vice versa.

Is it even possible to think of somebody in the past? One replaces another in what you call *Herz* and the light goes out. Your voice again; your eyes in the shadows, in the Augustiner Keller under the railway arches at Bahnhof Zoo in the snow, in the Italian restaurant Rusticano with the friendly waiter, in the Yugoslav Hotel Bubec on Mexiko-Platz, in the Greek place.

Today is your birthday; a Gemini like John F. Kennedy. The Nullgrab children call '*Nullgrab, det Datum wess ick nich, ick jlob et heesst vergiss nich.*' French kids go: '*Je te tiens, tu me tiens par la barbichette. Le premier de nous deux qui rira, aura une tapette.*' Your expressions were charming. You said 'the Hollands', 'trouts', 'copulations', 'intercourses'. You said: 'What do you think I

am – an animal in a box?' 'Yus,' you said, 'yus.' Oh,
quatsch!
   Doch-doch.

Do you recall the Isar flowing strangely in the wrong
direction, an invisible deer crashing through the undergrowth in the English Garden, the goose-shit around the
pond, the tattered tribes of hippies with their guitars
below the Minopterus, clustered about the hill? I felt
giddy under a tree, the sky whirled above us, it was the
beer, the wine, the Cognac of the night before in Schwabing. It was the air, the *Föhn*, the Bavarian day, the clouds.
The trees danced, the earth moved, the air was atremble
in a manner well calculated to bring on nausea. I lay on
my back on a public bench but it was no good, the earth
kept moving, the clouds passing overhead; the vegetation
danced above my head. You said 'Oh, *quatsch!*' and took
my head onto your lap, laid your cool hand on my heated
brow. The earth and the sky stopped their whirling, the
giddiness went. Your hand cool, the warmth of your thigh
on my neck. Leopold-Strasse was dug up; they were preparing an underground Metro system for the Olympic
Games, the killings to come. Our pillow-book was a
German translation of *In Watermelon Sugar* which you gave
me back into English at a table outside a restaurant in
Schwabing, or in bed in the big airy flat in Jakob-Klar-
Strasse. On the balcony opposite the retired boxer sat all
day, was handed out mugs of beer by his good *Frau*. Your
brief silences meant you were reconverting the words of
Brautigan into English. You bought a minute bikini in
the colour of *café au lait*. For me, it was always a giddy
time with you, dearest Schmutz. Perambulating in bright
sunlight and the air with an earthy smell, 17 degrees
centigrade in a very lush Bavarian spring.
   You suggested a siesta; in German you said it was the

little-shepherd-hour. You drew the long semi-transparent drapes, cool air blew in, we removed our clothes. The caterpillar's function is to gorge itself and grow. Linking we walked into the Tiergarten, walked hand in hand over spongy turf. It seemed relatively deserted. I offered to take you in the bushes. Excited Yugoslav *Gastarbeiter* with their shirts off were engaged in an untidy game of *Fussball*. The long column of the golden *Friedensengel* rose up into a clear (Bavarian-blue) Prussian sky. 'Yus,' you said, 'yus.'

The Ominous *Litfassäule*

Beauty is a projection or ugliness – I must have read it somewhere; the notion sounds vaguely French. By developing certain monstrosities we obtain the purest ornaments, argued Monsier Jean Genet with characteristically perverse ellipses. Certain dwellings, even certain ruins, and perhaps they most of all, reveal and betray the real Nullgrab.

The blackened ruins of the gutted and bullet-riddled Soviet Embassy had been left standing in a nondescript street not far from her parents' apartment. Lore showed it to me as if unwillingly; something that had to be seen but not something that one could be proud of, like her politics. An ingrained dread of Communism that she had inherited from Papa Schröder had induced her to vote for the Christian Democratic Party. Unsound politics; beware of German politicians who come from Bavaria, such as the wild man Strauss. Lore was very conscientious in casting her vote.

You were a child in a city selected for destruction. In a way that no other city could be, it belonged to the dead, the burnt-out capital of a country devastated. They were everywhere, and not only in the civil cemeteries between Mariendorf and Britz; Russian and German dead were overwhelmingly present. 'Let's move on,' you said. It was something shameful you showed me once. As, at another time, I had opened my fist and shown you the unspent cartridge I had found in undergrowth by the water near the Jagdschloss. Something I once showed to you. 'Throw it away,' you said.

Always you showed me the Nullgrab ruins with this odd diffidence, as if proud and ashamed at the same time. The shuttered Italian and Spanish embassies facing the Tiergarten, haunt of nocturnal whores. I thought of the liar Malaparte, Count Augustin de Foxa and Count Ciano. Go quietly, the ghosts are listening. Their embassies were empty now as beehives when the bees had gone, a wasps' nest when the wasps had been destroyed. They faced into the Tiergarten, side by side, dire presences long abandoned but not quite dead. A curious atmosphere surrounded them; centres of finished ambitions, as Stonehenge and Tara, the Alhambra in Granada or the great necropolis at El Alamein. Their absolute stillness was perhaps a shocked silence, as if the hectic life could begin again any day, that gross splendour and nationalistic fervour renew itself as monstrously as before.

In a tree-lined side street stood a *Litfassäule*, one of those essentially Nullgraber constructions as truly German as Parisian *pissoirs* are French. The real Axis soul had flown from the abandoned embassies and settled here. On its defaced surfaces a patina of print weathered by time and destroyed back into the acid; for no hand had removed the ordinances, propaganda become threatening even against its own people, and rotted back into a decayed repose – sinister as the anti-tank gun emplacement hidden in a turn of the road by the Rehweise sunken meadows.

I am reading Heine again, about the lovely nixies all dressed in green. Today, stricken with longing, I was thinking of you.

Playa de Burriana

For three days the *terral* blew, throwing dust about and making the palms dance. On Playa de Burriana the wind-surfers hung about on shore, the Nerja Ski School did little business, damp *Fräuleins* in minute bikinis swarmed in the surf. Back in the hot sand off the shore thoughtful bearded sunbathers adopted lofty Buddhist lotus poses, head resting on palm of open hand, watching the topless parade go by. A form of supplication.

A beautiful face and port from another time – ancient Egypt – her black hair turbaned in a white towel, maroon togs with plunging backline cut to the cleft with a gen-erous play of gluteus muscle, walks with a girlfriend by the Sapphic shoreline; the face hierarchic, remote. Two gays are skimming flat stones while other interested parties watch from behind boulders with bated breath and a stout Englishman in shorts with very tanned legs practises niblick shots with practice golf balls, chewing on a cigar.

For emphasis, with the English, the voice is lowered, modified to the consistent bleat of the tamed middle class, expressive of the all-in-oneness of their privileged status. With the Spaniards the voice is raised for emphasis, becoming louder lower down the social scale. Headsets are becoming fashionable among the young, for instant pop music all day long, the apparatus clamped to both ears like a hearing-device for the stone deaf, or electrodes for the brain-damaged.

A Spanish family in high excitement are erecting a Moorish-style tent in moss-green and raspberry vertical stripes with dark blue bands and an awning, bang in the midst of sunbathers. The paraphernalia that people take to the beach with them! Collapsible camp chairs, mats, inflatable cushions, hampers, beer coolers, beach umbrellas, transistors, toys for the kids, silent grand-mothers.

A parade of the halt and the lame go by, figures from Brueghel or Bosch. It is the day Real Madrid go down to Liverpool in the European Cup Final. Flies dance in the ammonia-and-piss reek of the beach privies. In La Barca *merendero* the waiters take orders at the double, darting about in blue singlets and white shorts, barefooted. Piercing blasts from the cook's whistle disturb the canary swinging in its cage and a hermaphrodite assistant grins through the hatch. A hairy-chested chef whips up cream in a thermos shaken vigorously near his ear as though preparing a cocktail. The missing Lord Lucan strolls through.

'Gude bhay ma luve, gude bhay!' a bull voice roars from an echoing place, apparently from a barrel. The canary is silent now, head sunken in its wing; piercing blasts come from the galley, the waiters dart about like Keystone Cops. A tractor harrows the sand where the surf has dampened it, and a saddleless horse is being ridden into the sea.

Playa de Carabeo is a small horseshoe-shaped beach diffi-cult to reach, the path down befouled by dogs and children between the wild begonia beds. The fishermen use the beach below as dormitory and open latrine, as fishermen have done since the time of the Redeemer and His Apostles. But then again it was always a dogs' paradise.

Heavy-beamed peroxided *Fraus* block the entrance of the *librería* in the Square of Martyrs behind the church of Nuestra Señora de las Angustias, Our Lady of Sorrows, hard by the bordello, fingering *Bunte* and *Stern*, German newspapers, and an upstart Spaniard drives past the Banco Andalucía in a new Cortina with an abstracted air. A sombre *Herr* with a *Mensur* scar is deeply immersed in *Frankfurter Allgemeine Zeitung* at a table outside the Bar Alhambra on the *paseo*, pays with a 5,000 peseta note. José the waiter in platform heels flips open his change wallet, accepts a small tip. He takes his *señora* for vacation into Portugal, Lisboa.

Rijeka Harbour, 1956

An awkward squad of Yugoslav soldiers in baggy pants and ill-fitting tunics lines up on the quayside near steps that go down into the still blue water of the harbour towards which a launch with some visiting dignitary aboard is moving, its flag fluttering in the breeze that blows across the harbour. A salute is fired and a small figure on the launch offers a brisk salute.

Then the launch draws in alongside the steps and a stout little man in a linen suit darts nimbly up the steps, where the stiff squad of awkward soldiers comes to attention as the white smoke of the gun salute drifts over the water. It is 6.30 in the morning and the August sun already hot in the port of Rijeka on the Adriatic Sea, in the long-ago and far-away, when I went there with you on the way to Cavtat, Mlini, Dubrovnik.

Thick Clouds Cover the Sky

Thick clouds cover the sky, then suddenly there is a rift and we see a wretched little paddleboat pitching off the Irish coast somewhere towards the end of the nineteenth century. On the exposed deck a young woman, seated. She wears a tweed ulster and poke bonnet and is gazing sadly out over the sea. Her husband sits close to her. A singular pale-visaged man in a brown moleskin greatcoat, one hand thrust Bonapart-wise into the breast. The sea wind bends back the brim of a brown felt hat held in place by a length of string which depends from the hatband, secured to a button on the greatcoat. He looks foreign, with his full disgruntled face, the troubled introspective eyes, the bleak regard; he looks ill.

Both are pale-faced, with suffering goitrous eyes; hers cast upward as if in supplication to a Greater Power, more in despair than hope; his probing the space between. Both sit bolt upright as if horrorstruck; just awakening from the conjugal dream. Plunged in deepest despair but united for the nonce in suffering, they stare out over the flying waters at the receding cliffs of England.

Turf Boat, 1979

The Scalp, Ballylee, Cruachmaa, thistles in a ditch, wind in Belharbour, in Gort, a handsaw sawing in Inchy Wood, water pouring over a low weir, crows over a copse of trees in Kinvarra, a ghost walking in broad daylight in Ballinmantane Castle. Esker, the Burren hills, a lad in a red gansey, geese crossing the road at Shagwalla, the briny Atlantic crawling in over Bundoran strand. The days full, the tyres hard, the saddle tight, the going grand. Don't let Connemara down! They wouldn't tell you a lie!

A turf boat is lying to with patched brown sails furled. And always the river – murmuring to the right, murmuring to the left, flowing under a humpbacked bridge – Lebane, Roxborough, a hare on the road.

Kies: the Passage of Time

The stone returned. Walk again on Burriana beach in the spring. On the sand there with my first-born Carlos. We collect stones, draw figures with a Bic pen.

Flies crawl over the boulders, the waters pour as if they'd always existed, as if I didn't exist. Other eyes, another spirit regard this evidence. Or again: small ants crawl over the rocks. The spirit troubled, conscience troubled. Tumbling water. Troubled water. Wheeling gulls. The riddled sandstone cliff. The high blue sky overhead.

Your guiding hand, your protecting love. Not to hear those three voices call my name again. There is perhaps no seductive alternative worth this loss.

Or again: call me by my pet name again (a guard against loss, like primitive music). For two days, Sunday and following windy *lunes*, both of you were savages with clubs, prehistoric men making obeisance to the tethered mule startled by these formal reverences, bowing down before him. Those three ghosts lately departed for Truss City. A batch of letters abandoned in a drawer. Your guiding hand. Your protecting love. The stone drawn on and returned.

The early departure in the dark, the two buses seen from the terrace, emptiness of feeling. Dozed for an hour and then walked to Fábrica de la Luz, by the ruin, *Al campamento 10 minutos*, the skull and crossbones, *Peligro ruinas*, the pool abandoned, Elwin's stone named with an extraordinary name.

What came out of the sea was no less than a horror: the owl's orange eyes aflame, a pointed beak, sodden plumage, underfeathers – an old man's skinny shanks in sagging drawers. Oh *búho real*, you eagle-owl, hissing at the Alsatian that kept its distance, what took you into the Mediterranean sea in a morning in May?

My middle son aged ten asked me: 'How can Elijah ascend to Heaven in his bodily shape?'

Autumn Acorns

An autumn of acorns in Highgate Wood and Queens Wood, where the mass graves for the Plague dead were dug; archaeologists unearth pottery made by Roman slaves. An autumn of conkers and red berries and an oldish man saying to his wheezing, waddling old dog: 'You're only a big overgrown puppy, that's all you are.'

On the sports field, the cricket pitch surrounded by the wood, the Royal College of Music CC v. Belsize Park CC. Two magpies tormenting a hawk in Ken Wood, mole-casts in the depression, orange and red berries in profusion. Sign of the end of the world?

Bailey the billygoat, not a normal goat by any means, but rather a sergeant-at-arms goat or company mascot at some military dress occasion, gallops through the wood.

What would winter be without the golden yellow flowers of *Jasminum nudiflorum*? Even the greyest coldest days don't dishearten this beauty for long. In Piccadilly Underground a lovely leggy girl squats before the call-boxes, her head down, eyes closed, curious coloured puke at her feet. All gape at lovely legs, thighs. A still for *I Am a Nymphomaniac* by the sodden steps leading to above-ground. The lovely girl vomiting by a dark man, her friend. Xmas spirit in London town.

Mahonia japonica is closely related to lily of the valley, scented flowers that last for months. Put your japonica in a tub at the foot of steps. Lemon yellow flowers on cold foggy evenings, there it is. Foliage for twelve months of the year, flowering for two or three months in winter, tolerant of lime and acid soils, penchant for shade. The lime-tolerant ones prefer shady forecourts. Sarcocolla, mahonias, skimmias on a north-facing wall, contrasting leaf-forms to delight the beholder. Poinsettias in winter in flower-shops of Notting Hill Gate and Holland Park. Red as red, a Christmas Box.

Under the Ice Shelf

One hundred and sixty years ago in the dreadful frost and snow at the beginning of 1814, kind-hearted Charles Lamb was out in all weathers visiting the imprisoned Leigh Hunt who had been put away for two years for ridiculing the Prince Regent. Hyde Park was then littered with dirty people and provisions (not that much has changed in the interval). Mary Lamb had toothache very badly and was about to go mad again. Insanity ran in the Lamb family like a streak through Brighton rock.

Trust I find you in fine fettle, friend. Stay well muffled up. Up here in the Pennines they still count sheep in the old lingo. *Bumfit.* Deep snow still lingering on here where none in their right minds would go marching. Down below in murky Birmingham it's all Bingobongobanga I can tell you. The soccer Yahoos prowl about with skulls shaven to the pluck in the manner of convicts in Dickens's day, invoking Magwitch and the hulks. Their looks of fixed hostility bode ill for old England. The pro football season gets into its swing with a ritual killing. But this generally happens away from the actual arena where 'supporters' or rival gangs of thugs are constrained behind moats and high wire fences, as in the days of chivalry when maidens were locked away in towers. The hot whiffling puppies run amok after the game, and the great mindless commonalty go in outright fear of them. But you know a nation is finished anyway when it produces postage stamps such as this with image of your dyspeptic sovereign affixed to this *carta.*

However, spring must pull us round again. This muck cannot endure for ever. Didn't I hear the children scream 'Yellow!' almost a month ago? Feathered songsters will soon be on the job. Weather will be dull but extraordinarily mild, with grass sprouting out of season, honeysuckle bursting prodigiously, awaiting another nip of frost to kill it. Geese honking whilst assaulting the wet uplands with soft grey shit, appropriate emblem for a whoreson year not unfree of general adversity, no by God. Keep thy head well covered.

I rarely venture down below except for absolute necessities such as Scotch and tobacco, carbon paper. From my bedroom I survey the rolling fells, a name I've always liked, the fells, where today a gruesomely active crow, very black against the virgin snow, feeds on the eyes of a dead sheep, only the stricken head emerging ghost-like from the drifts. The immediate ambience is now mercifully rid of the sound of polite handclapping followed by communal gusts of infectious laughter, for I have persuaded the obliging landlady to remove the offending Box. The times are even worse than those envisaged by Orwell who admittedly was ill; and we still have some way to go.

'I *still* value human life, in spite of everything,' I overheard a sagacious Parsnip say in a frightfully Punjabi-wallah-y voice from a lounge bar I just happened to stumble into a week or so ago. What kind of life had this wag in mind, do you suppose? The Gulf Oil man in natty blue company overalls spoke knowingly of pressures and borings to a hotel commissionaire who displayed all that starched and bluff rigidity that told of previous army training.

Mad scientists, said the Gulf Oil man, drilling through a lost undersea world beneath the Ross ice shelf in Antarctica, had come upon life-forms and fossils dating back fourteen million years, and were attempting to discover what kind of creatures could have evolved in waters which had not seen sunlight for more than 10,000 years, with water temperature hovering just above freezing. Wilkinson's blades for a close easy shave.

Meanwhile the long injurious winter is showing no sign of ending, releasing its iron grip. I live just on the snow-line, now general, in a peeling late Victorian mansion that might still appeal to Charles Addams, wrapped up in blankets before a coal fire in a house wanting repairs in all essentials, staring into the birch tree in the garden, in it some birds which I attempt to identify through opera-glasses bought twenty years ago in Canal Street for one dollar, when life was still possible there. Doors hang on their hinges by the skin of their teeth and the lot is mortgaged to the hilt. I snowshoe over the white fells to a rude bar patronised by those hardy souls who walk the Pennine Way, ending up in a far-off Escotia amid the hoar-frost. Below in the haunt of skinheads and punks, thick and squat or leery and lank, truculence and insolence inextricably mixed, you have coal-smog in the plundered glass-walled valley where the heart shrinks as the stench freezes the mind, converts it into authentic minerals. Some lost soul plays grim Baptist hymns on an old diseased church organ in a deserted church in Coke-on-Ende into which I happened to stagger, looking for grace but found only dark choirstalls, mildewed prayer books, a booming organ, the odours of bygone piety and lost congregations, the wind moaning through the leaded windows, and a redheaded lunatic in a chalky black smock pedalling away for dear life, head down as if passing into a head wind, drawing almighty wheezes from the antiquated pipes. I crept out, ashamed of what I had seen, as far as I can now recall.

The Venerable Bede of Jarrow did not hold overmuch with birthdays and suchlike frippery; what mattered more to him was the day of a man's death and the passage into everlasting life. So, *Glückwünsche und Mähs* (goat), as I believe yours falls about now and raise a brimming beaker in your direction. All the very best, friend. Stay well. Gather thyself unto the old things.

We live in squeamish times.

IV

Ronda Gorge

Sex magazines attest to contemporary glut; clipped to the kiosks the toothy photomodels expose a good deal more than their gums. The ancient mossy trees are still in old disarray near the dry riverbed where the last public garotting took place in Málaga. An empty taxi careers past with its indicator raised: OCUPADO.

The passing of the Generalissimo has seen Spain pass, rather awkwardly (there is no other way), into the latter part of the twentieth century, with strikes, pornography and terrorism. Porno movies feature the Fallen Abbess, Anne Heywood; she also features in *Buena Suerte, Miss Wyckoff* (dir. Marvin Chomsky). Charl Ton Heston (*sic*) bares his teeth manfully in *El Desesperado* at the Zaybe. In an alley on an old wall near a dusty door is painted TOD DEN JUDEN, in a street only fit for pogroms. There is a place for everything, even misfortune, in the Capital of Sorrow.

The very ancient port of Málaga stands for the past; here nothing essential ever changes. Pigs' blood flows into the gutter by the market. Time passes slowly at Portillo, in the shadowy bar Antigua Casa de Guardia (*fundada en* 1840). Black-clothed widows of Spain walk about in their day of perpetual mourning. Bulky men in grey uniforms convey packages to and from Banco de Bilbao, veritable *postillons d'amour*. In the woodsmelling wine bars stout men in braces are taking their first drink of Muscatel; '20' is chalked again and again on the knife-scarred counter, 20 pesetas for a shot of Dulce. Everywhere I hear that sad-sounding ordinary word: *siempre*. Around the *mercado* by night there's a dreadful smell of old prick. Málaga is full of fruit. *¡Admisión del Rector!* Athens and Málaga are oily cities.

Delicate touchers of cash registers and balancers of scales; something fresh and fishy is being weighed judiciously. And always the talk of money, *'dinero'* in the mouths of the pasty-faced Latin men – *'¡millónes!'* King Juan Carlos looks permanently constipated on the stamps. Men are blowing their noses gustily into clean linen handkerchiefs, while having their shoes polished. Market women squat on the steps by the bus terminus for Nerja, offering Scotch whisky and French cheese. Calle Córdoba smells, as always, of open drains, dissipation, mournful numbers: an abattoir stench in the streets of pickpockets, male prostitutes. Watch-sellers lie in wait near Portillo, a coach is pulling out for Cadiz. But little by little the pleasing things are going: Hotel Cataluña closed, the Café Español reduced by half. *Cine* hoardings are explicitly horrifying; a naked girl bound to a stake is fearfully impaled, a wooden dagger protruding from a mouth pumping blood, watched by bushmen or cannibals who crouch watchfully nearby. Some artist has rendered a pair of convulsively clasped hands, naked as fornicating nudes.

Andalucía, Talmudic as anything alive, is made up of contradictions: *cine* advertising become inverted Catholic iconography *outré* as ever (the Fallen Abbess); blood still flows. While a fat fellow with sunken breasts in a Jaeger jersey stands idle in the doorway of Viajes Marland, not expecting much in the way of trade. It's going to be another hot day in Málaga.

After dark in the Café Español nine ladies arrive carrying Menefis plastic shopping-bags, dressed in moleskins, with one fox fur; rather Germanic in mien, grim of mouth, with blue eyeshadow. Draping the furs over the backs of their chairs they order Coca-Cola and Cognac. An old-style waiter (Wicklow Hotel, Dublin, *circa* 1946) places a bottle of Cruzcampo at a judicious remove between a nervous young couple, having removed the cap with a wristy one-handed pass, looking elsewhere: a polished gesture of exquisite tact.

The grim-mouthed Ingebabies are now joined by three others dressed in more expensive woollen jackets, which they throw over the backs of their chairs. Is it a consciousness-raising session at coffee-break or Málaga wives out on the town?

Cat fur is worn aggressively by the gum-chewing transvestite whores at the Bar Sol y Sombra near the market. Vermilion lipstick goes ill with hair dyed off-yellow, saffron wigs, heavy make-up, stiletto heels and deep bass voices. They adjust false bosoms, study the effect in the mirror, eyes flash like Semiramis, ignoring the snickering of the young male barmen. Traffic is heavy to and from the *señoras*. None of them are being picked up – transvestite whores wild in appearance as pro footballers at a drag party.

Are the blind lottery-sellers really sightless, or have they induced blindness upon themselves by an act of will? They circulate about the cathedral, tapping with their white canes. There's much to be seen in Málaga; a strong sense of *déjà vu* permeates it; shoe shops for spastics, religious candles for funerals, china cats stare from shop windows; within, candelabras, dire reproductions of landscapes; casseroles and glassware, dinner-plates in opened crates of wrapping stuff. A fellow is artfully arranging a large fish on a slab. Smell of drains and dust; English faces scorched by the winter sun, a last opportunity to swagger a bit.

In the hotel bar above the Alcazaba overlooking the harbour and the bullring, von Stroheim, bald as a coot, riding-crop under one arm, sporting spurs, is throwing back double whiskies.

A pale-faced barman at La Campana wine bar is deeply immersed in a pornographic magazine printed in Madrid. The evening trade is drinking Seco Montes, P. Ximen, Agte, Seco Añejo and Málaga Dulce tapped from the large barrels ranged behind. The *servicio* is as old as all human ills; a dank place with water dripping from above. Málaga always meant the past. Snails are in. Service in the stationery shop is slow even by Andalusian standards; an unseen transistor plays 'Roll Out The Barrel' in a muted way. Girls in school uniforms, with hockey sticks, pass by. A powerful hose is played over a path to keep the dust down. The city never changes. A bird sings in a cage. Sallow-complexioned businessmen are ordering *sombras* with *churros* in what is left of the Café Español. The Bar Baleares has become yet another shoe shop. Málaga was obsessed by Yo-Yos. Victoria draught beer hard to come by.

Small sailors are propositioning the *chicas* who parade in pairs, giggling; their long hair freshly washed. They are all atitter; the attentive tars getting nowhere. A collection for the Asociación Protectora Malagueña de Subnormales. Landaus drawn by carriage horses in foolish hats proceed half asleep down Travesía Pintor Nogales, carrying tourists. Saigon has fallen, the English pound is dropping, American public opinion rising.

'TYRANNIQUE OU TROP CONCILIANTE?', cry the kiosks. 'SAIGON PANICS AS LAST AMERICAN LEAVES.' 'ANGRY

PICKETS LASH TOP JOCKEY WILLIE.' And in a heavy Dutch accent, *Algemeen Dagblad* announced: 'KANS OP CRISES BLIJFT!'

To keep up with the rest of Europe, the crime rate in Málaga has risen; port of call, furlong, of blind men, of graveyard statuary, ornate chess sets. In La Sirena fish-bar by the harbour the well-heeled clientele are flashing 5,000 peseta notes, not bothering to count the change. The barmen move as elegantly as dancers. Bar Pombo is closed for good. The lottery man is whistling the opening bars of Beethoven's famous Fifth, the so-called Symphony of Destiny. Blind men go tapping around the cathedral; inside the Orquesta Sinfónica de Málaga are offering *Ars antigua* (R. Diaz) and *Sinfonía sevillana* (J. Turina). Resident organist Christian Baude.

When the offices empty the port hums like a beehive. A vast Soviet tanker lies to in the bay. The wine bars open. Deviants lurk in the groves of the Alcazaba. In certain tall hotel rooms overlooking stairwells you would suppose yourself back in a previous century. Port of curious chess sets, stonemasons, shoeshine men selling lottery tickets on the side, vendors and deviants, blind men, operatic traffic policemen in navy-blue uniforms with white gloves and white pith helmets, sunglasses *de rigueur,* even in dark bars. Quiosco los Periquitos. Black swans with red bills paddle the dirty pond in the Alameda Gardens where a child dressed as a diminutive bride is being photographed by her adoring *papá.* It's time for lemon tea. Awkward soldiers with close-cropped heads are walking their girls. The sun coursing through the luxuriant overhang of tall palm trees lights up the inverts who watch from public benches. Not a crestfallen buttock in sight! ¡ASPIRINAS ASPROMANIS! The cathedral bell at midday. ¡EXPLOSIVOS RIO TINTO! Drawn by repetition of clever moves, White cannot escape the checks without letting the Black rook join the attack. And if his king tries to hide on 93, we may expect trouble. Platonou and Minic wiped off the board. *Adiós* Quinteros and Browne! The *mariposas* are in a perpetual froth of excitement in the clever mazes of the Alcazaba; lured by the stagy décor, the sudden appearance and disappearance of like-minded lads. *Todavía no me acostumbro a estar frustrado.* So much, as Plato politely phrased it, for such matters.

While modern Spain sprawls along the Mediterranean, busily going to hell, the ascending new road to Ronda is as extraordinary as the southern approaches to Barcelona. Cut off from the mess of the coastal 'development' and deep in the off-season, Ronda (850 *metros de altitud*; 32,049 *habitantes*) offers herself as a kind of Sparta. A bullfighters' town. From here came Pedro Romero and the great Ordoñez.

The coastal stretch from Málaga to Marbella is as ugly as the urban development from Salthill to Costello Cross on Connemara's Atlantic seaboard, allowing the Spaniards slightly better taste. Up here men with windscorched faces are talking intently to each other. They are addicts of circles and all shades of green, with the habit of contradicting you ingrained, a Moorish trait. In Ronda your thoughts fly upwards. Walk on the windy walls. To live here would be to marry a very strict but beautiful woman.

The surrounding countryside of undulating hills and far vistas rivals certain valleys in Yugoslavia near the Austrian border, or the Transvaal. Beyond the gasoline station (Zoco 500 *metros*) lies the veldt; land the colour of puma, Africa.

And do they love green! Oxidised bronze bells, washed and bleached army uniforms of Thai-like neatness, worn with panache under tasselled forage caps, introduce touches of green everywhere. Into the Bar Maestrol – just wide enough for you to turn around – twitches a griev-

ously afflicted beggar, calling '*¡BOOoojijjji!*' In an alleyway
off a nameless street a bar is crammed with soldiers in
green uniforms. PEÑA TAURINA ANTONIO ORDOÑEZ, the
sign says, swinging in the wind. A torture-picture: the sad
comedy of a reunion of friends.

In Piccola Capri, open at long last, the recorded voice
of Bob Dylan sounds like an unhinged aunt, singing sadly
over a sensational view of the gorge by night. Down there
gurgles the Guadalquivir.

I see a line of hanged victims carved in stone. In the
pedestrian walks you see the finite gestures of bullfighters,
jackets draped over shoulders in *torero* manner when the
weather permits. The wind sets its teeth into the *toreros*-to-
be, the Ronda girls rumpy as *rejoneadores*. Their shoulders
protrude like flying buttresses. Mauve slacks are worn by
these addicts of *alegría* who spit *pipas* in the street; flashers
of *mil* peseta notes, dislodgers of preconceptions, rel-
ishers of large mushrooms sautéed in garlic, child-lovers,
they themselves somewhat childish. A chess competition
takes place in what once must have been a Moorish
palace. *Peña: J. M. Bellón. Torneo Social Ajedrez.* For three
days the Levant blew a half-gale.

Men with convex eyebrows frown thoughtfully into
their coffee and Cognac. '*Poco diferencia,*' they say, always
ready with the qualifying clause, the caesura, the direct
contradiction. I have two eyes, I say to the man in the
late-night bar (we are discussing the 'invisible villages').
No, he says, you have four. It's true, I'm wearing *gafas.*

An old church, I say to the old man in the corner of
the *librería* where I buy carbon paper. No, he contradicts
me, not old, only two hundred years – of Iglesia Nuestra
Señora del Socorro.

In the Germanic Restaurant Jerez near the bullring a
distinguished grey-haired man arrives with a lady in furs.
The owner seems to know me, hovers about our table

and stares pointedly as if at a long-lost son who refuses to acknowledge his own *padre*. The noble-looking Frenchman in the neck-brace, hair a sable silver, pulls up his expensive tweed trouser leg to expose a calf of corpse-like whiteness to the lady in furs who bends forward, slowly removing her sunglasses – 'Ouch, *chéri!*'

In the long bar overlooking the plaza a stout man in a Panama hat set at a bullbreeder's angle sits at the counter, plunged in thought. He is joined by men in expensive leather jackets, with the swarthy faces of impresarios. A posse of purposeful men with bursting bellies now arrive, roaring for *cerveza.*

A calm nun in a powder-blue modern habit is transacting some business at the Banco Central. The waiter with the scorched face above his red jacket is playing in an old Simenon thriller, as is the lovely girl who sold me carbon paper in the *librería*, as is the contrary old man sitting in the corner. A thin bell is tolling. The cold in hot countries is absolutely poignant.

The bullring is the largest and most dangerous in all Spain. The New Town is a mess, a sort of Arab shanty town. A ring of towns with odd names face Portugal: Estepa, Eciza, Arcana. On the winding road to Marbella and the desecrated coast lie the 'invisible villages'; not to be missed on any account.

Soon the eastern coastline from Estepona near Gibraltar to Gerona near the French border will have gone the way of Marbella and Torremolinos, and it will be left for hardy souls to move to Pontevedre or La Coruña on the Spanish Atlantic coast. American bombing colonels out from the the airbase at Morón de Frontera drink Cognac like beer.

Over Ronda hangs a most Moorish moon and I never wish to leave it.

*

Torremolinos is a creepy place.

The intense light shed at noon in winter can produce an unhinged effect, like walking on water; a mescal dream on beer or gin – living as flying. Scandinavians now run bars (Bjarne) or manufacture ice cream (Bjorn), being an adaptive race out of their own country. The Irish Bar is run, wouldn't you guess, by a quiet Englishman.

Two truculent sailors from Dundee are huggermuggering at the Anchor. In the neon-lit surreal night a passive crowd of mixed nationalities, a little lost, go perambulating; an army of street entrepreneurs attempt to gain and hold their attention, always flagging, afraid of being done, moving on. Grisly prints are everywhere on view.

Here is a town of shifty characters always on the move. Flat at first, just a throughway, it becomes suddenly a maze of levels with flights of stairs descending; regions of mugging and lush-rolling. Keep your wallet buttoned up. In the English Bar, run by a Plymouth couple, an oil-tanker crewman, who likes to play a bit of golf, says that being cooped up for months on end in the belly of a big tanker can make a man go all funny. Has he come to the right place? Would not a fortnight here be tantamount to spending fourteen days and nights trapped in a Ferris wheel whirling? But people seem to like noise today, need it; silence augmenteth rage. We live in peculiar restless times.

Whores and pimps abound by night. Discos thunder, strobe lights flash, recorded voices bellow. The young are packed together in dark underground cellars; pay as you order, the light is poor, the recorded sounds deafening. I am offered a small sullen girl by a large Bavarian pimp in sombrero; seemingly quite at home (Schwabing?) in these Andalusian badlands. The quick turnover. French is spoken by the questing pimps.

Architecturally the place is a true nightmare. Grouped along the shore and turned inwards upon themselves high-rise apartments of depressing sameness appear to advance seaward – a breeding place for crime. It is a manner of building – one cannot call it a style – that suggests impermanency. Strange factor in a building, concreteness rotating towards illusion, no Johannesburg or Salisbury in Zimbabwe: poverty does not exist, provided you rise above it. Pie in the sky. Le Corbusier fathered this inhumanly scaled grid patterning, these elevated box-quarters piled on *ad nauseam*, offering an unreal cycloramic future in the here and now. Odd that a Frog should make such an error; a building style designed for transients, commercial travellers, call-girls, night owls. On twenty-first-storey terraces behind the high-wire fences Modular Man plays tennis for ever and ever.

Unamuno's 'ether of pure speculative contemplation' has no place here; but look away, not far off are wooded mountains and a lake, where few people go. Of the old village, the Tower-by-the-Sea, little remains, the market being the only authentic part left. But why are *gambas* so expensive? The Mediterranean fished out already? They used to be given away free with draught beer in Málaga.

Latins, the multitudinous forms of machismo; the gushing fountains, the bullring.

Multitudinous? Come, come; say rather the stereotypes. Behind Andalusian machismo lurks the Moor. Although departed several centuries – the fall of Granada and the discovery of America occurred simultaneously – in the body, some of his nature and character remains; the residue of his language, the ruins, his shadow. The Alhambra presumes inner space. And the true notion of the dignity of man is that all are extraordinary, at least potentially. A deeply Spanish conviction, this, not I think found in the doleful Gaelic philosophy of *An scath a chéile a mhaireann na daoine* (people live in one another's shadows or are dependent upon one another). Midway between Málaga and Nerja lies the tax *refugio* of Torre del Mar with a powerful stench of open drains. Its foreshore looks as grim as the Mexican wasteland of Buñuel's *Los Olvidados*. It has become a German colony. Hoffman's zone of empty high-rise apartments awaits more Germans from the cold hard cities of the North. A beach has been cleared and named; it will look fine in a colour brochure. A brothel has opened at Nerja.

From the mouths of mercenary men in the Bar Don Quixote the word *negocio* drops like mercury. Wads of *mil* peseta notes are flashed. Cured hams hang from the low ceiling. Dick and Tony have retired to Málaga. Two stout German *Fraus* with gross backsides packed tight into white flannel slacks pass by in the subdued company of a stout *Herr* with a nervous French poodle on a lead. A plump *Fräulein* in a pink bikini as brief as decency will permit walks along Burriana beach with a brown-skinned local manikin who is not right in the head; his features are squeezed together into a veritable snout. They go linking. Two dogs are copulating in a cove, observed by amused German sunbathers.

Again the constants: English hopelessness, German pushfulness, both lost in a language they will never learn, a culture they do not wish to know.

'How's our Kitty?'

'Are you near the end?' an exhausted female voice asks to my right, on the Balcón de Europa.

'Time to go back for lunch,' an elderly male voice answers, *sotto voce.*

At La Luna on the outskirts of Nerja (population 6,000 ten years ago, 16,000 today) bronzed German couples play tennis on the municipal courts. In the bar a Yorkshire JP, late of Burma, says he believes in capital punishment. Bring back the birch. He is for hanging Provos.

On the plateau, which ten years ago was a scrubland for the passage of goats to the river below, now has arisen a monstrous development of high-rise apartments. When the sun goes down behind El Capistrano, 300 Belgians stand on 300 identical balconies, watching it sink, before retiring indoors to flush 300 identical toilets.

The signs are up: PROHIBIDO ... PRIVADO; the guard-dogs alert, the sprinklers working – it might be a Cape Town suburb. Jesús has sold his fish restaurant and gone horse-riding in the hills. Paco Fernandez, son of an honest banker, is erecting a Mussolini-style mansion on Calle Carabeo on top of the poor quarter; an ingenious way of effacing want. Lady Blanche is in *constant* correspondence with the grandson of Richard (*Gatherings in Spain*) Ford. She has no trouble at all in understanding the mystery of the Blessed Trinity.

The Parisian psychoanalyst who dabbles in oils has painted a black bull that would pass for a black astrakhan hearthrug, such as might adorn the living room of Germans who decorate their heavy rich apartments from the advertising sections of *Bunte* and *Stern*. Business-women are selling insurance and steel tubing.

'Psychic death,' says the subtle Doctor Klaus from Berlin. Voodoo is back, the Evil Eye, witchcraft. He himself has a heart condition, being a gluttonous eater of meat, hardly reassuring in a doctor of medicine; would *you* be treated by a blind oculist?

'Most discoveries are economical,' says the homoeo-pathic doctor, who claims to have cured his own multiple sclerosis and can cure yours, at a price; having refused no less than five chairs at Gröningen. He hopes to open a sanatorium in the hills, become its Hofrat Behrens. He believes that the Soviet Russians are infiltrating Europe and have already taken secret control of Scandinavia. 'I started clearing up my kidneys with parsley soup.'

CUEVAS DE NERJA–FANTASÍA NATURAL, the sign says. But is it not the town itself grown so monstrously, that is the unnatural fantasy? El Capistrano, the clotting on the hill overlooking La Luna and the river, is a village in Spain the way a Butlin's camp is a village anywhere. T-shirts bear the name, so that the inmates of Casa Cost Enuff can recognise a friendly neighbour. Half the face has been cut off a mountain to make a quarry, and the construction trucks run all day. The main lingo of the beaches on Costa del Sol would seem to be German: '*Fleisch*' chalked above '*porc*' and 'meat' on the menu boards. A sinister breed of Germans have come down to the coast from Hamburg, Hanover, Essen. The vicious Bremen hippie is living with his seraglio near a waterfall on the way to Frigiliana. A morose German owns the *merendero* on Playa de Salon, serving German-style mugs of coffee with cream *dobles* for 62 pesetas to some early-risen English couples who speak in intense and compromising vagaries.

'How's Fritz and Kitty?'

'I know this for a fact because I've got friends in the Forestry Commission myself.'

For emphasis, the English lower their voices. Germans raise theirs. The favoured mode of address among Spaniards would seem to favour the half-shout, even when standing within touching distance.

On Burriana a group of idlers are much diverted by the antics of a *mono* on a lead, dressed in Turkish trousers and a red toque, diminutive, almost one of themselves but not quite.

A gaudy macaw leers from a cage suspended over Calle de la Gloria. The asters have withered on the columbarium where Miguel Rojaz sleeps his last sleep in the *cementerio,* with a fine view of the Cuesto del Cielo, over which shadows of passing clouds fall obliquely: *testimonio recuerdo.*

Over the swimming pool in the garden of *número* 32 Calle Carabeo Old Glory flies above the Spanish tricolour on the masthead, in the house now owned by one of the Rothschild brothers. We lived there once.

Behind Burriana beach the exploitation goes on, new roads cut out of the ochre sandstone, building sites laid out. The drains cannot take all that's been put into them. Stink of fish on the sand below the *parador,* stink of diesel oil offshore. Windsurfing must be the last late-twentieth-century distraction that is soundless; figures flying and floating prophetically out of da Vinci's sketchpads into the here and now. The Mediterranean has a nip in it in early May and few venture in. On a stalled *pedalo* off the Balcón de Europa within full view of all, a beast is forcing his attentions on a beauty in a *very* brief mauve bikini. Her scream hangs over the water. The tick-ridden stray dogs who have had a dip are now pissing against the rocks; soon to be observed complacently by the sun-bathing German group, strenuously copulating in a cove. At mid-morning a band of male Germans are roaring drinking-songs at Pepe Gomez's *merendero.* Where Leslie Marshall ('a very common name in Scotland') confides his fear of the wily Russians. 'The Rooskies are past masters at dabbling in troubled waters.' He recalls a Singapore brothel with a cherry tree bursting through the roof and the madam presenting him with a toothbrush wrapped in cellophane on leaving. It was 1937 and he was young. Now he's a dead ringer for James Joyce. The Nerja bordello stands behind the church. A local rapist out of prison knows the ropes there; 2,000 pesetas a knock.

On the five beaches sun-bronzed Prussian widows of

advanced years and flab go topless; sights for sore eyes, *nichts für ungut.* The pretty French and German girls also, sunbathing and swimming, suffering themselves to be kissed topless and generally move about as if in Eden and not in the Turdy Pleasure Grounds. In the prone position when oiled for sunbathing, the top of the bikini may be entirely removed and the bottom part pulled down as low as decency will allow; what Swift termed the dishonourable part may be fairly exposed. A young lecher wearing a peaked cap is on the prowl, armed with powerful binoculars.

On Carabeo beach the pretty long-haired tease who came skipping down the path with hair freshly washed is now perched elegant as a mermaid on a boulder and lighting up a Marlboro; presently to be metamorphosed into Mariposa the gay barman who mixes a strong Bloody Mary.

At Io's *merendero* the waiters run. Flies are dancing in the *servicios.* Petting and kissing occurs in the most public places, behaviour that in Franco's day would have resulted in jail sentences and even deportation.

Spaniards are given to hyperbolic excess; with them, silence is a form of impoliteness. The constants remain: stink of drains, the morning parade to Burriana. The helplessness of the English and the rudeness of the Germans; French *elán,* finickety manners, they turn *café-au-lait*-coloured in the May sunshine, the non-Latins go lobster-red, tumescent. Large Labradors and Alsatians strain at stool in public places. A smart Spaniard drives past the Banco Atlántico with a credit card clenched between his teeth, both hands on the steering column, the ultimate in chic. (The English like to be seen entering bars with car keys on leather tags held between the teeth.) The fish-bar smells vaguely of fresh vomit.

It's the dead hour of the day in Andalucía, four in the

afternoon; not much life stirs in the Bar el Kiko or the Bar Julian. The redheaded barman, who looks Irish but is a local man, helps himself to a quick shot of Terry in the swanky bar of the Hotel Balcón de Europa. A well-fixed native son is just wiping his Citroën in the forecourt of Apartamentos Playa de Torrecilla, which is owned by an Englishman. Rafael Fossy counts his night's poker takings laid out on his bed: half a million pesetas. The Aerolitos are giving out their dire space gruntings. An elderly boozer with hare's teeth and a squashed straw hat with a broken band is sipping red wine in the Bar el Santos. The engineer Manuel Herrera Bueno of Calle de las Angustias is without a job.

Alberto Joven the barman, who can speak four languages, addresses me as *¡Compañero!*; a great honour, coming from this human dynamo. I, the feeble *escritor.* He copies out the Octavio Paz poem that begins '*Controlador de serenos esclavizas . . .*' Reads it back to himself.

'This man is not happy,' he says. *Polvo* (dust, powder) in context has 'a metaphysical meaning'. If there is such a thing as the dignity of the working man, Alberto Joven personifies it.

Women seem to age better than men. Possibly they take better care of their bodies. The men don't give a damn, exposing hairy pot-bellies, the sagging paps of Tiresias. All women are not Helen, I know that; but all women hold Helen in their hearts. Strawberries are in. May lightning has blasted a tree in Berkshire, I am told. But the Land of *Lotería* is changing. Meaty handclapping drives intelligence out of the head. An eagle-owl staggers out of the sea. The *búho real!*

Which leads us back by a commodious *vicus* to the slaughterhouse all white tiles inside, a cow, a goat, two bleating kids, and a pig, along with some very innocently dressed butchers, that is no costume, not even workaday don't you know the informal touch, all grist to their mill, those gruesome things, *herzlich, mit freundlichen Grüssen*, sharpest knives in town, and the pig put up the best fight.

Dumb brutes they, all slosh and this and that, a view of the fields, the last view, a cauldron for shaving off the skin I suppose. Smiling faces gentle men, takes all types these days to remember anything, just guts and great swirling forms, start to see the abstract positive and negative, the throat takes, the tongue swells, but not until you get your right elbow halfway down the pig's throat groping for the heartstrings will the thick beast let go its life. No music if you please, I've got a timid system, inherent dizziness and garlic fillet with a stiff glass of beer or two, elbow at sides, yes even now I can taste the sour refrain.

The man's all ashake now how nice, a family bag secured tightly above the ears, leather I think, a young Scorpio friendly to the very end suggests I put something on my head, well there it is. I think the leather to absolutely muffle the screams, effective just as your arthritic itch of ageing relatives, cleaned in a damp toilet twice a year.

One eye going out here, the other there, almost defiance when you would fancy a look of trepidation, well that's not the way of the beast, no sir, beginning to cough up the innards. The least I could feel for the poor dead things hanging by their hooves down by the river which is named River of the Occasional Yelp, in Spanish. Well of course that's inaccurate, like most things, but the suggestion is certainly not far from yelping dog. Found a dog eating away, some spare intestines I supposed. And the hung things, the carcasses don't you know, bleeding away, bleeding away.

Our coach overtakes trucks loaded to capacity with orange *butano* containers, for cooking Spanish dinners, two racing cyclists in yellow and blue caps marked FIAT, going like hammers of hell, overtaking each other in quick bursts of speed, driving down hard on the pedals, speeding freaks from Jarry's *Supermale.* Heading for Valencia, that town of good white wine, swaying palms, wildly gesticulating heroic statuary. A spring is released and then something snaps; the freed spirit soars.

We pass orange groves protected by windbreaks of cyprus, pines about olive groves, peach interspersed with vines, the succulent South, a line of racing hills. Pine-covered hot hills, water cannons firing in a green field by sugar-cane plantations, three tiers of young porkers in a well-ventilated scarlet trailer bowling merrily along towards some distant abattoir. I have set out from Málaga to travel to Barcelona, 200 kilometres away, and then 170 to the French border, passing through Paris at night, reaching London on the third day.

Pylons now, orange flames shooting up from gas refineries into the clear air, the tall striding shapes of praying mantis are building cranes, the signs and symbols of modern industrial Spain. A series of linked motorways, *salida* 35, tollgates, tall cyprus trees in a cemetery passing, some haciendas, more palm trees buffeted by the wind, another flyover. B141, a sign seemed to convey, REUS, TARRAGONA, VALLS.

French cars heading for the border (do they arrive as fast as they depart?), Port Bou, Biarritz, racing by a fine aqueduct outside Tarragona. French drivers are dangerous half an hour before lunch and even more so before dinner. Dutch drivers are helpless in the Alps. But the approaches to Barcelona are as exciting as the approaches towards any modern city. B97.

One approaches it by long easy spirals, with Spanish

prosperity becoming more evident by the minute, unlike
the straight run into West Berlin across the grim DDR
and its darkness before the blue neon Schultz signs. The
hoardings began 82 kilometres out as the flyovers became
more frequent, the tollgates. Did a racing sign say
BARAMAR? Sitges sounds like an infirmity, not a place, and
Vendrell is hardly an improvement. I see a pith helmet
and a bottle of VAT 69 in the back seat of a German
Lancia; blue-domed churches are left behind and the
late-afternoon air becomes cooler. An intermittent stench
rises off the chemical-dosed land. The sky is alive with
feeding swallows. A sign cries LA CAIXE!

A fine church dome, as if dancing, is left behind with
a whiff of perdition off the land.

PINORD ... KENT ... SKOL ... BARCELONA 45 ...

The city's lighting system begins. Off to the right are
the new towns, Villanueva and a tormented anagram:
Geltru. Beyond lie Badalona, Matard, Tossa de Mar, San
Feliu de Guixols, Cadaqués, Patmos, the drums and
spheres and flames of oil refineries, Olympia Nuclear SA,
the piled-up drainpipes of an expanding city.

The courier gives his spiel patiently. We are booked
into the Hotel Apolo in the Ramblas. Take all you need
for the night. Dinner is on the company. The call is at 7
a.m. We depart 8.15 for France with two French drivers
who will remain with us until London.

The coach goes accelerating into the city alongside a
river. The first street signs loom, LIV AUTOMATICA; the
tentacles of the city close around us, we have become
part of a larger traffic movement. It's 5.30 rush-hour, 15
September. My feet have swollen. The ageing gay tour-
guide, with his arm about a young puzzled boy, assigns
rooms. 'We'll put Iggins wiff the Norwegian.'

I go drinking with Bjorn Engel (Angel Bear), who has
buried two wives in Denmark, left the heavy tax and the

dead wives behind him to start manufacturing ice cream
in Torremolinos. The riot squad are out in the Ramblas,
armed like combat troops. No more villainous-looking
armed fellows had I seen since the sallow-faced American
Army troops went on parade in West Berlin. Last week a
girl had been shot dead in a street demonstration. Watch
your wallet in the Ramblas. Don't run.

Morning departure as per schedule. France lies ahead.
The French drivers go with the expected panache,
windows refreshingly open. The two daredevil Spaniards
liked to supervise refuelling with lighted cigarettes
glowing under their mustachios. The rivers run with
waters under splendid bridges. After the ordered fields
of Perpignan the road markings become long white Gallic
lines with sporty stipple effects, Toulouse coming up with
red and black ovals, curved road signs.

The cones of the red-and-white wind indicators are
straining away from the motorway. After Arles Spain
begins to seem grubby. At Aix-en-Provence the roof tiles
change their contours: convex to the south, concave here
in the north. A coloured dwarf with a long university scarf
wound around his neck waits by the roadway alongside a
travelling-bag twice the size of himself.

Black September

Nothing upsets Bavarians more than the *Föhn*, a devious Italian wind that slips in over the Alps and whistles through the Brenner, whispering Latin things into German ears. Possibly repeating what *Il Duce* told Count Ciano: that Germans were dangerous because they dreamed collectively.

Be that as it may, when the *Föhn* blows, surgeons lay down their knives and publishers' readers cast aside typescripts, both knowing their judgement to be impaired. Remote objects, such as church spires, draw closer. The good citizens of Munich – where once more I happened to find myself in the Black September of 1972 – like nothing better than to sit for hours on windowseats or out on small balconies, stare into the street below, observe life passing.

In Jakob-Klar-Strasse in Schwabing the retired boxer takes up his position early, and is there all day, fortified by mugs of *Bier* handed out to him by an unseen *Frau*, become just a brawny arm. I was there in the *schwarzer* September of 1972.

A positively Latin feeling for blueness prevails. *Lividus* bleaching to the delicate washed-out blue of the Bavarian sky over the Englische Garten, in the watery eyes of the citizens, in the flag, on Volksbier labels: it's München blue.

'*Ciao!*' say the better-educated ones on parting; though in the old-style shops the *Grüss Gotts* ring out right merrily. Misha Gallé called, then Volker Schlöndorff with his wife Margarete von Trotta for *Tischtennis*.

From Riem Airport into the city the way was festively prepared with huge Olympic flags. My taxi was driven by a woman. I offered Prinzregenten-Strasse Fünf as my address, a Freudian slip if ever there was one, and was driven smartly up to Adolf Hitler's old address. I redirected her to a number in Schwabing.

Once again I began losing my bearings on the wrong side of *Der Friedensengel*, walking my feet off in this city of fine girls and spouting fountains. Greek goddesses with Bavarian thighs, eyes closed against the inevitable, supported on their shoulders heavy pillars pockmarked by bullets fired from afar. The great stone goddesses were protecting the bridges over the Isar, traversed at set intervals by a villainous low-slung black limousine packed with what I assumed to be Italian gangsters, who turned out to be Irish government leaders. *Der Friedensengel* balanced precariously on one foot, hopefully extending a palm branch. Across the plinth an activist had squirted in white aerosol: LIEBE DEINE TOTEN!

Preparations for the games had intensified throughout summer, with Police Chief Schreiber's men out in waders cleansing the old Isar of a detergent overflow from a factory. On 28 August *Süddeutsche Zeitung* reported that sportsmen and politicians were fascinated (*begeistert*) by an opening ceremony without military undertones. Lord Killanin was in control. Aged Avril Brundage had flown in from the United States. The fire too had come from afar: Greece. Whether this was a good augury or not, few were willing to predict. The American traveller and cynic

Theroux would write later that the games were of interest because they showed a world war in pantomime.

But something more disturbing than the *Föhn* (causing double vision) had slipped into Munich via Air France with false papers on 4 September when I arrived from West Berlin (where *Cauldron of Blood* was running at the outpost for occupying troops whose regimental motto had a threatening ring to it: HAVE GUNS WILL TRAVEL, and be damned to syntax) – Al Fatah. Their target: the Olympic Village. More particularly, Israeli coaches and weight-lifters, the heavy innocents stall-fed on milk and T-bone steaks, who were soon to lay down their lives in the German slaughterhouse prepared for them.

As bubonic plague, the Black Death, entered Europe as a flea on the body of a rat, so sophisticated international terrorism, late-twentieth-century style, entered Germany from the Middle East via Riem, in the person of Muhammad Daoud Odeh (code-name Abu Daoud), probably travelling on a forged Iraqi passport. He was to remain there, undetected by Schreiber, throughout the impossible ultimatums – one hostage to be slaughtered every two hours unless 400 or whatever Arab prisoners were released – and the carnage that followed, the self-immolation, the capture of three terrorists at Fürstenfeld-bruck military airport.

It was *Föhn* weather, Sharpeville weather, the girls out in summer clothes one day, scarves and coat the next. Police and ambulance sirens never stopped in Leopold-Strasse, the dogs barking after the fox has gone. In a mossy fountain, somewhat magnified in the water, small white eggshells broken in halves seemed to tremble. Shabby men were reading discarded newspapers in a public park protected by high hedges. Trams clanged around the steep corner at Max-Planck-Strasse, clinging to the wall. The black limousine was back, now strangely flying the Irish colours on bonnet pennants, with CD registration plates, still traversing old Munich. The Irish Taoiseach Jack Lynch was conferring with Willy Brandt in the country. Buttercups grew along the grass verge on Thomas-Mann-Allee. A woman wearing leather gloves was gathering red berries. Near the Englische Garten two sailors enquired the way to the archery contest, one of them drawing an imaginary bow. Men in shirt-sleeves were out. I walked by the embankments, saw the skyline drawn and painted by Klee and Grosz, two brown beauties in bikinis were sunning themselves near the weir where terns were wading; there two Americans had drowned the previous summer. It was a lovely September day, *anno Domini* 1972.

Two workmen in blue denim overalls sat silently at a table on which were arranged some empty beer bottles with the remains of their lunch, under acacia trees buffeted by the wind; a most peaceful scene, one would think. But on Luitpold-Strasse, leading to and from the Olympic Village, the sirens never stopped wailing; it was difficult to distinguish police from ambulances; destination lock-up, hospital or morgue. The call was for law and order; but what is that but disorder with the lid clamped down?

Why was an Irish Embassy car packed with Italian gangsters? Riddles. One handsome terrorist declared that he would have preferred death with his comrades who had blown up victims and themselves with hand grenades flung into the helicopter. A sombre choral work, then, to be expected in Munich. A style of killing had been set by terrorists who looked more like movie actors than political activists, acted and spoke like them too, in German and broken English, chain-smoking.

The leaves were turning. In shop windows now the signs read '*Hallo Herbst! Du wirst chic.*' The yellow press yelled

'MORDORGIE!' The headlines screamed 'MORDFEST!' *The Times* put it more diplomatically, more Britishly: 'STORM GROWS OVER WHAT WENT WRONG AT MUNICH'. *Der Spiegel* of 11 September stated bluntly: 'DAS MASSAKER VON MÜNCHEN!'

'The XXth Olympic Games resumed yesterday after a 24-hour suspension while Munich mourned the eleven members of the Israeli team who died at the hands of Arab guerrillas.' Mireille Mathieu was driven around the Marathon *Sporthalle*, standing in a white open-top Ford Capri, singing '*Ein Platz an der Sonne für jung und alt*': while *Papst* Paul VI, not to be outdone, was photographed in Venice, standing precariously upright in what was described as *eine Prunkgondel*, solemnly blessing some Venetian sewage, a clotting of flowers and scum. To the rear of the precarious vessel stood what appeared to be Roman centurians.

The Schwabing flat had been cleaned and the rugs had their colours renewed. Framed on the walls were strange tortured viscerae, possibly human, in monochrome. A single flower, richly red, damask, with streaks of sunflower yellow in its heart, hung in a small blue vase. Red of anther, hush of autumn, tread of panther.

We went swimming in Starnberger See, Erika and Wolfgang and I. Out there in the blue, insane Ludwig had drowned with his physician. The wooded hills rolled away. On Saturday the *Süddeutsche Zeitung* obituary notices faced pages of movie advertising of unrestrained lewdness. Marie Garibaldi was showing her all in *Amore Nudo*. 'MEIN TREUER LEBENSKAMERAD', the obituary notice declared with melancholy certitude. The dead could not cavort with Marie Garibaldi. Hitachi advertised, 'I am you', with Oriental guile. It was time for MacBaren's Golden Blend. It was time for Volksbier. Müller, the man with two left feet, had scored again, and was being ardently embraced by his captain Beckenbauer. *Tip-Kick Fussball* brings competitive fever (*Wettkampfstimmung*) into the home. A modern German family were shown in the throes of 'Tip-Kicking'. Charles Bronson was appearing in *Brutale Stadt*, Jerry Lewis elsewhere, a black detective appeared in *Shaft* ('*Der absolute Super-Krimi!*'). The girls of the DDR ran away with all the track and field events; a splendid example of specialised breeding and expert coaching achieving good results within three decades. An exhibition of early Bavarian folk art was showing at the Staatliches Museum.

Germans togged out for golf are a sight for sore eyes. They go in for overkill, armed with *Golfschläger*, but cannot laugh at themselves, unlike the English, who do it tolerantly all the time. Nor can they endure their own Germanic incompetence. A game without visible opponents disturbs; and at golf you are your own opponent, even in matchplay. How they suffer! They *detest* losing. By the eighteenth none are on speaking terms.

I played with the Wittys and their elderly female friend on a woody links in the Bavarian Alps above Chiemsee. The lake itself was invisible below in the haze. I spent most of the round searching for lost golf balls among trees; the lovely Hannelore flushed and peeved, saying 'Shit! Shit!' between clenched teeth.

Back to Munich by train with two well-preserved mountain hikers, man and wife, in deerstalker and *Lodens*. A relief to be off the *Golfplatz*. (Watch them tearing up the rough, cursing blind. It is a game unsuited to their temperament.) Back in München again, passing *Oktoberfest* tents and stalls.

Prone to a certain kind of spiritual narcosis with which they are afflicted, more so than most races, the Germans must *suffer* themselves. Your average Bavarian is a baleful mixture of sentimentalist and brute. Krüger has his trouser legs shortened by a Herr von Bismarck, Munich tailor, who asked him on which side he wore his shame.

It sounded grosser in German. Intemperance, fist-fights, puking, in those lovely Ember Days. Stay clean. Tripper and Raptus were on the rampage, Dominguin gored at Bayonne (*carneada* is always the fault of the *torero*). Nature abhors a vacuum. *Neu! Ajax mit der Doppelbleiche.*

Chefpolizist Schreiber negotiated with a terrorist whose head was covered with a woman's stocking. Itchy-fingered *Sturmkommandos* were dressed like frogmen in athletic tracksuits; they watched privily from their hiding places. *Omnipotenz, Super-Helden!*

The aneroid temperature registered somewhere between *Veränderlich* and *Verstörung,* or something between distraction and bewilderment. *Stern* displayed a corn-yellow blonde in the act of unpeeling a corn-yellow T-shirt, her only article of clothing; stamped on her backside were the joined circles of the Olympic symbol, most poshlustily.

Clouds pass over the roofs of Munich, a blue evening falls. The ex-boxer points down into darkening Jakob-Klar-Strasse, amused by something below. There are moments when I am able to look without any effort through the whole of creation (*Schöpfung*), which is nothing more than an immense exhaustion (*Erschöpfung*), wrote stout Thomas Bernhardt.

Gusty *stürmisch* wind-tossed weather; then a warm sunny day in Munich. The face on the screen, on high hoardings, was out in the streets, the violence let loose. Hands were constantly feeling and touching, groping and tapping. Fingers parted long hair, touched noses, brows, the bearded lips rarely smiled, the looks exchanged were just severe or merely sullen. Hands were never for one moment still, compulsively pulling and picking; plucking at the backs of leather seats, tearing paper, restless, agitated, never still, the eyes restless.

In the capitals of the West the same feature films were released simultaneously. *Little Pig-Man. My Name is Nobody* (*sic*). LIEBE was sprayed indiscriminately over walls. Amerika Haus was riddled with bullets. The riots squads sat in paddywagons behind wire mesh and bulletproof glass, parked in back streets near universities, out of sight, played cards, bided their time. A Judas-grille opened and a baleful eye observed us. In the heated bar the tall lovely unsober teacher Barbara König was swallowing ice cubes, pulling faces.

Ach ach; tich-tich. We cannot stop even if we wanted to, have become voyeurs watching atrocious acts. The lies are without end because the hypotheses are without end. It has become suspect to 'think'; all adults occupy the thrilling realm of moral dilemmas (civic inertia), political drama; *Strassentheater.* Dangerous blindness with a dash of singularity. Angels, for the man who cannot avoid thinking about them, wrote the pessimist Cioran, certainly exist. *So sitzt es mir im Gemüt.*

On the large screens of TV colour sets in the windows of banks the Olympic Games went on, in silence, in triplicate. The high pole-vaulter in the briefest of shorts lifted herself on unseen springs, collapsing in slow motion onto a large bolster. The DDR female athletes were pouring over the hundred-metre hurdles, elegant as bolting deer in a forest fire. From the rapt tormented expression of the long-legged high-jumper, one knew that track records were being broken now in the head. The athletes on the podium were crowned with the bays, gave clench-fisted salutes as their national flag flew on the mast.

In West Berlin at midnight, in the small white flat of a pregnant beauty, the phone rang, the ringing tone muted. A hidden voice, a Basque voice (not a Berlin accent) said into her ear: '*Es wird noch kommen!*' It would come . . . It still would come. Out in the Olympic Village the twenty-five hostages were still alive. The ultimatum was that one would be killed every two hours, beginning 15 *Uhr* or 3 p.m. Central European Time.

On Kurfürstendamm, advertising an empty cinema, two enormous Sapphic heads regard each other steadfastly with frantic blue-tinged eyeballs, across an illuminated movie façade. Something funny is going on between those two. On high hoardings opposite Marga Schoeller's bookshop the braced bodies of huge nude females proclaim a stressful poshlust, *luxuriante*. A nude female crawls into a tent, pursued by a nude male on all fours. Above the murderous traffic that runs all night, a cutout of the slain actress Sharon Tate looks over her shoulder at the human clotting below, the sandwich-board man advertising strip joints, the Berlin hurdy-gurdy man cranking out an old tune, the prowling beard-stroking hippies, the beads and bangles set out on the wide pavement, like a temporary camp in a jungle clearing. PIGS, her murderers had scrawled on the Polanski door; Manson's tribe. Disordered thoughts, *Chaos oder Anarchie* in the here and now. Karl Kraus had defined German girls: 'Long legs, obedience'; not any more.

All strove for a dissipated appearance; many achieved it. Sunglasses were worn indoors, even in ill-lit bars in the depths of winter. Insane seers and mad putative leaders sprang up, were applauded, discussed, shot at, vanished from the scene. Graffiti abounded. The young revolutionaries sprayed aerosol everywhere. ANARKI ELLER KAOS!, as though the terms were not synonymous. The message hardly varied. In the La Rouche district of Paris it ran: LIBÉREZ HESS!

An underground disco pulses redly: the Mouth of Hell. The pace is set to hedonism, gluttony, the here and now.

Frantic with betrayal, two inverts copulate near the Spree in the headlights of a parked car, in a thin rain. (The woodcock, wily bird, is said to dress its own wounds. Partridges sleep with one eye open. The Chinese, more observant than most, maintain that the rat changes into a quail, the quail into an oriole. The female muskrat, as everybody knows, is the mother of the entire human race. Unless I am thinking of the Eskimos' Sedna. Muskrats are barren when in captivity; if they breed, they devour their young. A young Munich *veterinario* blamed stress induced by crowded conditions; or, more likely, the fact of being under constant observation by humans.)

In West Berlin (population 2.2 million souls) every second citizen is over forty years; more than 25 per cent over sixty-five. Thirty-nine thousand die each year, with 13,000 more dying than are being born; every third citizen owns a dog.

Frau Meinhardt likes to curry-comb her two Airedales on the balcony, and curly orange hair floated into our morning coffee. She drove to Malta in a green sports car, a nice change of air for the nervous bitches, mother Anya and whelp, a classical allusion. There was no shade in Malta, it was bad for the dogs.

She, the war widow, never referred to her late husband; the fine house in Nikolassee was all that remained of that lost life. The old heart of the city was dead – Unter den Linden. She owned a house in Wiesbaden, let out the Berlin property; demonstrated how to work the vacuum cleaner, a *Walküre* model, adding on tubular parts and a rigid snout. When devouring dirt the bag swelled, set up a strident whine, began snarling, all snout and stomach. A true German machine.

Tall beauties paraded on Kurfürstendamm, displaying themselves in tight jeans; that was the accepted uniform of chic. The boutiques advertised a worn but not yet threadbare look; that was the fashion. Their manner implied: 'We belong to the streets'; and, by analogy – false – 'The streets belong to us.' *Strassentheater.*

Freedom marches followed protest marches, the squatters occupying empty buildings. They were untouchable, in a way. They, too, were in the dream, living the dream. They occupied the streets, seemingly at home there, some living a hand-to-mouth existence, squatting before lines of trinkets, metalwork. Wearing sandals like gurus and holy men, or going about barefoot; footloose as Rastafarians, Reb stragglers from the American Civil War, fuzzy-wuzzies from Abyssinia, Tibetan monks with shaven polls; the females were even more lightly dressed, as though in perpetual summer (*'La naturale temperature des femmes,'* quoth Amyot in a soft aside, *'est fort humide'*), their extremists more dangerous than the males. In West Berlin the Black Cells, the Anarchists, went among the passive resisters like hyenas among zebra.

Insistence on the unique and particular had spawned the microbe Duplication. The face on the screen was in the street. The violence there was let loose here, in the open, the dream gone mad. They were actors and actresses playing bit-parts in a continuing series. The face on the hoardings walked the streets. The Individual as such was disappearing, had disappeared; only remained, in a disordered milieu grown ever grubbier, more dangerous. The world's capitals had become *pissoirs.*

On fine summer evenings, in Málaga and Athens, Copenhagen and Munich, long cinema queues waited to watch a violent surrogate existence run on huge screens, the sound monstrously distorted. 'To learn is to have something done to one.' Why bother about Bach if a saxophone gives you an idea of eternity? Their own life had ceased to interest them. Huge hoardings displayed a Red Indian brave naked from the waist up, advertising a brand of shampoo. Rock cellars throbbed, their lurid entrances leading down into an inflamed red throat. *Schlagermusik.*

Hungarian camomile, asafoetida gum, aeroplane grease, cola nuts, Syrian rue, fly agaric, horsetail, skullcap, yohimbine, these were popular. In Absurdia the poor drank the urine of the high rich. Informed heads, *Tagträumer*, trippers, might tell of the so-called Jackson Illusion. Pepper, with a hole at one end and a cigarette at the other through which the entire contraption might be smoked to provide colourful and elaborate hallucinations.

Road-hippies on endless round trips sold their blood in Kuwait; took overdoses, observed the 'way-out' regions inhabited by the teeming poor of the miserable Third World. Lost ones blew their brains out. A huge organ was playing at noon in a department store heavy with controlled artificial air. Shoppers, passive as fish, stunned by pumped *Musik*, ascend and descend by escalators. Overpriced commodities were sold by ingenious advertising campaigns, an all-out 'psychological' war not on want but on plenty. Everything was oversold, overheated; fraternity too had become a Hell. The cities were splitting up from within, supermarts and car parks replacing cathedrals and concert halls. On fine summer evenings the long cinema queues waited silently in the north. To flee the world and dream, the past, was their intent; a sourceless craving now externalised, brought close. For them it would always be *Sperrmüll-Tag*: Throwing-Out Day.

Alcoholic professors taught their own version of history. The students were apprehensive to leave the campus. In the surrounding woods maniacs prowled all night, whistling. The young kept to their dormitories, debated much on their 'development', always making schemes. Schedules were drawn up, abandoned. Believing that life goes in steps, exclusively concerned with drugs of one sort or another, hard politics, India-Buddha teachings, claptrap about 'freedom'. Their future was grim. But the protestors went marching anyway. They were lost in the dream. Their own parents were the irrecoverable Past.

On which side do you wear your shame?

Faina Melnik in athletic hotpants was displaying the Popo look, said to have been imported from Japan. The discus was thrown an unlikely distance by an unlikely-looking female. The huge Israeli weightlifters were all dead, blown to Kingdom Come. The games had gone on. The so-called Day of Mourning had been nothing less than hypocrisy; too much money was invested, too many interests involved; national honour had been at stake. The word had come down that the terrorists were not to leave German soil with their victims. Too much was at stake. The terrorists themselves had shown less hypocrisy; they were not interested in deals or (even) human life. *Rheinischer Merkur* had its '*Mordorgie*'. 'Aroused Prussia' was a lard factory. A *mortadella* mincing machine.

'RUSS MAY BEEF UP NAVY IN MED', spoke out the *New York Herald Tribune*. 'BODIES OF SLAIN ATHLETES REACH LODZ, FLOWN FROM MUNICH' (American speaking). Lodz Airport, soon to receive its own baptism of fire from Japanese *kamikaze* terrorists. *Falsche Spekulation der Luftpiraten!* At the Staatliches Museum an exhibition of early Bavarian folk art was on display. Art, 'progress' (towards what?) comes from weaponry, not from the kitchen. The arms of the foot-soldiers, peasant conscripts, were no different in kind from their primitive work-tools. Art and progress were displayed in the finely decorated swords and pistols of their mounted officers.

Der Bomber (Müller) scores again.

In the Neue Nationalgalerie in West Berlin hang two

paintings commemorating the Student Uprising of '68 in Paris; Renato Guttuso's *Studentenumzug mit Fahnen* and *Barrikaden in Paris*. To the sad cliché of the street barricade, the hero with flag unfurled, the brave corpses, must now be added the Faceless Terrorist.

Leni Riefenstahl's extraordinary *Fest der Völker* was showing at the Arri (8 *Woche*). The XIth Olympiad at Berlin in 1936. In the old recruiting documentary the plumes of smoke rising densely black around the Imperial Eagle might have come from Hell itself. Wagner shows me a world I am not sure I would wish to enter. Stout Hermann Goering, the cocaine addict, shaken with helpless laughter; Hitler leaning forward, rubbing together his cold political hands. Hess, his putative son, all eyesocket and jaw, watched Jesse Owens, assuredly no Aryan, run away with all the track events. A cinema full of war widows watched in an uncanny silence. What was one to make of the spider in the web, before the credits rolled, and the scalped athletes running naked around a Berlin lake, through early morning mist? No symbols where none intended.

Misha Gallé had been permitted an interview when Leni Riefenstahl, still a handsome woman, had learnt that *her* father had been a Nazi judge. She told Misha Gallé that Herr Hitler had been a good man led astray by 'bad companions' (!). The homosexual Röhm? The war widows dispersing silently from the Arri, set their mouths in grim lines and, separated for *Kaffee und Kuchen*, were offering no comments.

Two months later a Lufthansa flight into Munich was hijacked and the three terrorists sprung from three high-security prisons sixty miles apart. When interviewed, they chain-smoked, spoke in broken English and were reported to be of 'terrifying' niceness. They had the rugged good looks of movie actors and justified their actions at length; somewhere in the world ravishing girls awaited their return.

In February 1973, Abu Daoud, now passing himself off as a Saudi sheikh, was arrested in central Amman by a Jordanian security patrol. His 'wife' was a fifteen-year-old girl carrying a handgun and ammunition clips, which, on being arrested, she dropped. 'Abu Daoud's' forged passport showed him to be the father of six children. His own father worked in Jerusalem as a labourer for the Israeli City Council.

September 16 had been the last day of the XXth Olympiad. All the shops were closed and the Schwabing streets deserted, a dead day. Misha Gallé played *Tischtennis* with Wolfgang. On the huge Olympic board the last farewells: 'AVRIL BRANDAGE' (*sic*) for all the world to see. Twenty *Grad* of *Bodenfrost* on 28 September. *Das Ende der Saison.*

Meanwhile the super-rat, immune to all poisons, had arrived in Rio. Six dead. Abu Daoud, where are you now?

The Opposite Land

Arrival

It's overcast over England. We descend through murky cloudbanks; a drab land reveals itself below. The 747 rolls into the loading bay.

In the arrival hall at Heathrow incoming passengers move in a daze, smaller than Americans, less colourful in dress, less self-assured in manner, paler than Canadians. Queues form up at the buffet. Service is slow, but presently the first pale, slightly moist ham sandwich is carried triumphantly past on a plastic platter smeared with mustard; also strange sausage-shaped objects like blown-up condoms – 'bangers' are a national delicacy.

Drinking civet piss in a soaking sweat, I try for a Copenhagen number but there is no reply. Passive as zombies, standing or seated, staring out of the long windows, pacing about, restless, those in transit put in time. At the bar – a sort of siding near the ever-ticking Arrivals and Departures board – a distinguished gentleman of colour orders a beer.

'Light or dark, sir? ... er, ale or lager?' the poker-faced barman easily amends the gaffe.

Hortative headlines scream from the front page of an

426

abandoned *Sun.* 'LIFE FOR MONSTER OF AA!' 'STARK TERROR OF RAPIST VICTIM.' The AA patrolman who had raped a stranded girl motorist stood 'ashen-faced' before a judge's wrath. Guilty of conduct that would have disgraced a 'primordial savage'.

I'm back in the horn-mad land of villainy. In this disunited kingdom ruled by two stern matriarchs, one autocratic, a distant queen, persiflage rules, disquiet spreads, bigotry is abroad. 'Winnie' and 'Monty' having passed away, only 'Maggie' remains, all true monsters. 'Nessie' has been sighted again, surfacing in Scotland. Rooks are building high in the Somerset trees.

Thuggery and pro soccer engage all interests as exchange fees move into the million sterling. Anything is possible on the downward path. Labour disputes alternate with mayhem and murder. Soccer hooligans are uneasily contained behind moats and barbed-wire stockades as in a POW compound; written about daily in the overly familiar parlance of the gutter press. But what is one to do? In the Midlands the cities are dying from within. Even the BBC radio serials are neurotic. 'She didn't like dreaming about a dead person.'

'Chat shows' are popular, a cheap form of commercial radio. The *Robbie Vincent Chat Show* on LBC is well calculated to set the fastidious listener's teeth on edge. Melanie of Maidenhead had the coil inserted last October and is still bleeding, what should she do? Oldish ladies flirt, the accents are various, posh to semi-literate, records of social disharmony and frustration. Robbie dispenses words of wisdom and advice.

Back in the departure hall a Mr Ledwich travelling to Munich cannot be found. And here again are all the travelling lovers and lost ones. They file by, dramatically silent or chattering like monkeys. The true new vulgarity of Britain, formerly 'Great', can best be studied at these airport entrances and exits. They go by:

the Hip Swayer,
the Exotic Tease,
the Busty Big Blonde,
the Lourer,
the Buoyant Bitch,
the Boy-Girl,
the Grey-haired Lecher,
Pouty Lips,
the Po-faced One,
the Misanthrope,
Hot Fudge,
the Pusher,
the Mule,
Mr Mountebank,
the Soul in Revolt,
the Hot-house Plant,
the Misfit,
Madame Majeska,
the Dark Note,
the Unhappy Vixen,
the Frightened Man,
the Jogger,
the New Suffragette,
Jump Suit,
Blow-Job,
Gadfly,
the Sneaky Old Beldame,
the Gruesome Party,
the Fellow-Who-Couldn't-Get-It-Up,
the Spanking Colonel,
Judy Chalmers (endlessly *en route*),
the Mad Monk,

his wife,
the Rich Digger,
the Right Bitch,
the Pain in the Arse,
the Gorgeous Gael,
the Shrouded One,
the Missing Link (could it be Ledwich?),
the Sedulous Ape,
the Sullen Baggage,
the Right Prick,
the Priest in Plain Clothes,
the Old Crud,
the Hard Case,
the Booted Cuban (with Good-time Girl in tow),
the Rough Rasta,
the Grim Counter-revolutionary,
Mickey the Dunce,
the Sheep in Wolf's Clothing,
the Sheikh of Araby,
the Girl from Ipanema,
the Merchant Banker,
the Anti-Christ,
the Après-Ski Exquisite,
the Sodomite,
the Israeli,
the Two-timer,
Embraceable You,
'Whispering' Golden,
'Silent' Busby,
William Faulkner's Double,
Joe Soap,
the Hard Man,
'Even' Stevens,
the Cad with the Pipe,

and the dead too, pacing gravely along, deep in private conversation, or silent, wrapped in thought:

> Podge Magee and Terry Butler,
> Gerda Frömel-Schurmann,
> Alex Trocchi,

and last but not least, pushing through the gates:

> the AA Patrolman, and
> the Girl Motorist,

and then a lone female dressed in black, high fashion not mourning, booted, mysterious even unto herself – possibly Bianca Jagger travelling incognito.

COPENHAGEN now appears on the departures board, the flying digits fluttering by, faster than eye-blink, constantly re-forming. My destination, after

MUNICH	14.40	BEA
BERLIN	15.10	BEA
NAPLES	15.20	BEA
MADRID	15.25	BEA
AMSTERDAM	16.00	BEA
COPENHAGEN	16.15	BA

In the duty-free shop a rotund little Japanese lady holds up a bottle of Harvey's sherry to the girl at the cash register. 'Shilly?'

The girl shrugs her shoulders.

'Shilly-*shally*?'

The girl looks away. Mr Ledwich cannot be found. The atmosphere is already densely Danish. The daughters masticate gum like ruminants. And now, the long-awaited:

COPENHAGEN 16.15 BA NOW BOARDING

I am boarding among solid Danes. No fraternising; all

are glad to be returning home. For me a five-hour wait is ending, the fruitless phoning of your new number, the Heathrow pay-phone connection ringing in an empty flat. Where could you be? I'll go anyway. All aboard for Copenhagen! We are flying out on a lovely sunny May day. To Kastrup Airport. Is it near the city? We file aboard in an orderly Danish way, the two silent daughters still chewing gum.

At Kastrup Airport a quiet crowd of Danes wait behind the grille. I have never been here before. You are not waiting for me. At security an Oriental girl, possibly Chinese, goes through my bag, not looking at me, her hands unzip, probe, feel – *next!*

I share a taxi into town with two pederasts bound for Jutland. One is English. Jutland is the place, he tells me, it's so peaceful there. In the slanting evening light now a quiet port appears: København.

Young women in headscarves ride old-fashioned cranky black bikes along cobbled streets. The taxi drops the other two at Central Station and I go on to your flat at Øster Søgade. And there is the lake, the watery blue quadrilateral, with three swans flying in. You are not at home. No message. The mad landlady Mrs Andersen is most uncooperative; of your movements or whereabouts she knows nothing. I ask the taximan for a reasonable hotel.

At the Østerport Hotel opposite the East Station a Japanese male receptionist takes my passport, issues me a key, points. I traverse a number of narrow hotel corridors, all deserted, until I find a narrow room facing the railway tracks. If you do not show up, I vow, I'll leave for London by air tomorrow, even if we have not met in four years.

I walk out under a drifting sky, passing through the

King's Gardens where Christian IV, 'the people's king', fell under the spell of a hard and beautiful woman, who let him down in his old age, went riding around with a guardsman instead, leaving the king to die alone with dropsy in his legs.

The transvestite carpenter works alone in the old street of whores. In the students' bars the style is to collapse footless across loaded tables and be set upright again, no apologies offered or required. The pimp for male prostitutes – a retired sea-captain – is guffawing away in the flower shop. The Marxist translator of Marquez brawls in the bars, drinks Mateus Rosé at home with his new bride. In Copenhagen the telephone rings in muted tones, subdued as the taxi intercom, as the voices of the people. This quiet city suits me. The musical sing-song voices are telling me that already it has begun. I am here, so it must have begun. But where are you?

In Dyrehaven the moles burrow deeper. Baroness Blixen is buried under her favourite tree at Rungsted-lund. Perhaps in spirit she is in the company of Denys Finch Hatton in the Ngong Hills with the lions, all lying down. This is the monstrosity in love, lady; that the will is infinite, and the execution confined; that the desire is boundless and the act a slave to limit.

Didn't you know? And where are you? How was I to know that you had gone to Elsinore Castle?

City of phantoms. Tired faces in May. Sailors on shore leave. Groups of German students leaving in a launch for a trip around the harbour; a view of copper domes, ornamental snakes. They speak German, naturally; I may follow them a little. In the streets Danish is spoken; this I cannot follow at all.

And where are you, my dearest? If I may call you that.

No lewd burlesque tonight at the Tivoli Gardens, where McEwan's Export play 'Hands across the Sea'. Staid middle-aged citizens parade in green *Lodens* in the parks, the people pale-faced after the long northern winter. In general appearance they are a racial mixture of German and Dutch, but sober. Sober observers; they look you in the eye. Their eyes follow you.

A bronze statue of a tortured peasant sits with head bowed, arms bound behind his back with bronze leather thongs, being pulled apart by his own weight, on the primitive torture-machine called *træhest*, a cruel Danish version of the old Saxon stocks.

Time passes. You arrive by night from Elsinore Castle. I leave the Østerport Hotel. In a small bar near a bridge, down steps, you order cold herring in aspic with schnapps and Tuborg. A candle burns on the bar counter. The woman who serves us is regal. You sit opposite me. Around us the port. The candle glows. Time passes. The ghost of Kirsten Munk drifts through the King's Gardens. Now that the people have left and the gates are locked for the night, all is quiet there. The night outside is quiet in a thoroughly Danish way; we have found this bar, this peace. After ten o'clock few pedestrians are about. The moon rises over the harbour. We return to your flat.

Then it's day again. We take a train from Østerport Station to Humlebæk, to visit Knud Jensen at Luisiana Museum. I open a window, the passengers stare critically at me. Danes do not like fresh air while travelling. We arrive at Humlebæk Station. It's not as I had imagined it. But what ever is? I am with you.

Jensen is away. You say you are hungry. Over the road is Humlebæk Inn, set among trees. We order fresh sole with chilled white wine, served by a dumpy little woman and set before us on green baize. Danish mourners pass our table, wish us good appetite. We take coffee and Cognac outside under a tree. Over there, you say (pointing), lies the Swedish coast. I saw something white: a nuclear station.

I taste Cognac. Do Danes and Swedes get along together? No, you say, Swedes consider themselves superior. You can speak Swedish fluently. Your Italian and English are adequate; now you are learning Greek. What more can you learn? I order more coffee and Cognac. A man serves us there under the trees.

In Humlebæk Kirke the jackdaws caw in a tod of ivy. On the road, climbing the hill, a father passes on a push-bike with his small son on the crossbar. The little boy licks ice cream and watches us as they pass, seeing a strange man with a goatee and a tall lovely brunette pacing about in a narrow cemetery of low box hedges, at Humlebæk Kirke.

From Humlebæk Havn we walked to the bus stop, took a number 1 to Central Station. We bought Rioja wine and returned to your flat. The days went by too fast, too fast. The well-tortured peasant on the Wooden Horse has expired at last. What could his offence have been, to merit such a cruel death? Traffic moves either way over the bridge at Øster Søgade. We were happy. Then came the last morning. Four days.

How many facts does a life story require? What is fact and what life story? It is not enough to live; no, you have to know as well. Go on.

Then the last day came. We drank Elephant beer with schnapps in Porno Street in the company of Jutlanders, about whom you warned me. Beware their drunken rages, their wild moves, their skinning-knives! Do not fall foul of a Jutlander. But I saw only two peaceable men seated at a small table with bottles of beer set out. A candle sent up a thin spiral of smoke into the thin sunlight that came slanting in. Behind the counter an old-fashioned radio played muted Danish film music from the 1930s.

A third Jutlander now joined the other two; all three of them were murmuring greetings, all wore woollen caps and had hot, weathered faces. It was my last day. The last day.

Departure

In Central Station I prepared to go. We embraced. I won't look back, you said. Porters in brown uniforms, with fuzzy hair erupting from under caps too small for them, walked by the moving train in a possessive way peculiar to railway employees the world over. The boat-train was leaving punctually for Esbjerg Havn. You walked quickly out of the station, not looking back. Now you are passing over by the Østerport Hotel, from which I had booked out four days previously, on the same day as I had booked in, as the train began to pull out of the station, the fuzzy-haired porters walking alongside it, deep in conversation.

The fare seemed on the steep side. I found I was travelling first class on a second-class ticket in the company of a sour Scot called Dick Gaughan, late of Glasgow. The ticket inspector came; Gaughan paid the difference on two second-class tickets. I would reimburse him when we stepped on board the boat for Harwich. The rest of the train was crowded.

Soon we reached the coast. At Esbjerg Havn the SS *Winston Churchill* was docked. We went aboard together. I found the exchange bureau.

We stood at the crowded bar. The dour Scot had been over for three nights at the Tivoli, three 'gigs' at £100 a time. They had cut a disc for their group: McEwan's Export. He was sick of Glasgow and planned to settle near Sligo. We drank Rémy Martin and his mood improved. A shy, somewhat sour, good-hearted gingery Scot. We got on all right.

Hard rock thundered from two thunder-boxes controlled by Tony Burton ('International Disc Jockey'). The metallic howling never let up, a male voice roaring out incomprehensible inanities, delivered at maximum pitch, the utmost volume, nothing human allowed to interfere. The Danish teenyboppers were galvanised, as though touched by electrodes. We ordered more Rémy Martin. Don't forget your shovel if you intend to go to work.

For'ard, away from the howling disco, we came upon another more sheltered lounge, where middle-aged passengers were waltzing sedately. Here they could tango to their hearts' content. A male half-caste vocalist took the hand-held microphone and into the phallic head imitated a hysterical girlish high-pitched squealing. Gaughan and I began ordering doubles. Leaning on the bar counter my Celtic friend was moderately amused.

The SS *Winston Churchill* was hugging the unseen European shore. England seemed far away. Denmark receding. Clutching inebriated partners the dancers waltzed by, the half-caste continued squealing. Somewhere aft below the teenyboppers would rock and roll into the wee hours. I spoke to a fellow who had once spoken to Rex Harrison, when *he* was courting Lilli Palmer, my old heart-throb, then appearing in *Blithe Spirit* at the Golders Green Hippodrome. It was rumoured that Rex would return to play Professor Higgins in the West End at an estimated fee of one million pounds. And I would reach Harwich a day late, having lost a day recrossing the North Pole, flying from Vancouver via Seattle on Northwest Orient, leaving behind sun and Pacific wind, the nudist beach, the big trees coming down to the shore, Japanese cherry in bloom, the opulence of Vancouver, the Chinese Quarter. I bade the dour Scot goodnight and retired.

At six next morning I was the only passenger stirring. The teenyboppers were flaked out all about me. An empty lager can was rolling about in the scuppers.

Just before midday the pilot boat *Valour* of London hove alongside. A vague ill-defined coastline appeared out of the murk on the aft side. Lowering vapours shroud the dim horizon. Could this be England?

Four jet fighters in tight formation tore the air to shreds above the SS *Winston Churchill.* The coastline began to drift by. Sealink passenger-liners followed each other towards open sea. Seaweed brushed past. A bell was tolling on a tilted buoy, a very old sound emitted now and then on the dirty swells. On the nearing coast a tall derrick rose up, then another. Dick Gaughan did not show up.

I recall: a bell ringing at a level-crossing, a stout Bornholm woman calling for Matthew, a herd of fallow deer, a man in forest green crossing a path, the bellowing of the stag, shadows on the grass.

At Harwich I was first off. The boat-train was waiting. Two elderly porters with the complexions of jailbirds serving a long sentence, their uniformed shoulders with a fine dust of dandruff, began punching tickets in a listless English way. Hard-faced youths with convicts' close hair-cuts were leaning against the train, swigging tinned beer, on the lookout for 'birds'. Presently the boat-train pulled out of Harwich Station. Two Danish girls sitting opposite me drew three-tier Danish sandwiches from their holdalls. They offered to the mild air a pair of flawless com-plexions.

Their first view of England: a wayside cemetery with thin Anglican steeple above a granite church, rising into a grey thoroughly English sky. And, sliding by, schoolkids at horseplay on a station platform. A bully striking a weakling caught in the act of flinching away, his schoolbag falling. Bullies and frightened weakling, faces of another strange people, another race, petrified as on a screen.

I passed through a London of slanted sunshine and spring shadows moved now by balmy breezes, a new growth, come full circle. *Dine kysser glemmer jeg ikke.*

V

Lengthening Shadows
(An Elegy for England)

Sombre

It was one of those dingy overcast London days that occur with such regularity at the tail-end of autumn; intimations of later foul weather coming off Dogger Bank in the long months ahead. In the muggy London Zoo, high in their dunged cages, the great condors were shifting about.

Nothing sadder than the Strand on a Sunday. Reaches of Mother Thames stank of diarrhoea. The open mouth of the tube was foul. A man was calling out on behalf of the Catholic Evidence Guild. Brassy sounds came from the Salvation Army band playing on Victoria Embankment Gardens near the flat of the fellow who told me his dream of death. He was three men. The weather was cold. Peter Duval! Why this is Hell, nor am I out of it.

I resume: Like fish immobile in a glass tank, they stare at the foolish movies. They seem tired of life in a way no fish can be, save dying fish; as though this incessant viewing of foolish movies was depriving them of even curiosity, that force which helps the young to grow.

441

In the foolish movie, the movie of the day, one of many, always the same; one day more of all the identical dull days spent in that stale-smelling viewing room where they congregate, now it is the old, old story of the father and the son. The story of the ambitious father who cannot let his son be.

The father is played by Malden and the son by Perkins. The father played for the famous Boston Red Sox. See him deteriorate, I beg your pardon, *demonstrate* the grip, the stance, with all the zeal of prosopography, as he faces the pitcher, to demonstrate most unconvincingly, standing holding the bat limply in a fashion thought to be resolute, nothing deterred, just standing there facing the unseen pitcher. Perkins.

Perkins and Malden play son and father respectively, in the foolish movie, both foolish in their respective ways, Perkins and Malden.

Remember Charley Craven's body-swerve? They say he once scored with 'is effin backside! Well, you wouldn't remember that but you've 'eard of 'im, yeah? Joe Robinson burst the effin net at Arsenal's bleedin ground. A right nutter 'e was. Remember Jack Waterman, Charley Craven, 'Cockles' Appelyard, the great Bestall?

I resume: A black Austin hearse with old-fashioned spoke wheels and running boards stands in pouring rain which will not let up, before the flintstone Baptist Church on Muswell Hill.

No mourners gather and the church doors remain closed, though the hearse is packed with flowers. The weeping printer has slipped into the Rathskeller off the premises and is dosing himself with Mild and Bitter in the gloomy public bar, looking about him furtively with scorched printer's eyes. Dracula's black hearse glitters outside like an infamous joke as the mourners gather about the closed church and stare up like fish.

Tell me, why do Baptists favour flintstone? Grey pebbles from the seashore, in their oddly shaped places of worship, so unlike the sombre grey granite of High Anglicanism with their uplifted spires in perpetual memory of Luther's eternally raised admonitory finger, the gesture of a stiff rationalist ever hostile to Roman Catholic hocuspocus? Which is more fattening – nuts or crisps? Has the cricket season started? I come here on Friday nights – what do you do?

Lady Genevieve and Sir Wilf

Lady Genevieve Goodsward or Godesward or Godsreward comes of an ancient and highly respected line known to Mysore and Delhi and the hill stations in a life before our time, wife of the decorated poet, snobbish as a Twitwell with a pendulous bust and a stiff hairstyle that makes her long face a mask, sits in an armchair, stroking a large comatose dog that lies half buried on her lap, of a species not readily determinable.

Absently she pulls at its matted hair, palping the beast as though it were her worry-beads, and speaks of the rights of vanished traditions in a cut-glass upper-class voice, fwaithf'lly naice.

Sir Wilf (whisper it) is thought to sleep with his teddybear Archy but would much prefer to chain himself to area railings or period lamp-posts or even period pillarboxes (symbols of an extinct past once glorious) or rope himself to area trees in parts of the city given over entirely to the modern automobile, in a manner made popular by suffragettes.

Master of the softly imparted aside, lover of the commonplace to say the least of it, at least in his poetry, his verse, lover of descant singing over secluded Quads, Gregorian chanting in school chapels, boys in distant playing-fields engaged in rough games in the rain, avid young beer-drinkers yet to be pickled in Old Bushmills; lover of the Worcester sauce bottle placed fairly and squarely on the spotless linen tablecloth, good breeding (a pure-bred golden Labrador savaging its fleas, a pedigree bull scraping its neck on a gate, a beetle in the morning tea; a tiny coda, large as all England).

Of all this Sir Wilf is greatly enamoured; doing good or with a will towards doing good (which is not quite the same thing) in the style that smacks of a curate's vaguely useless ways, of men in cassocks walking in glebe lands and offering the soft hand at the Rectory gate, softly imparting advice to subdued parishioners, to the sound of a quiet bell tolling and a vision of clouds over the Weald, the memory of a bottle of Worcester triumphant on the now slightly stained linen cloth; the softly spoken rebuff. Dead England – an inward-turning trouble.

Wearing gloves, with stout walking-shoes, a sturdy walking-stick, a decent hat, the old trusty gabardine, stumbling forward (always with a kind word) to the sound of a distant church bell softly tolling.

Now striding swiftly and resolutely towards an unseen destination; searching behind furniture for the object lost or mislaid, fetching up heavy sighs, drawing aside drapes, all period stuff in a living room alive with dogs, faithful animals dangerous to strangers who try to pet them but good when you know them, all family heirlooms pickled in Old Bushmills, the deserted dining room choked in chintz, the bedroom a familiar terrain of lost battles. All well-beloved objects (decanters, siphons, slippers, etc.) well cared for, Archy tucked up for the night.

Now wearing gloves, hatted and gabardined, the lost object retrieved (a pipe); fiercely inane expression of grim resolution (C. Aubrey Smith, Sir Winston Churchill), the light rain falling and then ceasing to fall and gabardine discarded for the nonce for light tweed overcoat, thrown casually over the shoulders as a cape, rubber galoshes sometimes known as gum-boots or wellingtons or overshoes, from the time of spats.

Striding forward now courageously into the teeming rain, followed by a pack of dogs, expression of the most absolute determination fixed on the flushed face, the unlit pipe clamped in the jaws; to the pedigree bull glaring hotly over the gate, the Weald obscured for the nonce in drizzle.

Onslaughts on the commonplace, pathogenic bacteria. Nothing. On.

Or: quite paralysed from the waist down, ever the brave display handkerchief in the breast pocket, leather patch for tweedy elbow, flower for the buttonhole in memory of Ascot, fixed expression of the most absolute determination, bulldog breed pipe clamped in the jaws as if struck by lightning in South Africa or Rhodesia or was it Ind'ja. Perhaps Cape Town or Kimberley, Krishnapur or Mafeking might it have been (I see a heavy ceiling fan revolving sedately and coloured – black – bar-waiters in scarlet ratcatcher quietly placing little bowls of salted peanuts on an oaken table beside a gin-fizz, taking a quietly spoken order), slowed by premature but quite crippling rheumatism, from the chill of the Home Counties, the English disease.

Behind it all once the lost herds, the holy cows, the Untouchables, remittance men with drink problems, to put it mildly, the long lines of the destitute of another race, descant song (surely not *there?*), the lost goldfields, the afflicted ones of another colour and creed, the bullwhips of a Rhodes or a Kruger, men of destiny with public parks named after them; the goldfields now in other

hands, their wise policy-making now disputed land settlements, deeds of possession in banks, all finished now, tied
and stamped with seals; given once with the left hand
(the hand that wavers); horrible opposites.

Most unctuous rendering of 'Sarie Maria' at closing-
down time with setting sun over rolling wheatlands that
stretch for ever but now reduced to a tiny pinprick and
then darkness. But now the mug of Horlicks and a flood
of wordplay or fatuous alliteration calculated to stun the
clever mind and obscure the meaning (if any), or worse
still, distort it, granted any meaning there in the first
instance (sound of derisive hooter on Thames).

Gone the carnation in the buttonhole, gone the toppers
at Ascot, gone the straw boaters at the Oxford–Cambridge
boat race and rivercraft of the most various kind hooting
in open derision, gone the upsetting wake disturbing the
banks; toffs at Lord's, strawberries and cream at Wimbledon, wistaria clasping itself in an almost human almost
painful way on the river-wall at Richmond. So much for
the Changing of the Guard and the *Guardian*'s editorial
matter.

> Land of hope and glory,
> Mother of the free;
> How shall we extol them,
> Who are born of thee?

Toff: I once met Kipling with a group of young people at
his place at Burwash in Sussex. Somebody asked him
about the English in Ind'ja.

'You want to know how we got the Indian Empire?' he
asked. 'I'll tell you. The British arrived at a given place
in the midst of squabbling tribes. And wherever the
British were the tribes could have their breakfast in peace
and go to sleep without fear. The British moved to a
further place, and once again there was security and

peace. And so it went on. We couldn't help it. H'rrmmmph.'

> Song:
>> Do fish make good mothers?
>> Yes they do, yes they do.

Grump: Take a number 102 to the Cock and Bull, then a W4 or 27 will do. An affable company of boozers are swigging cider by the ponds. Rough fellows are roaring truculently by the tube station. The umpires are offering England the light.

Paddington tannoy announcement: 'Train departures between Windsor, Eton Central and Yatton, as also to Worcester and Crud Hill, will operate with skeleton staffs, due to industrial dispute. But the services between Evesham may arrive 19 to 23 minutes earlier; while the Slough slow will be delayed until 8.01. But for our Didcot customers an extra commuter service will be laid on.

'The trains from Paddington are being delayed to all Western regions, the Reading service will be 35 minutes late, but Oxford on the hour and Worcester in 2 hours 18 minutes.'

Without more ado I left the station and sprang into a stationary double-decker omnibus that was moored outside and just then on the point of leaving for destination unknown (it turned out to be Mortlake garage) . . . where I descended and, feeling the need for a sobering drink, plunged into a local hostelry. Where who do you suppose was laughing his blooming head off in a corner, but the Baptist printer, drinking wallop and short ones in the gloom that was all mirrors and gashes of refracted light from the street.

A small news-sheet was set out before him, open at the page devoted to the nude of the day. And there she was, all spread out. Looking deadly serious, and naked as two plums – a sullen-looking baggage, that is the approved erotic style now, a suggestion of *Weib* and whip.

He was devouring the page with gusto, well accustomed to getting the hang of the odd morphology employed by the tabloids, a kind of passacaglia or montage of caps in heavy type, like yells, concerned with local and regional and then European and global calamities.

The printer was breathing heavily through his nose, bleary eyes big as saucers fixed on the crossword puzzle. Blimey, mate, I've just got the windowsill of a ship!

I stared at him, at a loss for a word. Who was he, this mysterious Baptist printer who certainly got around, staring before him now with compressed lips?

Now he started up from his reverie, wrenched his hands apart, which he had been holding convulsively clasped, and drawing the paper to him commenced making notations in the blank squares, as though another Greater Power guided his crabbed inkstained fingers, setting off with absolute confidence amidst its manyfold tomfooleries, as if impelled.

A rough: That's it, Len. Come an' sit by me an' do up
   yer flies an' all.
Another: 'ang on!

Hoyle Rules

Sometimes, not too complacently, I stare out of the front windows of this top-floor flat through which a Luftwaffe bomb passed during an air raid. The windows are arranged along one side of the living room which is the end wall of this block of flats; this being the topmost or fourth floor (it's really the rear end of an old galleon); and I can tell you that I've seen some pretty strange sights down below – what the disturbed ones get up to when they fondly imagine that they are not being observed, although that would hardly deter them, head-butters and lathe-turners on the spree. The flats, a breeding ground for broken marriages, form the truncated half of a triangle overlooking the Patch, where our children play ('Last up the fire escape is a lesbian!'). The sycamore that gave some shade has been cut, because its roots were undermining the stinking repair garage.

One afternoon whom did I espy but little Curly Hoyle gliding through the traffic that circles the public toilets of the Broadway, a public service used by drug-pushers for making contacts and as a sort of open-air gymnasium for coloured youths practising karate chops and kicks outside, and indeed inside, the women's section.

Did he remind me of dog, hare or little boy about my youngest son's age, and his best friend, his 'only friend in all the world', in his own words? In short, was he chasing (hunting) or being chased (hunted), or was he perhaps a mixture of all three: the hunter running, the hunted fleeing, or the little boy lost, running after the others?

For, caught up in some dream, and far away, surely he did not himself know? Dog or hare or little boy following (pursuing); or a mixture of all three, being the fourth state. Or, in the fifth state, more confusing than the first, a mixture of all four preceding: dog, hare, boy lost, hunter found, observer observing (like a fellow attempting to play the piano with his nose)? A treat for the chronically bored.

He moved wraithlike (was this the sixth and last state – the wraith?) through this region of incessantly circling heavy traffic; a place of Old People's Homes in the side roads of what was once country. A senior citizens' twilit zone with hospices, all under the kindly auspices of the Borough Council. Truth was never slummier and called for litter in the setting; leafy reveries were a thing of the past.

In a little while his innocent fancies will harden to something coarser, become belligerent; little Billy ('Curly') Hoyle grown older, in bovver boots and with a convict's shaven poll, a soccer supporter ('Arse Rules!') will set about the attack upon this relatively green haven of parks and ponds, where Dr Johnson, that irascible man, once walked by the stand of beech saplings.

Here the ponds proper to a seafaring race who now fish for minnows in stagnant or dead water by sewage plants and gasometers; fishing patiently and as like as not by night (for I have seen their lights glimmer under the umbrellas), below the defunct palace by the abandoned race track where no spectral horse has run, no horse at all since the turn of the century; now a grassy area for training police dogs.

By the empty palace, empty of royalty that is to say, for Indians hold banquets there and the middle-aged tango on Sunday afternoons, watched by a worker in brown boilersuit who is ostensibly cleaning the stone lion's mane, and appears to be combing it, Hoyle will begin his defacing attack with trusty aerosol gun hidden in his seersucker, squirting his hasty message on all likely surfaces:

HOYLE RULES!

Come to join all the other feverish imaginings – phrases of impatience, thud of William Blake's wings of excess, etc. – extruded by the noctambulists with little or no regard for grammar, leaving behind their white dripping spoor of 'full frontals' and hopelessly entwined lovers' initials, notes on themes of ardour and faithlessness, where a sullen Japanese girl in tight-fitting shantung waits patiently for a number 9 that comes with YAMAHA advertised on its red bodywork.

On a Highgate wall looking down on the blurred city, a wall near where Lamb had walked and Coleridge was treated for drug addiction and Lord Byron's funeral cortège had to pass *en route* to his country seat, a hand has scrawled

> cane my bum
> suck my tits
> fuck my cunt.

A desperado with horrid shaven skull and an intent deranged look carried a bundle of old newspapers into the toilet of the lewd old Cock in Edmonton where felons hung from a gibbet in the old days, on the site of what was once the Cockerel Tavern, near where Lamb walked, exercising Leigh Hunt's dog. Before that it had been a Roman thoroughfare to Peterborough, but now was merely the largest and oldest Ind Coope pub in London.

I see the disturbing word EMBRYO painted in black on a clapboard fence near the Employment Exchange and ALEC THE COPPER IS A SPIDER-LOVING CUNT scrawled on the chassis of a red double-decker bound for Barnet and Leyton Whipps.

THUG RULES is scrawled everywhere. Thug Rules and Punk Rules and Suck, Screw, Cane, Cunt, in the angry idiom of the disgruntled brigade who operate by night. The Tit-Bum-Cane cry become by some curious alchemy 'Paps, Oceans, Nature'.

The instinct behind it all – baffled human nature at odds with itself – become pure. Even 'CURLY'S HOLE RULES OKAY!!'

'IMMANUEL KANT RULES!' I read on a broken hoarding.

'The Scrots are Sick in the Winkle!' ELMS ROAD had by a simple adjustment become BUMS ROAD. And a desperate recidivist had squirted on the side of the steps below the dead palace:

PUKE ON THE DUKE!

But below it all and above it all and through it all, sometimes in the oddest places, the soaring blazon:

HOYLE RULES OKAY!

For Harold Pinter

¡Célèbre dramaturgo! The faithful, by definition, need no conversion. Last weekend I witnessed a ghostly end-of-season scratch game, in every sense of the term, that would surely have gladdened your cricketing heart.

The event took place at Crouch End. They now have a new pavilion almost as charming as the old one, the 1920s structure gutted by vandals, presumably soccer Yahoos opposed on principle to cricket. They even burnt down the temporary structure that replaced the original and broke into an adjoining pavilion to make a bonfire of the bats.

Cricket is an odd game, more difficult than appearances suggest. Like chess, which it somewhat resembles, in that the attack can be hidden, which must suit the English nature. Ceremonious under certain restraints, its logic coldly applied; a ritual performed mostly in silence by males dressed in white, nowadays wearing Greekish visors. Such white ceremonies on the greensward obviously appeal to the Anglo-Saxon mentality. Is it not so? The cricket season follows the annual migration of the swallows whom the Spanish call *golondrinas*. Beginning and ending the season and the air so sweetly assailed by their chirpy cries.

We were spared the 'I-would-have-thought' and 'I-should-have-thought' of that most tendentious commentator who shall be nameless, but you would know him, once one of England's Great Stone Walls. *À bas* Bailers!

It was a dreamlike scene, sir.

The umpire was lame and held the score-book to his chest, as a charge-hand might a scratch-pad or clipboard in a factory where nobody works any more. He answered all appeals, no matter how dubious ('how *was* he??'), with upraised finger. A stabbing of the air that would have done credit to the late Herr Hitler clearing up or emphasising some oratorical point. Or even Emperor Napoleon himself, of whom it was said (by Chateaubriand, I believe) that all his gestures wiped everything else off the table. At every turn he had to create *facts*. Neither of them could be disobeyed; they were accustomed to giving and signing orders that sent men to their deaths.

The umpire seemed anxious to keep the game going at all costs, this last game, and the fielders were also batsmen. It was an all-fielding team playing against itself. Sufficient to say the traffic to and from the pavilion was brisk, despite the obviously ineffectual nature of the attack.

The double of the late Cecil Beaton (yclept Sir Cecil before he breathed his last) stood at square leg, wearing a floppy sunhat. The same haunted face, same small delicate gestures. Presently he was thrown the ball by the skipper and took a turn bowling slow long hops.

A grossly corpulent medium-pacer (how he permitted himself to get into *that* condition I do not know) who resembled to a marvellous degree the fabled Billy Bunter of Greyfriars, then took a turn bowling twisters, but was accorded scant respect by the only fit-looking man on the field, who enjoyed a brisk knock of fifty odd, including three sixes in one over; this against an erratic pace-man with a queer green stain on flannels none too clean in the first place.

What with the tawny bronze leaf colours, the rare strokes of some suavity recalling the Nawab of Pataudi, but here the static figures, not all togged out in regulation flannels I regret to say, and a general air of benign incompetence, the umpire's upraised finger, all was a sober joy to behold.

A bit of the old Maecenas and no mistake – *Vita dum superest bene est*, what? While one's alive all's well, nothing but well and fair. Into the wind. What? How deuced pleasant, *Célèbre dramaturgo*, to watch the shadows lengthening, shoulders (no matter how incompetently) being opened for the last time, the vapour trails ravelling out like white barbed wire 30,000 feet up in the clear blue sky, in the last Saturday peace of this golden October day! The last yowls. *OOOoowww Waazzzzeee!*

Those curious rhetorical imperatives. The last 'Well bawled, sir!' ringing out, and the final loud guffaw from the pavilion which up till then one had supposed empty – for the batsmen came down to field as soon as they had unpadded, a sort of inept progress in reverse, the mockery of a game played with the utmost seriousness by sixteen incompetents.

Not forgetting the gentlemanly handclapping – they were supporters, crowd, as well as participants – absolutely *de rigueur* at these polite affairs.

A small coloured batsman (an Asian) who looked well set was run out attempting a quick single that simply was not on. Acorns were thick in Queen's Wood (sign of the end of the world?) in this Autumn of Conkers and the squirrels careless of hoarding their nuts. I thought of you. You should have been there, a well-knit figure striding purposefully towards the crease with a Middlesex cap drawn down in a threatening Boycott-like manner over the hooded eyes.

Discipline on the field of play was lax, but who cares? The white figures passing and repassing had become effigies, emblematic. Playing or rather, say, *conducting* themselves at a game whose rules and quaint terminology ('Ow waZZZy??') have barely changed in the course of its long and pleasant history. At least five matches were played at low tide on the Godwin Sands in the nineteenth century.

A game of detailed records and the keeping of records, which is not quite the same thing; this undermines boasting and must offer a strong appeal to the modest English character, being itself a form of hyperbole. Records, after all, cannot lie (you cannot cheat at chess, either). There can be no appeal against the umpire's upraised finger. Cricket, a game played in the mind.

That one went clean through him – as if he had a hole in him like a Henry Moore statue! Such punctilio – an off-drive from the batsman with his eye in was a quicksilver flourish on the flute. Arlott should have been there, sipping a Muscadet and recalling great figures and games of the past, never to return again.

Hobbs and Sutcliffe with his Brylcreem quiff, Compton and Edrich, Verity and Voce, Bradman and Ponsford. The quick and the dead.

Are you perchance, Maestro, familiar with the work of Richard Jefferies, favourite author of the self-made naturalist Henry Williamson, author of *Tarka the Otter*? In his *Field and Hedgerow*, the chapter on the July grass, he could tell the varieties and categories of all the weeds on a given hill. He'd have been in his seventh heaven at

Crouch End playing-fields, where the outfield is densely weedy.

A line of Heine came to mind. You may know it. '*Ich hab im Traum geweinet.*' I hath in mine dreams ge-wept, might be a tentative English rendering. Of course the Froggies and the Huns couldn't play cricket for nuts. It's not in their natures; heavy doses of *déjà vu*, which is the real kernel of cricket, what, what?

Believe me ever the admirer of those early stage *Stücke* of yours, *Landscape* and *Silence*, would that be correct, sir? I have the honour to sign myself

Amory

P.S. When are we going to see a bit of action in one of your plays?

A Pearl of Days

Vaults of bridges!

I think of the great metal bridge by the railway station of my old home. A sense of grit and the long reverberation of plates as the train went by overhead. It was a place without law. I felt that even then, obscurely. No one was really responsible for anyone else. Only a few ruins of walls were left of the castle Chaucer had hoped to build. The lord's home had been sold to politicians.

Blown spume, ruddy faces, thick ears, jug ears nothing daunted, briny smells, kippers and herrings, shelly seafood of Skegness, stinking tides, tidal motions, semen-stench of the great heaving ocean. Tar-pots and fish-heads of Deal, nets drying.

Porpoises portend Atlantic storms, dolphins in the Mediterranean. Provisions waxed scant and such were the extremities of these poor wretches in cold and wet than to have no better sustenance than their own urine for six days at a stretch. Tars puking their guts out in the rigging, gulls a long way from home, jolly sea shanties in the steamy fo'c'sle, the here-today-gone-tomorrow philosophy of a livelier time.

A time of sea kale, jugged hare and cherry tart, the sailor's hornpipe, the vigour of Cruikshank or Rowlandson. Cuckolds all awry, the old dance of England.

'I would rather be blown up than suck up,' Lady Astor (glaring fearlessly across the narrow Channel at the Nazi hordes massing) confided to Harold Nicolson, that old smoothie, who recorded the remark in his diary. 'I believe this to be true,' the diplomat noted with perfect sang-froid and not a hint of sarcasm or *noblesse oblige.*

Saw a tall well-made girl grimacing with embarrassment, leading her old father (bent double) across the crowded way. A scene of public distress not uncommon.

Bankruptcies up 30 per cent, a new record. One shouldn't be surprised. And one more species of butterfly (pale blue) extinct. I shouldn't wonder. Another wasted day, did I hear you say? Oh no, sirs. Never! Never a wasted day, in the strange withdrawn world of the Fish.

A Pearl of Days.

Rückblick

Love perfumes all parts.

Robert Herrick

Through the Abbey grounds sauntered the abandoned Vanessa, her spirits cast down. Coming onto the little bridge top heavy with ivy she felt the mossy path give way to shale under the thin soles of her Dutch shoes. She watched her reflection below but no *Jonathan* stood by her with powdered wig askew on his hot head, thinking of her hairy anus and panting like a Pekinese, suggesting morning coffee there and then. Drinking your coffee, Miss Essy, at mid-morning with the larks singing.

The current dragged and pulled at the tendrils of brown maidenhair and brown eelgrass straining away in the rushing stream and she felt the river throbbing and quivering under her feet, hitting at the arches, gulping and going swiftly on.

Short of breath and with all the blood drained from her face she had stood accused before him in a room that had become a nursery. In his terrible rage he had ridden over from Laracor with the damning evidence in his saddlebag; evidence of perfidy, of female meddling; had flung this evidence in her face – that was her own handwriting, those were her own words, accusing Stella, that was enough. Without a word spoken but for his hiss of breath he had departed on the big nag that should have been named Delirium. He with so many strong

458

words at his command (pox, bosom, rank, mischief) now had none for her; he was finished with her.

His two pure angels had grown to be not dolts but worse, Odious Animals. Lusty and breedy animals prone to squat and release stinks; their soiled underclothes and unseen dishonourable parts inspired a kind of horror in his bosom, as did their courses, their discharging of the necessities of nature. Every year on Stella's birthday he sent her a poem but not the one with the aghast refrain: 'Celia shits.' This fairly took his breath away, left him dry-mouthed, gulping for air. He conceived the notion of a small defenceless being at the mercy of monsters; then of a monster (Lemuel) tolerated by diminutive beings. Leaving London lodgings on his way into Ireland he threw the manuscript of *Gulliver's Travels* through the coach window onto the doorstep of his publisher. Ride on!

From Miss Vanhomrigh*

Dublin, 1714

Well! now I plainly see how great a regard you have for me. You bid me be easy, and you'd see me as often as you could: you had better have said as often as you could get the better of your inclinations so much; or as often as you remembered there was such a person in the world. If you continue to treat me as you do, you will not be made uneasy by me long. 'Tis impossible to describe what I have suffered since I saw you last; I am sure I could have borne the rack much better than those killing, killing words of yours.

* Miss Esther Vanhomrigh, alias Miss Essy, Vanessa, Skinage.

Sometimes I have resolved to die without seeing you more, but those resolves, to your misfortune, did not last long: for there is something in human nature that prompts one so to find relief in this world, I must give way to it, and beg you'd see me, and speak kindly to me, for I am sure you would not condemn any one to suffer what I have done, could you but know it. The reason I write to you is, because I cannot tell it you, should I see you; for when I begin to complain, then you are angry, and there is something in your look so awful, that it strikes me dumb. Oh! that you may but have so much regard for me left, that this complaint may touch your soul with pity. I say as little as ever I can. Did you but know what I thought, I am sure it would move you. Forgive me, and believe me I cannot help telling you this, and live.

From Miss Vanhomrigh

No date

Is it possible that again you will do the very same thing I warned you of so lately? I believe you thought I only rallied when I told you the other night that I would pester you with letters. [Did not I know you very well, I should think you knew but little of the world to imagine that a woman would not keep her word whenever she promised anything that was malicious. Had not you better a thousand times throw away one hour at some time or other of the day, than to be interrupted in your business at this rate: for I know 'tis as impossible for you to burn my letters without reading them, as 'tis for me to avoid reproving you, when you behave yourself wrong.] Once more I advise you, if you have any regard for your own quiet, to alter your behaviour quickly, for I do assure you, I have too much spirit to sit down contented with this treatment. Because I love frankness extremely, I here tell you now, that I have determined to try all manner of human arts to reclaim you; and if all these fail, I am resolved to have recourse to the black one, which [*it*] is said never does. Now see what inconveniencies you will bring both me and yourself into. Pray think calmly of it! Is it not better to come of yourself, than to be brought by force, and that perhaps at a time when you have the most agreeable engagement in the world; for when I undertake anything, I don't love to do it by halves. [But there is one thing falls out very luckily for you, which is, that of all the passions, revenge hurries me least, so that you have it yet in your power to turn all this fury into good humour, and depend upon it, and more, I assure you. Come at what time you please, you can never rail of being very well received.]

From Miss Vanhomrigh

Cellbridge, 1720
— Cad – you are good beyond expression, and I will never quarrel again if I can help it; but, with submission, 'tis you that are so hard to be pleased, though you complain of me. I thought the last letter I wrote you, was obscure and constrained enough. I

took pains to write it after your manner; it would have been much easier for me to have wrote otherwise. I am not so unreasonable as to expect you should keep your word to a day, but six or seven days are great odds. Why should your apprehensions for Molkin hinder you from writing to me? I think you should have wrote the sooner to have comforted me. Molkin is better, but in a very weak way. Though those who saw me told you nothing of my illness, I do assure you I was for twenty-four hours as ill as 'twas possible to be, and live. You wrong me when you say, I did not find that you answered my questions to my satisfaction; what I said was, I had asked those questions as you bid, but could not find them answered to my satisfaction. How could they be answered in absence, since Somnus is not my friend? We have had a vast deal of thunder and lightning; – where do you think I wished to be then? and do you think that was the only time I wished so, since I saw you? I am sorry my jealousy should hinder you from writing more love-letters; for I must chide sometimes, and I wish I could gain by it at this instant, as I have done, and hope to do. – Is my dating my letter wrong the only sign of my being in love? Pray tell me, did not you wish to come where that road to the left would have led you? I am mightily pleased to hear you talk of being in a huff; 'tis the first time you ever told me so; I wish I could see you in one. I am now as happy as I can be without seeing – Cad, I beg you will continue happiness to your own Skinage.

From the Same

— Cad, I am, and cannot avoid being in the spleen to the last degree. Everything combines to make me so. Is it not very hard to have so good a fortune as I have, and yet no more command of that fortune, than if I had no title to it? One of the D—rs* is – I don't know what to call him. He behaved himself so abominably to me the other day, that had I been a man he should have heard more of it. In short, he does nothing but trifle and make excuses. I really believe he heartily repents that ever he undertook it, since he heard the counsel first plead, finding his friend more in the wrong than he imagined. Here am I obliged to stay in this odious town, attending and losing my health and humour. Yet this and all other disappointments in life I can bear with ease, but that of being neglected by – Cad. He has often told me that the best maxim in life, and always held by the wisest in all ages, is to seize the moments as they fly, but those happy moments always fly out of the reach of the unfortunate. Pray tell – Cad, I don't remember any angry passages in my letter, and I am very sorry if they appeared so to him. Spleen I cannot help, so you must excuse it. I do all I can to get the better of it; and it is too strong for me. I have read more since I saw Cad, than I did in a great while past, and chose those books that required most attention, on purpose to engage my thoughts; but I find the more I think the more unhappy I am.

---

* Doctors perhaps.

From Miss Vanhomrigh

Cellbridge, 1720

You had heard from me before, but that my messenger was not to be had till to-day, and now I have
only time to thank you for yours, because he was
going about his business this moment, which is very
happy for you, or you would have had a long letter,
full of spleen. Never was human creature more distressed than I have been since I came. Poor Molkin
has had two or three relapses, and is in so bad a way,
that I fear she will never recover. Judge now what a
way I am now in, absent from you, and loaded with
melancholy on her score. I have been very ill with a
stitch in my side, which is not very well yet.

From the Same

Cellbridge, 1720

Believe me it is with the utmost regret that I now
complain to you, because I know your good-nature
is such, that you cannot see any human creature
miserable, without being sensibly touched; yet what
can I do? I must either unload my heart, and tell you
all its griefs, or sink under the inexpressible distress
I now suffer by your prodigious neglect of me. 'Tis
now ten long weeks since I saw you, and in all that
time I have never received but one letter from you,
and a little note with an excuse. Oh, how have
you forgot me! You endeavour by severities to force
me from you, nor can I blame you; for, with the
utmost distress and confusion, I behold myself the

cause of uneasy reflections to you, yet I cannot comfort you, but here declare, that 'tis not in the power of time or accident to lessen the inexpressible passion which I have for – .

Put my passion under the utmost restraint, send me as distant from you as the earth will allow, yet you cannot banish those charming ideas which will ever stick by me whilst I have the use of memory. Nor is the love I bear you only seated in my soul; for there is not a single atom of my frame that is not blended with it. Therefore, don't flatter yourself that separation will ever change my sentiments; for I find myself unquiet in the midst of silence, and my heart is at once pierced with sorrow and love. For Heaven's sake, tell me what has caused this prodigious change on you, which I have found of late. If you have the least remains of pity for me left, tell me tenderly: No; don't tell it, so that it may cause my present death, and don't suffer me to live a life like a languishing death, which is the only life I can lead, if you have lost any of your tenderness for me.

From the Same

Cellbridge, 1720

Tell me sincerely, if you have once wished with earnestness to see me, since I wrote last to you. No, so far from that, you have not once pitied me, though I told you how I was distressed. Solitude is insupportable to a mind which is not at ease. I have worn on my days in sighing, and my nights with watching and thinking of – , who thinks not of me. How many letters must I send you before I shall receive an answer? Can you deny me in my misery the only comfort which I can expect at present? Oh! that I could hope to see you here, or that I could go to you. I was born with violent passions, which terminate all in one, that inexpressible passion I have for you. Consider the killing emotions which I feel from your neglect, and shew some tenderness for me, or I shall lose my senses. Sure you cannot possibly be so much taken up, but you might command a moment to write to me, and force your inclinations to do so great a charity. I firmly believe, could I know your thoughts, (which no human creature is capable of guessing at, because never any one living thought like you,) I should find you have often in a rage wished me religious, hoping then I should have paid my devotions to Heaven; but that would not spare you, – for were I an enthusiast, still you'd be the deity I should worship. What marks are there of a deity, but what you are to be known by? – you are at present everywhere; your dear image is always before mine eyes. Sometimes you strike me with that prodigious awe, I tremble with fear; at other times a charming compassion shines through your countenance, which revives my soul. Is it not more reasonable to adore a radiant form one has seen, than one only described?

* *

Astride a sorrel mare the sour Dean of St Patrick's rode from Laracor in a very ill temper, incapacitated by gravel and wind and a stitch in his side, added to which was a further horrendous pressure that lay heavily on mind and stomach; the slyness and downright deceitfulness of his ward and secret love, Esther Vanhomrigh, alias Miss Essy, Vanessa, Skinage.

The beseeching angry letters demanding what she conceived to be her rights went out from Celbridge; but this recipient was having none of it; would accept no such infringements on Stella's (Esther Johnson) territorial rights.

The Liffey went babbling under the bridge arches and onwards through Celbridge. Seated at her desk, Vanessa pressed down hard on the nib which scratched the notepaper and spat ink in the lines scribbled at speed. She pressed down on the words as if exerting pressure on her own misery: Cad, Cad, Cad.

The man of muddy complexion, of sour and dyspeptic nature, the friend of Arbuthnot and Pope, rarely rode over, coming on the Lucan road, jogging up his liver, the sour face on him set like dough that wouldn't rise.

When I was but ten years old my mother took me to an auction of household effects held at Marlay Abbey, passed many times some years later when cycling down for the papers that came by bus from Dublin. My mother would put in a bid for a packet of assorted books among which were the two she wanted – Hemingway's *Green Hills of Africa* with woodcuts in the Putnam edition and Willa Cather's *Death Comes for the Archbishop*. Lady Gregory was selling up. Yeats writes somewhere of her 'saying goodbye to the rooms'. That was my first auction.

The next was at Greystones maybe fifteen years later, around 1952. I had hoped to put in a small bid for a rocking-chair (I must have been reading *Murphy*). J. P. Donleavy and his first wife had come from Kilcoole to buy bedlinen in the days when he was writing *The Ginger Man*. Behan had read it and was full of praise. Donleavy and I had the same barber, Josey, who also shaved and trimmed the male dead of Greystones. I did not know

Donleavy; Behan (usually roaring drunk in the Railway
Hotel) I knew to avoid.

Springfield, Celbridge, 13 August 1942

I am back in the nip and immersed up to the neck in the
cement tank into which I have pumped freezing cold
pure well-water that came up from deep below and
gushed from the spout until the tank overflowed. The
whole contraption shook as if with convulsions.

Russet-brown heifers watch me, rolling their submissive
oily eyes, scratching their throats on the bars of the gate;
with beshatten hindquarters they shift and stumble about
in their own shit, butting each other.

I immerse myself fully, holding my nose. Underwater I
hear the roar of the sea at Monkstown and surf pounding
the beach at Mulranny. Immortal water, alive even in the
superficies!

At Springfield near the Crooked Meadow between the
townlands of Straffan, Taghado to the north-west, Aderrig
and Stacumny, Kildrought to the north, Kilmactalway
beyond the Grand Canal where at Hazelhatch the steam
trains of the Great Southern & Western Railway take off
for Dublin, all remains tranquil. Pacing up and down on
the departure platform my progenitor is putting on airs
with the stationmaster. My mother calls this 'doing the
heavy', i.e., letting inferiors know their proper place.

The rotting humus in the lawnmower's box has a damp
and sweetish odour of warmth and cyclical corruption
which is also the stink of generation. Humus disturbs me
and yet stimulates my imagination, as the smell of rotting
apples stimulated Schiller's. He kept some in a drawer of
his writing-desk. The steamy imagination of *amigo* Trevor

Callus was fired by the pong of human excrement which he called 'ecrement'. Phew, the smell of the sea! 'Nine million tons of the stuff pours daily into the Hudson.' Such statistics made his brain reel.

The chemical composition of skatol, the volatile aromatic portion of human faeces, is very close to jasmine. These two odours have a common root.

Smell of the lawnmower's catch near the clump of high waving bamboo, smell of Málaga after rain, a brown ligneous aroma suggestive of standing water in the boles of partly rotted trees (half dead at the top). Maja-aroma, scent of juniper, Maja-scented evenings in the Alameda Gardens in Málaga, the young widow in black drinking lemon tea in a dim bar. Heady scent of incense at Benediction.

Andalusian summer dusk, dry earth, vapoury sky, scent of magnolia, ambergris of the sea; thermal evenings in the Alameda Gardens near the port in Málaga. The line of fishing boats stretches far out beyond the mole and the Mediterranean glints and sparkles with all its little mirrors; all the entrancing little mirrors of the Mediterranean sparkle. The most disturbing of all smells (inanimate) must be seaweed, for a Piscean, in the surges of the Atlantic pounding the back door at Salthill in Galway. No less disturbing is the odour (animate) of the open lip-between-the-legs of ladies, 'the intoxicating bouquet of roses and Parma violets' (Aldo Buzzi).

That which is past is past; that which is wished for may not come again, cannot come again. Certain scents even imply: the longing for that which cannot come again. The exuberance of the eternal lymph.

Notes on the Text

'Flotsam and Jetsam' (with added material) was originally published as 'Nightfall on Cape Piscator'.

'In Old Heidelberg' was originally published as 'Tower and Angels'; 'Berlin After Dark' as 'Winter Offensive'; 'North Salt Holdings' as 'Killachter Meadow'; and '*Lebensraum*' and 'Asylum' as originally titled, all in *Felo de Se* (John Calder, 1960), reprinted as *Asylum & Other Stories* (Calder & Boyars, 1972).

Parts of 'Catchpole' appeared as Chapters 18–19 of *Balcony of Europe* (Calder & Boyars, 1972).

'Helsingør Station', 'Sodden Fields', 'The Bird I Fancied', 'Frère Jacques, Bruder Hans', 'The Other Day I was Thinking of You', and 'Under the Ice Shelf' were published in the collection *Helsingør Station & Other Departures* (Secker & Warburg, 1989).

'Ronda Gorge', 'Black September' (originally '*Sommerspiele*') and 'The Opposite Land' were published in *Ronda Gorge & Other Precipices* (Secker & Warburg, 1989).

'Lengthening Shadows' is adapted from 'Texts for the Air', commissioned by BBC Radio 4.

LANNAN SELECTIONS

The Lannan Foundation, located in Santa Fe, New Mexico, is a family foundation whose funding focuses on special cultural projects and ideas which promote and protect cultural freedom, diversity, and creativity.

The literary aspect of Lannan's cultural program supports the creation and presentation of exceptional English-language literature and develops a wider audience for poetry, fiction, and nonfiction.

Since 1990, the Lannan Foundation has supported Dalkey Archive Press projects in a variety of ways, including monetary support for authors, audience development programs, and direct funding for the publication of the Press's books.

In the year 2000, the Lannan Selections Series was established to promote both organizations' commitment to the highest expressions of literary creativity. The Foundation supports the publication of this series of books each year, and works closely with the Press to ensure that these books will reach as many readers as possible and achieve a permanent place in literature. Authors whose works have been published as Lannan Selections include: Ishmael Reed, Stanley Elkin, Ann Quin, Nicholas Mosley, William Eastlake, and David Antin, among others.

SELECTED DALKEY ARCHIVE PAPERBACKS

PIERRE ALBERT-BIROT, *Grabinoulor.*
YUZ ALESHKOVSKY, *Kangaroo.*
FELIPE ALFAU, *Chromos.*
  Locos.
  Sentimental Songs.
ALAN ANSEN, *Contact Highs: Selected Poems 1957-1987.*
DAVID ANTIN, *Talking.*
DJUNA BARNES, *Ladies Almanack.*
  Ryder.
JOHN BARTH, *LETTERS.*
  Sabbatical.
ANDREI BITOV, *Pushkin House.*
ROGER BOYLAN, *Killoyle.*
CHRISTINE BROOKE-ROSE, *Amalgamemnon.*
BRIGID BROPHY, *In Transit*
GERALD L. BRUNS,
  Modern Poetry and the Idea of Language.
GABRIELLE BURTON, *Heartbreak Hotel.*
MICHEL BUTOR,
  Portrait of the Artist as a Young Ape.
JULIETA CAMPOS, *The Fear of Losing Eurydice.*
ANNE CARSON, *Eros the Bittersweet.*
CAMILO JOSÉ CELA, *The Hive.*
LOUIS-FERDINAND CÉLINE, *Castle to Castle.*
  London Bridge.
  North.
  Rigadoon.
HUGO CHARTERIS, *The Tide Is Right.*
JEROME CHARYN, *The Tar Baby.*
MARC CHOLODENKO, *Mordechai Schamz.*
EMILY HOLMES COLEMAN, *The Shutter of Snow.*
ROBERT COOVER, *A Night at the Movies.*
STANLEY CRAWFORD, *Some Instructions to My Wife.*
ROBERT CREELEY, *Collected Prose.*
RENÉ CREVEL, *Putting My Foot in It.*
RALPH CUSACK, *Cadenza.*
SUSAN DAITCH, *L.C.*
  Storytown.
NIGEL DENNIS, *Cards of Identity.*
PETER DIMOCK,
  A Short Rhetoric for Leaving the Family.
COLEMAN DOWELL, *The Houses of Children.*
  Island People.
  Too Much Flesh and Jabez.
RIKKI DUCORNET, *The Complete Butcher's Tales.*
  The Fountains of Neptune.
  The Jade Cabinet.
  Phosphor in Dreamland.
  The Stain.
WILLIAM EASTLAKE, *The Bamboo Bed.*
  Castle Keep.
  Lyric of the Circle Heart.
STANLEY ELKIN, *Boswell: A Modern Comedy.*
  Criers and Kibitzers, Kibitzers and Criers.
  The Dick Gibson Show.
  The Franchiser.
  The MacGuffin.

  The Magic Kingdom.
  Mrs. Ted Bliss.
  The Rabbi of Lud.
ANNIE ERNAUX, *Cleaned Out.*
LAUREN FAIRBANKS, *Muzzle Thyself.*
  Sister Carrie.
LESLIE A. FIEDLER,
  Love and Death in the American Novel.
FORD MADOX FORD, *The March of Literature.*
JANICE GALLOWAY, *Foreign Parts.*
  The Trick Is to Keep Breathing.
WILLIAM H. GASS, *The Tunnel.*
  Willie Masters' Lonesome Wife.
ETIENNE GILSON, *The Arts of the Beautiful.*
  Forms and Substances in the Arts.
C. S. GISCOMBE, *Giscome Road.*
  Here.
KAREN ELIZABETH GORDON, *The Red Shoes.*
PATRICK GRAINVILLE, *The Cave of Heaven.*
HENRY GREEN, *Blindness.*
  Concluding.
  Doting.
  Nothing.
JIŘÍ GRUŠA, *The Questionnaire.*
JOHN HAWKES, *Whistlejacket.*
AIDAN HIGGINS, *Flotsam and Jetsam.*
ALDOUS HUXLEY, *Antic Hay.*
  Crome Yellow.
  Point Counter Point.
  Those Barren Leaves.
  Time Must Have a Stop.
GERT JONKE, *Geometric Regional Novel.*
DANILO KIŠ, *A Tomb for Boris Davidovich.*
TADEUSZ KONWICKI, *A Minor Apocalypse.*
  The Polish Complex.
ELAINE KRAF, *The Princess of 72nd Street.*
JIM KRUSOE, *Iceland.*
EWA KURYLUK, *Century 21.*
DEBORAH LEVY, *Billy and Girl.*
JOSÉ LEZAMA LIMA, *Paradiso.*
OSMAN LINS, *Avalovara.*
  The Queen of the Prisons of Greece.
ALF MAC LOCHLAINN, *The Corpus in the Library.*
  Out of Focus.
D. KEITH MANO, *Take Five.*
BEN MARCUS, *The Age of Wire and String.*
WALLACE MARKFIELD, *Teitelbaum's Window.*
  To an Early Grave.
DAVID MARKSON, *Reader's Block.*
  Springer's Progress.
  Wittgenstein's Mistress.
CAROLE MASO, *AVA.*
LADISLAV MATEJKA AND KRYSTYNA POMORSKA, EDS.,
  *Readings in Russian Poetics: Formalist and
  Structuralist Views.*
HARRY MATHEWS, *Cigarettes.*
  The Conversions.

FOR A FULL LIST OF PUBLICATIONS, VISIT:
www.dalkeyarchive.com

SELECTED DALKEY ARCHIVE PAPERBACKS

FOR A FULL LIST OF PUBLICATIONS, VISIT:
www.dalkeyarchive.com